SENTINEL FLAME BOOK 2

TREE OF MEMORIES

A STORY OF FEAR, SUSPICION, DANGER, AND THE COURAGE IT TAKES TO OVERCOME UNIMAGINABLE OBSTACLES.

ADAM FREESTONE
ALASKA'S MASTER OF IMAGINATION

 PUBLICATION
CONSULTANTS
We Believe In The Power Of Authors

PO Box 221974 Anchorage, Alaska 99522-1974
books@publicationconsultants.com—www.publicationconsultants.com

ISBN: 978-1-59433-996-7
eISBN: 978-1-59433-997-4

Libruary of Congress Number: 2020925565

Manufactured in the United States of America.

DEDICATION

To Isaac

Though your actions went unrecognized, if not for you on that fateful morning, this book would have remained a dream and that dream would have died with me. Thank you for giving me an opportunity to write it.

ACKNOWLEDGEMENTS

SPECIAL THANKS TO THE BETA READERS
Kathy Bennion

Ashley Beatty

Jameson Beatty

Justin Freestone

Randi Freestone

Wendell Harrison

Dena Williams

Shoua Yang

CONTENTS

CHAPTER 1
MISTRUSTED

S poradic raindrops descended from the overcast sky, plinking softly against the roof of the cabin. It was a small rectangular structure, its walls made from smooth wooden logs, with dark green moss covering the roof and masonry of the chimney. It was a simple cabin, but many of the inhabitants of the nearby village, and those in the surrounding woods, considered it evil, where monsters and witches resided. Shrouding all mention of the cabin were wild and disturbing details. Most were stories intended to frighten young children from venturing near it—though such tales often encouraged the opposite reaction—and some intended only for discussion in the comfortable interior of the village tavern.

New stories had recently emerged about the cabin. These were less unsettling in many regards but shared similarities with those that had come up before. They included not only the usual unsavory details regarding the practices and dangers of witches and speculation of what else resided nearby, but they also included something more tangible. Something that occasionally visited the village and had, for the last few months, claimed the structure as its own.

The new something seemed harmless enough to most—for now—but it was still no less strange and unnerving. It was unlike anything the villagers had ever seen, and no one knew where it had come from or why it was there. It didn't seem like something to be allowed anywhere near the village, but their elders had decided that. Some attributed this decision to minds clouded by too much ale. The thing hadn't harmed anyone or stirred up trouble in the village; in fact, it had proven some-what of a boon to those who benefited from the furs it often traded. So most left the thing alone, regarding it simply as an oddity, something to gossip about, a guard against stalled conversations.

The thing could have been considered a monster in many regards. It stood upright on two legs like a man but had a snouted face akin to that of a wolverine, claws, and a covering of black and brown striped fur. However, the thing's thoughts and actions were no more monstrous than those of the villagers. It was actually quite timid. It didn't seem to want to harm anyone, but it would defend itself if needed—something a family of hunters had recently discovered. Oddly enough, the family had unofficially adopted the thing; his intentions were quite clear to them.

But there was something about his story of which no one in the village or the family of hunters, save for two, were aware. It was a dis-covery so deeply disturbing to him that it had not left his thoughts. He knew the secret was dangerous and threatened to throw his life into chaos. And it had almost cost him the life of his best friend.

Hyroc walked through the door of his cabin, the hood on his cloak up to guard against the rain, a quiver full of arrows on his back, and his bow at his side. Shutting the door behind him, he moved toward the foot of the mountain. He stopped at a nearby tree and looked up into it. The large feline shape of Kit was balanced on a branch, meeting his gaze.

"You coming with me today, buddy?" Hyroc called up.

Kit began swishing his tail but remained where he was. Hyroc shrugged—that seemed a probable no. Rarely did his companion leave the tree, and that never included accompanying him during trap checking or hunting. Not since his mind had endured the touch of a shadow demon.

Hyroc still had nightmares about the evil thing he had killed in the forest during the winter. He vividly remembered how scared he was seeing Kit writhing on the ground in pain. Then he went still. Dread had engulfed Hyroc, but relief quickly followed when he found Kit breathing; he only seemed to be unconscious. The relief lessened his fear, but he didn't know if another demon or more mind-controlled animals were lurking nearby. His cabin seemed a much safer place to move Kit. Not knowing what else to do, he had carried Kit back to his cabin with the help of Donovan and Elsa.

To Hyroc's surprise, when they had arrived at the cabin, neither one of his friends inquired about the thing he had killed. He knew they had seen it because they both fired an arrow into it. But from the looks on their faces, they were scared and deeply unsettled.

Kit had awakened the next day. At first, he was aggressive and confused, lashing out fearfully at Hyroc whenever he tried to touch him. When he eventually calmed down, he was timid, skittish, withdrawn, and he had been like that ever since the attack. Hyroc hoped he would snap out of it, but after a few months he was starting to think his companion wouldn't.

Hyroc moved past Kit's tree, continuing to the mountain to check his traps.

When he returned to the cabin, he held one wild turkey in each hand, along with a wood grouse and a rabbit hanging from his belt. Food-wise, this was turning out to be a phenomenal morning for him. He stopped at Kit's tree, dropping one turkey at its base. "I've got a turkey for you down here," Hyroc called up. Kit lay balanced on the same branch, staring at the turkey intently but made no move to come down. Hyroc sighed. "Well, it'll be right there when you want it." He went to the front of the cabin, sat with his back against the wall, and began plucking his remaining turkey.

As he finished with the bird, he heard the sound of distant voices. Looking toward where the voices were coming from, he saw two hooded figures moving up the trail to his cabin. He recognized the figures as Elsa and Donovan. From the aggravated hand gestures they were making, they seemed to be arguing about something, but as they drew close to the cabin, their argument seemed to vanish. Hyroc rose to his feet, pulling the last feathers off the turkey as Donovan and Elsa arrived. They exchanged a quick round of "good day."

"You doing alright?" Elsa asked. Ever since the attack, that was something she had started asking whenever she happened to see him. This question had never led to him responding with anything more interesting than "yes" or "I'm fine." There was far more hesitation in her voice than usual, and she seemed strangely nervous. Donovan looked tense and had a serious expression scrawled across his face as if he were ready for a fight.

"I'm fine," Hyroc answered.

Elsa nodded, but he could tell her politeness wasn't part of her normal idle conversation. There was something she urgently wanted to talk to him about, and she was greatly concerned about it. He had a fair idea of what that thing was. It was something he had been expecting and dreading ever since the attack. He had no idea how they might react to seeing that demon.

She shifted her gaze toward Kit's tree. "Is he doing any better?" she asked.

"He still won't go with me when I hunt," Hyroc replied.

"Do you know if he's leaving his tree at all?"

Hyroc nodded. "I keep finding his tracks all around the cabin, so he does come down."

"Good. Just give him some more time I'm sure he'll come out of it."

"I sure hope so," he said unenthusiastically.

There was a long pause. Hyroc knew the pause was just a precursor to whatever unpleasant thing she needed to tell him.

She turned to face him. "We haven't talked about what happened in the woods *that day*," she said. And there it was, the conversation that could decide his future here. Hyroc sighed. "You know what that thing was, don't you?"

Telling them wouldn't do any more damage than was already done. Hyroc took a breath. "Before the two of you go thinking anything about what I tell you, I only know this because someone told me a story about it when I was a lot younger," Hyroc said. "That thing was a Shade Hunter, a type of shadow demon."

10

"You knew it was a shadow demon this whole time!" Donovan cut in. Elsa shot him a scathing look.

"Yes, but the two of you haven't exactly given me an opportunity to tell you," Hyroc retorted. He grimaced, unsure why he had said it so bitterly. Why was he angry with them? They hadn't made this situation come about.

Taken aback, Elsa said, "We had no idea how to come to you with this. We were attacked by psychotic wolves and some kind of flaming monster that turned to ash after you killed it. Then there was something wrong with Kit, and you were trying to take care of him. We didn't want to bother you with this."

"But we need to know what's going on," Donovan said sharply, garnering another even more irritated look from Elsa.

"I don't know what's going on. Seeing that thing was as much of a shock for me as it was for you."

"Do you know if there's any more of them out there?"

"I have no idea."

"Hyroc, I've done my best not to pry into your past, and I know you don't like talking about it, but we need to know if there's anything from your past that could be dangerous?"

The Ministry was the only thing he thought he had to worry about, but the appearance of a Shade Hunter had thrown that logic into disarray. It seemed extremely improbable that anyone in the service of The Ministry would summon a shadow demon to hunt him down. Someone else had to have done that. Someone yet unknown to him. That fact had gnawed at his mind ever since the attack. But how would Elsa and Donovan react to this information? He had no clue. They would likely help him, but there was a risk that they might reveal him to The Ministry. Keeping it from them would only increase the chance of the latter happening; he couldn't afford to dodge the question. Many of his former fears now seemed irrelevant.

"Nothing from my past, no. But someone sent that thing here to kill me," Hyroc said. Elsa's expression turned more concerned, and Donovan's more distrustful.

"How do you know it was sent after you?" Elsa said warily.

Hyroc shrugged, there was no going back now. "Because it spoke to me, or I mean I heard what it was saying." Their expressions only deepened.

"And what did it say to you?" Elsa asked cautiously.

"Not much, it said that it wanted to kill me and wanted to fulfill a covenant with the one who sent it."

Elsa's expression relaxed a little. "And that's it? There's nothing else?"

"I promise, there's nothing else."

She took a relieved breath, seemingly satisfied with his answer.

"What is the name of the person who sent it?" Donovan intoned.

"I don't know; it never said his name." That was unless the word Wol'dger was that person's name, but in the context the demon was using, it seemed wrong for it to be someone's name.

"His name?"

"What?" Hyroc said, both he and Elsa shooting Donovan a perplexed look.

"You said, it never said *his name*. So how do you know if that person was a he?"

"Because the demon referred to that person as *he*."

Donovan had a skeptical look on his face. "And who's to say you're not just protecting that person?"

"Excuse me?" Hyroc said indignantly, warmth seeping into his face.

"Donovan!" Elsa exclaimed. "Knock that off."

"It's a fair question," Donovan said, shrugging off his sister's protest. "He was the only one of us who could hear that thing speaking, so who's to say he's telling us everything?"

Hyroc squared his shoulders, looking Donovan in the eyes. "You're suggesting I had something to do with bringing that thing to us? Are you a moron! That thing almost killed Kit, and that's a great way for your village elders to label me as a threat *and kill me*. Why in the name of The Hallowed, would I ever do that?"

"I don't know, maybe you made a mistake or were simply overconfident."

"And what part of that sounds anything like Hyroc, Donovan?" Elsa said.

"Well, he's very good at hiding things about himself." Donovan waved a hand, indicating Hyroc's cabin. "He hid right under our noses in this cabin for a month before we found him; how do we know he isn't also hiding something about what that demon said?"

"Alright, Donovan, that's enough, we're leaving," Elsa said irritably, moving toward Donovan.

Hyroc's face felt hot, and his fingers were tightening into fists.

"No, Elsa, it's not," Donovan said sternly. He pointed an accusing finger at Hyroc. "Whatever he's into affects you, me, and our entire family! We shouldn't risk everyone's safety because he doesn't want to talk about something."

"There's nothing else to talk about, Donovan," Hyroc said defensively.

"Is that why you ran away from Forna, then?"

Hyroc shot him a scathing look. "That has nothing to do with this. I ran away because The Ministry was going to kill me." He used his hand to indicate his face angrily. "Just because of this! Not because I summoned demons, or dabbled in witchcraft, or anything diabolical. That's also personal and none of your business. Is that clear enough for you?"

Donovan opened his mouth to speak, but Elsa cut him off. "Yes, that's clear enough for us," Elsa agreed. "Donovan, it's time for us to leave. Hyroc, I'm really sorry for my brother's behavior today." With a series of shoves, she forcefully moved her brother away from the cabin.

"I'm telling you, he's hiding something," Donovan protested, as Elsa led him away.

Hyroc watched them until they had disappeared from view in the trees, and the sound of an ensuing argument had faded. Hyroc blew out an exasperated breath. That conversation had either gone very well or very badly. Elsa still seemed to be on his side, but Donovan now seemed extremely distrustful of him. Enough so that his going to The Ministry seemed a distinct possibility. Everything around him was falling into chaos. The lonely wilderness may become his home after all.

He snatched up the plucked turkey, headed toward the nearby stream, and crossed it. He stopped at a birch tree on the other side. Unsheathing his knife, he severed the head of the felled bird. He then smeared the bloodied neck across the birch tree's light-colored trunk, leaving behind a trail of blood. There were already several tracts of dried blood near the fresh mark. He needed answers. She had told him to do this if he needed something important and anything related to the shadow demon seemed to qualify. Why wasn't she coming?

CHAPTER 2

SUSPICION

Donovan trudged down the thin trail, following his sister as they wound their way through the trees. He was still fuming from Hyroc's veiled explanation; and that Elsa had prevented him from getting more information. How could she be so content with the little he said? There had to be more to it. When he considered both Hyroc's appearance and the arrival of the shadow demon, the two encountering each other had to have been more than a simple coincidence. He had always suspected Hyroc was the product of witchcraft. He had been willing to overlook those suspicions when the elders decided Hyroc could stay. Hyroc had saved his sister from the wolf and acted about the same as any other person he had ever known. But the monster they encountered in the woods had been uncomfortably close to his family's home; they needed to know more about what was going on, to keep everyone safe. Hyroc was his family's closest neighbor, and if he was messing with some forbidden art, they needed to know. No matter how much he had grown to like Hyroc, their friendship wasn't worth getting anyone killed.

"How could you let him off with that?" Donovan called out, unable to handle the silence any longer. "We both know he's hiding something."

Elsa stopped and turned toward him. "Of course, he's hiding something Donovan," Elsa said indignantly. "I've known that since the first time I met him, but it seems a reasonable reaction for someone in his situation."

"Just because it's reasonable doesn't mean it's not dangerous."

"Do you know what The Ministry does to people like him?"

"Yes, they kill them."

Elsa nodded. "Or worse, they burn them alive."

"But those are some pretty bad people they do that to."

"Most of them, probably. But have you forgotten about the story Harold told us, you know the one with the little girl who healed the farmer's injured cow? Well, The Ministry killed her. She helped someone, and she died for it. Not everyone they go after is evil or has even hurt anyone."

"So what, you think Hyroc is one of those unfortunate souls wrongfully branded as dangerous when he isn't?"

"Yes, I do."

"Then why did we run into a shadow demon a few months after he arrived? Those don't just come out of nowhere."

"I don't know, but from what I've seen, all he seems to want to do here is stay hidden, stay out of trouble, and make a living. You saw how scared he was after he killed that thing. He seemed just as shocked as we were; he had no idea what was going on. So, I believe him when he says there is nothing else for him to tell us."

"Maybe he doesn't know anything else, but you should've let me press him a lot harder for answers instead of jumping to his defense."

"Yes, that would've gone over well if we brought up some very painful memories," Elsa said sarcastically.

"Elsa, we're involved in something dangerous here. We need as much information from him as we can get so we can figure out what's going on. I don't care if I violate his privacy by making him answer questions about things he doesn't want to talk about. We need to know everything to keep our family safe."

"I understand that, but needlessly aggravating him does not seem like the best way to accomplish anything useful."

Donovan studied her thoughtfully. "Maybe we should get Harold involved with this? These are the kinds of things he used to deal with."

Elsa gave him a shocked look. "*Are you serious?* Right now, only three of us know about what happened, and you want to get more people involved before we know what's going on. And of all people, you want to tell the ex-Witch Hunter. Harold's a good man at heart, but with what little we know, who's to say he won't prematurely jump to a decision that could harm Hyroc—severely. No, you're not to go to Harold with this!"

"Elsa, if we're into something dangerous, we may not have a choice in the matter, even if we're friends with Hyroc."

Elsa's eyes hardened into a glare. "I said no. You are not to bring this to Harold, not until we find out more about what's happening. Understood?"

Donovan shrugged and blew out a breath. "Fine, I won't go to Harold."

Elsa nodded satisfactorily. "Good." She turned and continued moving down the trail. After a moment, Donovan followed.

When they reached the road at the end of the trail, Elsa started walking toward their family's cabin.

With a perplexed look, Donovan pointed in the opposite direction. "I thought you said we were heading into town to get a few things after we talked to Hyroc," he said.

Elsa spoke as she walked. "No, I'm tired of your company for one day. I think I'll probably hunt some fowl at the lake. So, you can head to the village."

Donovan turned away and headed toward the village. He stopped at the village center, gazing thoughtfully at The Black Spruce Tavern. Harold frequented the establishment, and it was late enough in the day so he might be there. Explaining the situation to Harold was still an option, but was he willing to go back on his word to Elsa? His parents had always taught him never to lie. Was this instance worth disregarding their teachings? Donovan shook his head. No, he had a run-in with a *shadow demon*! That was not an event to take lightly. And that had occurred not too far from his family. For all he knew, his family was still in danger. There could be more of them out there. He needed to go in there and talk to somebody more experienced with such matters. That was the only way to be sure, even if it meant dishonoring his promise to Elsa. He could deal with those consequences later.

Donovan walked into the tavern. The air smelled a pungent combination of something roasted, beer and stale pipe-weed. Looking through the patrons, he eventually found Harold, stein in hand, among a group of men, talking. Donovan moved closer, waiting for Harold to finish retelling a story about the largest fish he had ever caught. When he had finished his tale, he took notice of Donovan. Donovan used his hand to acknowledge Harold and to signal he wanted to talk. Harold jerked his head to indicate an unoccupied table, and the two of them moved to it.

"Evening," Harold and Donovan said to each other in turn.

"How's your day been?" Harold said, then took a drink from his stein.

"There's something I wanted to talk to you about," Donovan said.

Harold gave him an intrigued look. "Okay, what is it?"

Donovan shrugged, a small stab of guilt nipping at his resolve. "It's about Hyroc." The look in Harold's eyes deepened. "A few months back, my sister and I were out hunting with him"—he paused, trying to figure how to phrase the next words—"and something happened."

Harold's expression turned serious. "Not so loud," Harold said in almost a whisper. He quickly glanced around to see if anybody had heard them. "Okay, please continue. What happened?"

For a long moment, Donovan didn't speak, deciding on the best way to word his explanation. "Okay, so, the three of us were out tracking a deer through the snow. We came upon the deer, and as Elsa was getting ready to shoot, it bolted for no apparent reason. That's when we saw a pack of wolves coming toward us. But these wolves were all acting strange. They were dead silent, no growling, and they had purple eyes." Harold's expression deepened. "Then, before we could get out of there, the whole pack came after us. We managed to kill all of them, but with all that was going on, Hyroc got separated from us. When we found him," Donovan paused uncertainly.

"Go on," Harold urged. "I need to know what you saw."

Donovan shifted in his chair. "I don't know how to describe what I saw. It was like somebody mixed a wolf with your worst, darkest nightmare, and it had what looked like purple flames for eyes. Hyroc was fighting with it. Elsa and I each put an arrow in it, but that didn't seem to do a whole lot to it. Hyroc then chopped its head off. When it was dead, its body turned to ash."

"Is that everything?" Harold inquired.

Donovan nodded. "Pretty much."

Harold was quiet a long moment before he spoke. "What you just described is a type of shadow demon. A particularly nasty one that can mind control animals."

"That's what Hyroc told us it was, too."

"You've talked with him about what happened?"

"Yes, both Elsa and I."

"How did he handle that?"

"Well, he seemed surprised and scared, but when we tried to get him to tell what he knew about what had happened, he kept saying he didn't know."

"And you don't believe him?"

"No, I think he is hiding something. I suspected from the first time I met him that he has secrets, but up until now, I had never thought of those secrets as anything I needed to worry about."

"I have often wondered about his past. My inability to identify what he is has made it difficult for me even to speculate, but witchcraft seems a likely part of his life before he came here. But to be frank, he never showed any of the usual dangerous characteristics exhibited by someone whose body has been altered, so I saw no threat that could come from him staying. And as a bonus that also allowed me to observe him further. But if he's involved with shadow demons, letting him stay may no longer be safe for the rest of us. I just wish you and your sister would have brought this to my attention much earlier. This situation may now have become much more dire because the two of you kept this from me."

"I'm sorry, we didn't know what to do."

"It's alright; we can deal with that some other time, right now we have more important things to worry about." Donovan nodded somberly. "Does anyone else know about this?"

"No, we haven't told anyone. Only the four of us—counting you—know anything about what happened."

"Good, it would be best to keep it that way for now."

"So, what are you going to do?"

"I'm going to pay Hyroc's place another visit and get eyes on what's going on for myself."

Donovan looked at him, surprised. "Is it safe to go up there all by yourself? What if there's more of those shadow demon dog things up there?"

"No, likely not, but causing a panic by informing everyone about something we don't fully understand could also be dangerous. If I don't come back from that cabin in two days, or I do but I'm acting strangely, inform the town elders. They'll know how to handle the situation. Got it?" Donovan nodded. "Good. Now, if you'll excuse me, I've got some work to get to." Harold stood and made his way toward the door.

Donovan watched Harold until he had left the tavern, hoping he hadn't just made a terrible choice.

CHAPTER 3

UNDERSTANDING

The morning dawned on Wolf Paw Mountain clear and warm, with only a mild breeze rustling the foliage. Steadily increasing light roused Hyroc from his sleep. He groggily slipped his feet into his boots sitting beside the bed and dressed into his clothes. Stepping over to the fireplace, he stirred the embers and added a fresh piece of wood. He snacked on a piece of deer jerky from a pack on the wall while gathering up pelts he had acquired from a variety of small animals over the last few weeks. He carefully laid them across his bed for inspection. Each looked acceptable for sale or trade in the village.

The only downside to going into the village was the potential of running into Donovan. Hyroc was in no mood for another interrogation, and if Elsa's brother even tried, he might end up with some knuckles to the face. Hyroc wasn't sure if he'd be able to control himself again, and the other villagers would not look too kindly on such an occurrence. But that might not matter for much longer. If Donovan's behavior continued the way it was going—or even if Elsa's thoughts changed slightly—it could only be a matter of time before someone else became aware of what had happened. Then things would immediately spin out of control, probably involving an encounter with an angry mob, and the wilderness would be his only remaining refuge.

Why did it always seem that right when everything started going good for him, something had to happen? Was it his fate to belong nowhere, endlessly roaming from place to place, never allowed to form a connection with anyone.

Hyroc shook his head, pulling his thoughts from such depressing things. Nothing had happened yet. And in the meantime, he had more important things to focus on, like who would be interested in his pelts. Maybe if he made enough flecks, he might be able to afford something to help break Kit out of his fear.

Nodding satisfactorily at what lay on his bed, he began belting on his sword and knife. When they were secure, he gathered his pelts and moved toward his cabin's closed door. Coming through the threshold, he caught the glint of metal moving toward him out of the corner of his eye. Tensing as a sword blade came to rest in front of his throat, he stopped, the pelts falling forgotten from his arms. Cautiously, he followed the blade with his eyes to the arm of its wielder, noting the raven tattoo of a Witch Hunter, then to the person's face. He recognized the person as Harold.

"I think the two of us seriously need to have a talk," Harold said, calmly but sternly.

Time seemed to freeze as Hyroc locked eyes with Harold. Instinctively, his hand began reaching down toward the hilt of his sword.

"Hold it," Harold commanded, taking notice of Hyroc's hand. "I swear I'll bleed you out before you even have a chance to draw it." Hyroc pulled his hand back into a resting position at his side. "If I wanted you dead, we wouldn't be having this conversation." Hyroc nodded slowly. "But you're going to answer a few questions for me. For instance, what's this I hear about you running into a shadow demon? And I would recommend you don't try lying to me either."

Hyroc, trying to keep a flood of fear from overwhelming him, silently considered the situation. Telling the truth hadn't exactly worked out for him lately, his present predicament was proof. But lying seemed a great way to get killed, so telling the truth was his only option, no matter the consequences.

"Okay," Hyroc said, speaking in a rapid, nervous tone. "Donovan, Elsa, and I were out hunting a few months ago, when there was still snow on the ground, and wolves with purple eyes attacked us. I got separated from them and I ran into a shadow demon, Shade Hunter, to be exact." Harold raised an eyebrow at the mention of the creature's name. "I fought with it and killed it with my sword."

"You killed it?" Harold said skeptically. "All by yourself?"

"Elsa and Donovan shot it, and then I killed it. So, no, I wasn't alone."

Harold was quiet a moment. "Even with their bit of help, I'm still having a hard time believing someone as inexperienced with blades as you—unless you're hiding something about that as well—managed to kill it without getting so much as a scratch."

The memory of the strange barrier he had somehow projected and the memory of the blue flames burning their way across the creature's face when he punched it, flashed through his mind. Those two instances were why he was probably able to kill it, but with a blade to his throat, informing Harold of his potential use of witchcraft, even unwittingly, seemed extremely hazardous. He should leave that information out altogether if he could help it.

"I just got lucky, sir," Hyroc said, hoping Harold would agree with his remark.

"Apparently so. That or you know more than you're letting on."

"No, sir."

Harold stared at Hyroc thoughtfully before speaking. "No? Okay let me ask you this, did you summon that demon?"

Hyroc shook his head. "No, sir, I didn't. I think it was hunting me."

"You do now? What makes you think that?"

Hyroc stared at Harold, stunned and unable to speak. How could he possibly answer that question and live through it? If he told Harold about hearing the thing's thoughts, he was liable to have his head removed. Hearing demonic voices was not something to be talked about with his present company. So, what was he going to say? If there was even the slightest doubt in Harold's mind about what he said, he was dead. It needed to be something believable. But what? He had absolutely no idea, and he was rapidly running out of time to come up with something.

"Because the truth is, it was tracking him, there need be no other answer," a familiar voice said.

Both Hyroc and Harold turned to look toward the voice. A swell of relief struck Hyroc as he saw the white-furred shape of a bear standing in front of Harold. It was Ursa!

Harold stared at her baffled. He moved his sword, so it was resting against Hyroc's throat. "Don't come any closer," Harold said. "I'll slit his throat if you so much as twitch an ear."

"I have no desire to come any closer, nor to hurt you, protector," Ursa said calmly. "But I must caution you, I will not let any harm befall my charge, and you would die before your blade would be able to perform its deadly action. I do not desire conflict, so please lower your sword." A deep guttural growl emanated from the roof of the cabin. Both Hyroc and Harold glanced up to see Kit crouched on top of the cabin, teeth bared, hackles raised, and he was staring directly at Harold. "And you would also have to deal with a clearly upset mountain lion currently in position to pounce on you."

Considering Kit a moment, Harold glanced at Hyroc. "And here I was starting to think you might have been an unwitting victim. I should've known that someone who looks the way you do was nothing but trouble." He then turned his attention to Ursa. "Now, who might you be, witch?"

"I am Ursa."

"Well, Ursa, even with the threat of that cat above me, why should I believe anything you say? What's to prevent you or that beast from killing me as soon as I comply?"

"My word. I promise I will not strike you, and his companion will not attack if you do not attempt to harm my charge."

Harold stifled a laugh. "You're going to have to do a lot better *than that*. I think I'll take my chances making my way back to the village with your charge. If things get too dire along the way, I can simply kill him because I don't believe your claim of being able to stop me. And even if, say, you can do me in, if I don't return to the village, everyone will know about his little incident with a shadow demon. That, coupled with my death, will make them less than compassionate."

Ursa sighed in mild annoyance. Her front paws flashed bright blue. Harold gasped in pain when his sword blazed orange with searing heat, and he dropped it. Hyroc took the opportunity to dart out of Harold's reach. Kit simultaneously ran across the roof, bounding to the ground, then stopping beside Hyroc, where he resumed growling at Harold. Recovered from his initial shock, Harold used his unburned hand to reach for a dagger on his belt.

"I would think you would realize such an action would be futile after what I just demonstrated," Ursa said calmly. "What's to stop me from making your dagger burn the same as your sword?" Harold grabbed the dagger but, considering Ursa's logic, refrained from drawing it. "And now, with you at my mercy, I have a prime opportunity to end your life. And yet, I do not. So, maybe you can rely on my word, after all."

"Yes, that is puzzling behavior for a witch," Harold answered.

"I am not a witch."

"You're not?" Harold said skeptically. "Could have fooled me; I've never heard a bear talk."

"No, I am not, protector, which, among other things, is the reason why you're still alive and relatively uninjured."

"That sounds reasonable, but it would go a long way toward me believing your intentions if one of you wasn't shadowing-bent on ripping my throat out." He used his eyes to indicate Kit, who was growling with steadily increasing intensity.

"Hyroc, if you would."

Hyroc nudged Kit with the side of his boot. "Everything's fine, buddy," Hyroc said, hoping that was true. Even in his present predicament, seeing Harold torn to pieces by Ursa wasn't something he wanted to think about. "He doesn't want to hurt me now; it was just a misunderstanding." Kit stopped growling, covering his teeth. His body posture became more relaxed, but he continued to glare at Harold.

"That's a little better," Harold said, releasing his grip on the dagger. "So, if you don't want to hurt me and you're not a witch, what are you?"

"I am a Guardian. And to make a lengthy and more precise explanation short, I hunt the evil things that would do harm to others and protect those I find in need."

"And is that why you didn't want to attack me?"

"Yes, but I also do not relish causing harm needlessly."

Harold pointed at Hyroc. "What does he have to do with all of this?"

"I am tasked with his protection and well-being."

Harold raised a questioning eyebrow. "Why?"

"That's not something you should be concerned with."

Harold narrowed his eyes at her. "It's not, is it? That seems fairly crucial information to explain. Then can you at least explain to me why he was involved with a shadow demon?"

"As I said earlier, it was hunting him. His only crime was nearly becoming its prey. He took no part in the summoning of the creature, and he is not a threat to your village."

"All I've been doing since I got here," Hyroc toned in, "is trying to make a living and get along with everyone as best I can. That I promise."

"And all I have is your word on this?" Harold said.

"His and my word should be all that is required. The restraint I have shown toward you is proof of that."

"Probably so. But what happens now?"

"Nothing."

"Nothing? I can just walk away?"

"Of course. But I must ask that you do not divulge any of today's events to anyone in the village, save you've cleared Hyroc's name of any wrongdoings."

"I can do that, but I must inform you there are others who know of his encounter with the shadow demon."

"Of that, I am aware, and I assure you no harm will come to them." Harold nodded. "If I learn of any danger to your village, I will inform you."

"You'll inform me?" Harold said skeptically. Ursa nodded. "I don't know how you could relay that information to me without someone in

26

the village seeing you, and it would look mighty suspicious if someone saw me talking to a white bear."

"I have my ways."

"Okay, you've proven your trustworthiness, I think." Harold turned his attention to Hyroc. "I apologize for my actions." Hyroc nodded his acknowledgment, though he wasn't quite ready to forgive the man. "And sometime we need to sit down and talk privately about all this." Harold retrieved his now much cooler sword and left.

Hyroc turned his attention to Ursa. "Thank you for that," Hyroc said gratefully. Then he began speaking with an acidic demanding tone. "But where have you been? Everything has been a mess. I've had so many questions. I had no idea how to help Kit after what that *thing* tried to do or if he was going to be okay. I even marked the tree with blood just like you said. So why have you been avoiding me?"

"I haven't been avoiding you, Hyroc," Ursa said. "I am well aware of your questions, but I had more pressing concerns to deal with since your encounter with the Shade Hunter. Though I knew it might be hard on you, I was confident you could handle it."

"How could you have had more pressing concerns? I thought protecting me was your sole focus?"

"I spoke the truth. I had to make certain there weren't more creatures hunting you; I had to eradicate any lingering traces of the demon's essence, including any animals that may have been corrupted by it. You should be grateful for my vigilance because there were more such animals than that pack of wolves, all of which would have attacked you or anyone else unfortunate enough to cross their path. You would not have enjoyed being attacked by a full-grown bull moose bent on your death. So, suffice it to say, I had my paws full these past months."

"Alright, I'll give you that," Hyroc said, suddenly finding it more difficult to maintain his anger toward her. "But do you know what it's been like between Elsa, Donovan, and me since they saw me with that creature? It's like they don't even know me anymore, like I'm no better than that necromancer they had to deal with years ago. I have been afraid that at any moment they were going to turn me in to the village elders because they thought I was dangerous. And considering what happened just moments ago, I would've thought preventing the entire village from turning on me would have still been a higher priority, at least until things calmed down."

"You never left my watch, and I could discern you weren't in any danger. Besides, those events you fear haven't come to pass and should be of no more concern to you."

Hyroc sighed. "Okay, that makes me feel a bit better. It would have just been nice for you to let me know about some of the things you were doing."

"Perhaps, but it was also unnecessary."

Hyroc rolled his eyes irritably. He had almost forgotten how infuriating she could be at times. "Okay, fine." He was quiet, thinking. "Were you able to find out anything about why that thing was after me?"

"Not much, I'm afraid. I perceive that it came from somewhere in the vicinity of the West and that someone from outside of The Ministry sent it, someone who wants you dead. Though I know not who, nor why."

"You don't?" That sent a small bolt of fear through him. Not only was The Ministry hunting him, but now there was some unknown person also after him. And if they were willing and able to summon a shadow demon to do their bidding, they were a seriously dangerous adversary.

Ursa shook her head. "No. My knowledge may be vast, but there are still many things unknown to me. And while you're my charge, I am forbidden to investigate. But it should comfort you that no more such creatures will slip past me unnoticed."

Hyroc nodded. "And what about Elsa and Donovan? How should I handle my situation with them?"

"In whatever way you see best. Harold cleared you of any wrong-doings, so once they know this, they should disregard any misgivings they previously held."

"So, things should go back to normal?"

"As normal as your relationship with them was before."

"And what about Kit? He hasn't been the same since that encounter."

"He should be fine. His coming to your defense is proof. And you should count him lucky; he was strong enough to stave off the demon's control long enough for you to sever the link and the creature's head."

"Okay, thank you."

"You're welcome."

Hyroc turned his attention to the pelts lying at his feet. He reached down to start gathering them up but stopped as a thought came to him. "Ursa," Hyroc said. "There was something else I needed to tell you. When I was fighting with that demon, it lunged at me. But right before it hit me, the air started to shimmer in front of me, deflecting the attack." Ursa gave him an interested look. "When it came at me again, it knocked me down and I punched it in the head. Flames came from my fist that seemed to burn the demon. Do you know what any of that was?"

"I may. Did it have any resemblance to this?" Ursa raised a large upturned paw, and a small blue flame blazed into existence above it.

Hyroc stared at the flame in surprise. Thinking back to the demon, the tiny flames he had seen had a striking resemblance to the one Ursa created, and the barrier also seemed to have a similar blue tint.

He nodded. "Yes, it looked exactly like that."

Ursa nodded, the flame fizzled out, and she set her paw back down. "It's called a Flame Claw."

"What is it, some kind of witchcraft?" Ursa shot him a look of annoyance. Hyroc cringed, remembering her irritation toward the words witchcraft or witch. "Sorry, I meant magic."

"Yes, a potent form of magic all Guardians utilize."

A sudden surge of inspiration struck Hyroc. "Oh, I see," he said happily. "That was you doing those things. I was too close to Elsa and Donovan for you to help me without them seeing you, so you used magic to help me from a distance."

She tipped her head sideways in a perplexed manner. "No, Hyroc, I didn't."

Hyroc's euphoria faded. "Wait, you didn't?"

"No, the flames came from you, not me."

"Hold on, you're saying I used some kind of wit—magic," Hyroc said, baffled.

"You were undoubtedly using the Flame Claw."

Hyroc flung his arms through the air in disbelief. "How could I have possibly used magic? I have absolutely no idea how to do that!"

"Of this, I am aware, but knowledge is not necessarily required. For those who possess the Flame Claw, the magic may react when they are in imminent danger, to help ensure their survival. The barrier you projected, for example, kept the demon from ramming you, and the flames helped disable it. However, magic used in this manner is unpredictable."

"Wow, so I was saved by unwittingly using magic. But what is it exactly?"

"That knowledge would be better divulged at a later time."

Hyroc shot her a questioning glare. "What do you mean 'it would be better divulged at a later time?' I used magic! That seems like something we should definitely talk about right now."

"No, we should not."

Hyroc sighed in aggravation. Why was it she could never tell him anything important? "Okay, fine, but I have your word; you are going to tell me?" he asked, defeated.

"I give you my word; I will tell you when the time is right."

"Okay. Now since it seems we have nothing else to discuss, and I don't think there's a demon waiting around to ambush me, I'm going to head into town to sell my pelts—again."

CHAPTER 4
HARD FEELINGS

Hyroc slowly pushed open his cabin's door, revealing a clear morning sky above. With his hand resting on the hilt of his sword, he cautiously peered from side to side. There was no one there. He figured what he was doing was unnecessary, but he wasn't about to risk another ambush. After stepping through the threshold, he carefully scanned his surroundings. There were still no signs of a would-be assailant.

Reassured, he closed the door to his cabin and headed off toward the mountain to check his traps. On his way to the mountain's foot, he became aware of something following him. Turning, he couldn't help but smile when he saw Kit trotting up to him. He had long anticipated this day.

"Hey buddy," Hyroc said eagerly, holding his hand out. Kit sniffed his hand before shoving his head into it. Hyroc obligingly scratched Kit's head as he dropped down into a crouch, then he began rubbing the big cat's chin. Kit closed his eyes, thoroughly enjoying the attention. After a few moments, he sharply tipped his head sideways away from Hyroc's hands, then rubbed his face across Hyroc's shoulder. "So, does this mean you want to come?" Kit gazed at him with what seemed a confirmation. Hyroc patted the back of Kit's head. "Alright, then we should get going." With that, Hyroc rose to his feet and continued toward the mountain, with his four-legged companion following.

Save for catching a rabbit in the trap at the creek and a deer–rabbit down by the one at a small pool of dirty stagnant water, the traps were empty. When they returned to the cabin, Hyroc dressed the two animals, offering the innards to Kit, who gladly accepted. When he finished, Kit wandered off to hunt solo while Hyroc headed into town to buy a few supplies.

Hyroc stopped at the village center, lazily looking from shop to shop, trying to decide which one to head into first. Eventually, he decided on Luna's shop to buy some twine. She was always nice to him or, at the very least, buying from her was never unpleasant. He was having a good morning, so why risk ruining it yet.

At the shop's door, Elsa's voice calling out his name caught his attention. Taking a glance toward her voice, he saw her walking toward him and waving. His good feelings then dissipated when he spotted Donovan skulking a few steps behind her. He was the last person Hyroc wanted to see after all the chaos his so-called friend had caused him just days ago. Then there was also the fact that Donovan seemed to think he was a dishonest sneak. If not for his fondness toward Elsa, he would have left already. He dreaded knowing she would inadvertently force him to talk to her brother. But as far as Hyroc was concerned, there was nothing to be said, nothing polite anyway—Donovan had betrayed his trust. That wasn't something to be easily forgiven. However, no matter the animosity he felt toward Donovan, he didn't want to be rude to Elsa. She had done nothing deserving of his ire, so he would endure the presence of her brother for a short time.

Hyroc returned her wave and began moving to her. "Good morning, Elsa," he cheerfully said in greeting, trying not to let his anger toward her brother show.

"Glad to see you in such a good mood after everything," she answered, sounding almost ashamed. She was quiet for a moment. "Look, I feel like I need to apologize for everything we caused."

ADAM FREESTONE

Hyroc was glad for her words, but he was confused about why she felt the need to apologize. She had seemed to believe him about the shadow demon, and it was doubtful she was responsible for sending Harold after him. If anyone needed to apologize, it was Donovan, not her.

"Harold told us everything," Elsa continued. Hyroc raised a questioning eyebrow. He felt a knot form in his stomach, hoping Harold hadn't told them *everything*. "He said you had nothing to do with summoning that demon, and he also found no indications whatsoever of witchcraft." Hyroc breathed a silent sigh of relief. Harold hadn't told them everything. "So, I'm sorry for any trouble we might have caused."

"It's okay, nobody got hurt," Hyroc said, though his words felt forced and insincere. "It was just a misunderstanding."

"I know, but it seemed a little uncalled for. "And," she turned toward Donovan, who had come closer but seemed to be trying to keep his distance. She made a beckoning motion with her hand, telling him to come over to her. Donovan obeyed with his head bowed, walking at a subdued pace. "And my brother here," Elsa said coolly. "Has something to say to you."

Hyroc folded his arms in anticipation and glared at Donovan.

With a reluctant sigh, Donovan raised his head to look at Hyroc. Elsa nudged his shoulder impatiently. "Well, Hyroc," Donovan said dejectedly. "I'm sorry for not believing you and all the hassle I might have caused you."

"You're sorry, that's it?" Hyroc scoffed.

"Well, what else do you want me to say?" Donovan retorted.

"I don't know, but you told Harold things I didn't really want to get around, things that could be dangerous for me. Oh, and you sent Harold—*an ex-Witch Hunter*—after me with *a sword*. He could've killed me! You know that, right?"

"Look, I'm sorry about all that. It was wrong and dishonest. I should've believed you. I'm sorry I sent Harold after you and put you in danger. I don't know what else I can say for what I did, but there it is and I mean every word of it. If you don't want to be friends anymore, I understand."

33

Hyroc studied Donovan thoughtfully. Cutting Donovan out of his life had crossed his mind recently. Everything Donovan had done made that reaction completely reasonable. But Elsa's brother appeared guilt-ridden over how he had behaved, the things he had done, and his apology seemed sincere. That seemed something a true friend would do. Besides, everything seemed to have turned out fine. Did anything really remain worth ending their friendship over?

"Alright, maybe I *can* forgive you for all that," Hyroc said.

"You can?" Donovan said, taken aback.

"I can, as long as you don't do anything like that again. You can trust me alright. Do you think you can handle that?"

Donovan nodded energetically. "You bet."

"Then I think we can still be friends."

"So, can we put all this behind us, let things go back to the way they used to be?"

"Yes, I would like that."

"Sounds good to me as well." Donovan held his hand out to shake on it. "No hard feelings?"

Hyroc studied Donovan's outstretched hand. "There's just one last thing," Hyroc said calmly.

Donovan looked puzzled at his words.

Hyroc made a fist and struck Donovan in the face. Donovan stumbled backward, falling onto his back in the dirt. His eyes glazed slightly, rolling halfway back into his head, but he remained conscious, though dazed. Elsa, with her hand over her mouth, laughed in a mixture of humor and shock.

"Now, there's no hard feelings," Hyroc said, turning away and moving back to the door of Luna's shop.

"Normally, I would have a problem with someone hitting one of my brothers, Hyroc," Elsa said. "But I'll have to admit, I had thought of doing that to him once or twice."

"Yeah, I probably deserved that," Donovan said, sounding almost drunk.

Hyroc pulled open the shop door and stepped inside. He felt much better now. It seemed today was going to be the best day he had had for quite some time.

CHAPTER 5
BIRTHDAY

Hyroc slowly crept toward a grouping of pines, holding his bow with an arrow at the ready. Water from a recently cleared rainstorm glimmered on their needle-covered branches like tiny balls of crystal in the midday sun.

Peeking through the branches, he saw two turkeys pecking through the sodden foliage. Kit trailed behind him in a walking crouch, his eyes firmly fixed on the same targets.

Hyroc nocked his arrow, lined up his shot on one fowl, and let it fly. The arrow struck its target, and the bird fell to the ground, hardly making a sound. Its companion took flight but Kit pounced on it midair. He slammed the bird down beneath his paws and dispatched it with a bite to the head. The big cat then proceeded to sink his teeth into his prize. Hyroc snatched the bird away from him. Kit instantly rose to his feet, giving Hyroc an irritated glare and a steady low growl. "Hey, stop that," Hyroc snapped. Kit stopped growling but maintained the glare. "Wouldn't you like me to pluck it first, so you don't get your tongue covered in feathers?" Kit settled down into a sitting position. Hyroc smirked. "That's what I thought."

Returning to the cabin, Hyroc found Donovan, Curtis, and Elsa waiting for him. One side of Donovan's face looked slightly puffy and discolored from bruising, and his eye had a fading purplish ring around it. The three of them exchanged a round of greeting. Kit, carrying a now featherless turkey in his mouth, made his way over to Elsa, showing no interest in her brothers. He rubbed against her hand, and she obliged him with scratching behind the ears. After a moment of her attention, he clambered up his favorite tree.

"How's your face?" Hyroc asked, indicating Donovan.

Donovan shrugged. "Just a little tender, nothing to complain about," he admitted casually. "But I've got to tell you, you've got a mean hook."

"Thought you had cold-cocked him for a second there," Elsa noted.

Hyroc nodded gratifyingly at the praise.

"And just so you know, that one was free, but next time I'm coming up swinging."

Hyroc cocked an eyebrow, and Elsa rolled her eyes. "Then let's hope you don't give me a reason to hit you again," Hyroc said, tossing his still unplucked turkey down in front of his porch. "So, what are the three of you doing here?"

The three of them gave him a strange look.

Elsa frowned. "You forgot, didn't you?" she said, brushing some of Kit's hair from her hands. "With all that's been going on around here, that's understandable."

Hyroc racked his brain, trying to figure out what he had forgotten. He had a faint recollection of discussing something with one of them before everything turned upside down, but he couldn't figure out what it was.

"It's your birthday," Donovan said.

Hyroc felt his face warm with embarrassment. "Oh."

"And now that we've established *that*."

"Happy birthday," the three of them said in unison.

Elsa then handed a honey pastry to Hyroc, who was starting to smile. "And when you're done with that, we've got a present for you."

Hyroc finished off the pastry and brushed the crumbs from his hands, with an expectant look on his face. Donovan handed him a leather sword belt with leaf designs stretching across its surface.

"Oh, you uh, you got me a ... a belt," Hyroc said, feeling a little confused. He was expecting something, something, well, that wasn't a belt.

"It was the only thing we could think to get you," Elsa admitted.

"The one you use to hold your sword and knife is kind of stained with blood," Donovan said. Hyroc gave his current belt a self-conscious glance, noticing the bloodstain for the first time. "But if you'd rather look like you ate somebody, then I'm happy to—"

"No, no, it's a really good gift," Hyroc interrupted sheepishly.

"And after all the trouble I caused, we felt the least we could do was get you something on your birthday."

"Well, thank you, all of you."

"You're welcome," the three of them said.

"Now go ahead and put it on," Donovan said.

Hyroc removed his sword belt and put on the new one. It fit comfortably, and along with being cleaner, it looked nicer than its predecessor.

"So, what do you think?" Elsa said.

"It's nice."

"Thank you. The leather's from a deer Donovan and I hunted, and Curtis did the designs. Harold and my father helped us while we were making it, but we did pretty much all the work ourselves."

Hyroc stepped over and lightly hugged her.

"Yep, I believe he likes it," Donovan said.

"Thank you; it's been a while since I had a birthday like this."

"And we were glad we could make it a good day for you," Elsa said happily.

Hyroc smiled; he knew this was where he belonged.

Later that night, while Hyroc finished with two squirrels he had caught that morning, he saw Ursa heading toward him.

"Evening, Ursa," Hyroc said in greeting.

She stopped to gaze at the horizon where peach-colored rays of the setting sun illuminated thin streaks of wispy clouds. "It appears indeed to be a good evening," Ursa said, turning her attention back to him.

"Was a pretty good day too."

"As I thought it would be for you. It's a very special day. Your sixteenth year. I believe now, in many respects, you are considered a man."

Hyroc paused in his work on the squirrel. He hadn't even considered the significance associated with this day. Sixteen was indeed the age in which he was supposed to become a man. He felt a swell of pride at that. No longer was he a child.

"Things will be different for you now."

"I suppose," he sighed, "I just wish June was here to share it with me."

"I'm sure she wishes that as well. Unfortunately, such displeasures are a part of growing up sometimes."

"It'd be better if it didn't have to be."

"That is something we both can agree upon."

CHAPTER 6

THE SPIRIT STONE

Hyroc hungrily bit into the hot meat of a freshly cooked piece of venison. He approvingly nodded as he chewed. He sat on a stool inside his cabin at the small table near the fireplace, in the deepening night. "How's yours?" he asked, with a full mouth, turning toward the still-open door. Kit lay just outside on the porch tearing into a deer haunch.

Given that the big cat had helped Hyroc kill the animal, he figured it was a fair reward. Smiling, Hyroc nodded in agreement when his companion showed no signs of hearing him. "Yeah, I think so too. Maybe if we're lucky we'll get another one this week. That'd be something."

Soon the fullness of night had crept onto the mountain, and the silvery disc of a full moon shone faintly through an overcast sky. As Hyroc finished stowing away the rest of the meat, he saw Ursa making her way toward him. She never visited him at this time of night; was something wrong? He wasn't exactly in the mood for her to inform him she had discovered another demon or some other potentially deadly creature.

"Is everything alright?" Hyroc asked her.

She studied him a moment before calmly saying, "Everything is fine, but you need to come with me."

He gave her a skeptical look. "If everything's *fine*, can't whatever it is wait until morning? It's late, and I was heading to bed."

"No, it cannot."

He shrugged. If she wasn't going to tell him, maybe if he saw what she wanted to show him, he could get some sleep sooner. "Okay," he said, throwing his hand up in annoyance. He glanced over at Kit, who lay sprawled out in front of the fireplace, resting the side of his head on his paws "You coming Kit?" His companion lifted his head, regarding him, then Ursa with a sleepy expression before lowering it back to his paw. "Well, if you're not coming, you still need to wait outside until I get back. I don't want you sneaking off with any of that deer." He nudged Kit's back with a booted foot. "Come on, out." With a groan, Kit reluctantly rose to his feet and sauntered out the door. Hyroc closed the door behind him. "Alright, Ursa, lead the way."

Ursa led him through the trees near the stream to an opening in the trunks. He was surprised to see a round pearly white stone, about the size of a pumpkin, with dark green spiral markings running across its surface. The stone sat suspended off the ground between two pines in a cradle of interlaced branches. He gaped at the stone in amazement. That was something new! He had been through these trees on many occasions, and he would've remembered seeing something like that.

"Did you do this?" Hyroc asked, awestruck.

Ursa regarded him with an amused look. "No, I didn't do this," she said.

"Then . . . umm, what is this?"

"It's called a Spirit Stone; I found it just as the moon was rising."

"Who put it here?"

"No one put it here."

He gave her a strange look. That was an odd answer, even for her. "Then where did it come from?" he asked, unsettled by her answer.

She shook her head. "That should be of little concern; all that matters is that it's here."

"Okay, then why is it here, and should I be concerned?"

She shot him a curious look. "It's here for you, of course," she said, sounding as if he should have already known that. "And assuming

41

I am correct in understanding your meaning, no, you're not in any danger from it."

"Okay, but what do you mean by 'it's here for *me*'?"

"I mean exactly what I said."

She still hadn't answered the question. Figuring she wouldn't elaborate, as disconcerting and vague as her answers were, he decided to move on to something else. "What am I supposed to do with it? It's pretty to look at and all, but beyond a decorative doorstop, I have no use for it."

"Touch it and see."

"Touch it? To see what?"

"The legacy of your lineage."

Hyroc widened his eyes into a startled but intrigued look. His lineage? Did she mean what he thought she meant? Would this stone really show him things about his origin, give him the answers he had so desperately sought his whole life? It almost seemed too good to be true. If it could reveal that mystery to him, he had to touch it, even if it posed a danger to him.

"You mean it could answer questions, right?" he said, gazing at the stone more eagerly.

"Some, yes. But you won't know until you touch it."

He gave her a thoughtful look. "Is something unpleasant going to happen to me in exchange for those answers? I've heard there's a cost for some of these things."

"There will be no payment required from you or anyone. How many different ways must I tell you it's safe?"

If she said it was safe, then it seemed reasonable to think he could believe her. She didn't seem to be deceiving him in any way he could tell. "I was just making sure. Large polished stones have never appeared to me out of thin air before."

Ursa regarded him with an inquiring look. "I should hope not."

He stepped up to the stone. He was ready to discover his past. Taking a deep breath, he tentatively pressed one hand onto its cold, smooth surface. The stone hummed like a purring cat, and a bluish glow began emanating from its core. The hum grew in strength and he soon felt a strong vibration throughout his body. His vision blurred, quickly fading to black.

"Be wary of the shadows," he heard Ursa say, before darkness engulfed him.

Hyroc opened his eyes to find himself staring up at a clear night sky, with the moon and stars spread across the velvety blackness. He jolted up into a sitting position. He sat at the center of a small grassy clearing surrounded by dark forest. In front of him, he saw a narrow trail with a point of starry light on either side. Sweeping his eyes above the treetops, he couldn't see Wolf Paw Mountain anywhere in sight. In the moonlight, he should still be able to see at least some part of it. If he couldn't see the mountain, then maybe the stone had transported him somewhere when he touched it. When Ursa told him he would get answers from touching it, he assumed those would come in the form of some sort of vision; he never imagined this would happen.

He should have known what she was offering wouldn't be as simple as she made it sound. Nothing ever was with her. And, well, she *was* a big white magical talking bear, that wasn't exactly normal—not that he could say much for himself there. But considering everything she did to keep him safe, he doubted he was in any danger.

Now he just needed to figure out why he was here. It seemed reasonable to assume Ursa was putting him through some sort of test. But that begged the question, what was the test? The other possibility was, there was something here he was supposed to find. Which brought him to almost the exact same problem as the previous question—to find what?

Unable to even guess at an answer to either question, he rose to his feet and headed toward the path. When he came to the points of light, he saw, with amazement, they were white glowing flowers. Looking down the trail, he saw more of the flowers lining either side, giving it an oddly inviting glow.

Another possible explanation popped into his head. He was dreaming. Maybe he had already gone to bed, and this whole situation wasn't actually happening. There was a quick way to find out. He smacked himself in the face. Other than making his face hurt, it did nothing. He sighed, deflated; no, it appeared he wasn't dreaming. Now rubbing the side of his face, he continued onward.

Farther down the path, wandering among the trees, he saw glowing animals with bodies that appeared made out of smooth, blue crystal of different shades. Most of them were rabbits, squirrels, and birds, but he caught a glimpse here and there of deer and foxes calmly walking through the trees. After passing the glowing animals, he arrived at an archway woven out of tree branches covered with flowers that had a pale azure tint to their light. He ran a hand across one leg of the arch, feeling the smoothness of the wood on the tips of his fingers.

Gigantic roots soon came into view on both sides of the trail. Their undulating shapes rose steadily in height until they connected above his head to the trunk of an enormous tree. He gaped dumbfounded at its size. Elswood village could have fit among its branches with room to spare. Blue crystal birds streaked through the air, twittering like wind chimes in a relaxing breeze. He arrived at a cavernous arched opening at the base of the tree's trunk. Dark green spiral markings adorned the arch. Emanating from within the opening, he saw an ethereal bluish glow. He felt strangely drawn to the glow, as if it were speaking to him, calmly urging him to come closer. Intrigued by the enticing glow, he stepped through the opening.

Piercing an impenetrable darkness ran a line of blue light toward a large area of bright illumination. When he stepped into the light, the glow dimmed, and he was startled to see a large crystal blue stag materialize before him. The stag sported an impressive set of antlers that came to sharp spear-like points. Despite its intimidating stature, there was a friendly air about the stag, and it seemed to beckon him to come closer. As Hyroc moved toward the stag, a brown and white deer buck with a full set of antlers appeared before him, running through the mottled shade between the trees of a forest in autumn. Its strides were long, and it moved with a swiftness he had only glimpsed after a missed shot. The buck slowed as the trees gave way to a large sunlit meadow. A herd of deer gathered in the meadow. The image shifted and the buck stood face-to-face with another male of equal stature.

The buck brandished its horns and scraped at the ground with a front leg; the other did the same. The challengers studied each other before lowering their heads and charging. Their horns locked together in a clacking cacophony of sharpened bone, each furiously fighting for the leverage they needed to force the other's head down. Back and forth, they fought for what seemed hours. Exhausted, the second buck eventually submitted, leaving the first as the victor.

The vision ended abruptly, and Hyroc once again saw the crystal stag. It stared at him with a hopeful expression. He felt a strange desire to reach out and touch the stag.

"Choose," a voice said softly.

Startled, Hyroc swept his eyes through the darkness, searching for whoever had spoken. To his right, he saw a crystal blue mountain lion. And continuing past that, he saw a line of even more animals.

"Choose," the voice said again.

Other than the animals, Hyroc saw no one. He returned his attention to the stag. "Are you the one speaking?" Hyroc asked the buck uncertainly.

"Choose," the voice repeated, but the stag's mouth didn't move.

"Choose what?" Hyroc asked. "Choose an animal?"

"Choose."

Hyroc figured that was as close to a confirmation as he was going to get. So, he needed to choose an animal. What was going to happen once he did? Was whatever animal he chose going to attack him, or would he gain that animal as a new companion? The thought of an attack made him nervous but so did the idea of having a crystal blue animal following him around, especially after his fiasco with the shadow demon.

"No harm will befall you," the voice said, seemingly in answer to his question.

"Then what'll happen once I choose an animal?" Hyroc responded.

"Choose," the voice said once more.

With a sigh, Hyroc returned his attention to the animals. Noting the earlier urge to touch the stag, he assumed that was how he was supposed to choose an animal. He thought the voice's assurance that he wouldn't be hurt was genuine, but that still left him with the question of what was going to happen once he chose an animal. But if choosing one was the only way for him to end whatever he was experiencing, then he supposed it didn't matter.

Considering the presence of the other animals, it seemed reasonable for him to believe that whatever animal he chose might do something different. There wouldn't be much point in having a choice if the same thing happened. He decided he would look through the animals and simply choose whichever one felt best.

The stag didn't feel like a good choice, so he moved on to the crystal mountain lion. As had happened with the stag, a vision encompassed his sight as he drew near the animal. He saw a mountain lion that resembled Kit. It crept across the boulder-ridden side of a mountain near dusk. The big cat walked silently, and its movements were sleek and careful. Soon a group of four goats came into view. The mountain lion crouched into Kit's familiar stalking stance and continued forward more cautiously. It entered striking distance without the goats taking notice. A ripple ran down the length of its body an instant before it pounced. The goats broke into a run as soon as they spotted the cat. They scattered, but one of the younger goats fell behind. The mountain lion had found his target. The goat weaved evasively around a large boulder, running for a steep incline. The cat leaped on top of the boulder, scrambled down the other side, and landed at the incline right behind the goat. The goat shot down the incline at a precarious speed. It jinked off to one side, where another slope ran perpendicular from the incline. The mountain lion pounced, landing on the goat. The goat shrieked in alarm before the cat dispatched it with a hard bite to the neck.

The vision faded. Hyroc studied the crystal mountain lion, but he felt less of an urge to touch it than he had felt toward the stag. Standing beside the mountain lion was another, more powerfully built cat nearly three times its size, its body covered in dark stripes. When the next vision appeared, he saw a large white and orange cat with black stripes. The cat walked through a snowy forest deep in the grip of winter. It too moved stealthily, but also seemed to radiate a sense of dominance, like nothing in the world could intimidate it. The vision shifted to the striped cat pouncing on a lone deer buck; its weight threw the deer off its feet. Before the buck could attempt to recover, the cat sank its teeth into the back of the deer's neck. With a powerful jerk of its head, the cat broke the neck of its prey. A black bear of moderate size then came into view. The striped cat lifted its head above the carcass, giving out a terrifying growl, exposing its large, blood-covered fangs. The bear stiffened alertly before running away. As the cat began to eat, the vision ended.

He once again felt an urge to touch this animal. He felt a strange connection to the cat after seeing it scare off a black bear as if it were a skittish dog, but something about the way it had killed that deer made him feel apprehensive.

The next animal was a large crystalline bear. The vision showed a brown bear, its face speckled with dirt. Using its enormous forepaws, it rapidly excavated massive amounts of earth from the side of a mound. It dug until Hyroc heard a small squeak. A ground squirrel bolted from the hole. The bear killed it with a quick strike of its heavy paw and snapped it up in its mouth.

Then the vision shifted. Wolves swarmed over the carcass of a freshly killed deer. They abruptly stopped their feasting when a brown bear came into view. Warning calls rang out through the air. Seemingly unconcerned with the warnings, the bear continued toward the carcass. Still issuing threats, the wolves moved reluctantly out of the way. The bear arrived at the carcass and, claiming it as his own, he began to eat. Two wolves moved in to harass the bear. The bear menacingly growled as it lashed out toward the wolves. The two wolves jumped back, then they and the rest of the pack headed off.

The vision shifted to a grassy windswept plain, with a male bear standing beside a much smaller female. Another male bear of equal size came into view. The bear beside the female took notice and issued a warning to the would-be challenger. Other than an initial pause, the new arrival continued forward unperturbed. The first bear charged. Both competitors reared up an instant before impact, slamming together while on two legs. They savagely bit and raked their clawed across each other with such ferocity, it made Hyroc's most vicious fight look like a polite argument. After receiving several bleeding gashes to the chest, shoulders, and neck, the new arrival relented. Now bloodied, the first bear returned to the female who had stayed to witness the fight, and the vision ended.

Hyroc had a very strong urge to touch the brown bear, but he didn't like seeing the bear steal from the wolves. After being beaten by bullies for most of his life, he loathed the idea of having anything to do with one, so he moved on to the next animal.

It was another bear. This one had a longer neck, lighter colored body with a dark nose, and was considerably bigger than its predecessor. When he came up to it, he saw an endless expanse of snow and ice. The air was bitter cold, colder than any winter night he had ever experienced, and a frigid wind cut through the air like a knife. A white bear came into view, its body silhouetted against a gray sky. The bear seemed unaffected by the severe chill as it trotted determinedly through the snow. It became excited by something it scented. The vision shifted, and the bear came to a slush-filled hole in the ice. The bear crouched down beside the hole, eagerly waiting for something to emerge. It lunged forward when a dark shape broke the water's surface. In a flurry of activity, using its jaws, the bear hauled onto the ice a round, streamlined creature with four flippers. The bear jerked its head from side to side, violently throwing the creature around by its neck until it stopped struggling. Then the bear began to eat its prey. The vision shifted and he witnessed a fight similar to the one he had experienced with the brown bear before the vision ended.

He had a stronger urge to touch this bear. It wasn't a bully, but he was disturbed by how violently the bear had killed that creature from the water. So, as with the brown bear, he continued down the line. Next was an enormous hawk. He felt an unexplainable familiarity with the bird as if he knew it far better than any animal he had so far encountered. He had no idea why; he rarely saw hawks circling above the mountain, and he had no real interest in the animals.

When he came close to the hawk, his breath caught in his throat when the vision opened to him looking down at one of the birds as it soared through the clouds. Below was a distant verdant blanket of forest stretching across the ground as far as he could see. He saw no snow on the trees, but the air held a wintry bite. He felt incredible freedom as he watched the bird bank to catch an updraft in its wings. The bird steadily rose on the invisible current for a short time before coming out of it. The hawk scanned the area below. It spotted something and entered into a dive. Hyroc felt his stomach drop, and he couldn't take a breath for an instant. The wind tore at his face, causing his eyes to water, and the deafening roar of air flooded his ears. When the hawk eventually leveled off, a flock of ducks came into view. The hawk barreled straight for the flock. The ducks quacked in alarm and scattered from their formation. Sifting through the birds, the hawk selected the slowest one and shot after it. The targeted bird jerked left and right, but the hawk easily countered each move. Using its superior speed and maneuverability, the hawk quickly closed in on the fleeing fowl and sank its talons into its back. The duck flapped its wings frantically before it died, hanging loosely from the hawk's talons. The vision shifted and the hawk came to rest in a nest beside its mate. Two fluffy chicks chirped vigorously for food. The two hawks used their sharp beaks to slice chunks from the duck and caringly fed their offspring. An instant later, the vision ended.

Heart still hammering with excitement, he nearly touched the hawk, but remembering how he had felt throughout the vision, he decided against it. When he looked toward the next animal, he was surprised to find it had flippers for legs. Its body had a shape similar to the animal the ice bear had killed, but not as streamlined and much less round. It had a large lump on top of its head that resembled a goose egg left from someone whacking it there, and its face oddly reminded him of a dog. He wondered if this creature was the *mermaid* he had heard stories about. How something like this could have a beautiful singing voice was beyond him.

The vision showed the animal gliding effortlessly through an expanse of seawater. Streamers of yellow-green plants covered in long slender leaves rose from the rocky bottom, mildly swaying from side to side like trees in a breeze. Blackish grey colored fish swam between the plants. Covering the seafloor, he saw spiky dark red creatures, brightly colored star-shaped things, crabs, and strange thick-stemmed pinkish flowers with tendrils. The fish-dog swam toward the bottom, causing a crab to scuttle for cover and, darting over to it in one swift motion, the fish-dog bit into it with a muffled crunch. Then the vision ended.

Although what he saw was intriguing, beyond wanting to pet the animal for the simple pleasure of touching something foreign to him, he felt no real desire to choose it. Continuing past the fish-dog, he realized, with slight disappointment, that he had reached the end of the line. He was about to head back through the animals when a shimmer in the shadows caught his attention. A bolt of fear shot through him when he saw eight spherical eyes staring back at him—it was a giant spider! His hand flew to his sword and grasped nothing. He glanced down and despairingly saw it wasn't there. The spider stepped forward, allowing a minuscule amount of light to reveal the rest of its arachnid shape. It had a similar crystal appearance to the other animals, but it was black like an onyx gemstone.

He saw a vision of a spider small enough to fit on a finger. The spider crawled to the end of a slender branch. Working its legs in a repeating motion, the spider pushed a web filament into a breeze blowing past the branch. Carried by the breeze, the filament drifted over and stuck to another branch. The spider pulled the filament tight then attached the unanchored end to the branch it stood on. The vision shifted to reveal the circular net structure of a completed web. A moth fluttered into the web. It struggled to free itself, sending ripples through the spokes of the trap. The spider scrambled across the web and sank its fangs into its prey. Once the moth stopped moving, the spider wrapped it in a web. The vision shifted to the spider feeding on the hollowed-out husk of the encased moth, then ended.

He had an urge to choose the spider. He felt a surge of alarm at the mere thought. The spiders that had nearly ended him dominated many of his nightmares. Why would he ever wish to go anywhere close to one of those horrors? The spider disturbingly waved one of its front legs at him in an inviting gesture. A chill ran down his back, and, in his head, he heard Ursa's voice say, "Be wary of the shadows." Her warning now made perfect sense. Shaking his head, he determinedly walked backward away from the spider. The spider studied him before sliding back into the shadows.

He took a deep breath. No matter what awaited him when he chose an animal, he was anxious to get this ordeal over with. Turning, he realized he had stopped at the ice bear. The white bear had lost none of its appeal. In fact, after encountering the spider, the incredible strength the animal possessed only made it seem more appealing. He lifted his hand toward the bear, but something about this choice felt incorrect. Choosing the ice bear didn't feel wrong, necessarily; he just couldn't shake the feeling there was a better option. He pulled his hand back and turned toward the brown bear.

As he considered the bear, he thought of a tough fight he had with a bully who had been heckling him back at the boarding school when he was younger. If he had been bigger than the bully, that fight would have gone much differently, and it might not have even occurred at all. He had always envied bears; no one dared mess with them. How many nights had he lain awake in his bed, unable to sleep because of the throbbing pain caused by a bully? If he chose the brown bear, it seemed he would never have to worry about another bully hurting him. Many bears might bully other animals away from things they want, but at the same time, this aggressive behavior also protects them from other animals that want to harm them. Just because they were bullies didn't necessarily mean everything about them was bad. Besides, they were just animals. It wasn't as if he was teaming up with one of his childhood bullies.

The brown bear was the right choice. Hyroc reached forward, laying his hand on top of the bear's wide head. The animal's skin was smooth like polished glass, but it was unexpectedly warm as if he were touching a living thing. The bear bowed appreciatively and indicated with its paw sit. He looked warily toward the place of darkness where the spider had been, but when he didn't see it, he sat. The bear raised its paw toward him.

Hyroc pulled back. "What are you doing?" he said.

The bear held its paw still and gave him a serene look. With that look, he somehow knew the bear meant him no harm. He returned to

51

his resting position, and the bear set its large glowing paw on his right shoulder. He felt a mild burning sensation on his skin. The feeling disappeared when the bear removed its paw. It gave him an obliged nod. Then everything went black.

He saw a woman holding a bundle of cloth in her arms. She stood in a room with walls made from polished wooden logs that shined with lacquer. The woman, to Hyroc's surprise, was covered in fur, had a snout, and shared many features similar to his own. She gently rocked the bundle in her arms and softly sang a relaxing tune. The song stirred a strange sense of familiarity within him. He felt as if he could almost sing along with it, though he had no memory of ever hearing it. The woman looked up, toward something outside of Hyroc's sight. Her eyes lit happily, and she smiled. Then the vision shifted.

He saw three piles of stones and the shape of a man backdropped by a smoke-filled sky at dusk. The man knelt in front of the piles with his hand resting on the hilt of a short-sword, the tip dug into the ground. Shadow obscured much of his features, but from what Hyroc could see, the man seemed to have a patch over one eye and also shared many of his familiar features.

"I've always tried to make the right choices," the man said. Hyroc felt a minuscule familiarity with the voice. He was unsure why. It seemed impossible that he could have ever been around someone who looked like him, and heard his voice. "We've never quarreled," the man continued, "and all I've ever wanted was to be a good brother." The man paused, breathing a little heavier as if what he was about to say was difficult for him to speak out loud. "I'm sorry I could not save you, I couldn't save them. I know they meant more to you than life itself. But I will not let your deaths go unpunished. I swear to you, I will avenge you." Then everything went black.

Hyroc felt as if he had slipped on ice and landed hard on his back. Opening his eyes, he saw a cloudy moonlit sky through the many branches of the surrounding trees. He sat up to find himself in the place where Ursa had led him. Sweeping his eyes around, he didn't see the Spirit Stone, nor did he see any evidence of the branch cradle it sat in

"Welcome back," Ursa's voice said.

"Back?" Hyroc said, turning toward her voice. "Okay, *what just happened?* Was that all real?"

"In a manner of speaking, yes, everything you experienced was real. But stay your questions; I need to know which one." There was a strange urgency in her voice, and she seemed unusually tense.

"Which one what? Do you mean those animals?"

"Let me see your shoulder, where it touched you."

"Why?"

"Just show me your shoulder," she growled. Curious to know what she was going on about, Hyroc unbuttoned his shirt. As soon as he exposed his bare shoulder, she came uncomfortably close, staring intensely at it. When he looked out the corner of his eye to see what could be so interesting about his shoulder, he was shocked to see a subtly glowing blue bear paw print. Ursa breathed a sigh of relief, and she seemed to relax.

"It's not one of the shadows; I was worried you chose from beyond the light."

"Ursa, *what's that on my shoulder?*" Hyroc said, alarmed.

"It's your *animal mark*. I thought you would have chosen a cat, or a bird, not a bear. Though I suppose it was still a fitting choice."

Hyroc spoke while running his hand over the mark. "Yeah, I chose a brown bear, but you told me going through whatever that was would give me answers; it didn't reveal anything to me."

"I spoke the truth; it revealed quite a bit more to you than you think. And it may take time for those answers to come, but at this moment, that is unimportant; we need to prepare for what happens next."

He snapped his attention on her. "Wait; *what?* What do you *mean,* 'prepare for what happens next?' There's more?"

"It'll be easier if you do as I say. Get down on your hands and knees."

"I'm not doing anything until you tell me how *THAT* answered anything for me, *and why I have a bear's paw print burned into my shoulder!*"

"I don't have time to explain; just do as I say!"

He started to feel an odd, warm, tingling sensation radiating from the mark. The sensation spread through the rest of his body. When it hit his stomach, he felt queasy.

"Ursa, what's going on? I don't feel right."

"It's nothing to fear, but you need to—"

By this time, the sensation had spread to his toes. The tingling intensified, and the warmth turned uncomfortably hot like he was sitting too close to a campfire. The hot feeling increased to burning pain. Uncontrollable nausea gripped him, and he doubled over to dry heave. Assuming this position lessened his nausea considerably. Intense dizziness followed. He fell forward, catching himself on his outstretched arms. He felt a sharp twisting motion and teetered over onto his side. His entire body started to feel heavier. There was a sickening pull on his innards like someone had reached inside him and moved something. An incredible strength began seeping into the muscles of his shoulders, arms, hands, and neck. Then both the burning and tingling sensations rapidly tapered off, followed by the debilitating dizziness.

When he put his hand in front of him to help himself sit up, it didn't look right. He blinked; it appeared he was staring at a bear's paw with large, thick white claws. Confused, he moved his hand, and the paw moved in exactly the same way. When he wiggled his fingers, they felt unusually stiff, and he saw the digits on the paw move. Then a horrifying realization dawned on him, *that paw was his hand!*

His arm was also far wider than it should be and appeared to be a bear's foreleg. His other hand and arm were in the same condition. He began frantically feeling his face with both paws. His nose, snout, and head felt enormous. His ears were also bigger, but they had become rounded.

Mind reeling with the implications of his situation, he stood up. Standing on two legs felt strange. Turning his gaze downward, he yelped in alarm when he saw the wide midsection of a bear. Not thinking clearly about his predicament, he took a step forward. His legs moved awkwardly, causing him to lose his balance and he fell flat on his enormous face with a *thud*.

"WHAT HAVE YOU DONE TO ME?" he yelled, thunderstruck.

"Me?" Ursa said, sounding almost insulted. "All I did was bring you to the stone; you did everything else. Besides, you're just a bear; I don't see—"

"A bear! Why . . . why . . . why would I want to be a *big, fat, bear*? I only wanted to get answers!"

"Hyroc—."

"My life is over! It was already hard enough to deal with people. How will they react to me now?"

"Hyroc, calm down—."

"*How can I possibly calm down*? Anyone who sees me now will think I'm a witch or . . . or some kind of monster and . . . *and they'll try to kill me.*"

"Hyroc, you need to *calm down*—."

"I doubt even Svald and Helen would believe otherwise. Maybe if I tell Elsa first, then she can convince the rest of the family it's still me."

"*Hyroc, if you'll just*—."

"She'll know it's me in this body; all I have to do is—."

A large white paw slammed into the side of his face with an incredible amount of force. Black spots burst in front of his eyes as his legs buckled, and he toppled over onto his side.

"YOU'RE NOT GOING TO STAY LIKE THIS!" Ursa roared.

Hyroc staggered to his feet and swayed wildly from side to side, struggling to keep himself from collapsing. His eyes began to focus, slowly the ground stopped flowing in front of him. He shook his head. Enough of his wits had returned to allow him to process what Ursa had yelled.

"Wait, *I'm not*?" he said, as a ringing chorus still sounded inside his ears.

"No, it's only temporary! That's what I *was* trying to say, *but you wouldn't shut up long enough for me to tell you.*"

"Oh . . . then . . . then turn me back."

"I can't."

"*But you just said*—."

"*I can't* because you have to do that yourself."

"Then show me how," he demanded.

"Don't worry, I will, just not right now."

"*AND WHY NOT?*"

"Because there are a few things you need to learn about this form first."

"I don't want to learn more about *this form*; I want you to tell me how to turn back to normal, and I want to forget any of this ever happened."

Nodding, she said, "Well, that's too bad; I'm going to tell you anyway."

"Why, I'm not going to turn back—," using a paw, he indicated himself with an up-and-down motion "—*into this*. It'll just be easier if you show me now."

She gave him an obstinate look. "The quicker you let me finish, the quicker you'll be back in your natural form."

He grumbled to himself before saying, "*Fine*, tell me so I can get this horrid night over with."

"You said you chose a brown bear, correct?"

"Yes."

"But yet, your fur is black?"

He lifted a paw and saw it was, in fact, covered in black fur. With all that had happened, he hadn't given thought to something as insignificant as his fur color. "I swear I chose a brown bear, not a black bear."

"No, you're correct, you are a brown bear; the hump makes it easy to tell the difference."

"*I HAVE A HUMP?* Are you saying I'm going to be a hunchback when I turn back into myself?"

Ursa shook her head half humoredly. "Of course not."

He breathed a sigh of relief. "Okay, good. I don't even want to think about how people would look at me if I also had a hump."

"The transformation doesn't turn you into the exact animal you choose; there are some minor physical characteristics that carry through like eye color, fur, and skin tone. That's why you still have the same coloration. But the characteristics of your animal form are never carried back through to your natural form. So, when you go from animal to your natural form, you'll look the way you did before the transformation."

"So, you're saying I'm a black, brown bear because I already had black fur?"

"Yes."

"Does that mean my stripes are also there?"

"It does."

He lifted a paw and studied it thoughtfully. "So, I am a black, brown bear, with blue eyes, white claws, and brown stripes."

"Correct."

"That's *not* confusing or anything."

As his eyes drifted up to his foreleg, it suddenly dawned on him he wasn't looking at the sleeve of his jerkin. Turning his gaze down to his enlarged body, he was shocked to see his clothes were missing; he was completely naked.

"WHERE ARE MY CLOTHES?" he yelled with sudden alarm, as he frantically felt around his midsection with one paw.

Ursa snorted in a mixture of amusement and irritation. "They're still there."

"*No, they're not.* I think I would know if they were."

"Yes, they are, you just can't see them."

"WHAT, *they're inside me!*"

"No, *they are not inside you.* Most of the time, whatever you're wearing is incorporated into your skin when you transform."

"So, I'll get them back once I become normal again?"

"Yes, but you're covered in fur, so I don't know what you're worried about."

He breathed a sigh of relief. "Okay, good."

"You gain no added protection from what incorporated clothing you were wearing before you transformed, but if you receive a cut while in your animal form, when you go back to your natural form, your clothing will have a rip in the same place, along with the corresponding injury."

He turned his head slightly and felt something metallic brush across his neck. It took him a second to realize it was his necklace. But why was it still there? If the transformation had changed his clothing, then shouldn't it have done the same to his necklace?

"Ursa, why is my necklace still here? Shouldn't that have also become part of my skin?"

"That necklace isn't as ordinary as it appears."

He cocked an eyebrow. "It's not?"

"It has an enchantment on it, allowing the chain to expand many times its starting length."

"Well, that would explain why I never had to get my necklace resized," Hyroc noted.

Ursa nodded understandingly before continuing. "But if your necklace didn't have that enchantment, you likely wouldn't have been able to transform in the first place. Metallic objects usually inhibit the transformation process. So, if you're wearing metal armor or a metal ring, you will be unable to transform until you take them off."

"Wait, hold on, when I touched the Spirit Stone, and went to the tree, I was choosing an animal to transform into?"

"Yes."

"And you didn't think something this shocking was worth telling me beforehand," he said acidly.

Ursa shook her head. "You needed no such indication, therefore you received none."

"Was what I went through with that Spirit Stone tonight, the reason you saved me from those three men and everything else that's tried to kill me?"

Ursa narrowed her eyes angrily. "That's *not* the only reason, and it's insulting you would think such a thing. You're my charge and, as such, it's my job to keep you safe until the *Choosing*. But even if you weren't my charge, I would've done the same thing. Those three men were going to kill you, and you were an innocent victim."

Hyroc shrugged. "That's good to know." He paused, looking at her thoughtfully. "The *Choosing*, is that the name for what I was doing with those glowing animals?"

"Correct."

He thought back to the line of animals and the spider. "What would've happened if I had chosen an animal outside that line?"

Ursa looked pained. In a biting tone, she said, "Be glad you didn't."

He knew pressing the issue was a lost cause, so he dropped it.

After a moment's pause, she spoke again. "Now, I'm going to show you how to walk like a bear."

"I already told you, I'm not going to turn back into a bear once you show me how to go back to my normal form. So, I don't see the point." Ursa fixed an obstinate glare on him. He sighed. "Never mind," he said in defeat, knowing that to argue with her was pointless.

"Stand," Ursa said.

He stood on his hind legs.

She shook her head. "No, not like that." She stood on her hind legs and took a couple of steps forward. She walked in a sort of waddle, with her forelegs hanging at an awkward angle, like someone wading through deep water. "Bears are fully capable of walking on two legs, but moving in this fashion is only effective over short distances." She dropped down to all fours and continued forward. Walking in this manner seemed more natural. "As you can see, walking in this fashion is significantly more reliable and less taxing. Now walk forward, on all fours."

With a conscious effort, he dropped down on all fours. "Good, now put one paw in front of the other and start walking." Very carefully, he lifted one paw and moved it forward. Then he did the same with the other, followed by his back legs in the same way. Then, repeating the steps, he started walking.

"Good, now try running." It took him a moment to acquaint himself with the required movements, but he eventually started running.

"Okay, I walked, and I even ran, can I transform back now?"

Ursa shook her head in annoyance. "Yes, now I will show you how to transform back to your natural form."

He breathed a sigh of relief. *Finally*! "Thank you," he said gratefully.

"Spread your limbs out, so you're putting an equal amount of pressure on each and keep your back straight." He did as instructed. "Now close your eyes. I want you to envision a full moon. Push every other thought out of your mind and only think about the moon."

He tried his best to do what she said, but his head seemed overcrowded with anxious thoughts about his bear form. He took several deep relaxed breaths. Slowly his turbulent mind calmed, and he was able to push all thoughts aside. Soon the bright silvery disc of a full moon coalesced within his mind. When he concentrated on it, he felt a strange, warm, tingling sensation in his right shoulder. The sensation spread through his body. When it hit his toes, he braced himself for imminent discomfort. He felt a subtle amount of pain and a mild increase in the warmth. His body steadily became lighter, and strength seeped from his muscles as they shrunk back to their normal state. Soon he felt like his normal self again.

Opening his eyes, he was ecstatic to see hands instead of bear paws. His clothes had also returned. When he ran his hands over his face, he was relieved to feel his own and not a big bear's. He seemed to be himself again.

"Thank you, I'm—," he stopped speaking when he saw Ursa. Her eyes were closed tight, her entire body was tense, she was panting heavily, and she bared her teeth in an uncomfortable grimace. "Ursa, are you alright?" he said tentatively. Ursa's eyes snapped open, and she gave him a frightening look. He saw pain in her eyes, pain the likes of which he had never seen before.

Ursa spoke in a sharp labored growl. "GO—HOME!"

He stiffened and hurried off toward his cabin. He didn't want to cause Ursa any further trouble by disobeying her request. But what, he wondered, could be causing her such pain?

Almost as soon as Hyroc came into the clearing surrounding his cabin, Kit appeared out of nowhere, bolting excitedly to him. The big cat came to an abrupt stop in front of him. His posture was suddenly cautious. Kit stared at him uncertainly, testing the air with his nose. "What is it buddy, what do you smell?" Hyroc asked, stepping toward his companion. Kit started, jerking back and issuing a low fearful warning growl. Hyroc studied the big cat's gaze. Kit wasn't looking at something behind him; his companion's had his eyes locked on him.

"Kit, it's okay. It's me, I'm not going to hurt you," he said in his softest and most friendly voice. Kit stopped growling and stared at him with a puzzled look. Very slowly, and as nonthreateningly as he could manage, Hyroc walked toward him. When he reached out with his hand, Kit recoiled. He stopped reaching, bowed his head, and held his hand where it was. Kit's eyes darted between his hand and downturned face. Kit very cautiously sniffed his hand. After taking a few whiffs of his scent, the big cat relaxed.

"See, it's me, silly." Hyroc breathed a sigh of relief. "I've had one crazy night, and I don't need you adding to it."

CHAPTER 7

MOTHS AND HONEY

Sporadic raindrops dripped from the cloudy, pale gray sky, splashing silently into the lake. Hyroc stood on the lakeshore across from the Shackletons' cabin, beneath the leafy umbrella of a cottonwood tree, with his fishing pole in hand. He cast his line in a high arc. When the hook plopped into the water, he slowly drew it back in. It had been a week since his otherworldly encounter with the Spirit Stone, and his resulting transformation into a bear. Thankfully, nothing else shocking had happened after that bizarre experience. He had hoped the whole thing was a dream. A dream would be much easier to accept. But the blue paw print on his shoulder proved otherwise. Still, he was determined to forget all of it.

He drew his line in, then cast it back out. Halfway through pulling it in, he felt weight on the line. He set the hook with a hard jerk. His line began swinging back and forth. Leaning into the motions, he slowly started bringing the fish in. After a short struggle, he landed a trout. As he dispatched his catch, he felt something cold and wet on his wrist. Looking toward it, he saw the swollen black body of an attached leech. Instinctively, he stuck the fish in his mouth to free up his hand, and using the claws on his index finger and thumb, pried the leech from his.skin and tossed it back into the water.

His eyes widened with disgusted horror when he realized he had put the fish in his mouth! He spat it out and, while trying not to gag, frantically wiped his tongue on his sleeve. Then taking several swigs from his waterskin, he tried desperately to cleanse his mouth of the sickening taste of fish slime. No matter how many times he swished and spat, an unpleasant aftertaste remained in the back of his throat.

Wiping his mouth, Hyroc stared at the fish, feeling unsettled. His mind drifted back to his fears from his time as a bear. Before any thoughts could take hold, he forced himself to think about something else.

My hands were full, he assured himself. *And that's why I put the fish in my mouth. That's all that happened, just an unpleasant mistake.* Determined to think about anything other than what he had done, he decided to head over to the Shackletons' to pay a visit to Donovan or Curtis.

When he arrived, beyond hearing Helen and Elsa's muffled voices from within the cabin, the only person he found outside was Svald scraping a deer hide near the shed. He and Hyroc exchanged a round of greetings.

"Where are Curtis and Donovan?" Hyroc asked.

"Oh, I think Donovan caught sight of some rabbits, and he and Curtis went out after them," Svald said. "They should be back before too much longer."

Hyroc nodded. "I was just coming by to see if either of them wanted to do something."

Svald's eyes lit a little. "We finished tanning a black bear pelt yesterday; would you like to see it?"

For some reason, the thought of seeing a bear's skin caused Hyroc a slight amount of discomfort. Shaking off the feeling, he said, "Sure," in a forced, enthusiastic tone.

"It's still in the shed." Svald set his fleshing knife against the back of the cabin and led Hyroc over to the shed. He brought out the pelt, carefully laying it on the ground.

Hyroc again shrugged off a disturbing feeling.

"Isn't that a beauty?"

Hyroc nodded his agreement. It was a nice looking pelt in good condition that was sure to fetch a fair price. "Mind if I touch it?" Hyroc asked.

"As long as you're gentle."

Hyroc crouched down and ran his hand over the length of the pelt. Touching it felt very wrong, and he had an urge to pull his hand back. He willed himself to keep his hand on the pelt. The excited barking of Dilo rang out nearby. Rising to his feet, he held his hand out in a welcoming gesture toward the dog. Dilo came to an abrupt stop out of arms reach. Her hackles rose suddenly into a ridge, and she bolted, yipping as she ran.

Hyroc had an inexplicable urge to dash after the dog and, alarmingly, the desire to sink his teeth into her neck. The desires suddenly vanished when he shook his head.

Svald laughed as he shook his head in disbelief. "Stupid skittish mutt, she probably smelled the pelt and thought there was a bear here."

"But I'm *not* a bear!" Hyroc blurted out before he realized he was speaking. He stared at Svald in wide-eyed mortification.

Svald gave him a strange look. "I know you're *not* a bear. Are you feeling alright?"

Speaking in a rapid embarrassed tone, Hyroc said, "Of course I'm fine, but I just remembered there is something I need to do and really should be going. Have . . . have a nice day." Trying not to run, he quickly headed away from the cabin toward the road, feeling Svald's eyes on him as he went.

When he was sure no one could see him, he put his back against a tree, lightly knocking his head against its trunk. He couldn't believe he had committed the words, "but I'm not a bear," into the air. He felt a renewed flood of embarrassment, envisioning how his behavior must have looked to Svald.

Soon the rest of the Shackleton family would hear about it too. Donovan would have an irritating quip readied for the next time the two of them happened across each other. He was not looking forward to that! His thoughts slowly drifted away from feelings of mortification, back to Dilo. Her behavior almost mirrored the way Kit had acted. Did they think he was a bear? He forced his thoughts away from the possibility; there had to be another explanation. If Kit truly thought he was a bear, his companion would not have calmed down. Some of Ursa's scent must have come off on him, but once he recognized who he was smelling, he relaxed.

Similarly, Dilo had probably caught a whiff of the bear pelt or Ursa's lingering scent, and that's why she became so frightened. He tried to think of the last time he had taken a bath and realized he hadn't done so since before Ursa brought him to that stone. All he needed to do was bathe and wash his clothes and everything would be fine. He felt silly; he had let his fears get the better of him when the explanation and solution to his predicament were so incredibly simple. Nodding satisfactorily, he headed off toward the village to buy soap.

He bought his soap, then remembering how bored Kit had seemed upon seeing rain this morning, he used his remaining coins to buy a leather ball. Heading back toward his cabin, he absentmindedly tossed the ball up and down. He had cleared the last village building when he noticed he had stopped tossing the ball and was chewing on a round object. Confused, he pulled the thing out of his mouth. He gaped in surprise when he saw the ball in his hand. He couldn't recall when he had stopped tossing the ball. Had it been in his mouth while he was in the village? Had anyone seen that? Consumed by hot embarrassment at the thought, he wiped the ball on his sleeve, shoved it deep within his pocket, and hurried back to his cabin.

Kit thoroughly sniffed the ball, then gave Hyroc an irritated glare.

Hyroc sighed. "I'm sorry," he said. "I didn't mean to put it in my mouth; one second it was in my hand, and the next, it was between my teeth. But I washed it in the stream. So, it's clean."

Seemingly pleased by his explanation, Kit fixed a murderous look on the ball.

Hyroc smiled. "So, you *do* still want it. Okay . . . go . . . get it!" With a quick wrist movement, he threw the ball past Kit's favorite tree. In a flurry of feet, Kit flew after his spherical adversary. He returned a moment later, dropped the ball at Hyroc's feet, and resumed trying to kill it. Mindful of the big cat's claws, Hyroc carefully extricated the ball from Kit's grip and threw it again.

After a few more rounds of play, he started cooking the fish he had caught earlier. When he went to put the fish in the fireplace, he irritably noticed he had forgotten first to get a fire going. He held his uncooked catch in one hand, and when he needed both hands to get a fire going, he caught himself moving the fish toward his mouth. *Seriously, I almost did it again?* Shaking his head in disbelief, he set the fish down on the edge of the fireplace. The fish only entered into his mouth later, when fully cooked.

The next morning, he found only a deer-rabbit caught in his traps. After lunch, he bathed and set about thoroughly washing every article of clothing he had been wearing the night he had some insight into the life of a bear. Nothing unusual happened that day: he didn't do anything strange nor did Kit act strangely in his presence. He went to sleep confident that the events of the prior day had no link to his transformation.

Awaking the following morning, he had a strange craving for carrots, honey, and something else he couldn't identify. When he opened the door after a quick breakfast, a large moth fluttered in front of him. His hand shot up, snatched the creature out of the air, and stuck it in his mouth. It made a slight crunch as he chewed, and the fuzz on its skin felt oddly pleasant between his teeth. He froze, his eyes widening as he became aware of what he had done. A wave of revulsion crashed on top of him. He felt sick as he vigorously spat out the masticated remains of the moth.

"Moths aren't *that* bad." Ursa's voice said humorously.

After swishing and spitting a large mouthful of water from his waterskin, he looked up to see her sitting beside the porch. Despite her part with the Spirit Stone, he was glad to see her.

"Ursa, I think . . . I think there's something wrong with me," he stammered.

"No, there's nothing wrong with you; everything that's happening is to be expected."

He narrowed his eyes at her, his gladness replaced with annoyed suspicion. "What do you *mean* 'everything that's happening is to be expected?' I just ate a moth!" He shivered a little at that. "Are you telling me you knew this was going to happen?"

"Yes . . ." she sharply raised her paw, cutting off his next angry question before he could begin. "You were clearly unsettled by what had happened the night of your *Choosing*. I thought it prudent to hold off on telling you anything more to give you a few days to process your experience."

"Well, thanks to your *prudence*, I made Svald, and probably half the village, think I'm not right in the head."

Ursa shook her head. "Most of the villagers already thought much worse of you. And regarding your pack leader friend, youth do and say strange things all the time; he won't think much about your behavior."

"That still doesn't make it any less humiliating."

"No permanent damage has been done to you."

He sighed irritably, knowing he should've expected a dispassionate response like that from her. "If you say so. Now, tell me how to stop this from happening again, so I can put this whole situation behind me."

Ursa sighed. "You continue to act as if simply ignoring what's happening to you—that will make it all go away. Do you think eating moths is the worst you have to worry about?"

His expression turned concerned. That didn't sound reassuring. "What do you mean by that?"

"Think back to the visions you saw when you looked at the brown bear. Did you see one steal the kill from a wolf pack?"

"Yes."

"Now, I want you to imagine yourself as that bear for a moment and substitute the wolves for people."

He gave her a dismayed look. "I hope you're not saying what I think you're saying. Are you telling me I'll start bullying people away from things I want?"

"More or less."

"So, you mean to say, I'm going to actually start acting like a bear? Fantastic."

"You already have."

"I don't want to become *like that*, tell me how to stop this, please."

"It is not as simple a matter as you seem to think. I cannot teach it with words alone."

"You're saying I'll have to be in bear form to learn this, aren't you?"

"Of course."

"There's a *big problem* right there—what if somebody sees me in my bear form? You know what The Ministry does to witches, and I'm positive turning into a beast fits into their consideration of a witch. Donovan, Curtis, and Elsa come by here quite often. What happens if they come to the cabin while you're teaching me something?"

"We won't be doing it where someone might see you."

"Then you must mean we're going to go off into the woods?"

"You can't properly learn to be a bear unless you spend time in their environment."

"I can't just pack up and leave, not now, not after everything I've done to make this place my home. I have friends here, people who genuinely care about me. It's been so long since I've had any of those. I can't . . . I won't leave all that behind."

"You're merely leaving it behind for a short time, and if you truly count those people as your friends, you will do this thing. If you don't learn how to control what's happening to you, you will become a danger to them. Would that not be worse?"

He sighed and nodded his agreement. He didn't know how he would live with himself if he were to harm his friends. "That would be *a lot worse*." He paused. "How long will I be gone?"

"That depends a great deal on you."

Hyroc shrugged. "You mean until I've learned it."

"Yes."

He took a deep breath. "Alright, when do we start?"

Ursa nodded approvingly. "We start tomorrow." He halfheartedly nodded his understanding. "But there's something else you're forgetting."

He shot her a puzzled look.

"Regarding the pack members you have befriended. What do you think they would do if you suddenly disappeared?" Hyroc gave her a thoughtful look, but after a moment's contemplation, shook his head. "They would come looking for you, and we can't have that."

"So, what, you're saying I should go tell them? No offense, but that seems like a terrible idea. Can you imagine how they would react to all this?"

"That is exactly what I'm telling you to do, but you need only to tell a single member of their pack."

"Who, then?"

"I believe you know."

"Elsa? No, that's still a bad idea."

"She has shown a tremendous amount of understanding and trust with you. Far more than any other person here."

"Yeah, but that'll change the instant she sees me turn into a bear! She'll think I'm a witch for sure, and everything in my life will crumble away again."

"I believe she may yet surprise you."

"After my fight with the Shade Hunter, she was very close to turning me in to the village elders, for fear I was involved in something dangerous; I could see it in her eyes. No matter how much I think I can trust her, this is not something I can tell her. It's just too risky. We need a better plan."

"You mistake what you saw. It wasn't fear in her eyes. It was concern, concern for you."

Hyroc gave her a quizzical look. "Me? Why would she be concerned for me, after what she saw?"

"Because she knows the kind of person you are and what's in your heart. She was afraid of what she saw that day, yes, but she knows you would never knowingly be a part of something so hazardous."

Hyroc stared down at the ground thoughtfully. Was it possible he had misread Elsa's reaction? Was she truly concerned about him? It seemed possible, and in the end, it was Donovan, not Elsa who had sent Harold after him. But could she be trusted with the knowledge of his newfound ability? Telling her was an incredible risk. If she told anyone in the village about this, his life in Elswood would be over.

Though, the idea of having someone to talk to about it besides Ursa was appealing. Maybe Ursa was right; maybe he should tell Elsa.

"Are you absolutely sure telling her is the best thing to do?" Hyroc asked, returning his gaze to Ursa. "If you're wrong, I lose everything I've worked so hard to build here."

Ursa nodded. "Yes. She can help cover for you while you're gone and to craft a believable story for the rest of the family and the village. Besides, it wouldn't hurt to have another informed ally, something you currently lack."

"Alright, if you think it's a good idea. What should I tell her?"

"That is for you to decide; though I may have more insight into her feelings, you know her much better than I." Hyroc blew out an exasperated breath. Of course, he should have guessed this is where her advice would end. "After you have completed this task, go to the other side of the river to the north. Shimmer will inform me when you have arrived. Pack only what is essential."

"There's one last thing you need to be aware of before I depart. If you choose to transform before we meet again, you must allow several hours to pass before you revert to your natural form; you will know when sufficient time has passed. Changing your form too soon is an extremely painful process."

"Wait," Hyroc said, puzzled. "Why didn't I feel much pain the first time I transformed back to my natural form? I couldn't have been in the bear form for more than an hour."

"Because I transferred the negative effects of transforming early to myself."

Hyroc's expression turned shocked. "Is that why you suddenly seemed to be in so much pain that night?"

"Yes, I was in considerable pain."

Hyroc felt a surge of guilt, knowing his impatience had caused her so much unnecessary pain. "I'm sorry if I . . ."

Ursa cut him off with a sharply raised paw. "No apology is necessary; I did it of my own volition. You had many things to consider that night, and letting you linger as a bear was not in your best interest."

Hyroc sighed. Even though Ursa held no blame against him for the pain she experienced, he felt awful knowing he caused it.

"Is there anything else?"

It took Hyroc a moment to overcome his feeling of shame to speak. "What . . . umm . . . should I do about Kit?"

"Bring him with you; it will be good for him to experience what it means to be wild, even if it's but a taste. Anything else?"

"No, I think I'm good, I just have to figure out what to say tomorrow."

Ursa nodded. "Make sure you get plenty of sleep tonight, you've got a long journey ahead of you."

She headed toward the back of the valley. Hyroc watched her go, feeling a mixture of curiosity and anxiety as he wondered what the coming days held for him.

CHAPTER 8
A RELUCTANT DEPARTURE

Hyroc nervously paced across the porch of his cabin anxiously awaiting Elsa's arrival. There were a lot of things he needed to explain to her. Part of him still feared this would go horribly wrong. But if Ursa said it was the best thing to do, it seemed reasonable to trust her. Or so he hoped.

He stopped pacing to glance over at Kit, who lay nearby half asleep. His plan was to transform as part of his disclosure to Elsa, and he wondered how his feline friend would react. He shook his head. One thing at a time. His priority needed to be on Elsa. That was the hard part. Handling Kit's reaction would be easy by comparison; Kit didn't have the power to bring an end to his life in Elswood.

Kit raised his head, looking toward the trail leading to the cabin. Hyroc followed his gaze, spotting Elsa. He took a deep breath. The dreaded moment had arrived. He hoped he wouldn't mess it up, that he could convince her to keep his secrets; he liked living here. Elsa waved as she approached, he returned the greeting.

"Pretty good day for hunting, isn't it," she said conversationally.

"Yes, yes, it is," Hyroc agreed, stealing a glance at the mildly overcast sky.

"Managed to shoot a sitting grouse at a pretty fair distance." Hyroc nodded his congratulations. "So, what is it you want to talk to me about?"

Hyroc scratched the back of his head nervously as he spoke. "Well, it's sort of, well, complicated." He made a gesture to forestall a question from Elsa. He removed a stool from inside the cabin and set it down beside the porch. "You . . . uh . . . you might want to sit down for this." She gave him a confused and intrigued look, but she sat without a word. "You . . . umm . . . know me, right? I mean, you know what kind of person I am, and that I would never do anything to hurt anyone."

"Donovan's face might disagree," she joked. Hyroc gave her a flat look. "Sorry I couldn't help it. Yes, I know you're a good person. Please continue."

"You also know I had nothing to do with that shadow demon, nor would I want to." She nodded. "And the same with witchcraft." She nodded again. He stared at her uncertainly, trying to gather his thoughts. He took a breath, stoking his courage. "Well, there's something, well, I don't quite know how to explain it, so it would probably be better for me to show you. I just want you to remember, no matter what you see, you're not in any danger and it's still me."

Her expression began to show hints of concern now. "Umm, Hyroc, the fact that you're trying so hard to reassure me isn't reassuring me. What are you trying to tell me?"

Hyroc had to force himself to resist the urge to blurt out what he was capable of doing. He quietly groaned to himself. "Just . . . umm . . . please just watch."

He lowered himself onto his hands and feet before envisioning the moon. When the warmth reached his abdomen, the debilitating nausea and dizziness he had experienced were far milder than during his first transformation. As the warmth reached his toes the heat intensified, but to a lesser degree than before. Then his body began to feel steadily heavier. He felt the disconcerting pull on his innards and, as before, an incredible strength seeped into his muscles. The sensations tapered off and, moments later, he was a bear.

When he opened his eyes, Elsa was no longer sitting. Her eyes were wide with shock, and she wore a baffled look on her face. Hyroc studied her, but he couldn't tell if she was about to scream, run away, or faint. The two of them stared at each other unblinkingly before she pointed a shaky finger at him.

"You . . . you . . . you just turned into a bear!" Elsa stammered.

Hyroc held a paw out and shrugged in agreement. "Yep, I'm a bear," he agreed. Glancing toward the porch, he saw Kit standing, looking puzzled and sniffing the air uncertainly. But he didn't seem afraid.

There was another pause before Elsa continued speaking. "How long have you . . . umm . . . been able to do *that*?"

"About a week." She gave him a mystified nod, then resumed her seat on the stool. *That's a good sign*, Hyroc thought. If she was sitting, that meant she wasn't about to run. But why wouldn't she run? She must think him some kind of witch now, and that should definitely concern her. Maybe Ursa was right; maybe his mistrust of Elsa knowing this was unfounded? But he also might be getting ahead of himself; he had only started.

"I guess I've always sort of wondered if you could do that," Elsa said thoughtfully. "Does it hurt?"

"A little, but—," he shot her a surprised look. "Wait . . . wait," Hyroc said, shaking his paw. "You're not . . . I don't know, freaked out by any of this?"

"Oh, no, that's the freakiest thing I've ever seen, but I know it's still you in there."

"But how do you know I'm not a witch?"

She let out a short nervous laugh. "Well, to be honest, other than mistaking you for a forest spirit when we first met, I've always assumed that's what you are. But I was okay with that because you never seem to want to hurt anyone, not to mention that first wolf incident." Hyroc nodded. He opened his mouth to speak but stopped himself when Elsa perplexingly stood and moved toward him. She held her hand out to touch his head, then quickly pulled it back, looking embarrassed.

"Sorry," Elsa said apologetically. "May I?" Hyroc shot her a quizzical look and nodded. Starting at his ears, she used her hands to feel across his head and face. Hyroc then obligingly lifted his paw so she could have a look at his claws. Similarly, Kit cautiously sauntered over and began sniffing him. "Sorry, I just had to do that," Elsa said after she had finished her inspection. "I've just never been able to touch a still-living bear. Or talk to one," she added, smiling. Hyroc nodded in humored agreement. "So, what happens now?"

"You can't tell anyone about this," Hyroc said.

Elsa gave him a flat look. "I already guessed *that*," she said indignantly. Hyroc waggled his head, annoyed at himself for stating the obvious. "Does that also go for my family and Harold?"

"Just for now; I'll get to telling them eventually."

Elsa nodded. "Is that everything you brought me up here for? Not that it's more than enough."

"Not exactly. I'm actually leaving."

"*Leaving!* What for?" She stood and indicated his body with her hands. "Because of this? I don't think this is a big enough deal for *that* kind of decision! Just . . . just don't use it around anyone."

"No, it's not like that. I'm only leaving for a little while."

She gave him a comprehending nod. "Oh, but what are you leaving to go do?"

"Well, I'm going off to be trained on how to use—," he used his paw to indicate himself, "—this form."

"Alright, but who's going to be training you?"

Hyroc silently chided himself; he never intended to tell her about Ursa. There was no hiding it now. "Well, this might sound a little odd, but I'll be doing it with—"

"A white bear?" Elsa interrupted.

Hyroc gave her a stunned look. How did she know *that*?

"Harold might have unintentionally mentioned something to me about seeing a white bear."

Hyroc nodded slowly, still feeling caught off guard by her knowledge. "Yeah, that bear would be the *who*, though Harold wasn't supposed to reveal that."

"Just curious, what's the bear's name?"

"Ursa."

Elsa nodded. "I'm glad, as your friend, that you've shared this, but—not to be rude—why? What's any of this got to do with me?"

"I need your help, but I'm still relieved to have told you; it felt wrong hiding it from you. I'm going to be gone for a while with this training, and it wouldn't be good to have your family come looking for me, thinking something happened to me."

"So, you need me to cover for you?"

"Exactly."

"What do you want me to say then?"

Hyroc sighed. "I . . . I have no idea." Elsa shot him a confused look. "I was kind of hoping you could help me come up with something."

"Okay." She paused. "Well, it needs to be something believable, something you might actually do. How long will you be gone?"

"Don't know that either, but it'll be at least a couple of weeks."

Elsa nodded. "Which means hunting is probably out of the question because no one I know goes out hunting for that long. You could be taking a trip."

"That was something I thought of, but to where? It might seem strange for me to just up and decide to take a trip across Arnaira."

"Not necessarily. What if I tell everyone you heard some rumors about people who look like you, and that's where you went, to check it out."

"I don't know, seems a little thin."

"Yes, but it doesn't have to be complicated. You're the only one of your kind anyone in the village knows about. So, to me, at least, it seems reasonable you would jump at any opportunity to find out more about where you came from."

Hyroc waggled his head in half agreement. That was indeed something he desperately wanted to know. "That might work."

"Don't worry; I can do it. But just so you know, my mother's going to be very upset with you for not telling her yourself."

Hyroc cringed at the thought. That was something that had completely slipped his mind. But there was no way of avoiding it. "Yeah, I know, but I don't see a way around that. I'll just have to deal with the consequences when I get back."

"Alright. So, when are you leaving?"

Hyroc sighed. "Later today." She shot him a dismayed look. He shrugged. "I know; it's very sudden."

"Well, if this is goodbye, for now, I have to give you this." She stepped over to him and hugged his big head. She released him and stepped back. "I guess I'll be seeing you."

"Bye, Elsa, and thanks."

"Bye, Hyroc, and you're welcome." She turned and headed away from the cabin.

Hyroc watched her until she disappeared from view. He then turned his attention to Kit, who was playfully pawing at his shoulder. "Well, once I have hands again, I guess it'll be time for us to finish getting ready to go. The next couple of weeks should be interesting."

CHAPTER 9

A BEAR'S FIRESIDE

H yroc, get up," Ursa said.

Hyroc groaned groggily and rolled onto his other side, eyes still closed. It had been four days since he left his cabin. He had spent most of the previous night tossing and turning, and when he was finally comfortable enough to doze, some flying thing would buzz into his ears. With his lack of sleep, he had no desire to get up any time soon.

Through Hyroc's half-conscious sleep haze, he was delighted when she didn't persist. He felt a droplet of water land on his head. He lazily brushed the wet spot with his hand. Another droplet hit. Grumbling unhappily, he brushed the second droplet away. Then a deluge of cold water drenched his head. He yelled out, flinging his eyes open. Hands flailing, he rolled out from under the stream of water, but his body caught on an enormous white paw. The paw pressed down on his chest and roughly rolled him back into the downpour. Sputtering, he scrambled to his feet in a confused blur. When his eyes focused, he saw Ursa standing in front of him, holding his water skin between her jaws.

"WHAT WAS THAT FOR?" Hyroc yelled crossly.

She set his depleted water skin on the ground. "I told you to get up," she said with a subtle hint of enjoyment. "And since you had no intention of doing so, I needed to be more . . . *persuasive*. Now, get something to eat, we're leaving shortly." She turned and trotted off.

Grumbling under his breath, Hyroc used the bottom of his cloak to dry his sodden head. He grimaced as the fabric of the cloak brushed against a scab on the back of his left ear.

For the first two days of the journey, the surrounding forest had seemed much the same as the areas he had hunted in. Then sometime after noon on the third day, Ursa led him into an area of rough terrain heavily overgrown with devil's club, wild rose, and wide swaths of nettle. Seeing the inevitable pain passing through here would cause, he had suggested they go around. Ursa responded by informing him that if anyone happened across their tracks, they would reach the same conclusion when they reached this spot and wouldn't want to continue after them. No matter how much he tried to convince her that no one would follow them, he couldn't dissuade her and was forced to continue down the miserable path. With some caution, he avoided the spiked plants, but the bladed foliage steadily closed in around him. Soon thorns were catching on his clothes and he was sure he was leaving behind an unmistakable trail of black, blood speckled hair that anyone could follow. About halfway through the stinging fauna, he had ducked under the low hanging branch of a tree, and the thorny stem of a wild rose plant embedded itself in his ear.

Stepping over to his pack, Hyroc removed a strip of jerky and his last slice of bread. He studied the slice thoughtfully before eating it, wondering how long it would be until he ate bread again. Kit joined him as he finished with breakfast, licking his chops, indicating he had made a meal out of some unfortunate creature.

After they departed from their campsite, a light rain began, which continued well into the day. The minuscule droplets eventually turned into a heavier downpour. The canopy of leaves overhead steadily diminished until they were traveling through a flat lonely expanse of pine trees. When they reached the end of the trees, the ground opened up to a muskeg bog. Hyroc expected Ursa to sink when she stepped onto the spongy ground but, remarkably, she continued across without difficulty.

Despite getting some water over the lip of his boots, he was able to traverse the spongy terrain without issue. Then the rain let up considerably. Normally he would have appreciated this, but since they were close to so much stagnant water without anything falling from the sky, a veritable swarm of bloodthirsty insects was attempting to make a meal out of Kit and him.

They traveled through the bog for most of what remained of the day before the semisolid ground gave way to forest. The number of winged creatures dropped off noticeably, though Hyroc still felt he had a substantial entourage of proboscis-faced bloodsuckers. Close to dusk, they arrived at a clear stream flowing around the base of a house-sized boulder covered in yellow moss.

"Here we are," Ursa said. "Welcome to your new home."

"I'm glad," Hyroc said gratefully. He was starting to wonder when she was going to stop. "Now, I can finally dry my feet."

"You get a fire going; I'll be back soon," she said, before trudging into the trees.

After shaking as much moisture out of his boots as he could, Hyroc headed off to collect firewood. Dismayingly, any he found was completely soaked, making the prospect of a fire unlikely. He stubbornly tried to get a fire going anyway. Despite his determination, after only managing sparks that frustratingly disappeared as soon as they touched wood, it appeared he would be spending the night without the warmth of a fire. He studied the wood thoughtfully, thinking back to the magic he had used while fighting the Shade Hunter. It was some kind of fire, so maybe he could use it to light his kindling. He stretched his hand out over the wood in front of him, concentrating hard on igniting it. Nothing happened. With a displeased sigh, he moved his hand back. *It was worth a try.*

Ursa returned before nightfall, dragging the biggest fish—outside of depictions of sea monsters—Hyroc had ever seen.

"Where . . . where did you get *that behemoth*?" he asked, awestruck, as he gazed enviously at her catch.

"Up at the river not far from here," she answered. "Where's the fire?"

Hyroc shrugged. "Every piece of wood I found was soaked," he said unhappily. "I won't be able to get a fire going until they dry, which probably won't happen until morning."

Ursa walked over to the pile of wet wood and held a paw over it. A blue glow emanated from her paw and the wood started glowing a matching color. Then the pile burst into blue flame, which slowly faded to a natural orange color.

"How did you do that?" Hyroc said.

Without looking toward him, she said, "I believe you have some idea, but it is unimportant."

"How can *that* be unimportant? I already know I can use magic; lighting tinder with the wave of my hand would save me a lot of time and effort."

"Hyroc, enough; learning such things is for another time."

Hyroc sighed. "Fine."

She indicated the fish with her paw. "Get that cleaned, and while you work, there's something I need to tell you."

Hyroc gave her a suspicious look. "Hold on, is something strange, like what happened with that stone, going to happen to me tonight?"

"I would not expect so; it's time you learned the origins of your kind; the Wol'dger."

"You know that!" Hyroc exclaimed, accidentally making a jagged cut into the fish's skin in his excitement. "*Why haven't you told me this before?*"

"You were not ready to know such things."

"How could I have not been ready to know?"

"Would you like to hear it now or should I wait for you to finish?"

He took a breath. "Sorry; I'm just *really* excited, I've wanted to know that for as long as I can remember. I'll be quiet now."

"Thank you, but you may not feel that way by the time I'm finished."

Hyroc cocked an eyebrow and opened his mouth to reply, but an irritated glare from Ursa made him close it.

"It is said that long ago, in the kingdom of Wulfren, there arose a people of great hunters. They never took more than the land could sustain and treated the animals they hunted with great respect. The people prospered, building wealth by trading furs and hides of creatures no one else dared to hunt.

"But their wealth did not go unnoticed. Seeking to take the kingdom's riches for their own, a vast army of invaders marched into the land. Although the people of Wulfren were lethal hunters, they had little knowledge of the ways of war. Though they valiantly resisted their enemy, all the lands of Wulfren were quickly conquered, save their mightiest city, but it was only a matter of time until that too fell.

"Wulfren seemed to be on the eve of its destruction, but their struggle had not gone unnoticed. Because of their respect for the land and its animals, they had unknowingly gained favor in the eyes of Wearla. The invaders treated the fur-bearing animals of Wulfren cruelly, seeing them as nothing more than a mere means to obtaining wealth and, because of this, Wearla had no desire to allow them to become the new masters of the land.

"She appeared before the king of Wulfren and his advisers in the form of a creature with enormous white wings, the head of an eagle, and the body of a lion. A strange and terrifying sight. But the fear felt by those in attendance gave way to hope when Wearla revealed her intentions.

"Wearla lowered her large wings to the floor. She then raised them, revealing a wolf, big cat, bear, predatory bird, and a stag. She then instructed the king to choose one. He pointed at the bear. The bear walked over to the king and placed its paw on his right shoulder. The king then transformed into a large bear. Wearla promised the change would not be permanent, and instructed all present, if they wished to do so, to also choose an animal.

"The king was grateful for her gift, but he did not know how to fight with claws and teeth, instead of blades and bows. Wearla indicated the animals with her paw and said, 'they will teach you.' She then instructed the king to bring to her every able-bodied man and women who desired this gift, so more could be taught.

"When his people had been trained to fight as beasts, the king led what remained of his army into battle. With this new power, the people of Wulfren were able to push the invaders back."

"I don't understand how the ability to transform into animals helped them push the invaders back," Hyroc interrupted. "The invaders were clearly superior fighters."

"Think about it: bears are brutally strong; they can be very intimidating and are surprisingly fast." She gave him a humored look. "I should hope I would be an expert in this, don't you think?"

Suppressing a smile, Hyroc nodded.

She paused to regain her line of thinking before continuing. "Wolves are fast, capable of running prey down over challenging terrain and incredibly long distances. As you know, big cats have enormous slashing claws, a deadly proficiency with their teeth, move silently, and are capable of lightning-fast bursts of speed. Deer can quickly traverse open ground and have sharp antlers they can use for slashing and stabbing. Now, the bird forms, they work a little differently. When somebody turns into a bird, that form is enlarged to more closely match the size of the other animals. These birds could easily carry off a grown man, drop a boulder onto the heads of enemies, or impale them with their talons. Now imagine an army of deer, wolves, bears, cats, and enormous birds, all possessing the ability to think like humans."

Hyroc nodded his understanding. With her putting it that way, he had to admit it would be pretty frightening.

"Mind you, the majority of the Wulfren people were frightened of this gift and did not accept it, so most of the Wulfren army was still comprised of people using human-made weapons. However, those people, combined with those fighting in animal form, now provided the Wulfren army with a substantial advantage over the invaders.

"A bloody battle was fought, with many lives lost on both sides, but Wulfren emerged victorious. When the king returned to the city, Wearla appeared before him a second time. She commanded that her gift was never to be used to take from others by force, except through the course of defending themselves from an aggressor. When she finished speaking, she vanished, leaving the people in the hands of her animal allies and the king. Her allies further taught the people how to use their animal forms in times of peace and times of war. And for many years, there was peace in the land."

"These allies you're talking about," Hyroc interjected. "Were they Guardians, like you?"

"That they were, as was Wearla."

Hyroc shot her a look of surprise. "Really, some of you can look like that?"

"Indeed we can, though we have not taken such a form in quite some time." Hyroc nodded. "At least I know you're paying attention," Ursa said.

She paused again before resuming the story. "For generations, the Wulfrens upheld Wearla's commandment and, with the assistance of her fellow Guardians, the kingdom continued to prosper. More invasions followed, but they all met an unfavorable end. After the final invasion had been thwarted, the people became prideful, sure that none could stand before them; not even Wearla and her fellow Guardians. Some even went so far as to seek out Guardians to test their strength against. At first, it was only the occasional person engaging in a fight. Other than that person receiving painful but relatively minor injuries as a reminder, nothing much came of it. These occasional acts of defiance continued for a time until someone foolishly attempted to kill a Guardian, tragically resulting in that person's death.

"An outcry for vengeance ensued, and in order to avoid needless bloodshed, the Guardians departed. A few ventured to the sacred places established for them to impart their knowledge to those who had remained loyal to their ways, in the hope they would continue to teach the people in their stead. Once this was done, those last remaining Guardians left for good.

"The Wulfrens naively saw the departure of the Guardians as a sign of their own unstoppable power. They turned their eyes to a small and wealthy kingdom on their border. Leading an army of men with the transformation gift, the king's son conquered the kingdom, returning home with substantial plunder. As punishment for their disobedience, Wearla cursed the people of Wulfren to forever look like the beasts they so adored, thus creating the Wol'dger."

All of Hyroc's excitement suddenly drained from him. "Hold on—I'm—*I'm cursed!*" he said in a bewildered tone. "My whole life,

I've been treated like I'm some *evil thing*; people have even tried to kill me on numerous occasions, and you're telling me that those people were right in doing so."

"I would not consider their blind fear of something they do not understand as justification for their actions," Ursa said.

Hyroc stared despondently into the fire. "That's why I look the way I do. I should've known better than to have expected anything better; I'm cursed," he said coldly. "How could there have been any other explanation? It was right in front of me this whole time, and I didn't see it. Everything Marcus said about me was wrong."

Ursa regarded him curiously. "Wrong? How so?"

Hyroc sighed mockingly. "I'm cursed," he said bitterly. "All those things he said about me being like everyone else were wrong. How could I be anything like everyone else when—," he sharply indicated his face with his hand "—I look like this?"

"Yes, you *are* cursed, but you are quite incorrect in your thinking."

Hyroc laughed humorlessly. "That shouldn't come as much of a surprise there; it seems I was incorrect thinking about things my whole life."

"This curse does not define you, what you—"

"Ursa, stop it!" Hyroc snapped. "You weren't the one constantly being reassured that despite how badly everyone treated you, there was nothing wrong with you. That the only thing that mattered was what was on the inside. But none of what I was told was ever true. There was something wrong with me, something that could not be covered up, and it was a curse that vibrantly showed itself. My mother had its affliction, and she passed it on to me."

"Yes, Hyroc, but—"

"No, Ursa, nothing you say will make this okay. I bear the shame of my ancestors and what's done is done." He could see a pained look in Ursa's normally stoic eyes, but he had no compassionate desire to acknowledge it. He shook his head irritably and turned to leave. "I want to be alone."

"And I will grant you this." She rose to her feet. "The next step begins tomorrow at first light if you still wish to continue." With that, she headed off toward the shadows of the trees."

Hyroc headed over to his gear, stopping at the trunk of a birch tree. He pounded the palm of his hand into its hard-papery surface, barely holding back tears. The telling of one story had unraveled every positive thing he had ever held onto. His whole life was a lie!

CHAPTER 10
DIVERTED

Keller looked eagerly across the grassy plains before him. The snow had melted, and he could now confidently resume his search for the Hyroc creature. Those long cold winter months spent quartered near the town of Rivermark, when he was unable to proceed with his task, had given him plenty of time to mull over his strategy. It was flawed. He had grossly underestimated the capabilities of his target. The lack of any evidence near the western wilderness or even a rumor made that clear. The Hyroc creature hadn't been making its way toward the closest area of the wilderness. It had potentially used some other course to get there or it had found someplace of refuge within Arnaira. He just had to figure out where. Searching toward the East was a good starting point since the plains offered considerable areas of unoccupied land that would be a prime place for the creature to make a new home where no one was likely to come across it. Soon maybe the Hyroc creature's threat would be eliminated. It was a nice thought, but considering his target's apparent ability for evasion, he knew it was improbable, and that he must brace himself for a very long, drawn-out hunt.

He drew in a long breath of the morning air, its cool freshness giving him strength. He turned toward a soldier of captain rank, who stood beside him. "Captain," Keller said, "order your men to break camp as soon as possible. I want to head out by this afternoon."

"Yes sir," the captain said, his tone eager. He turned and headed off to carry out his orders.

Keller saw the man stop, looking at something. He turned his head to see what the man was looking at. Coming up the thin, dirt path that divided his camp in two, he saw a carriage escorted by an entourage of mounted guards who bore symbols of The Ministry. It seemed an Inquisitor was paying him an unexpected visit. It wasn't uncommon for Light Bringers to check on his progress every so often, but never someone of this rank. Something was going on.

He brushed off his clothes and straightened out any wrinkles he could find. The escorts and carriage came to a gradual stop in front of him. A middle-aged Inquisitor emerged from the carriage, assisted by his aide. The man gave Keller an appraising look.

"Welcome, Inquisitor," Keller said politely. "To what do I owe the honor of your visit?"

The man glanced toward the camp, then back to Keller, before speaking. "Have you made any further progress with your search?" the man asked in an almost absent-minded tone.

"Not yet, but I have some new leads. We were just breaking camp and heading out."

The man nodded. "I am afraid I'm not the bearer of good news. I am here to inform you that you are to discontinue your search."

Keller shot the man a baffled look. "Discontinue?" he said in disbelief. "But I *have* new leads. We cannot afford to let that creature move freely through our lands."

The man's expression grew grim. "This is well understood, but we have a more pressing concern. A significant contingent of North Lander marauders has begun raiding the farmlands and villages to the east of the capital. We urgently need as many able-bodied soldiers as can be mustered to repel this barbaric intrusion upon our lands. You are to take your men to meet up with the rest of our forces east of the capital, where we will meet our foes on the field of battle. Are my instructions understood?"

"Yes sir, you can count on us."

"Good." The man signaled to his aide, who handed Keller a rolled-up scroll documenting his orders. "You have your orders, now get to it! And I would suggest you hurry." Keller saluted him. With that, the man retreated into his carriage and, after a moment, he and his entourage departed.

Keller rushed back into his command tent, unrolled it, and began pouring over the details it contained. The fulfillment of his task was finally within his grasp, but thanks to a violent band of savages, his success was in jeopardy and so too, undoubtedly, were countless innocent lives. He would have to turn his attention from the Hyroc creature for the time being, but the hunt was definitely not over.

"Captain," Keller said. "You heard the man; we've got a battle waiting for us. The men need to work faster."

"Yes, sir," the captain said. "I'll get right on that." He saluted Keller before stepping out through the tent flap.

Keller set the scroll down on a table, moving quickly toward a small wooden box full of rolled-up maps to plan the best route to his destination.

CHAPTER 11

A BEAR'S BREAKFAST

Hyroc sat on his deer hide sleeping mat, staring at the smoldering remains of the fire Ursa had made the night before. He had awakened some time ago, sleep proving somewhat elusive after what he had learned the night before.

Ursa came into view, heading over to him. She gave him a subtly surprised look, seeing him already awake and waiting for her.

"Have your thoughts changed?" Ursa said.

Hyroc shrugged. "No, they haven't," he said unenthusiastically.

The thought of abandoning his training had crossed his mind during the night after Ursa's life-shattering story. But despite how he felt, doing so didn't seem like it would accomplish anything useful. There wasn't exactly anything urgent for him to go back to. Besides, if what Ursa said about his becoming a potential danger to his friends was true, leaving wouldn't help the matter. They had nothing to do with everything in his life before Elswood going up in smoke. And for as much as he knew, their interactions with him were genuine. He might as well do what he could to preserve his current reality while it still existed.

"Good," Ursa answered. "From this point on, no matter how strange or difficult my guidance may seem, you must follow it. None of it is pointless. Do you understand?" Hyroc nodded his acknowledgment.

"You may, however, abandon this at any time, but be warned; if you do, you may not be able to resist the influence of your animal form fully and may become a danger to those you care about."

"I've never thought of myself as a quitter. Of course, that assumption could also prove to be untrue, just like many other things in my life. Who knows, maybe I actually am a quitter. But given the risk of possibly hurting my friends if I don't see this through, I have to try."

"Very well. Before we start, you need to first enter into your animal form."

"Can I have breakfast first?"

"I've already found breakfast for us, and it is much fresher than anything you brought, but I need you to be in your animal form."

Hyroc nodded and settled into position. Clearing his mind, he saw the image of the moon. Starting at his marked shoulder, he felt the familiar warm sensation spread throughout his body. He opened his eyes and was again surprised to see the thick forelegs of a bear where his arm should have been.

"Okay, I'm a bear, now what?"

"Hold out your right paw," Ursa said.

Hyroc tentatively held out his paw, making sure he wasn't going to lose his balance by standing on only three legs. Ursa put her paw over his, flexed the digits to get a grip, and closed her eyes. Hyroc saw a pale blue glow emanate from her paw. A hot sensation shot up his arm, settling at his shoulder. He had barely enough time to register the feeling before it vanished. Ursa released him from her grip.

"What did you just do?" Hyroc asked. He flexed the digits of his paw as he turned it over, trying to see if he could discern anything different. As far as he could tell, his paw was as it had been a moment ago.

"Nothing important," Ursa answered. "But now we can eat."

Trying to pry the answer out of her seemed pointless. The answer would undoubtedly manifest itself eventually, likely when it was the most inconvenient.

"What are we—"

Ursa put her back to him, walking away. She uprooted two fire-weed plants, and with them secured between her jaws, moved back over to him, dropping the green leafy stalks in front of him. Hyroc studied the plant, confused.

"Enjoy."

Baffled, Hyroc looked from the plant to her face and back again. He indicated the plant with a raised paw. "Umm, that's fireweed."

"It is."

"No, I mean, what's it for?"

Ursa gave him an amused look. "For eating."

His expression turned shocked. "What! Why would I want to eat *that*?"

"If you want to *think like a bear*, you need to *eat like a bear*."

"When you said *breakfast*, I thought you meant *food*, not some random plant you pulled from the ground."

Ursa raised her paw and indicated behind him. "If you feel this is beneath you, then as I made clear to you earlier, you may leave."

Hyroc cocked an eyebrow. "I didn't say that, no I—"

"Then *stop complaining* and eat your fireweed."

Hyroc sighed irritably at being interrupted, lowered his head to the fireweed, and gave it an investigative sniff. He looked back at Ursa. "This isn't some misunderstanding—you want me to eat this?"

"I would not have said it if I meant otherwise."

"But what does eating this have to do with learning how to use my bear form? I think I understand how to eat, even if I'm a bear."

"As I said, 'If you want to think like a bear, you need to eat like a bear.' This is what bears eat. Understanding why this is necessary is not required; all that *is* required is for you to do it. And if you will not, you may leave, it is that simple."

Hyroc sighed, returning his gaze to the fireweed. It was clear he wasn't going to win this argument. Leaving was an enticing option, but he dreaded the thought of becoming a danger to his friends. As unpleasant as this would be, he would do it. If he could eat cold-flour mush, he was sure he could handle eating fireweed.

Instinctively he reached forward with a paw to pick up the plant but immediately realized he couldn't do so. Now feeling somewhat self-conscious about making such a mistake in front of Ursa, he put his paw down, lowered his head, and reluctantly nibbled at one of the leaves. The flavor was more agreeable than he expected.

"See, it's not so bad." Hyroc rolled his eyes contemptuously. "And the entire plant is edible. When you're done eating, I'll show you what else bears eat."

Mid bite, Hyroc snapped his eyes toward her in alarm. "What! You mean, you're going to make me eat *other things like this*."

"Of course, you can't live off fireweed alone."

"But . . . but I . . . I thought you were teaching me to be a bear, not . . . *not a moose!*"

"Moose eat pine needles," Ursa corrected. "And you will not—nor should you—eat pine needles, even as a bear. However, bears can eat plenty of other plants in addition to meat, with their diet consisting mainly of the former."

Hyroc stared at her with a confounded expression, and Ursa obstinately returned his gaze. With an aggravated grumble, knowing what that look entailed, he turned his attention back to the fireweed, took an enormous bite, and chewed it angrily.

"I'm glad we've come to an understanding."

His anger faded when it occurred to him that Ursa was probably just demonstrating this purely for instructive purposes, and later he would be able to go hunting for some real food. Glancing behind him as he chewed another mouthful of leaves, he was horrified to find that his hunting gear, sword, the deerskin he had slept on, and everything else he had brought with him was nowhere in sight.

He hurriedly swallowed before yelling out, "Ursa, my things are gone!"

She answered in a calm tone. "Bears do not use tools, so neither will you."

Hyroc shot her a dumbfounded look. "WHAT! You mean to tell me you won't let me use any of my things?"

"That is correct."

"I came here so you could teach me how to be a bear, not for you to torture me and steal my things!"

Ursa gave him an annoyed snort. "Torture?" she scoffed. "I would hardly consider what I'm doing as *torture*. And you need not worry about your belongings, they are protected from the elements, and I promise you'll get everything back once you've finished with your training."

"I'm glad to hear *that*, but if I can't make a fire, and don't have something to sleep on, I'll freeze tonight."

Ursa shook her head. "I assure you; you won't freeze."

Hyroc shot her a look of disbelief. "How is that possible? The ground gets pretty cold at night."

"Your fur will keep you warm."

"No, it won't, it might during the day, but I'll still—," he trailed off, as a disturbing thought entered his mind. What if she wasn't talking about the fur of his natural form? "Hold on, what do you mean by *fur*?"

"A bear's fur is an excellent insulator; you won't get cold at night, even if you're lying on the ground."

He gave her a suspicious glare as a prickle of apprehension materialized in his mind. "Wait, wait, why wouldn't I be in my natural form?"

"Because I put a form-lock on you, you cannot go back into your natural form."

Hyroc felt a wave of dread slam into him. "WHAT! I'm stuck like this?"

"Only for the time being."

Why did everything have to be so complicated with this bear? She never told him the whole truth about anything. Everything came with surprises. It was almost as if she did nothing other than devise ways of deceiving him.

"So, what, I can't quit *even if I want to*?" Hyroc said scathingly.

"You assume incorrectly, the effects of the form-lock would dissipate by the time you reached your cabin, should you choose to quit."

"Well, that's a bit of a relief, but I still can't believe you would do something like this. I'm getting sick of you always keeping things from me."

She shook her head, dismissively. "You agreed to let me teach you and, by doing so, you also agreed to everything that accompanies it." She spoke in a more reassuring tone. "I know you're upset about this, but I assure you, you'll be fine."

Hyroc took a deep breath. It was frustrating. Ursa had stripped him of his things, trapped him in bear form—and she had done the latter to him without his knowledge—but, grudgingly, the more he thought about it, the more she made sense. He was learning how to be a bear, and spending his time as one might be the easiest way to learn, as unpleasant as it might be.

Hyroc sighed. "Okay, I *think* I understand. But I'm still angry you would spring this on me."

"I would be surprised if you didn't understand. But let me ask you this—would knowing about it before have altered your decision?"

Hyroc opened his mouth to answer but couldn't bring himself to speak when it occurred to him that it probably wouldn't have. Subduing a surge of embarrassment, mixed with irritation, he turned back to the fireweed and continued eating. When he finished, now in a slightly more subdued mood, he headed toward the stream.

"Where are you going?" Ursa said.

"To get a drink of water," Hyroc said sharply, though he was mostly looking for an excuse to get away from her.

"When you're done, meet me in the meadow beyond the trees where you went to sleep."

Hyroc nodded his acknowledgment as he continued toward the stream.

At the edge of the gently flowing water, he reached forward with one paw and tried cupping water into it. It then became apparent to him that the digits of his paw were not dexterous enough to accomplish this. He shook the moisture from his paw and bent down to drink the water straight up. On his second mouthful, he sucked in a water bug that had skirted too close to his mouth. Coughing, he lurched back. As his fit ended, the foliage further downstream rustled as something moved through it. He watched the spot anxiously, unsure what he should do if something dangerous appeared. Kit emerged an instant later, carrying a grouse in his mouth. He froze, and his body went rigid in a show of alarm when his gaze focused on Hyroc.

"It's me," Hyroc quickly called out.

Kit cocked his head, puzzled, but his body became relaxed. He studied Hyroc, then bounded across the stream over to him. As soon as he arrived, he began a thorough sniff-over of Hyroc's body.

"Well, at least one of us got something good," Hyroc said, as he patiently waited for Kit to finish his investigation. "Ursa made me eat two entire fireweed plants for breakfast. Can you believe *that*? I can think of several berry plants that would've made a much better meal. Helen made me some jelly out of fireweed once, but so far, nothing on that plant tastes anywhere close to what she made. And if that weren't bad enough, apparently I'm stuck like *this*—," he indicated himself with his eyes, "—until Ursa's done training me to be a bear."

Kit pulled his head back and affectionately rubbed against Hyroc's shoulder. Hyroc reached over with one paw to scratch Kit between the ears but ended up jabbing him in the nose. He cringed as Kit sharply recoiled. Kit answered with a vengeful glower.

"Sorry," Hyroc said. He flexed the digits of his paw. "I still haven't adjusted to not having hands yet." Seemingly satisfied by his apology, Kit offered him the grouse. Hyroc shook his paw dismissively at the lifeless, and nearly headless, bird. "You keep it; I just ate." Kit turned toward the stream, dropped the grouse on the ground, and stepped over to take a drink. Hyroc watched him inquisitively as he lapped up the water. There seemed little chance for choking on an accidentally swallowed bug that way. He ventured closer to the stream, and copying Kit, he tried lapping up some water. He was surprised at how well his tongue moved the liquid into his mouth. It was nowhere as efficient as drinking from a container, but it was good enough to sate his thirst.

Hyroc wiped his mouth with the back of his paw and happily said to Kit, "Thanks, buddy."

Kit stopped drinking to give him an indifferent look before turning his attention back to the stream. Hyroc carefully reached toward Kit and lightly rubbed his head with his paw. Kit stiffened in mild surprise then pushed up against Hyroc's paw. Hyroc tried smiling but found he was unable to make his face comply.

"I should probably get going; Ursa might decide to make me eat some bark if I keep her waiting." He turned and headed off in the instructed direction.

Through the trees, he arrived at a mostly flat, sunlit meadow, covered in dandelions, patches of clover, and a variety of other flowering plants.

"So, what do you want me to do now?" Hyroc asked as he approached Ursa, who sat at the edge of the meadow.

Using an outstretched paw, she indicated a patch of dandelions in front of her. "Dandelions are also edible; just avoid the roots."

Hyroc sighed and, knowing what she was about to ask, bit off the flower of the nearest dandelion. Unexpectedly, the flower part had a mildly sweet taste to it, but the leaves and stem were bitter.

Ursa nodded happily. "You may yet finish what I ask of you."

"How many of these do I need to eat?"

"Eat until you're no longer hungry."

He gave her a despairing look and sighed quietly before nipping off another dandelion flower. *It's not that bad. It's not cold flour. Thank goodness it's not cold flour.* He ate as many of the yellow flowers as he could stand before finding Ursa. She began leading him around the meadow, showing him edible plants while lecturing him about them. She did this for what felt like hours, many, many, boring hours, before heading into the surrounding trees. Mercifully the lecturing ceased when they arrived at a fallen tree.

"Please tell me you're *not* going to make me eat the wood on that," Hyroc said sarcastically. He wasn't expecting his earlier joke to come true!

Ursa gave him a strange look. "No, bears *don't* eat wood."

Hyroc breathed a sigh of relief. She did have a heart. "Good."

"We're after what's inside."

Hyroc shot her a confused look. "Inside? What could possibly be inside of it besides bu— *you're not serious.*"

Ursa spoke in a humored tone. "I'm quite serious, and they're called grubs."

"I don't care what they're called; they're still bugs! *And I am not eating bugs.*"

Hyroc saw a disconcerting glimmer come into her eyes. "You don't? Do you know how many bugs were on those flowers you ate? You didn't seem to mind eating them."

He felt a creeping shiver of revulsion at the thought. "Well . . . well, I didn't do it on purpose."

"Regardless, if you're going to stay healthy, you'll need more than plants to eat. This is no different than varying your diet by having bread with meat." Hyroc opened his mouth to launch another round of protests. Ursa cut him off by saying, "And before you waste your breath, you should know by now that you cannot persuade me otherwise. You must do what I say, or you will not proceed to the next lesson."

Hyroc loosed a loud, irritated huff. "*Fine*, I'll eat your stupid grubs!"

"I'm glad we've come to an understanding," Ursa said, in a voice laced with enjoyment. "Now I'll show you how to find one."

"I'll try to contain my enthusiasm," Hyroc said in a scathing tone, as he stepped closer to the fallen tree.

Ursa tapped the tree with her paw and moved an ear to its rotten bark, listening. She gave the tree another tap as she moved down its length. On the third tap, after lingering for a moment, she gestured for Hyroc to come closer.

"Put your ear here," she said. Hyroc put his ear against the indicated spot. "Now listen carefully." She tapped the tree. He did his best to listen for whatever he was supposed to hear. Other than the initial sound of her tap and the chirp of a sparrow soaring overhead, he didn't hear anything. "Did you hear it?"

"No."

"Close your eyes and listen carefully." He closed his eyes, and she tapped the tree again. He heard a subtle scraping noise.

"I think I hear something."

"Use your claws to strip away the bark from the tree where the noise is coming from."

Knowing what awaited him after his task, he reluctantly did as she said. Once his claws found purchase in the bark, he easily tore a large chunk free. Then he saw something white wiggle farther down a hole in the tree. Cautiously, he tore another piece off where the thing should be, revealing a fat, pulsating, white grub.

"Don't just stand there gawking at it, eat it."

"Do I really have to eat *that*?" Hyroc asked, disgusted by the very thought of putting something so repulsive in his mouth.

"Yes, you do, and if you continue trying to get out of it, you'll encounter something fast-moving flying toward your head."

Defeated, and understanding her meaning, Hyroc shrugged, returning his attention to the grub. He swallowed and hesitantly moved his face closer to it. He turned his head to look back at Ursa, hoping to elicit some form of sympathy, but when she gave him a warning glare, he knew there was no avoiding his fate. He closed his eyes and tentatively clamped his teeth around the wriggling grub. He felt its mandibles pinching his tongue. Then with an enormous mental effort, he slurped it into his mouth. As soon as he bit down on the grub, it exploded, filling his mouth with a grainy, rotten tasting substance. Staving off the urge to gag, he chewed the grub no more than was needed before swallowing. He felt violated doing so. The taste of dandelion greens or fireweed didn't seem all that bad anymore.

"See, it wasn't that bad. Ready for another one?"

Hyroc stared at her, horrified. "*Another one?*" How could she say such an awful thing? One was more than enough to understand this lesson.

"One isn't enough to sustain you. Eat another; then we can move on."

He forced himself to tap the tree and listen for the scraping noise. To his dismay, he found a grub on his second tap. This one was even bigger! When he put it in his mouth, the grub pinched his tongue hard enough for it to hurt. This one also exploded when he bit down on it.

"Good job."

Hyroc just gave her a sideways glare.

Ursa then resumed lecturing him on plants, and the rest of his day passed in this manner. When they returned to the moss-covered boulder, Hyroc glowered at the ground as he tried to figure out the best place to lie on.

Taking notice of his grumpy manner, Ursa said, "Hyroc, you need not sleep with nothing between you and the ground. Bears do make beds."

She walked over to an alder and waved a glowing blue paw over one of the branches, causing leaves to drift to the ground. She gathered the leaves into a pile, and using the side of a forelimb, slid it away. After spreading the leaves out, she tore a large chunk of moss from the side of the boulder. With it dangling from her mouth, she carried it over to the leaves and carefully laid it over them. When she was satisfied with the arrangement of the materials, she laid down on it.

"See, I now have something between me and the ground, but you can use whatever materials you prefer to make yours—just make sure nothing you use is poisonous."

Hyroc swept his eyes around and headed over to a lodge pine growing on the other side of the boulder. He snapped off five branches with his teeth then laid them down at the base of the boulder near where Ursa lay. Over the branches, he laid a layer of grass mixed with foxtail and covered the whole thing with moss. When he laid on the bed, he was impressed by the level of comfort it conferred.

Ursa gave him an accepting nod. "A wise choice of materials. Now, get some sleep, we've got more work to do tomorrow."

"I'll try," Hyroc grumbled under his breath.

He rolled onto his back. Lying in this position caused him to hold his paws at an awkward angle, so he rolled onto his side. This new position proved more comfortable. Glancing toward Ursa to see how she was lying, he slid one paw forward, set his head on it, and closed his eyes. His thick bear fur kept him surprisingly warm despite the chill of the night air on his nose but, without a blanket or fire, he still felt cold. No matter how tired he felt, sleep proved an impossibility. Just as the haunting nag of dismay at the prospect of dealing with Ursa without the reprieve of sleep was taking root, he became aware of the sound of footfall. Looking toward the sound, he saw Kit approaching from the direction of the meadow. Kit stopped at the edge of the trees looking from Ursa to Hyroc, figuring out which bear was which and headed over to Hyroc. The big cat gave him a short but equally thorough sniffing before lying down with his body pressed against Hyroc's back, and began cleaning a paw. Hyroc felt Kit's body heat pleasantly adding to his own.

"I owe you one," Hyroc said.

Kit stopped cleaning his paw and gave him a look that seemed to say, "No, you owe me *two* for today." He then resumed his cleaning. Hyroc put his head back down and was finally able to sleep.

The next morning, once he had relieved the stiff soreness of his body by stretching, he made himself a breakfast of dandelions, fireweed, and flowers from a lungwort plant. At the end of that, Ursa began showing him poisonous plants. When they stopped to eat at noon, rain clouds darkened the sky, and a substantial downpour commenced. Hyroc gladly stopped feeding on the greenery to take shelter underneath a tree.

"Hyroc," Ursa said, "What are you doing?"

Somewhat puzzled, Hyroc used his paw to indicate the sky and said, "It's raining; I don't want to get soaked."

"There's no need, now come, finish eating."

"But *I'll* get soaked; I don't think getting chilled will help anyone."

"Yes, you're going to get wet, but bears have two layers of fur—the outer is waterproof, and the inner will keep you warm, and if the rain starts to get through, you can shake it off."

"What, so you're saying I won't get cold even in this storm?"

"No, you'll still get cold—"

He shot her a confounded look. "*Then why are you making me stand out in the rain?*"

"Because a bear wouldn't let a little cold stop them."

Hyroc shook his head in disbelief. "But I'm not actually—"

"A bear? Yes, I know; you whine far too much to be considered one of us. A coyote would probably be a more apt description."

Hyroc narrowed his eyes, feeling his face warm. "*I am not whining. I just don't see—*"

"Then speak no more of the rain *and finish eating.*"

101

He loudly sighed as he headed out from under the shelter of the tree. Was Ursa teaching him to be a bear or how to be miserable? He was already well versed in the latter.

Unsurprisingly, within minutes, he was drenched and on the verge of shivering. He shook and shed nearly all the water from his body. Then an irritatingly short amount of time later, he was yet again soaked. He spent his next several hours shaking off water while doing his best to pay attention to Ursa's lesson. He was ecstatic when the sky lightened and it stopped raining. The rest of the day consisted of catching grasshoppers at Ursa's direction.

After breakfast, Ursa proceeded to quiz him on everything she had taught him over the last two days. He couldn't answer some of her questions, but she seemed satisfied with the information he had retained.

"There is one more task you must do before you can move on to the next lesson," Ursa said. Hyroc braced himself for whatever horrible thing she was going to make him do. "Bring me the flower of a lily pad."

"A lily pad?" he repeated, taken aback.

"Yes."

He swept his eyes around. "Don't those only grow in lakes and ponds?"

"Yes, they do."

"Umm, I haven't seen anything like that since we left my cabin. Are you saying I need to go *all the way back* to the lake near my cabin?"

"No, I wouldn't make you do that; that would be an unnecessary waste of time."

"Then where am I supposed to find a lily pad?"

"We passed an area with one on our way here."

Pondering Ursa's statement, he remembered the bog they had walked through. "Are you talking about that bog?"

"That I am."

"Lily pads grow in places like that?"

"Not usually, but there is a place there where some have taken root. It's not a big bog, so you should be able to find one and be back here before sundown."

"And all I have to do is bring you the flower?"

"Correct."

He nodded satisfactorily to himself. "That doesn't sound *too bad*. Okay, I'll be back with a lily pad flower." He paused. "Are you coming with me?"

"No."

"What if I run into something dangerous along the way? I don't know how to defend myself in this form."

"You need not be concerned with that; I made sure there was nothing of concern in the area."

Hyroc nodded, turned away from her, and headed off.

He figured he was getting close when his encounters with mosquitoes increased sharply. It then became apparent how truly inconvenient not having hands was. Other than using his paws to swat them off his head or twitching his ears, he was practically defenseless against his winged assailants. He quickened his pace and tried to ignore the itching bites.

Not long afterward, he reached the edge of the bog. He scanned his surroundings for lily pads. Farther into the bog, near a projecting spike of land with long spindly lopsided pines, he spotted a handful of unhealthy-looking lily pads.

As soon as he stepped onto the spongy ground, he sank. When he lifted his paw, he felt suction on it. He continued forward on this patch of the mushy ground until he arrived at a large expanse of stagnant water, leading to the lily pads. Reluctantly, he plunged into the cool dirty water. Mercifully, the water only reached below his chin, enabling him to continue walking.

When he arrived at the lily pads, he approached the only one healthy enough to have grown a flower and severed it from the plant with a quick bite. As he pulled back with the flower in his mouth, he saw a slimy black leech inching across the top of his nose. He reached up with one paw and slapped the leech away. Spurred on by the appearance of the bloodsucking slug, he hurriedly made his way back to where he had come from. He climbed back onto the patch of soggy ground, with streams of dirty brown water running off his body. When he shook, he saw a shiny black spot fly from him. Looking down, he was terrified to see leeches stuck to his abdomen and chest. He frantically tried to brush them off. A couple of the leeches lost their hold, but the others remained firmly attached as they fed upon him. No matter how many times he tried, he couldn't rid himself of his disgusting passengers. It took a tremendous mental effort to ignore the parasites and head back to camp.

"Good job, you got it," Ursa said when Hyroc dropped the flower in front of her at dusk.

"There were leeches in that bog!" he nearly yelled. "They were *on me*, sucking my blood, *and I couldn't get them off*; I had no choice but to let them finish."

"I thought that wouldn't have come as much of a surprise to you, but they won't cause you any lasting harm."

He used his paw to indicate his chest. "They made me bleed all over myself, and I think I'm still bleeding from some of the spots where they bit me."

"It is an insignificant amount they have taken from you; you won't suffer any lasting harm." Hyroc sighed irritably. "Just think of it like you've been out feeding ducks."

"How is this anything like feeding ducks; *Ducks* don't attach themselves to your body, *and they don't drink your blood!*"

Ursa gave him a humored look. "True, but surely you made those leeches happy."

"Yes, they must think *I'm delicious.*"

CHAPTER 12

THE ONE PROBLEM WITH HONEY

Hyroc grit his teeth as Ursa's paw sailed into the side of his head. After learning how to eat like a bear, how to sleep like a bear, and how to communicate with other bears, Ursa had announced that he needed to learn how to fight like a bear. He had attempted arguing the insanity of this, given that he had no plans of ever fighting with a real bear, but as with all her lessons, her mind was unchangeable. So every day since, he had been experiencing new kinds of pain and discomfort in the form of her lessons.

Pushing through the disorientation caused by the strike, Hyroc backpedaled on his hind legs as Ursa lunged toward him to lock his head between her paws. Now with nothing to grab hold of, Ursa stumbled. Seeing an opening, Hyroc jumped at her to throw his paws around her neck. She jerked upright, sidestepped his attack, and brought one of her paws down hard on the top of his head as he passed. He grunted as the force of the impact drove him onto the ground, forcing the air from his lungs. Then he felt the sharp pinch of Ursa's teeth biting into the back of his neck. Frustratingly, he was becoming accustomed to the uncomfortable sensation.

"You overcommitted," Ursa said, as she allowed Hyroc to rise on all fours. "If you make an opening for your opponent, they will take advantage of it." He waggled his head from side to side in reluctant agreement; he should have known better. "Ready?" With a sigh, Hyroc nodded, and the two of them stood up on their hind legs. "Just remember not to over-commit this time; it'll do you no good."

Ursa wrapped her paws around his neck and started pulling. Hyroc twisted out of her hold and retaliated with a paw swipe to her face, throwing her head sideways. He gripped her neck with his paws and began pulling on it. Ursa shoved him back with a push to his chest. He lost his hold but, other than a slight stumble backward, maintained his balance. Ursa lunged forward, locked his head between her forelimbs, and wrenched his head to the side. Hyroc bent his neck forward to loosen her hold, then yanked his shoulders back. She lost her grip and he narrowly avoided a nip to the neck.

Hyroc sidestepped Ursa, but before he could take advantage of his positioning, she turned toward him. She threw a paw strike at his head. Hyroc leaned back out of the way, feeling the wind pull at the fur beneath his chin. He lunged forward, put his paws around her neck and, hoping to unbalance her, yanked her toward him at an angle. Ursa staggered forward, throwing a paw onto his shoulder to steady herself. Then, to his amazement, she lifted her head to bite his neck before she had fully regained her balance. Hyroc jerked his upper body sideways away from her head. She missed his neck, but he felt a sharp pain as she sank her teeth into his shoulder instead. He yelled out in pain, immediately abandoning their sparring match. Ursa grabbed his snout and neck with her paws, pulled his head down, following through with a light nip to his neck.

Hyroc shoved off her and dropped down on all fours. "YOU BIT ME!" he yelled, glancing at the growing spot of blood soaking into his fur. He could tell it wasn't a bad injury, but he was irritated Ursa had bitten him hard enough to draw blood.

Ursa gave him a curious look. "Of course, I bit you," she said calmly. "In a real fight with another bear, you're going to get bitten."

"That really hurt!" Hyroc said indignantly. "*And I'm bleeding.*" He pushed his shoulder forward to show her the extent of what she had done to him.

She spoke without acknowledging she had hurt him. "If a bear bites you, you should expect to bleed, and you should expect it to hurt."

Hyroc rolled his eyes as he sighed unhappily. "I already know *that*, I don't see the lesson to be learned in *you* biting me like that."

Ursa shook her head in annoyance. "It was apparent you had acquired a solid understanding of sparring and were ready to move on to something closer to an actual fight."

Hyroc slammed his paws down in anger, turned away from her, and stormed off toward the opposite end of the meadow. He had had enough of this conversation.

"Hyroc, where are you going?" Ursa said.

"To get something to eat!" Hyroc glowered, without turning around.

He found a small patch of dandelions and savagely tore their brightly colored heads off. It was infuriating how Ursa could justify hurting him. He already knew what pain felt like; his bullies had taught him that lesson. Learning how to fight like a bear made some sense, but to purposely injure him during a practice sparring match was going too far. It was a bit of a cheap shot, almost as if she wanted to ensure he lost. That wouldn't surprise him much, considering her habit of throwing unexpected things at him.

Footfall sounded behind him. He growled. "I'm *not* quitting," he said sharply. "I just want to be left alone for now." A moment passed before the footfall resumed toward him. Turning toward the sound, he said, "*You're not listening*, I want to—"

He found Kit standing in front of him with a puzzled look on his face. "Oh, sorry, I thought you were Ursa." He grimaced, thinking back on his lessons. From the beginning of his training, Ursa had reprimanded him whenever he apologized, saying, "It is a sign of weakness, and you would do well to avoid it." He couldn't understand why it was so hard for him to avoid apologizing.

Glancing around the meadow, he was relieved Ursa was nowhere in sight. He held out his paw. Kit affectionately rubbed against it before moving on to his face. The mountain lion paused, then cautiously sniffed the blood on his shoulder.

Hyroc sighed. "Yeah, that's where Ursa *bit me*," he said grumpily. "Can you believe she actually bit me?" He shook his head. "And it wasn't a soft bite either. Then she tried to convince me it was a good thing. I don't know how wounding me could be a good thing."

He grimaced at the sharp sting in his shoulder as Kit began licking the wound. He jerked away. "No, don't do *that*, your tongue's like sandpaper, I'll take care of—." He paused, suddenly wondering how he was going to tend to his injury. Some yarrow would probably take care of it, though without the use of hands, how was he going to apply it to his shoulder? Washing it in the stream was another option, but he would have to soak most of his body just to get his shoulder in the water. Despite his thick bear fur, the water was still cold. His injury didn't seem severe enough to warrant that. He squeezed his eyes shut as a disturbing thought crept into his mind. "Oh no," he said unpleasantly. "That means I'm going to have to use . . . my tongue." The idea was somewhat uncomfortable, but it was his own blood, after all. Sometimes, in his natural form, when he accidentally cut himself, he would suck on the wound until it stopped bleeding. This wasn't that different. He turned his head to lick the wound on his shoulder but he couldn't turn his head far enough to reach the injury. Defeated, he turned toward Kit who wore an expectant look.

Hyroc shrugged. "Alright, you win," he said in an accepting tone. He lay down on his side. Kit studied him before resuming his treatment of the wound. Trying his best not to flinch, Hyroc grit his teeth as the stinging pain resumed. Slowly the discomfort faded to a dull throb. Then the wound was clean. "Thanks, buddy." He rose to his feet and gave Kit another round of petting before moving off toward a patch of fireweed. He had finished eating one plant when Ursa approached him from the trees.

"Look, I just needed a break," he said. "I'm not quitting."

"Nor did I think you were," Ursa answered. She paused. "I will not, however, show weakness by apologizing for biting you; it may have been uncomfortable, but it was a necessary part of the lesson." Hyroc rolled his eyes. He already guessed an apology was too much to hope for. Ursa paused. "There's something I want to show you."

"Since it's probably going to be something unpleasant, can it wait until I'm done eating?"

Ursa gave him a humored look. "I have a feeling you'll appreciate it more if you see it before you've had your fill of fireweed. Now come." She turned and headed toward the trees on the other side of the meadow.

Hyroc was suspicious, but knowing she was probably going to force him to deal with whatever it was before he could move on to the next lesson, he followed her, shaking his head.

As he entered the trees, a bee ran into Hyroc's face, and he swatted it away with his paw. Then another ran into his nose, causing him to sneeze. Bees continued bumping into him with a steadily increasing frequency and force. He became aware of a buzzing in his ears. Thinking a gnat or mosquito was trying to fly into it, he started swatting at his ears with his paw. The buzzing persisted at a steadily increasing volume, and he felt a sense of alarm creep into the back of his mind.

"Ursa, what's that buzzing?" Hyroc said anxiously.

Ursa came to a stop at a small gap in the trees and said, "You will see."

He looked around the clearing; all he saw was the wide trunk of a recently fallen cottonwood tree lying on the ground beside its splintered stump. He gave Ursa a suspicious look. "What exactly am I supposed to be seeing here?"

Using her paw, Ursa indicated the stump. "Look closer."

Focusing on the stump, at first all he saw was the dead remnant of a tree's base, but soon he spotted a bee emerging from a crack in the bark. Just as that bee took flight, another landed and crawled into the same crack. He watched as the rest of the bees came and went. It was a beehive!

"Oh no," Hyroc said, bowing his head in dismay. "You can't be serious!"

"I am serious," Ursa said. "I want you to bring me a piece of honeycomb from this beehive."

Hyroc jabbed a paw toward the stump. "But *that's a beehive!*" Though, even as he spoke, he had a strangely powerful desire to get at the golden syrup within, despite how much he knew doing so would hurt.

"I am well aware. I have informed you of your task, now get to it." Hyroc sighed and forced himself to walk closer to the beehive. "They tend to go for the eyes, so make sure to keep yours closed as much as possible." Her advice only heightened his feelings of anxiety.

Great, I might not have eyes after this.

When he drew close to the stump, an ominous buzzing rose from it, almost in a challenge to his presence. He suddenly felt he was somewhere he shouldn't be! He gave Ursa a pleading look. She returned his gaze with a cold, unsympathetic look. Reluctantly turning back toward the stump, he took a deep breath and continued toward it. The buzzing grew louder and angrier. By the time he reached the stump, it was the only thing he could hear.

He did his best to ignore the feeling of impending doom as he looked for the best way into the hive. He cringed, feeling the sharp burning pain of a stinger stabbing into the skin on top of his head. Shrugging off the pain, he persisted with his search, though more feverishly. After enduring another bee sting, he found a split near the top of the stump, wide enough for him to get his claws into. The wood crackled as he pulled it apart. Hyroc pushed his claws through the opening and ripped off a large chunk of wood, revealing the pale, waxy top of the hive. The instant the chunk ripped away, bees began pouring out of every opening in the stump. Spots of fiery pain blossomed across his face. He closed his eyes and, fighting through the pain, continued digging into the stump. An ever-increasing torrent of bees boiled off the stump. Stinger after stinger found its way into his flesh. His whole face felt as if his fur was on fire. Desperate for relief, he frantically rubbed his face with both paws to shake off the bees. The motion of his paws seemed only to spurn the swarm into an even more frenzied attack.

Gritting his teeth, and by sheer force of will, he compelled himself to resume his assault on the stump. He felt an uncomfortable tightening of the flesh all over his head as his skin began to swell. Opening one eye a sliver, he saw he had removed enough of the stump to get at the hive. He delved into the waxy shell. His claws seemed to dig agonizingly slow. All he found was wax, a seemingly endless supply of it. How could such tiny creatures possibly produce so much wax?

His whole body felt like one massive burning sore. Right when he was about to cut and run, he felt something sticky ooze out from between his digits. Not caring to open his eyes, he shoved his snout into the hole and tore a chunk from the hive with his teeth. Sweetness spread across his tongue. For an instant, he felt nothing of the fire immolating his body. He yanked his head from the stump, his prize between his teeth, and took off running from the enveloping cloud of stingers. He ran until he thought he was at a safe distance from the hive. As he slowed his pace, his elation vanished when several stingers stabbed into his rear end. With a shocked yelp, he resumed his flight at a higher speed. He ran until he was winded, and when he stopped this time, nothing stung him. Relieved—somewhat—he dropped the chunk of honeycomb, collapsed onto the ground, covered his face with both paws, and promptly filled the air with loud moaning noises.

He heard Ursa's footfall moments later. When he attempted to open his eyes to look at her, one was almost completely swollen shut, and the other would only open halfway. He resumed his hideous song of pain.

"Well done," Ursa said proudly. Hyroc groaned in response. There was a long pause; at least Hyroc thought it was long, the pain seemingly skewing his sense of time. "Thank you for the gift. As a reward for your *generosity*, the rest of the hive is yours."

"I don't care about that *stupid* hive," Hyroc groaned, still covering his face with his paws. "I'm not going anywhere near it again."

"As you wish. It's just a shame to waste something you worked so hard to get." Hyroc felt wind pass over his face, then the pain and uncomfortable tightness of his flesh melted away. Confused—though extraordinarily grateful for the relief—he moved his paws to the side of his head and easily opened his eyes. He blinked. "Especially since the bees aren't there anymore."

Hyroc gave her a blank stare. "What do you *mean* the bees aren't there anymore? It's a beehive! That's where bees live. And they clearly don't appreciate bears attacking their home."

"It *was* a beehive," Ursa answered smugly. "That is, until you cracked it open."

"But I only took a little piece of honeycomb from it; I doubt I did enough damage to destroy the hive."

"Go back, and you will see what I mean."

"Okay," Hyroc said skeptically, as he cautiously headed back toward the hive.

No bees bumped into him as he approached, and when he arrived at the stump, everything was strangely quiet, devoid of buzzing. He studied the hive from the edge of the clearing but saw no activity. Mustering his courage, he watchfully made his way to the stump. Peering down into the hive through the opening he had created, he saw no more than a handful of bees wandering around in a disoriented manner. The hive appeared dead.

He turned to Ursa. "I don't understand, why did all the bees leave? I didn't think I did *that* much damage."

"No, you didn't," Ursa said. "But you did *enough*. You made the bees realize their hive was no longer safe in the fallen tree. And because of this, they, and by *they* I mean the queen, decided to take what they could carry and move on to a safer location. This would've happened eventually, but by attacking them you expedited the process."

Hyroc gave her a baffled look. "I had no idea they could do that."

"There are many interesting things in nature about which you are as yet unaware." She was quiet a moment. "You should probably get your fill of the honey before the smell starts attracting scavengers. Meet me back at the meadow when you're done." She turned and headed off.

Hyroc wet his lips before greedily digging into the sweet innards of the hive. After all the misery he had endured, he deserved this. He ate until he felt sick. Then, energized by the bee's sugary substance, he happily made his way to the meadow at a brisk pace.

When he arrived, Kit emerged from the trees to join him. Hyroc extended his paw to receive his companion's usual greeting. Kit sniffed at his snout, paused, then began licking. Hyroc laughed, realizing Kit was licking off some leftover honey that adorned his face.

CHAPTER 13

STEPPING INTO THE CURRENT

Rain streaked down from the seamless mass of dirty gray clouds covering the sky. Wind pressed the droplets sideways and gave the air an uncomfortable chill. The endless patter of windswept rain was the only sound in the air, as no bird dared venture their calls out into the storm.

Hyroc's head slammed into the sodden grass of the meadow. As usual, he felt Ursa's bite on his neck an instant later. This loss, however frustrating, wasn't nearly as bitter as those proceeding it. He had come close to biting her neck.

He coughed as Ursa stepped in front of him. She shook, causing him to shy his head away from the shower of water.

"You did well," Ursa said. "You almost got me."

Hyroc coughed a final, loud cough before speaking. "I should've got you," he said indignantly. "I wasn't expecting you to try choking me!"

"Unexpected things are part of fighting."

Hyroc gave her a suspicious look. "I suppose, but considering what I've seen thus far, I don't think strangulation is part of a typical bear's technique."

Ursa gave him a mildly sheepish look. "Well, I might've gotten a little carried away."

"So does that mean I won then?"

Ursa laughed. "Of course not."

He shrugged. As he rose to his feet, he felt a painful sting on the underside of his front left leg. Turning it over, he saw a trail of drying blood emanating from a cut just below the wrist. He studied the injury thoughtfully, unable to remember when he had received it. During his first sparring session of the day, Ursa had given a hard bite to his uninjured shoulder. It had hurt, but it hadn't bled. Then following this, she had given him a nasty gash on the side of his neck with her claws; that too had bled. Despite the nature of his injuries, they didn't bother him anymore. That seemed strange because he remembered how much it had hurt and how angry he was when Ursa had first bitten him. Something had changed with him. As he pondered this conundrum, using the paw of his injured forelimb, he absentmindedly scratched at the itchy scab of a bee sting on the side of his snout. He paused, remembering the beehive and the corresponding awful fiery pain. That was probably the single most excruciating experience of his life. Since that experience, the things Ursa had done to him seemed insignificant.

"You're wondering why pain seems to affect you less?" Ursa asked, as if reading his thoughts.

Hyroc glanced from her to the injury on his forelimb and back again. "It was the bees, wasn't it?" Hyroc asked.

Ursa nodded. "They hurt, didn't they?"

"Yeah," Hyroc said dryly. "A lot."

"Pain is an interesting thing; once you've experienced severe pain, everything at a lesser degree doesn't seem quite so bad."

He sighed in reluctant agreement. "But, I am not thanking you for purposely hurting me."

Ursa laughed. "I would think there was something wrong with you if you did."

"And—and I'm also very angry with you," he said in a forced tone, feeling no such thing.

Ursa laughed, shaking her head. "I can tell," she said in a tone that bespoke her disbelief. "That's enough sparring for one day."

Hyroc nodded and shook the rain from his back. "There's something I've been meaning to ask you. What would have happened if I had chosen something other than a bear during the Choosing? Let's say I chose a deer."

"Then you would have turned into a deer."

"I understand that part, but what would have happened after that, with my training, I mean. Deer and bears are almost nothing alike. How would that have changed things for me?"

"Yes, you are correct, deer and bears share little in common. It would have made it more difficult for me to instruct you, but all Guardians are knowledgeable about most animal forms. Your training wouldn't have been as complete if you had chosen a deer, but your understanding and abilities would have been sufficient."

"And what if I had chosen a bird?"

"Well, then that would have changed things. Though I possess sufficient knowledge of ground-dwelling animals, and even some that reside in the sea, my understanding would not have been enough to train you as a creature of the sky. Hyroc nodded his understanding. "If you had chosen a bird, I would have summoned another Guardian, who, in my stead, would have properly trained you."

"So, I would have had a bird as my mentor?"

"Precisely."

"But what would have happened to you?"

"The new Guardian would have taken my place, and with my commitment fulfilled, I would have departed."

Hyroc gave her a saddened look; he didn't like the idea of a stranger coming to train him. He felt an attachment to Ursa, and had to admit things wouldn't be quite the same without her, even though she did cause him a considerable amount of discomfort.

"One last thing. When I was deciding which animal to choose, it seemed that a lot of animals were missing. I only saw cats, bears, a bird, and that strange fish dog. Why didn't I see a wolf?"

"Because you are not like a wolf."

Hyroc shot her a strange look. "What do you mean?"

"Wolves are pack hunters, and they work as a team to take down prey. You are not particularly fond of working with others, preferring to do things on your own."

"Well, that's because people generally don't want me anywhere near them. This whole curse thing and looking like a monster being the probable cause."

"Regardless of the reason, the fact remains. You don't work well with others, so, with a few small exceptions, you were only provided with solitary animals to choose from."

"So, you're saying because of the way I think and behave I was only able to see certain animals?"

"Yes. Your personality and disposition effect which animals are available to you."

"So then why did I see a giant spider?"

Ursa gave him a subtly surprised look. "You may not want to hear this, but despite your trepidation toward such creatures, you have a lot in common with them."

"How can I possibly have anything in common with one of those disgusting creatures?"

"Because you set traps as a spider would with its webbing, and you ambush whatever prey you're stalking."

Hyroc quivered at the thought of being like a spider. "Well, I'm still glad I didn't choose one."

"As am I."

"Thank you for explaining—even if it was somewhat disturbing."

Ursa nodded.

Hyroc turned and started toward the trees at the edge of the meadow. "Where are you going?" Ursa asked.

He turned back with a confused look on his face. "You said we were done sparring; I was heading over to the trees to get out of the rain. I know my fur mostly keeps it out, but I still don't enjoy getting wet."

She shook her head. "It's now time to move on to your next lesson. Go get your friend; we're leaving the meadow and won't be back for some time."

"May I ask what we're doing?"

"There's a river not far from here; I'm going to teach you how to fish like a bear."

He felt a spark of excitement at the idea of eating something decent for once. With a nod, he happily hurried off toward the tree where he had spotted Kit earlier. As hoped, he found Kit sleeping soundly on a branch high up the tree.

"Wake up, Kit," Hyroc called up from the base of the trunk. "We're going fishing." One of Kit's eyes slid open partway. He gave Hyroc a lazy stare, then closed it again. Hyroc rolled his eyes. "Kit, get up, you can sleep when we get to the river." Other than turning his ears, Kit showed no signs of stirring. Hyroc sighed. Running his eyes along the trunk of the tree, he saw claw marks scraped into its bark; Kit had been marking it. Hyroc's eyes lit mischievously. He placed both paws over the nearest mark and raked his claws over it. Looking upward, he saw Kit with both eyes open, giving him a malevolent glare. "Come down, and I'll stop." Kit remained where he was. "Okay." Hyroc scratched the trunk more deeply. Kit growled in frustration and scrambled down.

"I knew that would—." As soon as Kit was on the ground, he whacked Hyroc in the head with his paw. The strike was nothing compared to how hard Ursa hit, but it still had a surprising amount of force behind it. Hyroc pulled his head back. "Hey, *that was uncalled for*!" Kit lunged forward and nipped Hyroc in the ear. Grimacing, he gave Kit a subdued push with his paw. "Okay, that was low." Kit dropped into a playful crouch. "Oh, you want some more," Hyroc said, flexing his paw. Kit wiggled his backside and lunged forward. Hyroc ducked the paw swipe that followed, then answered with a backhanded swipe to the side of Kit's head, careful not to hit hard enough to inflict pain. Kit staggered sideways. Hyroc threw himself into the cat, bowling him over. Kit yelped in surprise as he was flung onto his back. Hyroc leaned forward and poked Kit with his paw. Kit slapped eagerly at his paw as he came in for another jab.

"I'm glad to see the two of you are having fun," Ursa's voice said, startling both Hyroc and Kit. "But we need to get going."

Hyroc used his paw to indicate Kit, who now stood beside him. "He . . . he started it," Hyroc said in an embarrassed voice. Kit gave him a contemptuous glare.

Ursa shook her head. "I don't care who started it; we need to go. So, come." She turned and headed back toward the meadow.

"You were actually the one who started it," Hyroc said under his breath. Kit playfully pawed at his nose.

It was close to noon when the three of them arrived at the relatively straight stretch of a gently flowing river, thickly lined with tall grassy foliage. Rocks lay throughout the flow, causing grayish bowl-shaped eddies to interrupt the placid surface.

Using her paw, Ursa pointed toward the middle of the river where the water was deepest, and the dark shapes of fish glided through the current. "I'm going right there, find a good spot to watch without coming too close; I don't want you scaring the fish away." She waded into the water, fish darting out of her path as she went. Hyroc took a couple of steps into the cold water, while an interested Kit looked on from the shore. Ursa gave the two of them a confirming glance and faced into the current.

"Catching a fish in this form is pretty straightforward," Ursa said. "Face into the current, move as little as possible, and wait for a fish." She scanned the water, focusing on a nearby fish. "Then, when the fish comes close enough, you, . . . *strike.*" In a flash of movement, she pounced on the fish, holding its wriggling body beneath her paws. She spoke quickly. "You pin it beneath your paws and sink your teeth into it!" She brought her head down to the fish, sank her ursine teeth into it, and pulled it from the water. It squirmed desperately from within her jaws before going still. Trudging through the water, she dropped the fish on the shore. She gave Kit an inviting look. The mountain lion watched her a long moment before cautiously approaching the fish. Ursa stepped away and turned toward Hyroc.

"That doesn't seem too difficult," Hyroc said. "But do I have to use my mouth?"

Ursa gave him a humored look. "How else are you going to grab it?"

He waggled his head from side to side in embarrassment, realizing he had asked a stupid question. "Forget I said that."

"As you wish. Now, go catch a fish."

Hyroc waded out into the middle of the river, where the water came up to his chest. He found a spot behind two large submerged rocks that would serve to funnel fish toward him, and he faced into the current.

When the first fish came through the rocks, he aimed and pounced. He made a considerable splash, soaking his body in a deluge of cold water, but he missed. With a shrug, he shook the water off and readied himself for another attempt. With the next fish, he aimed more carefully before pouncing. He felt the slimy brush of fish flesh beneath his paws before it too escaped. He got the third fish beneath his paws more securely, but it was small enough to slip out from under his grip and escape in his ensuing flurry of splashes as he desperately tried to catch it. With each failure, his technique slowly improved. He pinned the following fish beneath his paws, then hesitantly clamped his teeth around it. The instant the tips of his teeth touched the fish's flesh, it began thrashing and managed to work its way free. Hyroc lunged at it, throwing up a spout of water, but it was gone before he landed. He grumbled as water streamed off his head.

By now, he had nearly lost all feeling in his feet, and after so many failures, a break from his chore seemed appropriate. Ursa gave no complaint as he headed for shore. The ground felt pleasantly warm beneath his leaden feet. The rains had stopped, and the sun was peeking through holes in the clouds. He wiped his feet on a patch of foxtails before lying down on his stomach with his legs tucked beneath him for warmth. Once he regained sensation in his toes, he stood and headed back toward the river.

He found Ursa occupying his spot. Figuring she was just using it because it was a good fishing spot, he trudged over to her and patiently waited for her to move. An awkward minute passed without Ursa showing the slightest inkling she was even aware of his presence.

"Umm . . . Ursa," Hyroc prodded. "You're in my spot."

"I'm well aware of that," Ursa said, keeping her eyes fixed on the water.

Another awkward silence descended. "Then, can I have it back now?"

"No, if you abandon a good fishing spot, another bear will claim it."

"But this is just practice, I barely even know how—." Ursa's paw shot out of the water, whacked him in the head, and dunked him face-first into the river. "What was that for!" Hyroc said, spitting.

"This is *my* fishing spot."

"No, it's not, *you stole it from me.*"

"I did no such thing; you were the one who left it."

"My feet were cold."

"Maybe next time you won't let some discomfort get in your way."

"But—"

Ursa interrupted him with a deep growl. "Unless you wish for something longer lasting than a damp head, I suggest you leave."

Hyroc groaned angrily, heading away from Ursa in search of another fishing spot. Farther upstream, he found a partially submerged fallen tree sticking out into the water, which would force any fish close to the shore to swim near the tip. Taking up position behind the trunk, he waited for a fish. What felt like hours passed before the shape of a fish emerged from the other side of the tree. He aimed carefully and, taking a breath, pounced. He landed off target, but with a rapid read-justment of his paws, he managed to pin it down before it could escape. Moving swiftly, he clamped his teeth around the fish. It began thrashing violently, threatening to wrench itself from his hold. Without even thinking, he bit down harder. He gagged as slimy fish blood filled his mouth. It took all of his concentration to keep himself from dry heaving. Fighting off the nausea convulsions, he hurriedly made his way to dry land. He dropped the now lifeless fish on the ground, spit out a mouthful of fish blood, and enthusiastically gargled water.

"Good job," Ursa said.

Hyroc spat, causing himself to dry heave unexpectedly. "Thanks," he said halfheartedly. "So, how am I going to cook this?"

Ursa cocked an eyebrow. "Cook it?"

Hyroc's heart sank. "You're not seriously going to make me eat this fish raw, are you? I mean won't that—won't that make me sick?"

"I wouldn't expect eating that fish to make you sick!"

"But . . . but it's *raw.*"

"Have you ever eaten raw fish?"

He gave her a flat look. "Of course not!"

"Then how do you know you won't like it?"

He gaped at her, unable to think of a valid response. He shook his head. "How am I supposed to get the innards out then?" He held his paw out in front of her and flexed it. "It's not like I have hands, or even a knife, to gut it with."

"You know how to clean a kill; I'm sure you'll figure it out."

Hyroc opened his mouth to protest, but Ursa was already heading away from him. He sighed irritably, lowering his gaze to his catch. He held his paw out in front of him to examine his claws. They weren't as sharp as Kit's, but they did remind him somewhat of his hunting knife. Pondering this detail, he decided to try using them like a knife. He pinned the fish's head beneath one paw, pushed the claws from his other into the fish's belly, and slowly split the fish open, causing blood to spill over his paws.

Through an embarrassingly jagged opening in the fish's underside caused by his imprecise claws, he carefully reached inside and started scooping out the innards. After removing the innards, using his mouth, he dragged the carcass to the shore and dipped it into the river, letting the water wash away anything he might have missed. Once finished, he set the fish on dry land and bent his head down for a reluctant nibble. To his amazement, beyond the slimy texture, the raw fish was oddly satisfying. And more strangely, other than the occasional poke to his gums from a fishbone, he hardly even noticed them. With a shrug, he took another bite, hating to admit that Ursa was right. He ate everything on the fish up to the spine, head, and tail, then pushed the remnants into the river. Then acknowledging he wasn't full, he headed back out into the river.

His first attempt failed due to a fish unexpectedly leaping from the water an instant before he pounced and bouncing off his head, but the next one was a success. By the time Hyroc had cleaned and eaten his second fish, the glowing band of dusk had spread across the horizon, signaling the end of the day.

"I see you shed your earlier reluctance toward the consumption of raw fish," Ursa noted.

Hyroc nodded reluctantly. He paused as a thought occurred to him. "Why did I enjoy those fish so much?" Hyroc asked. "It's my animal form, isn't it?"

Ursa studied him quietly a moment. "Yes, bears eat raw fish; therefore, you also enjoyed raw fish. And well, as you likely noticed, fish taste much better than fireweed." Hyroc happily nodded his agreement. "Now get some rest, we've got more work to do tomorrow." With that, she headed into the trees.

After a short foray into the trees beyond the riverbank, beneath the sheltered umbrella of a tall cottonwood, Hyroc found a conical opening between two alders that would keep the wind off. Finding no lodge pine or moss in sight, he spread out dry leaves across the opening and overlaid them with some yarrow to keep the mosquitoes away. It was a poor substitute for his bed at the meadow—not that he considered it very comfortable either—but it was better than nothing. Just as he settled into it for the night, Kit found him. Before Hyroc could offer his usual greeting to his friend, Kit rubbed against his face, smearing him with some cold substance. Subduing a myriad of disturbing thoughts about what that might have been, Hyroc rubbed his face through the branches of the alders until he felt adequately clean, then laid down to sleep.

CHAPTER 14

FIGHT OR FLIGHT

The insistent buzzing of a fly drew Hyroc into wakefulness. He groggily swatted at the disturber of his sleep with one paw as it darted erratically toward his head. Dodging his paw, the fly touched down in the middle of his snout. A quick headshake returned it to the air. Ribbons of clouds streaked the pale blue sky and long insubstantial shadows stretched through the forest as the sun lazily made its way above the horizon. It was still early, too early for Ursa to wake him. He considered going back to sleep, but his mouth was dry and relieving it was a more pressing issue. He yawned, stood, stretched, and made his way to the river.

When he had cleared the trees, he saw Kit standing atop the dead tree that had fallen partway into the river, staring down into the water. Noticing his presence, Kit lifted his head attentively. The big cat regarded him before excitedly dropping into a crouch as something in the water caught his attention. Kit jerked forward, throwing one paw into the water, then yanked it back out an instant later. Showing teeth in an irritated grimace, he flicked the water from his wet paw. Hyroc stifled a laugh as he trudged through the cool water over to him.

"Morning," Hyroc said, taking up position on the downstream side of the tree. Kit sheathed his teeth, giving Hyroc a blank stare. "Don't worry, you'll get one, it just takes a little practice, that's all."

Kit returned his attention to the river. Curious, Hyroc silently watched his companion. Kit's whole body tensed as another fish came into view. The big cat waited until the fish was within striking distance and threw his paw into the water. Then, as before, he pulled his paw from the water and shook it in aggravation. He gave Hyroc a frustrated glare.

Hyroc sighed sympathetically. "You're not going to be able to catch a fish that way. You need to use both paws; watch, I'll show you." He stepped forward into a better position near the end of the tree and watched for a fish. When one came into view, he pinned it beneath his paws with a pounce, then sank his teeth into it. With the flailing fish in his mouth, he rushed to the shore, where he finished it off with a bite to the head. He turned toward Kit as the cat ran up to his side. He spat before saying, "See, just like that." Kit glanced toward the water with a dubious look in his eyes. Hyroc waved his paw dismissively. "And you're also going to have to get wet if you're going to catch a fish." Kit glared at him derisively and flicked his tail in annoyance.

"Don't give me that look. That's how it is. Whenever you get wet in the rain, you don't seem to mind, so I don't see what the problem is." Kit growled. Hyroc rolled his eyes. He clamped his teeth around the fish and tossed it down in front of Kit. "Here, you big baby." Kit sniffed at the fish before starting to eat it. Shaking his head irritably, Hyroc headed toward the two-rock choke point near the middle of the river.

Less than an hour after arriving, a fish came within reach. He pounced, but one paw landed off-target, allowing the fish to wriggle free from his grip. He splashed through the water, frantically scrambling to capture the fish. In the fish's desperation to escape, it grounded itself in a shallow patch of water at the shore. Hyroc rushed over, pinned the fish beneath his paws, and dispatched it with a bite. He beamed triumphantly at Kit. "I *still* got it."

After Hyroc finished his breakfast, Ursa arrived. The two of them exchanged a "good morning."

"I assume you've already eaten?" she said, giving his fish carcass a passing glance. Hyroc nodded. "Good, we're moving on from here."

"Where are we going?"

Ursa studied him thoughtfully. "There's a better fishing spot a day's walk from here." Hyroc's eyes lit up—he thought this was a pretty good fishing spot, and a flurry of enticing ideas about this "better spot" began circulating through his mind. "Are you ready?" Hyroc nodded. "Then we should be going."

Other than frightening a black bear and having a squirrel chatter angrily at them when they get too close to its tree, the rest of the day was uneventful. They traveled until the dull orange glow of dusk spread across the sky, stopping at the base of an enormous spruce tree. To Hyroc's dismay, his dinner consisted of fireweed and dandelion flowers. The surrounding area was lacking in bed making materials, so he opted to lie on a patch of clovers at the base of the spruce.

When Hyroc woke the next morning, the sporadically spread clouds had formed into a more solid mass.

"Almost done?" Ursa said, not long after Hyroc had started on his breakfast.

He swallowed down a mouthful of fireweed leaves before saying, "That was my last bite. Just let me go get Kit, and we can head out."

"He will need to remain here."

Hyroc shot her a startled look. "What, we're leaving him here, *alone*? Why?"

"His presence will only serve as a distraction during this next lesson."

"He hasn't distracted me yet."

"I understand your reluctance, but no harm will come to him in your absence, and it will only be for a few days."

Hyroc glanced toward Kit, who lay across one of the lower branches of the spruce. From the time he had found the mountain lion, the two of them had never been separated for more than a few hours. The thought of leaving him alone in an unfamiliar part of the forest far from home, gnawed at him. Many bad things could happen in a few days.

"You *promise* he'll be safe?"

"I give you my word."

Hyroc knew that if Ursa promised that Kit would be safe, then Kit would be safe. He sighed. "Okay, can I at least tell him bye?"

"You may; don't take too long."

Hyroc nodded and continued toward the towering tree. "Kit," he called up. Kit stretched, giving him a groggy stare. "I need you to come down." Kit watched him curiously a moment, then scrambled down. Hyroc spoke after letting the mountain lion rub against his outstretched paw. "I have to go away for a little bit." Kit stopped rubbing and gave him a cautious look. "But it will *only* be for a couple of days," he added hurriedly. "Ursa doesn't want you around me for her next lesson, and she promised you'll be safe." Kit gave his shoulder an affectionate rub. Hyroc reached out with his paw and stroked Kit's head with it. "I'll be back before you know it, alright?" Reluctantly, he slowly turned and headed back to Ursa. "I'm ready to go."

Ursa nodded. "This way." She turned away from him.

"Wait, if you're going with me, then how are you going to watch over Kit?"

Ursa put her head to the side and indicated a nearby tree. "Look up into that tree to your left." There Hyroc saw a crow watching Kit attentively. He nodded his understanding. Ursa resumed walking forward. Hyroc looked back at Kit before following.

About an hour after departing, when the gnawing guilt of leaving his companion behind had faded to an ever-present thought in the back of his mind, Hyroc detected the smell of something rancid carried on a gust of wind. But it was too faint for him to identify. The odor steadily grew in strength the farther they walked.

"What's that smell?" Hyroc said unpleasantly.

"You'll find that answer soon," Ursa answered evasively.

Hyroc shrugged. The smell was somewhat familiar. In the trees ahead of them, he saw a white and gray mass lying at the base of a tree. When he came to it, he found the decaying remnants of a fish carcass. But most unsettling, he saw the faded tracks of multiple bears passing by the carcass. Alarmed by the tracks, he rushed after Ursa, who was starting to get away from him. By the time he caught up with her, she was standing at the edge of a river twice as wide as the one they had left behind.

His breath caught in his throat. All along the shore, he saw brown bears! The biggest bears he had ever seen stood congregated around a ledge of rock he judged to be the height of his shoulders, forming a tiny cascade of water to his left. From the ledge, the river flowed for a relatively straight stretch before gently curving around a bend.

"Ursa, I think we should get out of here!" he yelped. "There are bears everywhere."

"Of course there are bears here," Ursa said flatly. "You can't expect a good fishing spot to go unnoticed."

Hyroc gave her a confounded look. "This is *that* 'better fishing spot' you were talking about? How is this possibly better?"

"There are more fish here."

He cocked an eyebrow and, in a waving motion of his paw, indicated the numerous bears lining the river. "And there are also *bears* here!" he said indignantly.

"I am well aware of this."

Hyroc felt a sudden sense of dread creep into his mind. What wasn't she telling him? He spoke warily. "You *are* coming down there with me?"

"I am not."

He gaped at her with terrified astonishment. "You . . . *you what!*"

"I will *not* be coming with you for this task."

"I'm going to get *killed* if I go down there alone; do you see the size of some of those *bruisers*?"

"We would not be here if I did not believe you were ready to face this task. You've demonstrated yourself to be more than capable of fighting in this form."

"Maybe against another bear close to my size, but I'll get murdered if I try fighting one of those big ones."

"Then, I suggest you avoid them."

"And what am I supposed to do when one of them, I don't know, *tries to EAT ME?*"

Ursa laughed. "You don't need to worry about *that*; there are too many easily obtained things swimming in this river for any of these bears to even bother with trying to eat you."

"Okay, but what if one of them charges me?"

127

"Well, if that were to happen, then you should run."

"WHAT, you told me *never* to run from a bear."

"Over territorial matters, but if you are woefully outmatched, running is usually the wisest course of action. Most of the bears here wouldn't chase you far for risk of losing their spot."

Hyroc sighed, unable to think of any further rebuff. He knew she would make him do this regardless of anything he said, no matter how logical. Well, he did have one other choice; but choosing it would mean he was not who he thought he was. "Okay, fine. So, what am I supposed to do while I'm trying not to *die?*"

"You need to get at least one intact fish, no partially eaten carcass, *a whole fish*, and do your best to stay within sight of the river for the next three days."

Hyroc gave her a look of utter disbelief. "THREE DAYS? You're going to make me stay here for *three days!*"

"Yes, three days."

Hyroc sighed loudly, throwing all of his frustration into it.

"You can complain and moan all you want, but you will do this, or you will leave, the choice is yours."

"I'll do it," he grumbled, even if it was the craziest, most suicidal thing he had ever done.

"Good. But I will offer you this before I go—avoid the ledge because the biggest bears congregate around it, and if one wants your fish, consider your course of action carefully. Lastly, if you venture too far from the river, I will know about it, so I'd advise against trying to cheat." She paused. "Now, I leave you to your task. Good luck."

She turned and headed back the way they had come. Hyroc watched her until she disappeared, before turning his attention back toward the river. He carefully studied the scene in front of him, trying to discern the best fishing area where he was least likely to lose his limbs. The ledge was the most dangerous area, he knew that, but beyond that, he honestly couldn't tell if any place was better than another. He would just have to head out and see what happened.

Taking a deep breath, he watchfully headed closer to the water at a comfortable distance downstream from the big bears, toward a congregation of smaller ones. All the bears here appeared to be females with cubs. Two of the nearest mothers took notice of him and affixed him with a deadly warning glare. Knowing that getting anywhere close to a mother's young would result in him getting his head torn off, he made a wide arc around them over to the bend in the river. The bears here were close to his size, with some bigger ones spread throughout. He found a promising patch of water between the shore and a small oval-shaped rise that split the river in two. Flanking either side of the rise, he found two of the bigger bears fishing. The two bears stood apart, and there seemed to be enough room between them for him to take up position without disturbing them. Warily passing a bear fishing near a boulder, he made his way toward his spot. As he drew close, the two bears stopped fishing abruptly, giving him a threatening look. One began to growl, and knowing he would get killed in a fight with it, he hurried away; there were plenty of other spots to try.

Further downstream, a clump of cottonwood trees sat on a dome-shaped run of shore that protruded into the water near where the river began a sharp turn to the left. Other than garnering some curious and cautious looks from the bears he passed, none seemed bothered by his presence. He found a decent spot to fish in the shade of the cottonwood-clump, where the shape of the shore created a minute swirling motion that would temporarily disable any fish swimming through it. Taking a glance over his shoulder, he reaffirmed none of his neighbors were charging toward him and settled into position to catch a fish. A loud moan from behind broke his concentration. Looking in the direction of the sound, he saw a larger bear lashing out at a smaller bear. The bigger bear slammed its paw into the side of the smaller bear's head, then sank its teeth into the other bear's shoulder. Hyroc grimaced sympathetically. With a grunt of pain, the smaller bear broke free of its attacker and bolted. The bigger bear pursued for several strides, turned back, and took up position in the smaller bear's former fishing spot.

Hyroc felt a twinge of anger at that bear for bullying the smaller one. He pushed the thought aside; that line of thinking was pointless here. Movement near the cottonwoods caught his attention. He saw the smaller bear that had been forced from its fishing spot, moving through the trees. Blood-soaked fur covered the bear's shoulder, and it was walking with a slight limp. The bear paused, studying Hyroc carefully. Hyroc did his best to relax and convey a lack of aggression. Seeming to understand his intentions, the bear stopped at the cottonwoods, sat, and began licking its wounds. Hyroc returned to his fishing, glancing up at the injured bear from time to time.

Eventually, a fish came into sight. As he had expected, the eddy pulled the fish into its grasp, causing it to turn sideways and drift uncontrollably. Hyroc pounced, but the erratic motion of the fish caused him to miss. Splashing through the water in a series of quick lunges, he captured the fish in his jaws.

He then heard splashes that sounded an awful lot like something large running through the water in his direction. He snapped his eyes toward the splashing and his heart began hammering away in his chest as he saw the thief-bear from earlier nearly on top of him. The bear threw a swipe at his head. Hyroc had barely enough time to duck the incoming paw. The bear gave a look Hyroc surmised to be astonishment at his unexpected movement. The look disappeared as the bear followed through with another strike. Hyroc dodged it by rearing up on his back legs. The thief followed suit.

Hyroc's eyes widened fearfully as the bear stood much taller. Using its towering height advantage, the bear whacked him squarely in the head. Dark purple spots popped in front of his eyes, and he felt the weight of the fish fly from his mouth. He struggled to maintain his balance as the world spun chaotically. The bear grabbed him by the shoulder and thrust its teeth into the side of his neck. Hyroc gasped in pain as he put both paws on the bear's chest and delivered the hardest shove he could muster. The bear stumbled backward, losing its hold on his neck, then it instantaneously regained its balance and lunged forward for another bite. Hyroc countered by latching his teeth onto the bear's jaw. While the bear attempted to shake free, he struck the thief in the side of the head with a hard paw strike. The bear pulled back to reposition for a counterattack. Taking advantage of a subsequent opening, and knowing he wasn't going to win this, Hyroc dropped back down on all fours to flee. As he turned to run, he felt a sharp pain in his hindquarters as the thief-bear's teeth sank into his flesh. With a yelp, he took off toward the cottonwoods. He ran through the trees, barely aware of the cool greenery slapping against his face.

He came to a stop well past the trees. Wheeling around, he watched for any signs of pursuit. He found none. Listening intently, the only thing he heard was the murmur of the river and the beat of his heart in his ears. With a long drawn out sigh of relief, he dropped down into a sitting position. He jolted back onto his feet when he felt the bite on his rear end sting. Growling, he turned toward the ground where he had sat, trying to judge the severity of his injury from the blood left behind. There was a thin, light red smear across the ground about as long as one of his claws. It didn't seem bad. Slowly, he lowered himself again into a sitting position until he felt the stinging. When he focused on the pain, the injury still didn't feel serious; it would just make sitting difficult.

He could not believe he had been bitten on the butt! Of all the injuries he had received, that was the most frustrating. And to make it all the more infuriating, his fish had been stolen. He forced any more thoughts on the subject from his mind; there wasn't any point dwelling on it. He stood back on all fours and turned his attention to the wound on his neck. Turning his head, he felt a mild sting in his neck. His fur felt damp with coagulating blood, but this injury also seemed nothing to be concerned about.

Unable to sit comfortably, he stood on the shore and took in his surroundings while he waited for his racing heartbeat to return to normal. To his right lay the end of the bend where he had been fishing. From the bend, the river straightened, continuing in like manner for a short distance, then made a curve to the right before eventually curving left again and running out of sight. A few bears stood on this stretch of the river spread apart, but they weren't anywhere close to him.

He headed toward a promising place where a large dark brown rock poked up through the surface of the river. The current was noticeably stronger around the rock. He would need to aim carefully when he pounced, but it was still a decent spot.

He studied the bend in the river, searching for signs of the thief-bear. Finding none, he began watching for a fish. When a fish came into range, he pounced, but the current pulled it along at a higher speed than he had expected, causing him to miss. The fish was already too far away by the time of his next pounce. Shrugging off his catch's escape, he refocused his mind on his task. Before long, another fish swam near the rock. Taking into account the strength of the current more accurately, he pinned his quarry beneath his paws. The fish managed to wriggle out from his grip. Lunging forward, he caught it in his jaws.

A succession of splashes sounded behind him. He froze. It couldn't be true; his luck couldn't possibly be that bad. He whipped around. His heart sank as he saw the thief-bear barreling through the water toward him. He attempted a warning moan, but the fish occupying his mouth snuffed out all semblance of threat. The bear made a hard swipe at the left side of his head. He yanked his head back and turned it out of the way. He felt a rush of cold water flow across the side of his snout as the strike missed. The bear immediately followed through with another strike from his other paw. Hyroc had barely any time to move his head out of the way. He felt the bear's claws hook into the fish, and there was a hard yank on his teeth, but his hold held firm. He countered with a strong swipe to the side of the bear's head, digging his claws in as his opponent pulled back. He felt a sense of justice as blood welled up around a painful-looking gash in the side of the thief's neck. Pulling his eyes from the injury, Hyroc dashed into the trees with his fish.

He ran until he felt he had reached a comfortable distance from the thief, then watched and listened for any signs of pursuit. When he found none, he took a deep breath. He felt a wave of euphoria; finally, he had caught and kept a fish. Eagerly, he dropped the fish on the ground. His mouth fell open in bewilderment as the severed tail of a fish flopped down in front of him. He stared at what remained of his catch, suddenly unable to think. When coherent thoughts filtered back into his mind, he lifted his head skyward and, with his eyes closed, moaned as loud as he could.

With a frustrated sigh, he despondently nibbled at what tiny bit of meat he could find. Then he headed back toward the river, making sure to avoid the area occupied by the thief. He walked down the shore toward the part of the river that flowed out of sight. Past this point, the river picked up speed, forming a swath of churning white water. Determined to find a spot where the thief wouldn't harass him, he made his way along the shore. The rapids continued until the river entered a scythe shaped curve that returned the river to a more fishable condition. There were no bears in sight.

He headed halfway up the curve in the river, over to a long, shadowed indent in the shore. His stomach growled. He felt a surge of aggravation at the gnawing hunger. Twice he had been moments from eating something! But here, he was sure he would actually be able to eat his catch. Looking skyward as he walked, he was dismayed to see the sun nearing the horizon. It would be dusk soon, and he didn't expect fishing in the dark was a good idea. He settled into the shadows at the end of the indent. Just as the sun touched the horizon, a fish swam past his position. Leaping from the ledge structure of the shore, he pounced on his target. He landed directly on the fish and sank his teeth into it.

With the fish hanging from his mouth, he scanned his surroundings. He heard no splashing, and, best of all, he didn't see the bulky shape of the thief-bear charging toward him. Breathing a massive sigh of relief, he happily climbed back onto the shore. He dropped the fish on the ground and was about to gut it when he heard an enormous splash emanate from the opposite shore. His eyes widened with disbelief. It made no sense; he had walked all this way; there was no logical reason for the thief to have pursued him over that distance! He cautiously turned toward the sound, ready to defend his catch. Two smaller bears stood on their hind legs at the water's edge on the opposite shore, their paws wrapped around each other's neck. They were sparring. Suddenly taking notice of him, the two bears stopped their match and watched him warily. He felt a strange kind of satisfaction from the way they watched him. They were worried about him. Being bigger than them, he could steal fish from them if he wanted to. Ursa never specifically said he had to catch his one fish. He pushed the feeling aside. He shouldn't be thinking like that, even if they were just bears. With a relieved sigh, he turned back toward his catch.

He narrowed his eyes in confusion; the fish was gone! All that remained of it was a bloody stain on the grassy plants that had been beneath it. Movement ahead caught his attention. Focusing on it, he was enraged to see a black bear running off with his fish. "Get back here, you little sneak!" Hyroc bellowed as he tore after the fleeing bear. Right as he caught up with the bear, it bolted up a tree. Hyroc dug his claws into the tree's trunk and began hauling himself up. After only climbing a single body's length, he felt himself slipping. He dug his claws in with all his strength, desperate to maintain his hold. One by one, his claws slid free until he plunged back onto the ground. He gasped as pain radiated from the bite on his rear. Gritting his teeth, he stood up on all fours and looked up toward the black bear. The bear sat on a branch, its back against the tree's trunk, holding the fish between its paws as it gnawed hungrily at the head. Hyroc glared at the bear contemptuously. The bear returned his gaze with an irritatingly curious look. After banging his head against the tree, Hyroc unenthusiastically headed back toward the river.

The river glowed orange like a sheet of beaten copper in the fading light, and deep enveloping shadows spread from the trees. Hyroc squeezed his eyes shut and groaned. There was hardly any light left, and he still needed to find a place to spend the night. Bending his head down to the surface of the river, he drank until his stomach was swollen tight. The water would help stave off his hunger pangs for a while. Then with his head bowed depressingly, he headed back the way he had come. He found a patch of moss on the ground, tore it out, and made a bed under the sheltering branches of a pine tree. Over the moss, he laid horsetail and covered the whole thing in a layer of ferns. Gingerly, he lowered himself into his bed then rolled onto his side. He focused on a long finger of a sunbeam shining through the trees in front of him. *Tomorrow would be a better day*, he assured himself. When the light faded away, he closed his eyes and did his best to sleep.

The crack of a twig yanked him from his blissful slumber. The deepness of night now obscured his surroundings, but he could still make out the shapes before him. He got to his feet, ignoring the discomfort emanating from his rear end. He scanned his surroundings for any sign of movement. Another crack and the rustling of bushes sounded to his left. Turning in that direction, he thought he saw the brush moving. The rustling continued to get closer. There was definitely something coming toward him. He loosed a warning moan. The rustling stopped. A long silence descended before the rustling resumed. A large brown bear came into view. It was the same size as the bears he had seen near the ledge. It was too large for him even to consider fighting. He popped his jaws in a desperate attempt to fend off the unwelcome visitor. The bear paid no heed to his warning and continued toward him. Hyroc then let out the loudest moan he could muster. The bear stopped, watched him for a second, then broke into a charge. Struggling to control himself through a breaking wave of panic, Hyroc bolted underneath the lower branches of a nearby tree. The bristly branches scraped against his face as he tore past the trunk. He emerged from the other side of the tree and broke into the fastest run he could manage. He ran until he was winded. His breath came in ragged gasps as he anxiously watched for signs of pursuit.

When it became apparent he was safe, he began searching through the darkness for another place to sleep. Eventually, he found what seemed a good spot in front of an alder. Forcing aside his growing frustration, he settled down to sleep.

He was again wrenched awake. He scanned his surroundings, trying to figure out what had roused him this time. A warning moan sounded in front of him. Looking toward the noise, he thought he saw the shape of something against the night. Before he answered with a warning of his own, a bear came charging toward him. It wasn't nearly as big as the bear that had chased him from his mossy bed, but what it lacked in size, it made up for in attitude.

He dodged a paw swipe with a quick sidestep. Moving with incredible swiftness, the bear caught him on the outside of his shoulder with another swipe. Claws raked down his forelimb. He countered with a strike of his own, but as he swung, the bear slammed a paw into his face. Two more strikes followed before the bear sank its teeth into his left shoulder. Growling at the pain, he lurched backward, swiping his paw through the air in front of him, causing the bear to pull back from another strike. He held his mouth open and issued a warning as he slowly backed away. The bear came forward with its mouth open, intent on tearing another chunk out of him. Hyroc lined his mouth up with the bear's, blocking the bite. The bear lurched forward, striking the ground with its paw, but remained where it was. Hyroc continued backing away, not daring to turn his head away from his attacker to look at what lay behind him. He kept going until the night engulfed the bear. Then he turned and ran. When he seemed safe, he settled down to take stock of his new injuries.

The outside of his shoulder was bleeding, and he had a nasty gash across his chest, which was also bleeding. Numerous scratches covered his upper body, and he seemed to have lost a few patches of fur. He began licking his wounds.

What had he done to incur the wrath of *that* bear? The bear had attacked him as if its life depended on driving him away. Maybe it was a sow with cubs? That would account for its smaller size and probably the ferocity of its attack. He saw no cubs, but that didn't mean they weren't there. It just seemed unfair; the only thing he had done wrong was get in her way. He shrugged. If she was just defending her babies, he couldn't get angry with her for that, no matter how infuriating the situation had been.

He finished licking his wounds, then, not caring to search for a better spot, he laid down to sleep. The exhilaration of the fight prevented him from relaxing, and he couldn't stop thinking about what he could have done differently. If he had run away the moment he had awakened, none of that would have happened. He lay there for what felt like hours, looking up at the stars through a small hole in the clouds.

He was thrust awake for the third time. Low hanging branches somewhere in the darkness began rustling. Too tired and sore to risk another encounter with something dangerous, he ran in the opposite direction. He tripped over a root not long afterward. He lay on his stomach in the position he landed in and went to sleep.

The chittering of a squirrel roused him from his slumber. Glancing up into the tree, he saw the shape of an agitated squirrel staring down at him from a branch overhead. He narrowed his eyes; it couldn't be morning already! Looking skyward, he saw the sun poking above the treetops. Squeezing his eyes shut, he whimpered angrily. It was already morning! He hadn't gotten any sleep.

It might be morning, but that didn't mean he couldn't still sleep. If anything, this might be a better time for him to sleep since all the bears would be at the river. He rolled onto his side and covered his eyes with his paw. His stomach growled. Groaning miserably, he stood and picked his way in the direction he thought would lead him to the river. Nothing looked familiar, and after wandering through the trees for nearly an hour, he realized he was lost. A raven settled on the branch of a nearby tree and squawked angrily. Glancing toward the bird, he recognized Shimmer.

Hyroc shrugged. "It wasn't my fault," he said grumpily. "I had to keep running from things during the night, so back off." Shimmer fluttered his wings irritably. Hyroc sighed. "Sorry, I didn't get *any* sleep last night." Shimmer stopped fluttering. "But I'm a little lost; could you point me in the right direction?" The bird studied him, focusing on a point to his left. Hyroc nodded. "Thanks." He headed in the indicated direction, arriving at the river not long afterward.

The only bear he saw was one of the smaller bears from the night before, further upstream. Tracking along the shore, he found his former fishing spot at the indent. He dunked his head in the water, its bracing cold shocking his lingering drowsiness into submission. After shaking the water from his head, he drank and, with a yawn, settled into a fishing position. When a fish came into sight, mind-numbed by lack of sleep, he lazily watched it swim into range. It had nearly passed him entirely by the time his mind snapped into action. In a startled movement, he turned and bolted after the fish. He pounced at his quarry, but missed, subsequently losing track of the fish. Irritated, he slogged back to his fishing spot.

An hour passed without another fish sighting, then another and another. Now ravenously hungry, he headed downstream in search of a better spot. He found another stretch of white water. He followed the shore until it became obvious it would be some time before he found a proper fishing spot in this direction. Reluctantly, he headed back, making his way past the indent and the rapids toward the area where he had lost his second fish. There were more bears here but, after studying each carefully, he couldn't recognize any of them as the thief.

He found a good fishing spot near the straighter part of the river. As he settled in, he heard a warning moan and sounds of a commotion. Looking toward the disturbance, he was dismayed to see the thief-bear bullying another smaller bear. He abandoned his spot and quietly walked into the trees. Then he snuck around the quarreling bears, heading toward the spot at the cottonwood trees. Maybe if the bear didn't see him go there, it would leave him alone. He found the spot unoccupied, but another bear of a concerning size stood nearby. Keeping a close watch on this bear, he came to his spot. He froze when the bear turned its head in his direction. The bear watched him, sniffing the air. Then after a tense moment, the bear returned its attention to the water. Breathing a sigh of relief, Hyroc started fishing, while still keeping his guard up.

After half an hour of waiting, a fish got caught in the eddy. He captured the fish in his jaws and wasted no time heading for the trees. He had stepped from the water when the thief-bear emerged from the trees in front of him. Startled by the sudden appearance of the other, the two of them stared at each other in mirrored surprise. The thief-bear broke into a charge. With a yelp, Hyroc dropped his fish, wheeled around, and ran. He reached the midpoint of the river when he realized the thief wasn't pursuing. Turning around, he found the thief lying on its belly, eating his fish.

He felt an upwelling of anger at the sight of the bear tearing into his fish. His rear end and shoulder hurt because of that bear, he had gone to bed hungry because of that bear, and he still hadn't had anything to eat. He didn't care how much bigger or stronger that bear might be; he was sick of it causing him misery. He didn't care how much it was going to hurt. He was going to make that bear pay!

He roared as loud as he could and exploded into a charge straight at the thief. The thief-bear snapped its attention on him in confusion, clearly wondering why a smaller bear would challenge him. Hyroc was already within striking distance before the thief made a move to stand. He raised his paw and brought it down as hard as he could on top of the other bear's head. With an audible impact, the bear staggered beneath the force of the blow. Regaining its composure, the bear retaliated with an angry swipe. Hyroc sidestepped the strike and dug his claws into the side of the bear's neck. It took another swipe, but again he dodged out of the way. He lunged forward, slamming his upper body into the bear's chest, forcing both onto their hind legs. The thief sank its teeth into the uninjured side of Hyroc's neck above the shoulder.

Only caring about punishing his opponent, Hyroc struggled through the pain and sank his teeth into the bear's shoulder. He bit down hard, tasting blood. The bear's teeth retreated perceptibly from his flesh; the thief was hurting. Hyroc mercilessly jerked his head from side to side, opening an even larger wound. The bear unclenched its jaws and attempted to pull away. Mustering all of his strength, Hyroc fought to prevent the thief's escape; he wasn't done yet. He stopped biting, yanked his head back, and sank his teeth into the bear's flesh farther down its forelimb. Growling in pain, the thief managed to lift its other paw and whacked the side of Hyroc's head. Hyroc felt himself lose his hold with his mouth and lunged forward, throwing all of his weight into his opponent. The bear lost its balance, toppling over onto its back. Hyroc's nose slammed painfully into the bear's shoulder as they careened into the ground. Ignoring the stinging discomfort from his wounds, he tore a chunk out of the bear's chest. In a panicked flurry of desperate movements, the bear managed to throw off his hold. The bear flew to its feet and tore into a run toward the cottonwoods. Hyroc pursued up to the trees, stopping when the thief showed no signs of slowing.

Feeling supremely satisfied with his actions, he turned back toward the partially eaten fish behind him. The bear that had been fishing close by stood over the fish eyeing it eagerly. Hyroc roared and charged. He had barely made it one full stride before the bear fled enthusiastically. Hyroc stepped past the fish and stamped his paws down in front of him. Every nearby bear was watching him warily. He felt a burst of pride.

He turned his attention to his reclaimed fish. Most of the head was missing, but the majority of the body remained untouched. He deftly ripped open the belly and cleaned out the innards. Then ravenous from hunger, he began to devour it. The taste far exceeded any of the fish caught at the other river. He had never expected raw fish to be so incredibly delicious.

CHAPTER 15
A BEAR'S NOSE

Hyroc drifted reluctantly from his dream of a massive bonfire, whereupon he cooked fish covered in an absurd amount of honey. He lay on his side in the shaded recess between two of the cottonwoods populating the dome-shaped protrusion near where he fished. The pale orb of the sun spilled its light across the river, and jagged clouds drifted lazily through the sky. A cool breeze blew off the river, tainted by the smell of putrefying fish. Aware of some presence, he snapped his eyes open. He found Ursa watching him as she sat with her back against a cottonwood. He lifted his head and growled involuntarily.

Ursa cocked her head in amusement. "I hope you understand that what you're doing is not a particularly welcoming gesture," she said.

He stopped growling, feeling a flood of embarrassment. "Habit," he said apologetically.

"It's understandable, considering your neighbors."

With a yawn, Hyroc got to his feet. He groaned as burning pain shot through every scratch and bite from the day before. Why did everything suddenly hurt so bad?

Ursa spoke as she stood. "And it should come as no surprise that you're in pain. That's what happens when you fight a much larger opponent and allow them to sink their teeth into you." Hyroc shrugged. She walked over to him. "Now, I need to check your wounds."

"I'm fine; I made sure to wash everything in the river."

"I'm sure you did, but I'm going to check anyway; no reason for you to risk getting an infection. Now sit." Hyroc rolled his eyes and sat. He winced at the stinging in his rear end, garnering a quizzical look from Ursa. He hoped he hadn't just betrayed the presence of that injury to her; his ego couldn't handle the thought of explaining it. She lowered her gaze to his shoulder and began a thorough inspection of his injuries. He breathed a silent sigh of relief. "You got too close to a mother with cubs, didn't you?"

"No, *she got too close to me*. I was lying on the ground, trying to sleep when she came across me. I must have startled her or something because before I knew what was going on, she was trying to rip my face off."

"Well, I hope that encounter showed why mothers are the most dangerous."

"Yeah," he agreed.

Ursa paused. She leaned forward and began licking the side of his neck. Hyroc jerked back away from her as renewed pain spread across his injuries.

"Don't touch it!"

"You can't reach that wound, and you haven't cleaned it properly. And if it gets infected, it'll hurt a lot worse. So, hold still before I pin you to the ground." Hyroc relented, allowing her to continue cleaning his wound.

"So, since you're here, does that mean I completed your task?"

Ursa pulled her head back, keeping her eyes fixed on his injury. "You've demonstrated you can take care of yourself in this form, so yes, you completed the task." She resumed licking his neck.

"What's next?"

She gave his neck a few more licks before pulling her head back to answer. "We head back to the meadow."

"No, I meant what's—"

"You'll find out when we get there."

Hyroc sighed to himself. What type of torture had she cooked up for him in this next lesson? Would it involve running through thorn bushes or trying to kill a live porcupine? He forced his thoughts from what awaited him. Speculations would only heighten his anxiety. He would find out when he got there.

"You might bleed a little on your neck," Ursa continued. "But everything else looks fine."

Hyroc spoke as he stood. "Okay, I'm going to go get a fish before we leave." Ursa gave no objection, so he turned and headed toward the eddy in the river.

"How did you receive a bite there?" Ursa asked.

Hyroc froze, feeling a flood of warmth across his face. He turned back toward her, forcing a look of confusion on his face. "Bite, a bite, where?"

Ursa sighed irritably. "*On your hindquarters.* I saw your reaction when you sat. And there's no point in you trying to hide it."

He bowed his head shamefully and spoke in a reluctant mumble. "I was . . . I was running away."

She shook her head. "I told you, if you're outmatched by your opponent, running is an acceptable option, but you need to do so without hesitation and in a manner that doesn't leave yourself open. Otherwise, you invite injuries upon yourself in some not so admirable places." Hyroc stared at the ground, too humiliated to think of a response. Ursa sighed. "Stay there so I can get a better look." Reluctantly he stopped. She was quiet a moment. "It seems to have scabbed over properly; it'll just hurt for another day or two." She paused. "Okay, go get yourself a fish."

Hyroc eagerly headed toward the river. Bears dotted the surrounding shore, but none were close to his spot. Most of his mortification faded away at this. Now that he thought about it, there really wasn't anything for him to feel ashamed about. Sure, he had been bitten in a less than valorous area, but he had fought a bigger bear, *and he had won.* The bite on his rear was just the cost of victory.

He caught a fish, gutted it, and ate it.

"Okay, you've had your fish," Ursa said after Hyroc finished his breakfast. "Now, it's time to leave."

He used his paw to wipe a spot of fish slime from his snout. "Can I catch one more?" he asked. "For Kit."

Ursa studied him thoughtfully. "You may."

"Thank you."

"But you realize you'll be carrying that fish in your mouth?"

Hyroc paused with a dismayed look on his face; he hadn't considered that. But after eating raw fish for the last few days, it didn't seem all that bad. Besides, he figured getting a present for Kit was worth it.

"I know," he answered.

"Very well."

He returned to the river and resumed fishing. It was a much longer wait before the next fish came by. He pinned it beneath his paws and finished it off with a sharp bite.

"Okay, you got your *second fish*," Ursa said. "Now, we're leaving."

Away from the river, the rancid smell of rotting fish steadily lessened until the air regained the pleasant fresh smell of pine needles and sap. Then they arrived at the large spruce where they had left Kit.

Hyroc scanned his surroundings, but Kit was nowhere in sight. He dropped his fish and gave Ursa a puzzled look. "Where's Kit?"

"Trust me, he's here," she answered calmly.

He called out Kit's name and heard a strange answering call from behind the tree. When he called again, the answer was louder. Kit slipped out from under the skirting branches of the spruce.

"Kit," Hyroc called out happily. "I'm back."

The mountain lion broke into an excited bounding run. Hyroc held out his paw. Kit rubbed his head eagerly against it, and Hyroc carefully stroked his head. The big cat turned his attention on the fish. "I brought you a present." Kit regarded it eagerly. "Go ahead; it's yours." Kit dropped down on his belly and began eating. Ursa waited patiently for the mountain lion to finish before resuming their journey back to the meadow.

As they walked, Hyroc saw the blue-tinted peak of Wolf Paw Mountain sticking above the trees. A sudden sense of longing struck him. It drew his thoughts back to his cabin, to his traps, the taste of freshly baked bread and cooked fish, but most of all, he thought of his friends. By now, the rest of Elsa's family had probably noticed his absence. A sense of guilt swept over him; he hadn't trusted them enough to tell them what he was doing. Were they worried about him? Had the false story he and Elsa came up with helped to alleviate their concerns, or had it only made things worse? He squashed any further thought on the subject; he would deal with that when he was done.

When night arrived, they made camp at the foot of a small hill overgrown with fireweed and pine saplings. An overcast sky and wind greeted them the next morning. Then sometime around midday, they crossed the small river where Ursa had taught Hyroc how to fish, arriving at the meadow not long afterward.

"So, what's this next task?" Hyroc asked.

Ursa gave him a thoughtful look. "You'll be learning how to use your nose."

He cocked a questioning eyebrow. "My nose? What could you teach me about my sniffer that I don't already know, even if I am a bear?"

"You know much less about it than you think. A bear's sense of smell is in the magnitude of ten times more powerful than a bloodhound's, which, if you are not already aware, is far beyond the capabilities of your natural form."

He gave her a puzzled look. "But if it's that much stronger in this form, then why does everything seem to smell exactly as it did when I was in my natural form?"

"Because that particular capability is currently blocked."

Hyroc shot her a strange look. "Blocked? Why is it blocked? Beyond maybe inhaling water, I don't see how I could possibly misuse my nose."

Ursa raised her paw, and a blue glow emanated from it. She made a sharp swiping motion in front of his nose. His nostrils stung, causing his eyes to water. He sneezed and wiped his eyes on the back of his paw.

"It is now unblocked."

"You could have warned me," he said indignantly, though he wasn't surprised she hadn't.

He felt a myriad of smells flood into his nose. He smelled pine needles, grass, fireweed, dandelions, and innumerable plant odors, all twisted together in an incomprehensible tornado. The scent of mice permeated the meadow. In the surrounding forest, he detected squirrels, rabbits, lynxes, the pungent odor of weasels, a burrow full of fox kits, the dusty smell of bird feathers, and the musky scent of deer. There were so many smells! He couldn't shut them out! A sense of dizziness engulfed him. He felt a fuzzy tickle on his nose and the sweet wispy smell of dandelions overpowering everything. The dizzy feeling vanished. Forcing his eyes to focus, he found Ursa holding a dandelion flower against the end of his nose.

"Hyroc, slowly drop down on to your stomach," she said calmly. He did as instructed, while Ursa held the dandelion in place. "Then, I want you to take the dandelion from me; make sure it stays on your nose." He lifted his paw, allowing Ursa to transfer the flower to him. She took a step back and sat. "Now that your sense of smell is at its full potential, you need to learn how to control it. Such a vast increase to one of your basic senses is more than the mind can handle unless properly attuned to it. If it weren't for that dandelion, you would be unconscious right now.

Hyroc gave her a sluggish nod. "When you're ready, take the dandelion from your nose and breathe shallowly. And if you start to feel dizzy again, put it back. Understood?" Hyroc nodded. He took two more breaths through his nose before taking the dandelion away and breathing shallowly. Quickly the smells overwhelmed him, forcing him to return the dandelion to his nose when he felt dizzy. He sighed. "Don't get frustrated; this will take some time. As with a young cub that learns to focus its hearing on important sounds and tune everything else out, so too must you learn to do with what you smell."

"Well, how do I do that if I get dizzy every five seconds?" Hyroc asked irritably.

"You'll get better. When you next take the dandelion away, try only focusing on the smell of dandelions, block out everything else." Nodding, he took another breath before removing the dandelion. Again, he was overwhelmed by the smells in an aggravatingly short period. "Just keep doing that, and you'll slowly extend your time without the dandelion until it is no longer needed."

On the next several breaths without the dandelion, he had little more success, but eventually, he smelled a tug of something else that smelled like a dandelion. Warily he ventured a sniff toward the new smell. The odors of his surroundings punctuated the smell, but he was able to focus the majority of his concentration on just the new dandelion smell. He took a breath through the dandelion in his paw then sniffed the air. He was positive the new smell was a dandelion. Looking in the direction the odor had guided his nose, he saw a large patch of dandelions. He continued breathing through his nose without feeling dizzy.

"Good, you're breathing without the dandelion," Ursa said. "And from the look on your face, I'm assuming you identified the smell of dandelions. Now, focus on the smell of pine needles."

He sniffed. The smell of pine needles and sap were nearly overpowering. It wasn't hard for him to discern that odor, as it was the most prevalent.

Ursa nodded approvingly. "Good. Now try smelling for fireweed."

He sniffed. It was much harder for him to identify the particular scent of fireweed as it smelled similar to the grasses covering the meadow. Then to further compound the issue, the pine needle smell obscured everything with its aroma. Pushing through the masking smell of pine, he sifted through the grasses. He was eventually able to discern something that didn't quite smell like grass. It was subtle, but it was different. He couldn't be sure it was fireweed without looking at it. He got to his feet and headed toward the targeted smell, with Ursa following close behind. Sure enough, he found fireweed.

Chapter 16

TRACKER BEAR

Hyroc sat at the edge of the meadow, indifferently chewing a mouthful of fireweed beneath an overcast morning sky. Oddly enough, his improved sense of smell seemed to give the leafy plant a more robust flavor. And it pleasantly lacked the gum-irritating scales of a fish, bones that got stuck in his throat, and unpleasant tasting slime. But it still tasted unappetizingly similar to grass. He shook his head humorously. He had never thought he would compare the qualities of raw fish to anything beyond other types of bait. The raw fish was more satisfying; there was just something about eating uncooked meat that had never settled quite right with him. No matter how much he disdained eating fireweed, doing so felt more natural. He swallowed, bent his head down and took another bite from his fireweed. Nearby he smelled mice. He had yet to see one of the tiny animals scurrying through the grass and if he hadn't smelled them, he would have never known they were there. If he wanted to, he could follow their scent trails to a burrow. Maybe if he got bored later, he might.

As he chewed, he detected Ursa's scent wafting past his nose; she was entering the meadow. Based on the other mildly sweet smell that accompanied her, Hyroc guessed she had eaten berries recently. It still surprised him how accurate his nose was, though he also had a hard time controlling it. Often, he would smell something unfamiliar and almost of its own accord, his nose would force itself into the air and make him sniff.

"Are you finished?" Ursa asked as she came up to him. Hyroc nodded as he swallowed. "Today you'll be learning how to hunt in this form."

Hyroc wasn't entirely surprised by this. After his fishing task and his nose lesson, he had suspected hunting was not far behind. "As in deer?" he asked.

"It really wouldn't do a bear any good to waste its time with animals any smaller."

Hyroc nodded knowingly. "Well, at least I won't be going into this one blind."

Ursa gave him a surprised look. "*No complaining*," she said, sounding sarcastically aghast. "I never thought I would see the day."

Hyroc scowled. "Well, this lesson actually makes sense."

She snorted. "*Now* you say one of my lessons make sense." She shook her head in annoyance as she turned and started back in the direction she had come. Assuming he was supposed to follow, Hyroc headed after her.

Ursa spoke when he had caught up with her. "Hunting in this form isn't like what you're used to; you can't rely on bows or setting traps to do the work for you."

"I guessed as much," Hyroc said. "Which means, since I can't use a bow, I need to get within biting distance to kill whatever I'm hunting, without alerting it to my presence."

"More or less. But most predators have one major advantage over their prey."

"Their sense of—," Hyroc sidestepped a patch of devil's club blocking his path "—their sense of smell?"

"Exactly. Humans, for example, must track their prey by identifying prints or other such indications it may have left behind. Most predators lack the eyesight and, of course, the mental capabilities required to recognize these signs, but as you pointed out, they make up for it with a substantially heightened sense of smell. They can follow scent trails, so, for the most part, finding prey is the easy part. Now, keep in mind scent trails are vulnerable to the same environmental effects as tracks. If it rains, the scent trails will be washed away."

"Hold on, you said, 'most predators lack the eyesight and mental capabilities required to recognize these signs . . .'"

"My meaning was, most animals don't possess human-like intelligence as we do. We can still use visual tracking when tracking by smell is not enough."

Hyroc nodded.

They arrived at a clearing with a thicket of pines near the center. Past the thicket, the ground sloped downward until it eventually flattened out. The gray trunks of fallen trees dotted the incline and the terrain at the bottom. Here, Hyroc saw the freshly killed carcass of a deer buck with fuzzy buds of horn adorning its head. He followed Ursa down to the kill.

He looked at the deer and sighed. "You're going to make me eat part of the deer, aren't you?" he asked unenthusiastically.

"Just until you've had your fill, but you may avoid the innards if you wish."

"But won't eating the blood make me sick?"

"I wouldn't expect it to. Besides, since you'll mostly be using your teeth to kill prey, you will need to get used to the presence of blood in your mouth."

With a shrug, he stepped closer to the deer carcass; there wasn't much point in arguing; he just wanted to get it over with. The buck's neck was bent back at an unnatural angle. Blood still oozed from a wound where a large chunk of flesh was missing, and lumps on the back of the neck indicated dislocated vertebrae. He felt a strengthened twinge of revulsion at the thought of eating anything from this mangled section. The animal's back was more appealing. After taking a breath, he bit down into it. The taste of fur mixed with bloody meat washed through his mouth.

He took another bite and gagged on a wad of deer hair. When he tried to spit, the wad splintered, covering his mouth with abrasive hairs. Using his teeth in a raking motion, he started scraping the hairs off his tongue, but only got a few. He sighed, and figuring there was no effective way to rid his mouth of the hairs, took another bite. He continued to eat, spitting out gobs of hair every other bite until he had all that he could stand of the meal.

"Done?" Ursa asked.

Hyroc wiped his mouth with the back of his paw and, suppressing the urge to gag, he said, "Yes."

Ursa nodded. "Then we may begin on what happens next." She lifted her head, gazing at something behind Hyroc. He turned to see Kit cautiously plodding down the slope.

Hyroc called the mountain lion's name in greeting. He turned back toward Ursa with a curious look on his face. "Wait, is Kit part of the lesson?" he asked.

"No," she said calmly. "The next part will occur away from here. This way." She started walking away from him.

"Hold on," Hyroc said. "Should we be leaving Kit here with the carcass?"

She stopped to answer him. "You're not going to eat it, are you?"

"Well, no."

"Then you need not worry." She resumed walking.

Hyroc shrugged and followed alongside her. She stopped at a gap in the trees where an animal trail came through. She pointed to the beginning of the trail with her paw. "Sniff there." Hyroc did as she said, becoming aware of the scents of five different deer. "Three of the deer you're smelling are bucks, but two of them are not; I want you to pick out the scents of those two."

Hyroc closed his eyes and sniffed, concentrating on the scents. Three of the scents stood out with a strong musky smell. He took another sniff. He discerned two faint scents beneath the three musky ones. Focusing on those two, somehow, he knew one of them belonged to a doe, and the other deer had a much weaker scent. It seemed to suggest that the second deer was a fawn or yearling.

"One's a doe and the other, I think, is a fawn," he said, opening his eyes

151

"Very good," Ursa replied. She headed down the trail, and Hyroc followed. After a few strides, she headed off the trail toward a grassy patch of ground beneath a gap in the canopy.

"Tell me what they did here," Ursa said.

Hyroc sniffed and coughed as a fetid smell flowed into his nose. He had a fair approximation of what it was.

"If the look on your face is any indication, no further discussion is required, nor do I think you wish to."

"You think!" he said sharply, assuming she had probably done that to him on purpose.

She headed back to the trail and continued down it.

Tracking the two deer for another hour, Ursa slowed, moving from the trail at a careful pace, and Hyroc did his best to mimic her. Through the trees, he spotted the mother and fawn resting in the shade beneath the canopy of a cottonwood.

Ursa came to a stop. She spoke in a whisper. "Hyroc, describe what their scent tells you now."

Hyroc closed his eyes and took a deep whiff of air into his nose. The deer's scents were sharply defined, making it much easier for him to sort through what he could tell about them. Coming from the female was a sliver of a strong smell that reminded him of dried blood.

He spoke in a whisper. "I smell a faint, bloody scent coming from the mother, so I think she had a scrape with something earlier in the day."

"And has that injury weakened her?"

"I wouldn't expect it to."

"Very good. And if you find that an animal is injured, that injury may make all the difference when you move in for a kill, so it's always worth investigating. You may discover that an animal normally beyond your capability of taking down is injured and therefore vulnerable."

Hyroc gave her a disturbed look. "We're not going to kill these two deer, are we?"

"No, that would be wasteful." Hyroc breathed a sigh of relief; he didn't relish the thought of killing a baby animal, especially when he would be doing so with his teeth. "But never dismiss the thought entirely; fawns are easy targets, and if you are in desperate need of meat, killing a fawn may make the difference between survival and starvation." Hyroc nodded, trying not to think of a situation where he would have to do that. "Now, I want you to—"

Ursa stopped speaking when the bushes began to rustle behind them. The two deer bolted the instant they became aware of the sound. Both Ursa and Hyroc spun around. They saw Kit making his way toward them with something white and black in his mouth. Hyroc stepped in front of Ursa to greet the big cat. He suddenly smelled something pungent that stung his nose and irritated his eyes. The smell sent a shiver of alarm down his back.

"Kit, what do you have?" Hyroc asked warily. Kit dropped the black and white thing on the ground. It hit with a muffled thud and growled. Hyroc yelped when the animal scrambled to its feet, revealing the white markings of an infuriated skunk. The skunk wheeled around and flared its tail. Hyroc dove out of the way as the burning stench of skunk spray filled the air. He heard the patter of liquid impacting leaves, but amazingly, he was dry. The skunk growled and, with its tail still held erect, trotted away.

Hyroc breathed a sigh of relief as he stood. "Well, that was close," he said, as he turned around. "That skunk almost—." His words caught in his throat when he saw a murderous glare in Ursa's eyes. Her eyes were rapidly reddening, and yellow skunk spray soaked the fur on her head.

"HAVE YOU NOT LEARNED ANYTHING?" Ursa roared. "YOUR STUPIDITY ASTOUNDS ME. IF YOU HADN'T SQUEALED LIKE A DYING PIGLET, I WOULD'T HAVE GOTTEN A FACE FULL OF SKUNK SPRAY." Hyroc's eyes were beginning to burn from the stink, but he didn't dare show any signs of discomfort for fear of what Ursa would do to him. "You *will not* move from this spot till you ponder the proper way to handle an agitated skunk." Hyroc opened his mouth to utter the sincerest apology of his life but slammed it shut when she rushed forward, putting the end of her nose against his. "And if you so much as whimper, you will be cleaning my face off *with your tongue*. Now I'm going to go TAKE A BATH."

She turned and stormed off, violently bending the branches and stalks of any plants unlucky enough to be in her path.

Hyroc let out a breath he didn't know he was holding. He wheeled around to glower at Kit, who stood stiff-backed in a frightened stance. "You idiot!" Hyroc hissed. Kit's ears flattened against his head, and he angrily growled. "*Why would I ever want you to bring me a skunk?* I don't even know how you didn't get sprayed. Now, thanks to you, when Ursa gets back, she's probably going to make me eat nothing but grubs for the next week." Kit's expression changed into what seemed mockery. "Oh, *you think that's funny. I'll show you something funny!*" He charged Kit. He was nearly on top of the big cat when the squawking of a raven shot through the air. Grimacing, he stopped; Ursa had Shimmer watching him. Kit gave him a derisive glare and headed away from him. Fuming, Hyroc angrily flopped down on his rear. "Thanks a lot," he said bitterly in Kit's direction. "I *was* having a good day."

CHAPTER 17

FOLLOWING A TRAIL BY NOSE

Hyroc trotted down the incline where, the day before, he had followed Ursa to the dead deer. The sun shone intermittently through gaps in the clouds, and a mild breeze flowed through the branches of the trees. Ahead he could see the remnants of the dead animal. Crows stood on and around the carcass, squawking as they fed on the carrion. Even at this distance, he detected that the smell of rot had already seeped into the flesh. Trying his best not to breathe through his nose more than was necessary, he continued past.

A frighteningly familiar pungent odor drifted from the carcass. Hyroc whipped his attention in the direction of the smell. Just behind the shoulders of the deer, he spotted a skunk. It poked its head over the deer and gave him a defiant glare, daring him to come any closer. There was a good chance this was the same skunk that had sprayed Ursa. The resulting scolding was still very much fresh in his mind. Ursa's mood had improved somewhat after her bath, but upon her return—after forcing him to stare off into space for hours—she had given him a thoroughly unpleasant explanation on how he should have reacted. And she threatened him with bodily harm if he caused her to get sprayed again.

He gave the carcass a wide birth as he continued on his way. This morning after a breakfast of grubs, Ursa had informed him that his task was to kill a deer and bring it back to the meadow. He wasn't looking forward to dispatching his quarry with his teeth, especially knowing it would make noises. At least fish were incapable of wailing out in pain.

He moved to the animal trail at the edge of the clearing where he had seen the fawn and its mother. Lowering his nose to the ground, he smelled for a scent trail. A twisted rat nest of trails sprang into existence all around him. He picked out the smells of deer, but intertwined with them was a mess of other animal scents that made it difficult to separate one trail from another. Why had it seemed like there weren't any other trails the previous day? He rolled his eyes, feeling annoyed with himself—the carcass was the reason why. Any animal in the vicinity with a taste for meat would come to investigate when they smelled something rotten. That was what Ursa was probably counting on. It had seemed odd she would simply leave a deer carcass out to rot, given her disdain for wastefulness.

He sorted through the scents, often walking in circles as he did so until he managed to discern one he could follow. The scent led into the trees away from the mother-and-fawn-trail. It had a strong musky smell about it, so it likely belonged to a buck.

Tracking along the winding course of the musky scent trail, he spotted a buck grazing among some bushes near the bases of three cottonwood trees that formed a misshapen triangle. Mindful of the brief explanation Ursa had given him earlier on the hunting techniques of bears, he did his best to creep toward the deer. He rustled the branches of an alder. He winced as cold dread trickled down his back. The deer turned its attention on him. They stared at each other for an instant before the buck dashed out of sight.

Hyroc shrugged. If he had been using his bow, he would have gotten that deer. He pushed the thought aside—thinking like that wasn't helpful. Putting his nose to the ground, he sniffed. Another fainter scent trail curved off to his left. This trail was less musky, like that of a female. There was only one scent, so he shouldn't have the complication of a fawn to deal with. He headed along that trail.

An hour passed before he spotted a lone doe resting in the mottled shade of a birch tree. Despite his best efforts to move carefully, he still made too much noise while moving through the foliage, alerting the deer to his presence before he was close enough to attempt a run-down. He watched helplessly as the deer bolted. Disheartened by this second spectacular failure, he wandered over to a patch of sunlight piercing through the forest canopy and flopped down on his stomach. While he sunbathed, some of his frustration melted away. When he felt a little better, he resumed hunting.

Doubling back the way he had come, he found the scent of the first deer and followed it. He spotted the buck resting between two trees with its eyes closed. Bushes and dry leaves covered most of the area surrounding his quarry. With his last two failures weighing heavily on his mind, he searched surreptitiously for a quieter way to his target. He discovered a course clear of bushes and dry plant matter coming up behind the deer. Taking a breath, he started sneaking down the path.

As he neared his target, his heart began pounding with excitement. Another few yards and he would be close enough to run it down. He should be able to get this deer. With each step, his excitement grew until he felt like he would explode if he didn't start running. Suddenly, the deer's nose twitched, and it darted into the forest. Hyroc stood there, staring flabbergasted at the spot where a deer had just been lying. His shock swiftly turned to angry frustration. He was so furious, he clamped his teeth onto the stalk of a sapling and ripped it out of the ground.

It didn't make any sense; the deer was asleep. He hadn't made any noise on his approach, so how did it know he was there? He felt the cooling touch of a breeze blowing across his face. Then the realization of what had happened hit him. Now that he thought about it, when he first spotted the buck, he remembered feeling a breeze. He was so thrilled by the prospect of finally getting a deer, he had forgotten about one of the most important things a hunter has to keep track of—the wind. Some features of the terrain must have sheltered him from the moving air until he walked into the breeze, and that was when the deer scented him.

Now feeling extremely embarrassed for forgetting something so rudimentary, he walked over to a tree and pounded his head into the trunk. He finished berating himself, then made his way back to the sloped clearing, only stopping to nibble on some spruce tips. Sifting through the scents, he discerned another fresh deer scent weaving past the rapidly putrefying deer carcass. Following the new trail, he glanced in the direction of the carcass, searching for the skunk. The skunk was still there. He couldn't see its face clearly, but he imagined it giving him a vulgar glare.

At the opposite side of the clearing, the trail began a gentle bend into the trees. It continued in this manner for a short distance before shifting erratically. As Hyroc fought to maintain his track on the confusing trail, he thought he smelled a rabbit. He growled his annoyance; a rabbit had spooked his deer. The clumsy hare would only serve to make the deer that much harder to sneak upon. He growled again, noticing he had just lost the trail. Resisting the urge to give up, he backtracked until his nose picked up the trail again. Not far from where he had originally lost the trail, the deer scent coalesced into a mostly coherent trail. The erratic nature of the trail slowly smoothed out, making it much easier to follow.

Another hour of tracking had drifted by when he caught a shift of movement out of the corner of his eye. He stopped mid-step, focusing his attention on what had moved. He saw a small buck with two knobs of horn on either side of its head. A ridge of root-riddled dirt ran along a bank of pine trees, which sat at an angle from the near side of the deer. The trees grew too close together on the ridge, and if he tried to move through them, the deer would know he was there and run long before he could pursue. Following along the ridge with his eyes, it continued straight for a few yards, gradually curving in the direction of the buck's back end.

Hyroc dropped down on his belly and warily crawled along the ridge. At the curve, he stole a glance at the deer. The top of his head brushed the edge of a branch. He saw the deer's head turn, and instantly yanked his head down. His heart was now hammering away within his chest. An uncomfortable silence settled around him, but he didn't hear the sound of feet thundering across the ground. He waited for what felt like hours before he worked up enough courage to take another look—making sure his head didn't hit anything. The deer was still there, though it seemed more on edge now. Hyroc breathed a silent sigh of relief. Carefully, he continued around the bend. Past it, the ridge's slope flowed into a flat patch of open ground directly behind the deer. He was upwind from the deer, and there weren't any branches to brush against here. There shouldn't be any reason for him failing to get this one.

Rising to his feet in one smooth movement, he started across the open area toward the deer. With each step, his confidence grew. Nothing would stop him this time. In a few steps, he would be within range to break into a run. At that distance, it wouldn't matter how much noise he made. Something dry crunched beneath his foot. The deer snapped its attention in his direction. Hyroc felt a cold stab of dread as he met its gaze; he wasn't close enough yet! The deer shot to its feet and bolted.

Hyroc flew after the fleeing deer. His legs seemed to move at an impossible speed, faster than he had ever expected in this form, but the deer was faster. It jinked to the side, and Hyroc followed in an aggravatingly slow arcing turn. The deer bounded over the trunk of a fallen tree. Knowing he wasn't agile enough to attempt such a maneuver, he turned and darted past the tree. The turn slowed his pace enough for a substantial gap to form between him and his quarry. He could feel the strength rapidly draining from his limbs, and his body steadily demanding more air than his lungs could supply; he couldn't maintain his pace for much longer. The deer dashed around the skirt of a pine. Hyroc barreled through the branches, feeling their abrasive needles scrape across the sensitive tissue of his nose.

Ahead he saw a thick line of trees in a crescent shape. If the deer attempted to run through, it would get tangled up in the branches and trip, so Hyroc assumed it would avoid them. He curved toward the far end of the crescent, heading to intercept the deer. As expected, the deer turned sharply in the direction he was heading. He was almost at his intercept position when the strength in his legs began to give out. He felt a burning stab of fear in his chest. He was so close! No, he wasn't going to fail, not again, not like this! He fought through the protests of his body. He wasn't going to give up until his body gave him no other choice.

Using what remained of his strength, he forced himself at his target. The deer, seeing its doom, jerked away. Hyroc countered with the sharpest turn he could muster, nearly toppling over in the process. He threw himself onto the deer. They tumbled to the ground in a desperate flurry of flailing hoofs. Hyroc grunted, as a rapid succession of hard kicks from the deer's hind legs found his ribs. He slammed the struggling deer to the ground by its shoulders, pressing down to maintain his tenuous grip. The deer yanked its head back, slamming the knobs of its horns into Hyroc's chin. Hyroc's teeth clacked together and he tasted blood. He lunged forward and sank his teeth into the deer's neck. The deer's desperate writhing became more frenzied, making its kicks much more painful. Almost without any conscious thought, Hyroc savagely jerked his head around in a series of brutal twisting motions. He felt the disgusting snap of something within the deer's neck, and it instantly went still. He held on until he was positive the deer was dead, then let go. He drank in the air with heaving gasps as he sat.

Ursa's earlier explanation had made hunting as a bear sound almost as easy as taking down game with a bow. No wonder bears liked fish so much—all they had to do was wait for a fish to come by. And it was even easier with plants since they were incapable of trying to escape. He glanced back in the direction he had come, and nothing looked remotely familiar. Confused, he scrutinized the terrain. He saw a distant patch of ground and was barely able to make out what appeared to be the end of the ridge. That couldn't have been where he had run from. Was he running *that* fast? He sighed happily—no wonder he had felt like he was about to pass out.

He stood and turned his attention to the deer. His heart sank when he remembered he was supposed to take the carcass back to the meadow. He squeezed his eyes shut and groaned; it would take him the rest of the day to do that. With a deep sigh, he clamped his jaws around the deer's neck and dragged it off. The carcass slid awkwardly across the ground, and he tripped over the legs every few steps. Despite the fact he was carrying the carcass by his mouth, he found the deer surprisingly light. He would have needed to construct a sled to do the same in his natural form.

Close to dusk, he arrived at the meadow with a growling stomach.

"Good job," Ursa said. Hyroc dropped the deer and settled into a sitting position. An awkward silence descended. Ursa spoke in a disapproving tone. "Unless you wish for this task to be considered a failure, you had better eat a portion of that deer."

Hyroc shrugged. He bent his head down and took a bite from the deer's back. The meat was still not something he wished to eat, but it seemed to taste a little better. He hoped he wasn't getting used to eating raw meat. He shivered at the idea.

He swallowed, resisting the urge to gag. "So, am I almost done with this training thing? There really can't be many more things left for you to teach me."

"Yes, you are indeed nearing the end."

Hyroc nodded, and reluctantly took another bite of the deer. He spoke when he finished his mouth full of cold meat. "So, what are you teaching me next?"

Ursa studied him pensively a long moment. "I won't be teaching you anything."

He gave her a surprised look. "You won't?"

"No, you now know everything I can teach you."

"Then, do you mean I'm done?"

"Nearly; two tests remain."

"What are they?"

"They wouldn't be good tests if I told you before-paw." Hyroc waggled his head from side to side, unsurprised by her answer. "Make your way back to the meadow, and what remains of the day is yours."

CHAPTER 18

ANOTHER?

Keller's sword clashed against the blade of a North Lander soldier. He pulled back from the soldier, parrying a strike aimed at his chest, then answered with a blow of his own. The soldier gasped then fell over dead as Keller's blade found its mark.

Similar scenes played out all around Keller as numerous Ministry soldiers engaged the North Lander marauders.

Keller had scarcely enough time to catch his breath when a burly North Lander came charging toward him with a two-handed battle ax. He lurched back to avoid a downward swing, then ducked under a lateral slice. The North Lander countered his evasion by kicking him in the abdomen. Keller felt a flare of pain as he fell on his back. Before the North Lander was able to finish him off with a powerful downward strike, Keller managed to slice into the man's leg. The soldier yelled out in pain and fell to one knee. The North Lander used one hand to swing his ax at Keller. Keller rolled out of the way and jumped to his feet. Arrows from some nearby archers whistled past him and struck the North Lander, killing his opponent. Keller glanced back to see a group of Ministry soldiers rushing past the archers toward him. He joined their charge as they ran farther into the fray.

Keller stood in an open field, using a wet rag to wipe the accumulated blood from his sword. Bodies littered the ground, and the air held the reek of death. Crows and vultures circled the sky above, eagerly awaiting the departure of those that still lived. The battle with the marauders had been fierce, costing the lives of many Ministry soldiers, but they had emerged victorious over their adversary. The North Landers had fled once it became apparent to them that they were outmatched and their casualties had reached unsustainable levels.

It was a common occurrence for the North Landers to raid the settlements along the east and northeastern border every few years, but a force of this magnitude was unusual. Most raiding parties were small, consisting of fifty to a hundred North Landers. This force had been easily five times that and was far more organized than any raiders Keller was aware of. He wondered if this change in tactic was due to a new High Jarl coming to power and deciding to challenge The Ministry. Their barbarous home was frequently in a tumultuous state, with much infighting, and often experienced sudden changes in leadership. But whoever their current leader should be—if they had survived the battle—he knew better now.

Out of the corner of his eye, Keller glimpsed someone coming toward him. Turning, he saw a soldier, a captain approaching with a disturbed and extremely concerned expression scrawled across his face.

The man gave Keller a quick salute before speaking. "Sir, I don't know how to say this." The man's tone was nervous. "Well, there's a, there's sort of a—"

"Out with it, soldier!" Keller cut in irritably. "There's a what?"

"It's hard to say, sir. I think maybe it would be best just to have you see for yourself." The man beckoned for Keller to follow him.

Keller followed the man as they weaved their way through the bodies of the fallen, arriving at the other side of the field. He felt a surge of shock when he saw what the man had led him to. He now understood why the captain had been having difficulty explaining this to him. Before him was a soldier attired in North Lander armor, but it was not of their kin. The soldier had a snouted face, and covering his entire body was black fur with whitish-gray stripes running across it. His instinct was to assume this was the Hyroc creature, but this specimen seemed bigger, and its coloration was wrong. He was indeed looking at a second creature.

His head spun with the implications of what he was seeing. He had assumed the Hyroc creature was simply some sort of aberration and that it was a unique creation. But the appearance of this second creature dissolved all of his reasoning. There were more of them out there! There was more to this predicament than he could have imagined. Who knew how many more of these creatures could be inhabiting lands across Arnaira? He needed to bring this immediately to the attention of his superiors.

"You did right bringing this to my attention, captain," Keller said thankfully. "Have you found any more of these creatures?"

"No, sir, just the one." Keller nodded. "I hope you don't mind my asking, but what is it?"

"Something dark and dangerous," Keller answered. "Captain, I need that creature's body loaded up on a cart, then preparations made to transport it to the capital."

"Yes, sir, right away." The captain saluted, then hurried off to carry out his orders.

Keller studied the body thoughtfully. "And now there are more," he said absentmindedly. "There's more work to be done."

CHAPTER 19

FEAR

Hyroc was roused awake by a large paw shaking him. He opened his eyes to see Ursa standing over him in the cool darkness of morning.

"Get up; there's something I need to show you," Ursa said.

Hyroc's thoughts immediately jumped back to the night she led him to the Spirit Stone. She had said almost the same thing then. Was he about to have another similar experience? He didn't know if he could handle that again. What, was he supposed to choose another animal to turn into? His training as a bear was already hard enough as it was. But the addition of learning the movements and characteristics of a whole different creature would make it almost impossible. He would leave if that were what she was proposing, consequences be damned, that was just too much.

He raised his head and yawned widely before speaking. "What's going on, are you taking me to another Spirit Stone?" Hyroc asked cautiously.

"Yes," Ursa answered.

Hyroc gave her a strange look, surprised at her candidness. Her behavior was more disconcerting than anything. "Why?" he said. "What's waiting for me when I touch it this time? Am I going to turn

165

into some other animal? Because if I am, I'm gone, and there won't be any stopping me."

"No, your body will stay as it is. This one is different."

"Different, how?"

"It's only intended to show you something." Ursa raised her paw to forestall another question from him. "And before you ask what that something is, I cannot be certain. You'll have to find out when you touch it."

Hyroc studied her face thoughtfully, trying to discern if she was deceiving him in any way. Finding no indication of deception, he rose to his feet. He raised his paw toward her in an accepting gesture. "Alright, lead the way."

She led him to the far side of the darkened meadow. As with the previous stone, a cradle of interlaced branches from a tree held it suspended off the ground. But instead of the swirly markings being green, they were red.

"So, I'm assuming I just touch it like I did last time?" Hyroc said. He turned toward Ursa. She wore a look of concern on her face. He wondered what she could be concerned about when the stone was just supposed to show him something. What was he about to see?

"Yes, simply place your paw on it."

Hyroc nodded. "Anything else I need to know?"

Ursa shook her head. "No."

"Okay."

He moved to the stone, and, stoking his courage, placed his paw on it. As before, an intensifying vibration moved through his body. Then a reddish glow emanated from the core of the stone. The edges of his vision darkened. As everything went black, he heard Ursa say, "You can fight the darkness, it does not define you."

Hyroc opened his eyes to a darkened forest and clear night sky dominated by a full moon. He scanned his surroundings, searching for the glowing flowers to indicate his path but, strangely, saw none. Ursa said he would see something, and without the flowers to guide him, he assumed he was supposed to find that something on his own. There was more than one way to do so as a bear.

He lifted his nose skyward and sniffed for a scent. He found one, but it was not what he expected. It was blood, a subtle scent, but definitely blood. That wasn't exactly a comforting sign. He had come this far with his training, though, and wasn't about to let the fear of an unpleasant sight stop him from completing it.

Following the smell, he wound his way through the trees, never sighting any of the blue crystal animals. The blood smell steadily grew in strength until he arrived at the entrance of a cave descending into the ground. It had a gentle grade beyond the entrance, and there was a reddish glow emanating from within. This glow didn't seem to be inviting him to come closer. It seemed to be urging him to flee, as if warning him of danger. He felt some trepidation as he headed into the imposing darkness.

The slope continued for a short distance before flattening out. The reddish glow provided enough light for him to see where his footsteps landed, but not enough illumination to see the walls of the cave. He walked through the reddish void encompassing him until he heard something. Listening closely, he thought it sounded like someone crying. Moving toward the sound, he spotted a figure running through the darkness. He picked up his pace, and the figure resolved into the shape of a small child. With a terrified yell, the child spotted him and ran at a faster speed.

"Wait, slow down," Hyroc called after the child, breaking into a run. "I'm not going to hurt you!" He easily caught up with the child. The child ducked behind a stalagmite jutting out of the ground. Hyroc came to a stop a few steps away. "It's okay; I'm not going to hurt you." The child warily poked his head around the stalagmite to have a look at him through reddened eyes. "See? I know I look big and scary on the outside, but I'm friendly. I promise I'm not going to hurt you." The child studied him thoughtfully, then let out a frightened yell and resumed crying. "No, don't cry; you don't need to be afraid of me."

"You're not what he's afraid of," a cold male voice said.

Hyroc spun around to see the speaker. Standing in front of him was a large black bear with glowing red eyes and two dark brown stripes running from its eyes down its back.

"Who are you?" Hyroc asked, a feeling of apprehension growing in the back of his mind.

The bear cocked his head in amusement, then laughed humorlessly. "I think I should be insulted that you don't know who I am," the bear answered. There was something strangely familiar about the bear's voice. Hyroc was sure he would remember meeting another talking bear. But that didn't necessarily mean anything considering the other-worldly quality of what he was currently experiencing.

The bear raised his paw and flicked something dark from his snout. "Why don't you be a good boy and move aside?" He used his eyes to indicate behind Hyroc.

Hyroc stole a quick sideways glance at the boy behind him. "Why? What do you want with him?"

The bear shook his head and laughed again. "To do what the strong have always done to the weak."

Hyroc narrowed his eyes. "Do you mean kill him?" He asked guardedly.

"Of course."

"Why, what has he done to you?"

"Nothing, he is my prey."

"Prey?" Hyroc felt a surge of revulsion at the mere thought of viewing people as game. This was what he was supposed to see? This was just sick! Why in the world did he need to see this? "So, you want to kill him just because you can?"

The bear laughed. "Still holding on to the idea that you would never do the same?"

"Because I wouldn't!"

"You can fool yourself all you want, but I know better."

Why was this bear acting as if he knew him? Beyond this form, he had nothing in common with this bear. And his voice, why was it so familiar? "Who are you?" Hyroc asked.

The bear sighed in annoyance. "You still don't recognize me?" He shook his head. "I'll be more than happy to explain after I've dealt with my little friend back there. Move aside. This won't take more than a second." The bear took a step to move around Hyroc.

Hyroc stepped sideways to block the bear's path. The bear stopped in an almost surprised manner. "I'm not moving," Hyroc said sternly. "You'll have to go through me first." This was only a vision brought on by the Spirit Stone, but he still wasn't about to stand by and witness this animal killing a child.

The bear let out an icy chuckle. "Ah, so the cub wants to play? I'd be more than happy to oblige."

The bear charged! Hyroc's opponent moved so swiftly he barely had enough time to ready a strike aimed at his opponent's head. The bear ducked the strike and rammed into Hyroc's midsection. Hyroc gasped as the air was knocked out of him. This bear was much stronger than he was. He slid backward on his hind legs, unable to counterattack as he focused on maintaining his balance under the continuous push. The bear stopped while simultaneously rearing back and delivering a hard strike to Hyroc's skull.

Dark spots popped in front of Hyroc's eyes and a flare of pain shot across his head. A succession of paw strikes drove Hyroc to the ground on his front legs. The bear used its weight to pin Hyroc beneath it and wrapped its paws around his shoulders to restrict movement. Its mouth hovered so close to his head, he could feel its hot breath on his ear. He struggled against his attacker, but couldn't break free.

The bear laughed coldly. "I'll let you in on a little secret while we have this quality moment together. You want to know how I can tell what you're thinking?" the bear said. "That's because I'm you."

Hyroc froze, a wave of ice shooting through him. Was this bear him? How could that make any sense? It was most definitely not him. This bear was bigger than he was, it had red eyes, and his own eyes were blue. But even as he thought that he was struck by familiarity with its markings, its stripes looked like his and were in exactly the same place. He didn't want to believe it, but that's why the voice was so familiar—it was his. This bear was him. But how? It acted nothing like him. It enjoyed killing and wanted to kill a child simply because it could. He could never think such a thing, let alone carry it out.

He twisted his upper body and slammed the back of his head into his attacker's jaw. The bear's grip loosened, and Hyroc was able to break out of his opponent's grip. The instant he was free, he wheeled around, nailed the bear in the head with a hard strike, and lurched backward.

The bear laughed and lifted a paw to touch a bleeding spot on his mouth. He studied the blood on his paw thoughtfully before lowering it back to the ground. "I didn't think you had that in you."

"Come at me again, and you'll see a lot worse!" Hyroc yelled.

"Oh, I plan to. I was surprised, not finished. It will take much more than a little blood to stop me."

The bear rushed forward and grabbed Hyroc's shoulder and head. It wrenched Hyroc's head sideways, following through with a bite to the side of his neck. Hissing through the pain, Hyroc lifted his free paw and struck his opponent in the side of the head. Then as his paw dropped, he hooked his claws in the bear's shoulder and pulled as hard as he could. Growling, the bear pulled his head back and sank his teeth into Hyroc's shoulder. Fighting through the pain, Hyroc readied another strike. Before he could follow through, the bear savagely jerked its head sideways. Hyroc yelled out, unable to push his way through the disabling wave of pain. Taking advantage of the distraction, the bear used both his paws to deliver a powerful sideways shove. Hyroc lost his balance, and the side of his body slammed into the unforgiving cave floor. Then before he could recover, the bear was on him, pinning him down.

"Why fight it, Hyroc?" the bear said. "We both know it's pointless."

Hyroc thrust his shoulder up into his opponent, attempting to make an opening so he could roll out from under him. His move failed, and the bear retaliated by striking Hyroc in the head. Hyroc's chin slammed onto the ground, and his attacker applied more pressure.

"You can't win against me. Give in."

"No," Hyroc growled, struggling futilely to get out from under the bear.

"You're wasting your energy. Just accept it. To everyone, we're a monster, that's what we've been our whole life, and that's all we will ever be."

"You're the monster!"

The bear laughed. "You don't see the truth of the matter. You're a Wol'dger. You have no choice. The curse made us into the monster we are. Why deny it? The outcome is already decided. Give in to it."

"I won't do anything you say!"

"I know you don't believe that for a second. Deep down, you know I'm right. You've felt the urges. The desire to dominate, to kill. Why fight them? You are already the monster everyone fears you to be. All you would be doing is confirming their judgments about you."

"I would be making them right."

"Justification is irrelevant. Right or wrong, both are meaningless. The only thing that matters is the taking, the getting of what you want."

"You're sick. There is more to life than just getting what you want. What about friendship and family? Those are much more valuable than taking from others."

The bear snorted derisively. "Friendship," he scoffed, "a pointless concept. Those weaklings you call friends care nothing for you. To show you their gratitude for saving them from the shadow demon, they sent the Witch Hunter after you."

"That was a misunderstanding with Donovan. He didn't know what else to do."

"The moment they laid eyes on you, they saw you as a monster. Elsa said it herself. She was scared when she first saw you. Then her brother and father captured you. Svald even threatened to kill you. They'd turn on you the moment it benefited them. The only way to protect yourself is to make them fear you. Give them one choice; submit to you or die."

"You're wrong. They changed their minds, even apologized; they were just scared of something they didn't understand. I could never hurt any of them."

"Then you are a fool! Many others have had no qualms about tormenting and hurting you. Some have even tried to kill you. How many restless nights did you spend wishing you could stop those who caused you pain? Now, you can see those desires fulfilled, and yet you refuse to exact retribution."

"Because doing what you say is evil."

"Evil? Ah, falling back on Marcus's teachings now, are we? Everything he taught you was woefully inaccurate. He merely condemned that which did not fit into his view of reality. A cat killing mice is not evil. It is simply in their nature as the monster is simply within yours. There's no fighting it."

"Don't you dare speak ill of him! He gave me as much as he could."

"Are you sure? He made your whole life a lie. And then he left you! He cared nothing about you. He only sought to benefit himself."

"Shut your mouth, that's a lie!" Hyroc yelled. "He was a good man."

"These are not my words; they're yours. You admitted everything he had ever taught you was wrong."

Hyroc grit his teeth, the emotions from the night he learned of his curse flowing through his mind. He had been angry, scared, confused, and nothing in his life seemed to make sense anymore, not even the happiness he had experienced in Forna. But now, the things he had said about Marcus that night filled him with shame. Shame for thinking such horrid things about the man who raised him and had done everything in his power to keep him safe. He deserved far more consideration. Then there was June. Even though she couldn't protect him as much as she desired, she too cared for him deeply, loving him no less than Marcus. Nothing they did for him was ever a lie. He was foolish for believing such a preposterous thing. And he would not dishonor their memory by becoming a monster. He had to fight it! For them and for everyone else he cared about.

Hyroc flung the back of his head into his opponent's chin. The bear's head bounced back with an audible clack of teeth. Hyroc furiously rocked his shoulders back and forth until the bear lost its grip. Then in a frantic series of movements, he scrambled out from under his opponent, turning to face him.

The bear stood, spitting out a mouthful of blood. He fixed a furious look in Hyroc's direction. "Not a smart move," the bear said irritably. "I guess more pain is in order before you're convinced. I'm glad; I wasn't quite ready for our little game to end."

The bear charged. It was too fast for Hyroc to counter. Instinctively, he flung his paw out to shield himself from the incoming attack. Heat shot through his forelimb and into his paw. A blue shimmer appeared in front of Hyroc, glowing purple in the reddish light. The bear collided with the shimmer, rebounding back from it. He shook his head dizzily then shot Hyroc an astonished look. Hyroc lifted his head, relieved by the presence of the protective shimmer. The bear rushed forward and struck the barrier with a strong paw swipe. This yielded no better result. Growling in angry frustration, the bear slammed both paws into the barrier. When this failed to breach it, the bear flung himself into it, coming away with a cut to the nose. Finally, he roared.

"What trickery is this?" the bear bellowed.

Hyroc smirked half humoredly. "You don't remember this, do you?" he said.

"I demand you come out and fight me, coward!"

"Gladly, you don't scare me anymore."

Hyroc shook his paw, and the shimmer slowly diminished until it disappeared. The moment it was gone, Hyroc and his opponent broke into a run. Hyroc ducked an attacking swipe from the bear, answering with one to the side of the bear's head. Prior to impact, his paw glowed blue. It struck with far more force than Hyroc was capable of applying. The bear staggered backward, barely maintaining his balance

"You cannot beat me!" the bear yelled

He charged again. Hyroc sidestepped the brunt of the charge, receiving a swat to his side. Seeing an opening created by the ineffective strike, he bit the bear in the shoulder and shoved him back. The bear stumbled, dropping down to all fours.

"Your strength was the only thing that mattered to you," Hyroc said.

"I do not require tricks to get what I want."

"And you don't need family, friends, or anyone who cares the slightest about you."

"These are only distractions, constructs to keep the strong from claiming their rightful place over the weak."

"No, you're wrong, these are all important things to be cherished, and I refuse to live without them."

"Then you can die with them!"

The bear charged. Hyroc dodged out of the way. When his opponent turned to attack, he struck first, delivering a glowing strike to one of the bear's forelimbs. There was a cracking sound as the bear stumbled sideways, and when he came to a stop, he couldn't put pressure on that leg anymore.

"You were right, I do know you," Hyroc said. "Or I know what you are."

"I'll rip your head off for that!" the bear roared. But even as he spoke, his words were laced with fear."

"You're what I might have become if my life had gone much differently. What might have happened if it were not for Marcus, June, Thomas, Elsa, Donovan, Curtis, Helen, Svald, and Ursa caring so much for me. Never treating me like I was a monster."

"All lies. They cared nothing for you."

"You're the liar. You're the monster here, not me."

"No!" the bear growled savagely.

"And you have no place with me."

"I'll kill you!" the bear roared.

He broke into a limping run toward Hyroc.

"I'm not afraid of you anymore, leave!"

The bear came to an abrupt halt in front of Hyroc and wailed out in pain. Quickly the body of Hyroc's opponent dissolved to ash, and all traces floated out of view into the darkness.

Hyroc turned toward the stalagmite where the child was hiding. The child walked steadily away from cover, never taking his eyes off Hyroc. He stopped and happily smiled his thanks. Before Hyroc could return his gratitude, everything went black.

Regaining consciousness, he felt as if he had tripped and fallen. Feeling a surge of alarm, he jerked up onto all fours. Darkness still obscured his surroundings, but they were familiar. Looking skyward, he couldn't see a full moon. He took a deep breath, relieved. His experience with the stone had ended and he was back.

"You mastered it," Ursa's voice said with relief.

Hyroc turned to see Ursa sitting a few steps away. "Ursa, what in the *sunless plain* was that!" he yelled thunderstruck.

"A test."

"A test of what, how much I could enjoy killing people?"

"It was a test meant to challenge your ability to resist the tendencies of your animal form."

"Well, I have a very hard time believing those tendencies would ever drive me to become anything remotely close to that thing."

"Perhaps, but it was the only way to be certain of your resolve toward resisting them. The test demonstrated the tendencies of your animal form and forced you to confront them. It showed you the consequences of giving in to those tendencies and how dangerous you would become to those around you."

"So, what I saw was just some twisted version of myself if I went down an extremely dark path?"

"More or less."

"Okay, but was it necessary for my shadow self to insult me in such personal ways?"

Ursa studied him thoughtfully. "Yes. The night you learned of your curse, you were in a tremendous amount of pain. Your whole life seemed a lie and in that was a danger of you giving in to the tendencies of your animal form. With you believing you were the monster people thought you were, you may have begun to disregard what you knew of morality. And as you did so, resisting the tendencies of your animal form would have seemed less and less important until you gave into them entirely. Then you would have become something similar to what you saw. Therefore, confronting you with those thoughts and bringing to light the error of believing them was an important component of the test."

"So, you're saying that thing I faced was a possibility, partially because of what I thought?"

"Yes."

"And all the things Marcus taught me were actually preventing me from going down that path?

Ursa nodded.

Hyroc shook his head. "How could I have been so stupid? How could I have let myself believe such ridiculous things? My time with Marcus and June could never have been a lie. What they taught me was the truth. They saw the good in me, not the bad, and only wanted to bring it out. I was never a monster. My curse means nothing. It has no bearing on my choices; those decisions lay with me and me alone. I've been cursed my whole life. It didn't determine who I was before, and it won't determine who I am just because I know about it."

Ursa gave him a proud look. "Yes, you now understand. Your curse is not what defines you; only your choices define you. Your fate is your own."

"Thank you for that, Ursa. Am I right in assuming that since I defeated my other self, I'm now safe from becoming like that?"

"Yes, but you are the master of your destiny and are truly the only one capable of preventing yourself from heading down such a path."

Hyroc nodded. "I don't know if I could handle not having friends and thinking only of myself."

"I would not dwell on such possibilities; be glad you have such things and do not take them for granted."

"I won't."

Ursa paused. "The rest of the day is yours; you may do with it as you wish, only remember to prepare yourself for your final test tomorrow."

"Will it involve another Spirit Stone? I'd be very happy not to see another one again."

"No, definitely not."

Hyroc nodded. "Anything you want to tell me about it?"

"No, as I've already stated."

Hyroc sighed humorously. "I had to try."

"As I've come to expect."

CHAPTER 20

THE FINAL TEST

A gust of wind rippled the fur of Hyroc's head, and with a half-conscious grumble, he rolled onto his side. His cheek bumped into the hard surface of a root protruding from the ground. With another more aggravated grumble, he slid his face off the root, settling it on his paw. All he wanted was to sleep a little longer, and everything around him seemed bent on preventing that. And his choice to sleep in such an uncomfortable place at the base of this tree was not one of his better ideas. Then it occurred to him he hadn't laid down for the night at the base of a tree. The air smelled of cottonwood, but that struck him as odd because there weren't any close to the meadow. Also, the scent of pine was much stronger than he remembered, and the area lacked the smell of nearly all the other plant odors that should have been there. Something wasn't right.

When he opened his eyes, he saw the trunk of a towering cottonwood. The sky was overcast, and a chill wind blew across the ground. Sweeping his eyes around, he saw pines surrounded the cottonwood. He wasn't in the meadow. A feeling of alarm crept through him. How had he gotten here? Had he been sleepwalking the night before? Surely he would have noticed at some point if he was a sleepwalker. He sat up into a sitting position, pushing his hind legs out in front of him.

Checking his feet, he found no dry mud or any other refuse that might have stuck to them if he had been walking recently. So, unless he had miraculously only walked on dry ground during the night, it seemed unlikely he had been sleepwalking. This brought him back to his original thought—how had he gotten here?

"Kit," Hyroc called out. The only sound he heard was that of leaves rustling in the wind. He called his companion's name louder, but still got no response. He then tried calling for Ursa, with the same result. He wondered if this was the beginning of the final test Ursa had mentioned the day before. The thought was calming, but what was he meant to do? She hadn't given him any instructions. He had assumed those would come in the morning; he hadn't expected he would wake up in a completely different place than where he had gone to sleep. For the time being, he would forgo the question of how that was possible, and figure out what he was supposed to do.

He glanced across the ground, his eyes settling on a white rock a few steps away. The rock had an unnaturally smooth surface as if someone had polished it. Thinking it might somehow be part of the test, he stepped over to it. He gave it a sniffing, but it smelled unremarkably like a rock. Then he placed his paw on its cool surface.

"Hyroc," he heard Ursa's voice say. Startled, he pulled his paw back and wheeled around to look behind him. There was nobody there, and his surroundings were still empty.

"Ursa," Hyroc called out. No response. "Ursa, are you there?" His sense of calmness steadily decreased. He swore he had just heard her voice. Warily, he turned his attention back to the rock. Studying it, he replaced his paw on it. "Don't be alarmed," he heard Ursa's voice say. He pulled his paw back. Giving his surroundings another glance, he still saw no one. Was the rock talking? He put his paw back on the rock.

"You're not hearing things. I've enchanted this stone so that when you touch it, you can hear the message I etched into it. I know you're probably confused and a little unsettled to find yourself in a different place, but this is the most effective way to start your test. Your task is to claim territory for yourself. Once you've established yourself in that territory, you must live off whatever you find in the vicinity for four days. There are other bears in the area, so you will likely have to fight to keep your territory. I will be watching you throughout the task, but whatever happens, no matter how dire, I will not come to your aid. That is to say, you can die during this. Then after those four days, you may find your way back to your cabin. We will be waiting for you there, as will all of your things. I wish you luck, and remember, you defeated the shadow of yourself; you can accomplish this."

When he heard no other words, he pulled his paw from the stone. So, there was a chance he could die during this test? His task suddenly gained a far more serious tone. Injury had become a near guarantee throughout his training with Ursa, but nothing remotely close to death. His situation hadn't been dissimilar after leaving the boarding school, and he had gotten through that, but he felt strangely vulnerable knowing this. He took a deep breath, smothering a spark of forming fear. Ursa wouldn't have put him to this task if she didn't think he was capable of doing it. And after everything she had taught him, what did he have to be afraid of? He was a *bear*, one of the toughest creatures in the forest. The only thing that had any hope of hurting him was another bear. He felt a surge of pride, remembering how he had fought off the larger thief-bear when it stole his fish and then the psychotic specter of himself. That in itself proved he knew how to handle himself. Still, he would need to be careful about running into the big males; he held no delusions he stood any chance against them, at least not for a few years yet. He smiled a little at that thought. How big was he going to get? He shook his head, shedding the thought. That was probably the most pointless thing he could think of right now.

Okay, so he needed to find a spot to claim for the next four days. His priority should be to find a source of drinkable water, followed by food. He lifted his nose and took in a deep whiff of air. Through the screening smell of pine, he couldn't pick out the scents of anything potentially useful. Studying his surroundings, he spotted the long depression of an animal trail threading its way through a gap in the trees. That seemed a good spot to start, so he began following it.

As the trail randomly curved around trees, the surrounding forest remained relatively unchanged. Hunger pangs began to gnaw at him.

The only thing he managed to find in the unchanging terrain was spruce tips, and a moth flattened against a trunk, but those barely took the edge off.

Most of the morning had melted away when a steep overgrown hill barely tall enough to clear the trees broke the monotonous surroundings. The trail continued on to the rise, and drifted to one side. Eager for a better look at the area, he trudged up to the top of the hill and reared up on his back legs. At an angle from the side of the hill where the trail passed, he saw a rough oval-shaped patch of open ground. Then from the side opposite of this, there was another taller hill with a bowl-shaped rise jutting from its flanks. The hill blocked sight of what lay on the other side, but few trees poked above the rise, suggesting there might be a swath of open ground there also. And where the ground was open, there was a likelihood he would find something to eat. He swept his eyes around, scanning for a gap in the trees where a stream might be. He saw none.

Looking from the hill to the oval of open ground, he decided to head toward the latter. If there weren't anything useful there, he would make his way to the hill; it was tall enough, he would still see it above the trees.

Away from the hill, the ground undulated with deep ruts, making for slow progress. Beyond this, the ground rose mildly, then inclined down. From here, the terrain remained mostly flat to the clearing.

Fireweed dominated the majority of the clearing, with intermittent patches of sweet clover, wild strawberries, Labrador tea, and dandelions. From the other side, he heard the faint murmur of flowing water. Everything he needed was here; this was a good spot to spend four days. He sauntered over to the strawberry plants and started picking through the ripe berries.

As he chewed, enjoying the sweet taste of his find, his eyes drifted past the plants to the trunk of a dirty-bronze colored birch. About halfway up the tree, he saw four deep scrape marks. He stopped chewing, focusing more closely on the scrapes. They looked awfully close to the shape of bear claws. He shifted his gaze to another tree, finding it too bore the same marks. He stiffened in alarm. Someone had already laid claim to this area! At the same moment, he heard the sound of growling to his right. Whipping his attention toward the sound, he felt a thrill of fear when he saw a massive male brown bear glowering at him malevolently. The instant they locked eyes, the bear broke into a charge. Hyroc had only enough time to take a single step back before the bear nailed him in the head with a paw swipe, wrenching everything above his shoulders sideways. Ears ringing, he managed to dodge out of the way when the bear lunged forward to lock his head between its paws. Instinctively, Hyroc bolted for the trees, the bear tearing after him in pursuit. He quickly outpaced his pursuer, losing the bear with several well-placed weaving motions between trees.

When he was sure the bear was gone, breathing heavily, he leaned against a tree. His ear began to sting. As he reached up with one paw, the stinging increased at his touch, and he saw blood when his paw came away. The bear must have nicked his ear with its initial strike. It was nothing compared to what could have happened. He felt irritated with himself; he had just started the test and had already gotten himself into a dangerous situation. He could get *killed* during this and needed to be more careful. Dying would be a pretty bad way to end his training.

Running his eyes along the tops of the trees, he spotted the top of the taller hill. He waited until his breathing slowed, and headed in that direction. Maybe he would have better luck there.

After encountering a rough patch of ground and a line of trees growing so thickly he had to go around, he picked his way over the far most rise of the hill. As he had thought, there weren't many trees here, but mingled between them were alders, some small sweet clover patches, sporadic groupings of dandelions, the occasional bush, and a dirty pool of mosquito-water. Disheartened by the lack of food here, he trotted over to the dandelions and started eating the flowers. After the dandelions, he ate as many of the bitter-tasting catkins from the alders as he could stand, then made his way to the top of the hill. Halfway through his ascent, he saw a black bear mother with two cubs. The cubs called out in alarm, and the mother gave him a warning moan. Hyroc backtracked before continuing on his way in a curve away from the bears.

From the hill's top, he couldn't discern any clearings of notable size but, about a mile away, he saw what looked like a gap in the trees where a stream flowed through. Moving his eyes along the horizon, he spotted the tall rocky shape of Wolf Paw Mountain reaching skyward. The mountain seemed far away, but at least he now knew which way to go at the end of his four days here. Turning his attention back to his task, he sniffed, making sure no bears were in his path, and started toward the stream.

After covering about half the distance to the stream, the terrain roughened considerably, and devil's club sprang up in nearly every opening leading through the trees, slowing his pace considerably. By the time he had navigated to the stream, it was afternoon.

He was relieved to find water flowing in a straight stretch of stream. He sated his thirst, then keeping the water within sight, ate some fireweed he spotted among the trees, before continuing along the shore. Past the straight stretch, the current was more subdued as the stream bent mildly to his left. Here, cattails lined both shores, and an eagle resting on the top of a tree watched the water attentively. At the terminus of the bend, the stream hooked sharply in the opposite direction, and the speed of the flow increased.

Away from the stream, the trees thinned out, and an opening appeared. Hyroc made his way there, warily watching the trees for any signs of ownership. He saw alders through most of the clearing, but growing against them he saw the ridged leaves of wild raspberry bushes. Then, filling what little space remained, were fireweed, lungwort, and black lily. There were birch trees and some cottonwoods spread along the side of the clearing closest to the stream. He inspected the trees but found no indication that anybody had claimed this spot. Relaxing a little, he came up to the nearest fireweed and ate it. Then he carefully picked through the raspberry bushes, doing his best to avoid getting a thorn in the face.

He looked skyward as he chewed. The sun was two finger lengths from the horizon; only a few hours of daylight remained. He shrugged. It had taken him all day to get here. Though he supposed it didn't matter. There wasn't exactly anything pressing to accomplish.

When he had satisfied his hunger, he chose several trees at random to rub his back against. Then he made claw marks on the tree's trunk as high up as he could reach. And just for good measure, relieved himself in places along the tree line. Now that the clearing was his, he snapped off some branches of pine and arranged them in a sheltered recess beneath an alder. Next, he laid down the branches of a leafy bush, over which he set yarrow. He then started uprooting ferns and setting them across the yarrow.

As he set the final fern in its place, the scent of something wet and musky entered the clearing. Watchfully, he stepped out from under the shelter of the alder. When he turned in the direction of the scent, he saw a brown bear emerge from the trees in front of him. The bear saw him, its body went rigid, and it growled as it continued forward. A sinking feeling struck Hyroc. This bear clearly had no interest in sharing the area. How was his luck this bad?

He studied the intruder thoroughly. The bear was bigger than he was, but the size difference was slight, slight enough that the bear's victory was far from assured. He could fight this bear, and there was a good chance he could win. This place was the perfect area for him to spend the next four days, and after all the hard work he had devoted to making his bed, he wasn't going to walk away.

He made his own body go rigid and issued a defiant warning moan before repeatedly popping his jaws. Aggravated by his insolence, the bear thumped its paws down on the ground. Hyroc answered the threat with a stiff-legged stamp. The bear's ears flattened, and it bowed its head. Hyroc responded in kind, readying himself for what came next.

Time seemed to pass at a lethargic pace as the two of them stared unflinchingly at each other. Then the bear burst into a charge. Hyroc reared up on his back legs, lurching backward out of the way of a paw swipe aimed at where his head had been. He nailed the bear with an angled strike to the head where the ears were. Shrugging off the hit, the larger bear rose on its back legs. The two of them lunged forward, throwing their paws around the neck of the other. The bear positioned one of its paws improperly, leaving enough of an opening for Hyroc to bring his head forward to bite the side of its neck. Growling in pain, the bear repositioned its grip and yanked Hyroc's shoulders sideways, unbalancing and surprising him. Hyroc grit his teeth as he received a retaliatory bite to the front of his shoulder. Pulling through the bear's grip, he regained his stance and shoved his adversary backward. As his opponent stumbled, he struck with his paw, raking the side of the bear's chest with his claws and opening up a bleeding gash. When he attempted to wrap his paws around the bear's neck, his opponent nailed him in the side of the snout. Hyroc gasped at a surge of pain when the bear's claws slashed open a swath of flesh halfway across his snout and up onto his cheek. Blood soaked through his fur, dribbling down into the side of his mouth. For an instant, the only thing he could concentrate on was the pain shooting through his face.

The bear hurled itself forward, throwing all of its weight into Hyroc. Hyroc's foot slipped under the force of the impact, and he was knocked down onto one knee. Fighting through the pain, he strained against the bear's push as it tried to force him onto his back. Then the bear stood straight and brought its upper body down on him hard. Hyroc lost his balance, slamming down on his back. He pressed his paws against his opponent's chest, preventing the bear from burrowing its teeth into his face. The bear slipped its paws behind his shoulders and started pulling him toward it. Hyroc shoved back as hard as he could but he could feel himself slowly being drawn toward the bear's waiting jaws. The bear turned its head, lining its jaws up with the front of Hyroc's neck, and shoved its head forward to rip his throat out. Hyroc snapped his head toward the bear's head, latching onto the side of its jaw. The bear's teeth brushed across his fur but were unable to bite. Yanking its head back, the bear made a sharp twisting motion, sending a shock of pain through Hyroc's face and shaking his teeth free of its flesh. As the bear lunged forward for another attempt, Hyroc moved his hind legs onto the bear's belly and pushed against its gut as hard as he could. As the bear struggled against the push, he threw his paws onto the bear's shoulders and, with a sharp wrenching motion, threw the bear off. He scrambled to his feet an instant before the other bear did the same.

Hyroc charged, slamming into his unsteadied opponent, and mauled the bear's face. He tore open a wound that promptly began issuing blood. Growling savagely, the bear grabbed Hyroc's head, yanked it downward, and sank its fangs into the side of his uninjured shoulder. Hyroc clenched his teeth and hissed through them. He threw his upper body at the bear, making his adversary stumble. As the bear struggled to regain its balance, Hyroc shoved with all the strength he could summon, driving the bear backward in an attempt to knock it off its feet. The bear grabbed him by the shoulders, digging its claws into his skin to maintain its balance, and began pulling on him. Hyroc stumbled forward. In a quick motion, he shoved off his opponent. The two of them staggered away from each other, falling onto all fours. Hyroc spat out a mouthful of blood riddled saliva and wiped his mouth on the back of his paw. He narrowed his eyes at the bear, then growled. The bear gave the branches of an alder a threatening swat. Hyroc understood from that gesture that this wasn't going to end anytime soon. But he wasn't going to abandon the clearing over a couple of scrapes. This place was his! He exhaled loudly, and charged.

The sharp gray crescent of the moon rose above the nighttime horizon, bathing the darkened forest in its silvery sheen. Hyroc stood in the clearing, heavily breathing as he glowered at the intruding bear, which stood at the trees growing closest to the river. His limbs burned from exertion, and numerous wounds covered his chest, shoulders, forelimbs, and parts of his head, neck, and snout. The opposing bear was in no better condition. The last few hours were a blur of blood, claws, teeth, and pain. Hyroc knew he should take advantage of the weakened state of his opponent by charging, but his legs refused to obey. He was so tired! All he wanted now was for the fight to end. Why wouldn't the bear just leave? There were other places where the bear could go.

He felt himself beginning to sway. Deciding it was better to go down by his own accord, he dropped down into a sitting position. He had nothing left to fight with. A moment later, he saw his opponent collapse. He sighed; the fight was finished. At this point, he didn't care what happened as long as he could rest. Gazing down toward one of his forelimbs, he saw a patch of half-coagulated, dirty blood oozing out of a substantial break in his skin. The injury needed cleaning. He was exhausted but leaving it unattended, risked infection. With a sigh, he laboriously climbed to his feet, then limped haggardly toward the stream. He dipped his forelimb into the water. It stung as the cool liquid flowed over the openings in his flesh. Grimacing, he stepped into the stream, exposing every one of his wounds to the cleansing touch of the flowing water. His breath caught in his throat at the sudden increase of pain but, at the same time, it felt strangely pleasant, like the sensation after taking a much-needed bath. When everything seemed as clean as it was going to get, he trudged back to the clearing. The bear was lying on its side when he arrived, and he wondered if the bear was dead. Almost in answer, the bear gave him a cautious look. Hyroc groggily bowed his head in a nonthreatening gesture, not caring if he did it properly. When the bear dropped its head back to the ground, Hyroc moved over to his bed and collapsed. He never thought a bear nest could be so comfortable. Sleep took him an instant later.

He awoke to the sun beaming down on his face through the thin branches of the alder he lay beneath. When he stretched, every muscle in his limbs shrieked in an anguished choir. He felt a sharp sting in his neck as one of the wounds there split open and resumed bleeding. He groaned miserably; what madness had made him think going through such a severe fight was worth this clearing? It wasn't as if somebody's life depended on him winning. His stomach growled. He groaned again and thumped his chin frustratingly on the ground. All he wanted to do was lie here on his plant bed and not move. With a sigh, he carefully got to his feet. Sweeping his eyes through the clearing, he found that the other bear appeared to have departed. He sniffed and shrugged happily. There was only a faint scent of the bear lingering in the clearing. It seemed, after all the misery of the previous night, his opponent had decided the clearing wasn't worth any more trouble. At least one good thing had come from all that pain.

After eating two fireweed plants and a mouthful of lungwort flowers, he limped to the stream. He quenched his thirst, then returned to his bed. He rolled onto his side and closed his eyes. The rest of the day passed in a similarly lazy manner, with him only rising to eat, drink, or to relieve himself.

Early the following morning, he awoke to rain and wind. All desires he had to spend another day resting beneath the alder vanished. When he stood, soreness still plagued his forelimbs, causing him to limp, but it was much less debilitating than it had been the day before. He sated his thirst at the stream, then started picking through the raspberry bushes. As he did, the familiar scent of a bear wafted over to his nose. It seemed his adversary hadn't given up on the clearing after all. He stepped away from the thorny berry bushes and wheeled around to look at the scent's source. His expression turned puzzled when he spotted a small brown bear, barely old enough to be away from its mother, peaking cautiously around the sides of the cottonwood trees at him. The bear wasn't big enough to pose a threat, and it even looked a little gaunt as if it hadn't been eating well. He was unsure of how to react to this. The bear he had fought the night before wanted him gone so it could claim the clearing for itself, which made his decision obvious. But what was he supposed to do here with a bear that posed no threat? Running it off was the easiest option, but it seemed callous to chase the little bear away, especially if it was hungry. He could share. There was plenty of food in the clearing for both of them, and he wouldn't mind having some company that wasn't intent on tearing his throat out.

He entered a relaxed posture. The bear studied him a long moment before lifting its head into the air and sniffing out his scent. Unsure of what else he could do to show a lack of aggression, he returned to scrounging through the raspberry bush, while keeping a watch on the bear out of the corner of his eye. Eventually, the bear emerged into the clearing. It studied him thoroughly, body tensed, ready to bolt if the need presented itself. Seeming to decide that he posed no immediate danger, the bear sauntered over to a patch of fireweed and, maintaining a watchful gaze, started eating. Hyroc turned his head slightly and sniffed. The bear's scent was tinged with weakness, as he expected, but he realized it was a young female. He was unsure why, but this made him feel even better about deciding against chasing her off.

When he had his fill of berries, he ate some fireweed, then headed toward the stream to explore more of his surroundings, staying well away from the young bear. At the shore, he glanced back to see her sniffing at the raspberry bush he had eaten from. He turned his attention from the bear and started limping in the upstream direction of the water. Past where the stream hooked, it ran straight, then bent sharply around a ridge on the opposite shore. Close to the bend sat the trunk of a dead tree dipping into the stream. Away from the bend, the stream ran straight again before turning to the right and flowing out of view. Hyroc had moved halfway up the straight stretch when he caught sight of a hill on the opposite shore poking above the treetops. He crossed the stream and made his way through the intervening trees, only altering course to avoid a nasty looking clump of wild rose bushes.

About a quarter of the way up the hill, fireweed grew in an unbroken swath. Toward the top, cow parsnips punctuated with rhubarb sprang into view. Hyroc uprooted a fireweed plant, then, with it held it in his jaws, ascended the slope. Once at the top, he began eating his fireweed. Looking around as he chewed, other than what he had passed on his way to this area, he couldn't see anything of interest. As he brought his gaze back to the severed fireweed stalk to take another bite, a flash of light-colored fur in the forest below caught his attention. Instinctively, he sniffed. He caught the scent of a deer. He hadn't cared for the taste of raw venison, but tomorrow would be the last day of his test before he began the journey back to his cabin. And it might not be a bad idea to have a substantial meal before then to help maintain his strength. With any luck, this would be the last time he would have to eat uncooked meat. He took a breath and started down the hill. He circled the bottom until he found a solid scent trail; he surmised the deer was a male. A buck would have more meat than he could eat, but maybe his guest would pick up the smell. It would make him feel good if she got some of the kill. Was this what it felt like to have a little sister, he wondered?

The scent trail headed away from the hill, pooling at a grouping of wild strawberry plants before winding back to the stream. It followed along the shore, becoming concentrated where the deer had stopped to drink. Then the scent suddenly vanished. He saw the deer's tracks turning toward the stream, and spotted more on the opposite shore leading into the trees. Swimming across, he rediscovered the scent trail and resumed following it. The trail curved erratically through the trees before bending back toward the stream. As before, the trail vanished at the edge of the water, only for him to discover it on the other side. Then after what felt like hours of tracking, he spotted the deer through a gap in the trees grazing on ivy leaves.

There was no discernible wind to carry his scent, but between him and the deer was a latticework of branches. There was no feasible way he could approach without making noise, but since the obstacle was close enough to the deer, it was likely he would be able to take the deer down even if it heard his approach at that point.

He stealthily crept up to the branches as a gust of wind swept over his back in the direction of the deer. The deer's nose twitched. Repressing a curse, Hyroc barreled through the branches just as the deer bolted. The soreness of his muscles flared into existence as he pursued his quarry. Almost seeming to sense his discomfort, the deer quickened its pace. Hyroc attempted to match the deer's speed, but his legs refused to move at their maximum potential. The deer was rapidly pulling away from him. He felt a wave of disappointment, but he wasn't all that surprised. He should have known better than trying to run down a deer so soon after such a strenuous fight. There was no way he was going to catch the deer. As he began to slow, the deer rushed toward the grey husk of a fallen tree, and one of its legs caught on a branch lying across the ground, causing it to trip. Feeling a thrill of excitement, Hyroc spurred himself forward as fast as his legs would allow. He pounced on the deer as his quarry regained its footing. He immobilized the deer by locking his paws around its neck. Then he buried his teeth into its neck, and in a sharp twisting motion of his head, broke it.

After taking a few recuperative breaths—knowing how lucky he had been that the deer tripped—he started eating the meat from the deer's back. When he had his fill, he dipped one claw in the deer's blood and smeared it on the uninjured part of his other forelimb. He hoped if the she-bear smelled the deer's blood on him, she would go looking for the carcass. Then he started dragging his kill toward the hill.

After depositing the carcass at its base, he hurried back to the clearing, doing his best to avoid washing the deer blood off in the stream. The she-bear was lying in the shade of the cottonwoods when he arrived. She scrambled to her feet and hid behind the trees. Hyroc sighed in annoyance, wishing he could simply tell the bear he wasn't going to hurt her. He walked into the middle of the clearing near the trees and laid down. He rested his head on one paw, trying to appear as if he were sleeping. Maybe if he laid here long enough, the bear would pick up the smell of deer blood on him. He kept a watch on the bear through half-closed eyes. As he waited for her to come out from behind the trees, he began to consider naming her. He sighed humorously when the name Pip came to mind. He knew it was odd to name her when he was going to leave and likely never see her again.

Pip took a few tentative steps out of the safety of the trees. She jutted her nose into the air repeatedly as she smelled the deer blood. Still sniffing, she rotated to face in the direction of the deer carcass. Pulled by her nose, Pip walked toward the stream. Hyroc lifted his head and watched until she disappeared. Beaming with a burst of happiness, he stretched and returned to his bed beneath the alder.

At dusk, Pip returned with a smear of dried blood across her snout. She gave Hyroc the same wary look, but she seemed more relaxed and less concerned about keeping as much of a distance between them.

"You're welcome," Hyroc whispered. He settled his head on his paw and went to sleep.

When he arose, light-colored puffs had replaced the rain clouds of the previous day, but the wind remained. Most of his soreness had disappeared, and he no longer walked with a limp. As he started eating fireweed toward the southern end of the clearing, Pip emerged from the cottonwoods to do the same at the edge of the tree line. They couldn't talk, but he enjoyed her company nonetheless. He wished he could do more for the little bear. He would leave her this clearing, but he knew it was likely a larger bear would claim it shortly after he left. That short amount of time here was still something she could benefit from.

He finished with his fireweed then headed over to the stream to have a drink. He stared into the surface of the water thoughtfully, listening to the murmur of the flow. What should he do today? Exploring didn't seem useful since he was leaving tomorrow, and hunting was unnecessary. He fought down a sudden longing for his bow, reminding himself it would just be a matter of days before he could transform back to his natural form. The hill he had found yesterday had a nice view and food, so he decided it was a fitting place to go for a while.

The hill was exactly as he had left it, and the surrounding forest was just as dull looking as he remembered. He made his way to the spot where he had stashed the deer. He was disturbed to see the deer's belly ripped open, and the meaty parts of the body mutilated. It definitely looked as if a bear had fed upon it. With a sigh at the bad table manners of his small guest, he started eating meat from the few remaining places on the carcass that hadn't been mangled. When he was full, he made his way to the top of the hill.

Aside from the distant calls of a hunting eagle circling overhead, the afternoon came and went in a haze of boredom. There wasn't that much for animals to do for entertainment—no wonder some of them liked eating people, Hyroc thought in a humorous shadow. He shook his head. He shouldn't think things like that, especially after what the last Spirit Stone had shown him. He needed to get back to Elswood and transform back to his natural form; his mind was starting to wander in strange directions.

A gust of wind blew up the side of the hill. Hyroc grimaced as he smelled the deer carcass. It was already beginning to rot. He hadn't expected it to smell that bad for at least a day or two. He sighed irritably, remembering what Pip had done to it and realizing he had made the mistake of leaving it out in the sun.

Another gust of wind swept up to him. He rolled his eyes, annoyed with himself for tainting the air with the smell of rotting deer. And with the deer's innards hanging out, he had no desire to move the body. As he stood to leave, he discerned an unfamiliar scent. It reminded him of a fox, but with a much wilder and dangerous tone. Then the air stilled, snatching away the scent. Maybe that scent belonged to a coyote or a wolf. Even if he had smelled a wolf, there wasn't much he had to fear from them. He wasn't yet fully grown, but in this form, he was still big enough to give a wolf pack pause. Still, he wouldn't press his luck by sticking around a pack. That was asking for trouble, and he didn't want to end up in another fight.

He stretched and made his way down the hill, following the stream past his clearing. Pip peered through the trees at him as he passed. Where the flow of the stream slowed near the cattails, he stepped into the water and bathed. He had nothing better to do, so removing deer blood and other grime from his body seemed the best way to spend his time. Afterward, he backtracked to the clearing. He startled Pip when he entered at the cottonwoods, but she quickly relaxed. Hyroc then spent the remainder of the day resting in his bed. He was ecstatic when he saw the sunset. The test had ended; all he had to do now was sleep through the night and in the morning, begin his journey back to his cabin. He looked toward Pip's shadowed shape, feeling a twinge of sadness at the thought of leaving her. Trying his best to push all thoughts from his mind, he laid down to sleep.

The howl of a wolf thrust him awake. He flew to his feet, sweeping his eyes through the darkened clearing as he sniffed for a scent. Nothing moved in the clearing. He picked up the same scent he had found on the hill, but it was distant, coming from somewhere downstream. He stiffened with alarm, suddenly realizing he couldn't smell Pip. Another wolf howl sounded. A cold prickle of dread crept up his back as the distressing thought that the wolves were hunting Pip struck him. How could they be going after her? They would have had to run past him, and he was positive their footfall would have woken him. Then a disturbing thought occurred to him. What if they hadn't come into the clearing, what if Pip had gone to the carcass and their howls had frightened her, and she tried to run away?

Alarmed, he dropped his nose to the ground. Pip's scent sparked into existence. Her scent led away from the cottonwoods in the direction of the hill. When he arrived there, her scent moved to the carcass, then sharply away from it, and it had the faded quality of a fleeing animal. Hyroc swore, flying along Pip's scent trail. Her scent led to the stream near where he had originally killed the deer. Then her trail vanished. It was too dark for him to see any tracks on the opposite shore. He made his best guess as to where she had crossed and trudged through the water. Her scent reappeared where he made landfall. Another wolf howled; it didn't sound very far off. He broke into a run. Leaves slapped against his face, and branches scratched at his snout.

He soon heard a cacophony of growls and snarls. The trees thinned out, opening up into a break in the canopy. Toward the middle, he saw the jostling shapes of five wolves in a half-circle, and in the middle of that circle stood Pip. She snapped savagely at one wolf when it feigned a lunge. But as she did so, another wolf jumped forward and nipped her hind leg. Pip snarled, twisting around to strike at the attacking wolf. Then the whole pack tensed, all five of them lunged, piling on top of the she-bear. Anger flared within him, and he loosed the loudest roar he could muster as he charged toward the pack. Three of the wolves fell away from Pip in alarm, wheeling around to face him. They howled a desperate warning, but Hyroc paid them no heed. He charged over to Pip and nailed one of the wolves still on her with a sideways paw swipe. With a yelp, the wolf tumbled sideways across the ground, regained its footing, and shot into the trees. The remaining wolf had scarcely enough time to snap its attention on Hyroc before he sank his teeth into it, and with it firmly gripped in his jaws, threw the wolf into the trunk of a tree. He turned toward the remaining wolves and roared. The wolves shied back two steps. Growling, Hyroc lunged forward, swatting the air in front of the wolves with his paw. They lurched back and scattered. He gave a sharp nod of acceptance as he watched them flee.

He wheeled around to face Pip. The small bear lay on the ground, breathing heavily and bleeding from several wounds on her hind legs and rear end. The wounds looked painful but not serious. Pip clambered to her feet and made a startled jump away from him. She swept her eyes through her surroundings in a shaken and bewildered manner, seemingly unsure of what had happened. So as not to risk stressing her any further, Hyroc lay down on the ground. She studied him in a dazed manner, then slowly walked toward him. Tentatively, she leaned forward and gave him a sniffing. Hyroc remained motionless. She pulled her head back and walked past him in the direction of the clearing. Hyroc felt a stream of pride flow through him as he stood to follow Pip. In some small way, it seemed she had said, "thank you."

He saw one of the wolves still lying on the ground, and it unsettled him when he realized it was dead. Even though he had killed that wolf while defending Pip, it troubled him how easily he had done so.

CHAPTER 21

ROAMING

Hyroc dug eagerly at the ground encasing the bulb of a black lily. Pip watched his actions with intrigue from an alder not far away. Since this was probably the last day he would ever see her, Hyroc had decided it would be a nice parting gift to show the little bear how to get at the bulb of a black lily. Pip's wounds were healing well, and there didn't seem any risk of infection, though it was hard for him to tell because she wouldn't allow him to come close enough for a good inspection. Despite this reluctance, during the night she had remained somewhat close to him. It wasn't much, but it was good knowing she felt safer around him. And if the wolves had any sense at all, they must have fled the area and wouldn't even dream of coming back anytime soon.

He extricated the bulb from the moist earth, gave it a few shakes, set it down, and used his paw to wipe off as much of the remaining dirt as he could. Then he ate it, leaving a tiny portion of the bulb for Pip to taste. He headed toward the nearest tree, raked it with his claws, and did the same to every tree until he had made a proper perimeter with his marks. Maybe he could trick a bear intent on bullying Pip out of the clearing to move on for fear of angering a larger bear. It was a bluff, but there was a chance this would offer her some protection. When he finished with the trees, he relieved himself in numerous places along the edges of the clearing. He turned toward Pip to see her sniffing at the black lily. He felt a prick of sadness as he watched her take a bite. It was now time for him to say goodbye. With a deep breath, he made his way toward her. She stopped eating and gave him a quizzical look.

It took him a moment to force himself to speak. "Pip," he said. He knew she wasn't going to understand anything he said, but informing her of his departure felt like the right thing to do. He subdued a stab of guilt, knowing his friends at the lake were also deserving of that, much more so than the she-bear he had just met. Pip tipped her head and gave him a strange look, clearly confused about the new noise he had made. Trying not to grin at her expression, he continued talking. "I've marked the trees around the clearing with my claws, and my scent should remain for a few days, so you should be safe from most other bears for a little while." He paused uncomfortably. "Pip, I liked having you around, and I'll admit the last few days haven't been quite as lonely because of you, something I'm very thankful for. But now it's time for me to go." She gave him a look he could trick himself into believing was her saying farewell. "I wish you the best and hope you stay safe; goodbye."

He stared at her awkwardly, then taking a breath, headed toward the stream. At the water's edge, he glanced back to see Pip still watching him. He carved her into his memory, then headed along the stream, retracing the trail that had brought him to this place four days earlier.

When the top of the tall hill came into view, unsure how long it might be before he found another source of water, Hyroc drank from the stream until his stomach was swollen tight. Then he made his way to the top of the hill. Looking in the direction of Wolf Paw, away from the hill, the ground steadily rose into a line of broad rolling dark green hills. Sparing one final glance in the direction of the clearing, he made his way down the hill and started toward the distant rise. He followed an animal trail about halfway there, abandoning it when its course ran in the opposite direction of the inclining terrain. At the base of the rise, he encountered a short ridge lined with devil's club. He circled this, but when he arrived at more easily traversed ground, he was dismayed to find it covered in an even thicker growth. Positive he was going to look more like a porcupine than a bear by the time he crossed through the horribly thorny plants, he searched for a way through.

He found a break, but it was narrow. Mindful of every step, he slowly made his way through. A couple of strides into the patch, his foot caught on an obscured root, causing him to stumble. The side of one paw brushed against the spiked stalk of one plant as he regained his balance. He felt a sharp stinging as several of the needlelike thorns snapped off the plant, stabbing their way into his flesh. Examining the afflicted paw with a hateful grimace, he saw translucent spikes protruding from the area of his wrist. He wanted to dig out the spines, but given the narrowness of the path, he was likely to rub against another plant in the process and end up in a whole lot more pain. The thorns could be safely removed only after he had passed through the patch; he would just have to deal with the pain. Gingerly he set his paw on the ground. A sharp, burning, itching pain flowed through his skin around the protrusions. He continued through the devil's club, gritting his teeth whenever he put weight on or moved the afflicted paw. He agonizingly made his way to the end of the patch. Finding a comfortable patch of moss to sit on, he brought his paw up to his mouth and gently closed his teeth around a thorn. Then hissing, he guided it out of his flesh. After spitting out the bloodied thorn, he started removing the remaining barbs in likewise fashion. On the last thorn, he bit down too hard and snapped it off right at his skin, leaving nothing to grab. With a growl of frustration, he began the uncomfortable task of chewing the thorn out of his paw. Eventually, he got it.

He licked the stinging punctures clean, then got to his feet. Taking stock of his surroundings, he couldn't see anything that resembled food. He picked his way to the top of the rise. Here he found an open patch of ground covered in fireweed. Below, the terrain sloped more gently, flattening into a slender swath of ground that merged into a willow flat sprinkled with the occasional cottonwood. The sun had begun dropping toward the horizon, and only a few hours of light remained. He figured he could reach the edge of the flat by nightfall. He quickly ate some fireweed, then started toward the bottom.

A little way from the bottom, he lurched back in alarm as the ground suddenly disappeared from in front of him. The cliff before him had been hidden from view by a concealment of thick foliage. Taking a deep breath, he followed along the cliff until he found a slope leading to the bottom.

It was well into dusk when he arrived at the edge of the flat. He scrounged up a few ripe berries from some unhealthy-looking wild strawberry plants scattered through the vicinity and dug up some black lilies. He then constructed a bed out of lodge pine and a patch of moss. After working out a stubborn lump caused by the arrangement of branches, he lay down and watched the sunset before settling in to sleep.

He awoke early the next morning, early enough that dew still covered the plants. After not having anything to drink since he left the stream yesterday, he soothed his dry mouth by eating plants laden with the cool moisture. The sun rose lazily from the horizon, accompanied by thin strands of clouds. It was going to be a sunny day, but for the only time he could remember, he wished for rain so he would have something to drink.

When he finished eating, he made his way to the edge of the flat. Initially, the willows grew far enough apart for him to walk through without difficulty, but branches were soon poking and scratching across his body. He pushed through to a space of empty ground. An animal trail ran parallel to him, weaving a clearer path through the willows. Studying the entrance and the exit of the path, he decided on the exit. He quickly lost track of his progress amid the unchanging view of innumerable willow branches as the path wound its way through. He spotted a strange elongated object on one side of the trail. Taking a closer look, he found two moose skulls with their antlers locked tightly together. It appeared the two animals had gotten their antlers stuck together and had starved to death as a result. The thought of dying literally face-to-face with an opponent made him shudder. Stepping back onto the trail, he moved onward, trying not to think too hard about the long-dead moose.

The trail forked, and he took the path that seemed to head in the direction of Wolf Paw. Time passed in a similarly dull manner on this trail, broken only by a single cottonwood shading part of the path. Past the cottonwood, an opening formed in the willows, and he caught sight of a light brown shape dashing out of sight. Testing the air with his nose, he identified the smell of a fox. He shook his head humorously. It seemed almost unfair how easily he could identify animals now. From here, the path made a series of wild curves before arriving at a shallow stream. Hyroc nibbled on a cattail—grimacing at the taste—then drank until his stomach could hold no more.

It took him the better part of the day to find his way out of the flat and into the familiar sight of pines. He stopped at dusk in a tiny clearing dominated by dandelions. There weren't any bed making materials here, so he slept unhappily on the cold ground.

The stars were out, and Hyroc had, as of yet, been unable to find a comfortable position to sleep in. Frustrated, he flopped on his back to stare up into the sky. As he lay there, he began to wonder if Marcus was watching him. He felt a surge of guilt at the terrible things he had said about his foster father when he learned of his curse.

Then his thoughts drifted to his current form. Would Marcus even recognize him now? Would June? He felt a stab of loneliness at that thought. Would anybody even recognize him as a bear, an unstable beast, the thing they had always acted like he was? He cinched off those thoughts; it was too painful for him to think about. It wasn't as if he was going to transform when he was in Elswood; he would have very few, if any, uses for his bear form when he got back. Although, he thought hunting as a bear with Donovan and Elsa would be extremely beneficial. He grimaced. Elsa knew about his ability, but would the rest of the Shackletons understand? He pushed the thought aside, deciding he would cross that bridge after he got home. He turned his attention skyward and tried to trace the constellations. His eyes steadily grew heavy, and he drifted off to sleep.

It was nearing noon when he arrived at the edge of a river the next day. The air was heavy with the smell of rotting flesh, and he had passed numerous fish carcasses on his approach. Knowing what that likely meant, he glanced up and down the shore looking for bears, but he didn't see any. Was this the same river where he had learned to fish as a bear? He glanced toward Wolf Paw—the distance from the mountain indicated this was the same river. He would have been tempted to fish if the air didn't smell so bad. With a dismissive shrug, he plunged into the water and started across. Stepping onto the shore, he shook the water from his back. He started when a bear's growl sounded from the tree line in front of him.

Shifting his gaze toward the sound, he saw a male brown bear with small scars punctuated throughout the fur along its side, staring at him. The bear wasn't big enough to have an overwhelming advantage, but there wasn't any reason for the two of them to fight. Hyroc began chuffing and loosed a startled warning moan when the bear broke into a charge. It stopped a body's length from him and made a stiff-legged stamp. With his head bowed, Hyroc repeatedly popped his jaws while backing away. The bear remained where it stood, content to let him leave. When the bear showed him its back, Hyroc breathed a sigh of relief, then turned and cautiously continued into the trees.

Away from the river, the rancid smell of rot steadily faded from the air, replaced by the aroma of pine needles. He encountered another wide rise, but when he crossed over to the top, the other side was much steeper, forcing him to head down at an accentuated angle. At the bottom, the ground roughened and continued in this way for half of what remained of the day. Then a series of short lumpy hills rose out of the ground, terminating about an hour before dusk.

An animal trail he had been following led into a clearing with a bowl-shaped incline dotted with fallen trees. Sweeping his eyes around, he found bones scattered throughout and a faded reddish stain toward the middle. He recognized it as the place where Ursa had made him eat raw deer for the first time. It felt like months since he had done that. He made his way up the incline and, not long afterward, arrived at the meadow he had called home for so many weeks. It looked as it had before he had been miraculously transported to an area two days' walk away. He still couldn't figure out how it was even possible for that to have occurred without him remembering anything. Even if a giant bird had picked him up and carried him to that spot, he was sure he would have woken up.

Night was rapidly approaching. He ate some fireweed and as many strawberries as he could find and drank his fill from the stream. Then he found what remained of his moss bed. From its shredded appearance, something had either been taking pieces of it for bedding or eating it. With what light remained, he repaired as much of the bed as he could. He looked eagerly toward the looming shape of Wolf Paw Mountain. It was only four days away. Four more days and he would be back at his cabin, sleeping with a roof over his head, no longer fearing it might rain during the night. It was then hard for him to sleep with a constant flow of eager thoughts running through his mind.

CHAPTER **22**

HOMECOMING

I t was well past noon when Hyroc made his way along the eastern edge of Wolf Paw Mountain. Soon, he arrived at the back of the valley, and his cabin was finally within sight. Eagerly he trotted up to the front door. He had been dreaming of this moment since he had left, and it had finally arrived! He found Ursa resting in the shade of the large spruce beside a deer carcass.

"Congratulations," Ursa said proudly, rising to her feet and making her way over to him. "You made it back in one piece."

"I'm done, right?" Hyroc asked, hopefully. "*Please tell me I'm done.*"

"I have nothing more to teach you about your animal form. You now know everything I have to offer you."

Hyroc breathed a sigh of relief. All the discomfort of his training was finished. He had started to wonder if it was ever actually going to end. He fixed his eyes on the deer. "Is that for me?"

"Well, it's actually for the three of us."

Hyroc perked up. "Wait, where's Kit?" he asked, sweeping his eyes around.

"He'll be here soon."

Hyroc nodded, making his way over to the deer. "Okay, then let's make sure to leave him some." He bent down and opened his mouth to take a chunk out of one of the deer's hips.

"Hyroc," Ursa said, stopping him mid-bite. "Are you sure you want to eat it—," she indicated him with the sweep of a paw "—like that?"

Hyroc glanced down at his forelimbs, unsure what she meant. He felt a twinge of embarrassment when he realized she meant him in his bear form. "Oh, that. I suppose I don't." He paused. "So, I can just transform right now?"

"Of course, the form lock wore off some time ago."

He nodded. It took him a moment to remember how to transform. He put an equal amount of pressure on each limb, then closed his eyes, focusing on the image of the moon. It seemed more difficult than he remembered to make the moon's shape appear in his mind. A mild tingling sensation spread throughout his body. He felt his body steadily becoming lighter, strength seeping from his muscles.

When the process had completed, he was delighted to feel the warmth and comfort of clothing on his body and the feel of boots enclosing his feet, but most importantly, he was ecstatic to have hands again. How much he had missed his beautifully dexterous appendages; he would never again take them for granted. Reaching out to grab a rock, he felt the clothing on his shoulders and parts of his legs slide down. When he turned his attention on himself, he was surprised to see large raggedy tears in most of the clothing that covered his upper body.

He yelped in dismay. "There's hardly anything left of my clothing! There's no way I'm going to be able to fix all of this."

Ursa shook her head in annoyance. "I already explained to you that your clothing became part of your skin when you transformed. So, whatever damage occurred to your skin also occurred to your clothing."

Hyroc sighed. "Okay, but it's going to take me a long time to replace *everything I'm wearing*. What am I supposed to do—run around half-naked until then? I'm sure *that* won't draw the attention of the villagers or *anything*."

Ursa gave him a humored look. "That's not all that different from what you were doing while I was training you."

He glared at her. "*I was a bear*, but since I don't plan on being in that form very often, I need to wear clothing!"

Ursa shrugged. "I am well aware of *that*. I was enjoying the irony of your statement." She walked over to him and held her paw up. A flash of blue emanated from it, and then his clothing knit itself together until everything had been restored. He ran his hand over the material on his shoulder, mesmerized by what had happened.

"Thank you," Hyroc said.

Ursa gave him an accepting nod. "You're welcome."

"So where are my—"

He trailed off when Ursa used her paw to indicate a bundle of gear beside his cabin's door. "Everything's right over there, except of course for any food you might have brought with you. It would've gone bad by now, so I took the liberty of eating it for you."

Hyroc waggled his head, making his way over to the bundle. Everything within looked so foreign to him. But when his hand settled on his bow, its function and that of each object, seeped back into his mind. He beamed as he remembered how good cooked meat tasted. Grinning, he placed some firewood in a pile away from the cabin and got a fire going. Then he got to work gutting the deer. Right after he finished, he spotted Kit.

"Kit," Hyroc called out excitedly. The big cat stared at him in surprise before breaking into a run. Kit rammed his head affectionately into Hyroc's chest, nearly knocking him on his back, and began rubbing against him hard. Hyroc wrapped his arms around Kit's neck and hugged him. "I missed you, buddy," he said, scratching under Kit's chin. "Did you miss me too?" Kit pulled back to look at him, then pressed his head into his hand. "I'll take that as a yes." He paused. "And look what Ursa brought for us." He got to his feet and sidled over to the deer carcass. "Meat that I CAN COOK." Kit gave him an excited look. Hyroc grabbed one of the deer haunches and roasted it on the fire as Kit watched, impatiently flicking his tail.

When the meat finished cooking and was barely cool enough not to burn the roof of his mouth, Hyroc took a massive bite. He sighed happily at the taste of the hot meat. There wasn't much of a comparison between cooked and bloody raw meat. Kit stood by begging. Hyroc cut a large piece off and tossed it over to the mountain lion. Ursa then stepped over to the carcass and tore a chunk off.

Hyroc swallowed before speaking. "You know, I can cook that for you if you want," he offered. Ursa gave him a gleeful look, and he was baffled to see the meat sizzling within her jaws. He gave her a strange look and shook his head. There was a long pause. "Ursa."

She swallowed. "Yes?"

"I'm done with the training, so what happens now?"

She gave him a thoughtful look. "Whatever you want to."

"I mean, how do I use my bear form now that I'm back?"

"That I am unsure of, I am not you." Hyroc rolled his eyes humor-ously. "You know what you are capable of doing as a bear, so you must figure out for yourself how best to employ that capability."

Hyroc nodded. "But how am I supposed to—," he made a sweep-ing motion with his arm in the direction of Elswood "—do that here?"

"Yes, it will be more difficult to use your form here, but you must discover the answer to that question on your own. But I will say this. Keep it hidden as much as possible." Hyroc shrugged; he had already figured that part out. Ursa studied him thoughtfully for a long moment. "I'm sure there are things you wish to attend to, so I will leave you to them."

"Hold on, I'd like to ask you one more thing before you go," Hyroc said.

"Yes?"

"The night I first turned into a bear, when I came back from the tree, I remember you were relieved I hadn't chosen that animal from beyond the light, the spider. I know I tried asking about this before, but I want to know what would have happened if I had chosen it?"

A look of deep sadness and pain entered Ursa's eyes. "You were not ready to know this, but now I believe you have a right to." She took a deep breath. "You are not my first charge. Before you, many seasons ago, my charge was a young female Wol'dger, named Speara. She was smart, strong-willed, and in many ways the two of you are alike. Her parents were killed by another Wol'dger some months before she went through The Choosing. I helped her cope with her grief and showed her that her world hadn't ended. I used the time before The Choosing to guide her away from the animals beyond the light. She had the advantage of knowing what awaited her, enabling me to discuss the topic openly with her. But despite my warnings about what lay in the shadows, she showed an unusual interest in the animals residing there. She always wanted to know more about them and their abilities. Then the night of The Choosing arrived. And as I had feared, she chose a spider from beyond the light.

"Training her in a constructive and useful way was immensely difficult for me because she possessed unfamiliar and strange abilities and utilized many more legs and eyes than I was accustomed to. Still, I was able to guide her through the completion of her training successfully. My initial concerns faded away as she thrived in her spider form. Some months afterward, she did the most spectacular thing I've ever seen. In a grove of trees just outside the town she lived in, she had fashioned the most beautiful web imaginable. The silk shone in a kaleidoscope of colors, and the sunlight spilled onto the ground like a stained-glass window. Visitors from afar even came to admire her fantastic web-work. The years came and went, and her abilities continued to improve, enabling her to weave her webs into more and more complex and beautiful patterns. She found a mate, and I had the privilege of seeing them married."

"I began to reconsider the validity of steering those going through The Choosing away from the animals beyond the light as she seemed to demonstrate that those animals were no different than any other. But then something slowly started to change in her. At first, it was small things, decisions here and there that seemed to defy rational thought, things that could be overlooked as simple mistakes. Then it turned into more noticeable things. She started spending most of her time in her animal form, becoming reclusive and reluctant to stay around anyone, including her mate. She stopped staying in her home, preferring only her webs. Next, she would only take sustenance as a spider. She even started trapping prey with her webs. She lashed out at anyone who came near her, and soon the townsfolk were afraid of her. Her mate ventured out to her, desperate to talk reason back into her. He failed and she killed and consumed him." Ursa closed her eyes and tipped her head back sorrowfully.

"We don't fully understand why the shadowed animal forms have such drastic effects on the minds of those choosing them. But those who choose such forms always inevitably sink into madness. It could simply be that the bodies of those animals are so foreign to the senses that the mind cannot cope."

"Ursa, what happened to Speara after her husband died?" Hyroc asked tentatively.

Ursa was quiet a long moment, then she turned her head and opened her eyes to look at him. "I killed her. I had to. Her madness had made her a danger to everyone around her." Tears were streaming out of her eyes, the dampened white fur below them now appearing gray. "Now, you understand." She took a deep breath, wiping her eyes on the back of her paw. "But that is in the past," she continued. "Rest for the next few days. I'd advise you to take a bath and wash your clothes before you talk to anyone." Hyroc nodded. "Good night."

"Night," Hyroc said, feeling sick. She turned to leave. "Ursa, wait." She gave him a somber look. "Thank . . . thanks for showing me those things." She gave him an appreciative nod and headed off.

Hyroc put his hand on Kit's shoulder. He blew out an exasperated breath "I now understand everything she put me through. It was for my own good, to keep what happened to Speara from happening to me. I wish I had known that; it would've made me more cooperative. But she was probably right. I wasn't ready to know that."

CHAPTER 23

THE HARDEST LIE

Hyroc stood beside the creek, feeling the wind on his face and ears as he stared thoughtfully into the water, trying to remember if he had set all his traps in their proper places. Kit nudged his leg, breaking him from his thoughts. He looked down to see the big cat wearing an irritated expression. Having spent most of the morning reassembling traps, it was likely well past the time the two of them usually ate lunch. If there was anything wrong with the position of his traps, he would have figured it out by now. He nodded his agreement, turned, and headed back in the direction of his cabin with Kit eagerly following close behind.

At the cabin, he cut himself a chunk from a left-over deer leg and tossed the rest outside to Kit. The mountain lion wrestled the leg to the ground as if it were still attached to a live deer and tore into the hip enthusiastically. Hyroc set his coin bag on the table and counted its contents as he ate. There was enough for him to buy at least one loaf of bread. After what he had eaten during his training, the thought of eating soft, warm bread was irresistible. But that would mean venturing into the village. The idea of so many eyes watching him was disconcerting. It would be impossible to ambush anything there without being noticed. He cocked an eyebrow at the strangeness of the thought. Of course, he couldn't ambush anything there. Game would never venture into the middle of the village. With a dismissive shrug, he cinched the bag shut.

When he finished eating, he made his way down the trail toward Elswood. He stopped when the Shackletons' cabin came into view through the trees. Guilt swept over him; it had been almost a month since he had departed to train with Ursa. Beyond Elsa, he hadn't said goodbye to anyone. To them, he had disappeared to go on a trip to some unknown place. What had that done to the Shackletons? He felt a knot form in his stomach. How were they going to react when they found out he was back? And what was he going to tell them when they asked why he had left in that manner. Telling them the truth was out of the question. They wouldn't understand, and he couldn't risk his secret getting out. He sighed, hating the situation—everything about it felt wrong. It didn't seem right for the reunion with the family to be so uncomfortable.

He studied the cabin a long moment, then squeezed his eyes shut in frustration. He couldn't bring himself to walk over there and face the discomfort that awaited him. Irritated with his reluctance, he continued down the trail. It seemed a little ironic that he could fight off a bear, but he couldn't handle the thought of a few uncomfortable words from his friends. Ursa would have something demeaning to say about that if he asked her for advice. After he got his bread, he would face them.

At the edge of the village, he pulled his hood over his face as far as it would go. Even with his hood pulled out, everyone in the vicinity stared at him with the familiar looks of shock. How much more shocked would they be if he suddenly turned into a bear, he wondered mischievously?

He made his way into the center of the village and headed toward the bakery. When the baker, a portly brown-haired woman, saw his face as he entered, she yelped in surprise and nearly tossed a loaf of bread she carried on a tray across the shop. Doing his best to avoid showing any signs of amusement at her reaction, Hyroc held out his Flecks and asked for some bread. She responded with a long awkward stare. Then holding one hand over her heart, she set the tray down, never taking her eyes off him, and warily handed him a fresh loaf. Hyroc then hurried out of the shop. When he was a comfortable distance away, he eagerly tore a chunk off and stuffed it into his mouth. He sighed happily.

"HYROC," a familiar voice called out. Turning, he stiffened in alarm when he saw Helen tromping toward him with a furious expression scrawled across her face. He nearly started chuffing as she approached. She thrust a finger at him pointedly. "*Don't you move,*" she ordered. "You stay right there!" Hyroc took a deep breath, steeling himself for the scolding she was about to inflict upon him. Helen stopped in front of him, putting one hand on her hip, and fluttered the other through the air angrily. "You don't tell us you're leaving; *you're just gone,* leaving it up to Elsa to let everyone know! We were worried sick and thought something terrible had happened to you when you didn't return!"

"I . . . I . . . I'm sorry," Hyroc choked out.

She narrowed her eyes. "*Sorry,* that's all you have to say after what you did? What made you think it would be okay to just up and leave like that?"

Hyroc felt a knot form in his stomach. It took all of his resolve to prevent the truth from spilling out of his mouth. Every part of him screamed for him to tell her, and it hurt not to.

"I needed to go alone," he lied. His insides burned with shame when he finished speaking.

"Were we unkind to you?" she snapped back.

Hyroc grimaced. "No—"

"Did we ever treat you like you weren't welcome?"

"No—"

"Then explain to me *why* you thought you needed to travel alone."

"Please believe me, it wasn't anything you or your family did, you've been kind to me, kinder than anyone has been in a very long time. I just needed to be alone, to figure some things out, that's all. I just lost track of time."

Helen gave him a scathing look. "Well, maybe *sometime* you'll explain to me the *real* reason, and you had better not do anything like this ever again. Am I understood?"

Hyroc grit his teeth in an uncomfortable expression. "I won't, and I'm sorry for any grief I caused, I didn't mean for that to happen."

Helen nodded. "That's good to hear. Now, tell me what happened there," she said, gesturing at his snout.

He felt a renewed flare of alarm. What could she be looking at? Was there some part of his features that hadn't reverted properly? He quickly lifted his hand and felt along the area she had indicated. His fingers found lines of scabs running across his snout and upon his cheek. It took him a moment to realize she was looking at the remnant of the cuts he had received from the last bear he fought. He relaxed slightly. "Oh, that . . . it's nothing; just a scratch, Kit got a little excited one day when I was playing with him."

"You should be more careful when you're playing with him; he's not a house cat, you know, and from the looks of those scrapes, you're lucky you didn't lose an eye." Hyroc nodded. She paused, her expression softening. "Now that you're back, I expect you over for dinner tonight. But don't think for one moment this means you're off the hook." He nodded somberly. She sighed. "But no matter how angry you made me, I'm still glad you're back." He nodded again, purposefully staring at the ground. "I'll let you get back to what you were doing. Everyone will be glad tonight to see that you're well." She gently touched him on the shoulder, then turned and headed off.

"Hyroc," another voice said quietly. Hyroc lifted his gaze to see Curtis holding a supply-laden basket in the crook of one arm and waving at him with the other. He gave a halfhearted wave back. Curtis turned and hurried after his mother. Hyroc stamped his foot in frustration. He felt horrible lying right to Helen's face. And he would probably have to do it many more times during dinner tonight. He didn't deserve any of their hospitality. All he wanted was a way out of this.

Long shadows surrounded Hyroc as he made his way down the trail leading to the Shackletons' cabin. Exiting the end of the trail, he heard the excited barks of Dilo ringing through the air. The hound tore around the front of the cabin toward him. She stopped a few strides later, turned around and darted back the way she had come, whining and yipping. With a shrug, Hyroc continued to the front door. He found Curtis sitting at the edge of the porch, whittling at a block of wood with his knife.

Curtis lifted his head and gave him a welcoming smile. "I'm glad you're back," he said eagerly. "I was starting to miss you."

"And I was starting to miss everyone," Hyroc admitted. He paused, giving Curtis a strange look. "You're not mad at me?"

Curtis cocked an eyebrow. "Why would I be mad at you?"

Hyroc gave him a confused look. "Because *I left without letting you or your brother know.*"

"But you came back." Hyroc smirked humorously. "Why did you—"

"Hyroc," Elsa's voice called out from behind. Grimacing in false displeasure to hide his glad feelings from anyone who might be looking, Hyroc turned to face her. She stood with her hands on her hips and bore a displeased expression similar to that of her mother earlier, though he was sure she felt no such animosity toward him. "You put it all on me to tell everyone about your trip instead of letting them know yourself. And you didn't think one of us would have liked to come with you? Were we really that hard to be around?"

"It was nothing to do with you or your family."

"Then *why* didn't you tell them you were leaving?"

"I—," he pulled his mouth closed, unable to think of a direction to take his words.

She turned her attention to Curtis, who was watching their exchange. "Curtis, mother needs your help in the kitchen." Curtis nodded and headed inside the cabin. "Fine, Hyroc, if you don't want to—," she trailed off, leaning back on her heel to get a better look through the cabin's door. "Okay, I think he's gone," she said in a whisper, all pretense of anger disappearing as she started to smile. "Welcome back."

"Thanks," Hyroc said, relieved.

"Everything go well with your training?"

Hyroc nodded. "Yeah, I now know pretty much everything there is to know about being a bear, including some things that'll make hunting so much easier."

"That's good to know."

"Did that story you came up with work okay?"

She nodded. "I think so, but I don't think Harold bought it. From the way he was looking at me when I told him, he knows something's up." Hyroc nodded. "When are you going to tell the rest of the family?"

"Right after everything settles down from me being back. I'd like to tell your brothers first. That way, they can help us break it to your parents and Walter. But until then, when other people are around, I need you to keep pretending like you're mad at me for leaving without anyone coming with me. That okay?"

Elsa nodded. "That's fine, but try not to keep me doing this for too long."

"Don't worry. I won't. Oh, one more thing. How's your brother taking this?"

Elsa shrugged. "I don't know, I couldn't tell. I think he missed hunting with you."

"Dinner," Helen called out, holding the cabin's door open. "Come on."

Elsa affixed Hyroc with a fake look of anger.

Hyroc trudged into the cabin. He took a seat in a chair at the left side of the table as Helen studied the contents of a steaming pot hanging in the fireplace. Elsa avoided eye contact with him as she set a stack of bowls nearby. Hyroc helped Helen fill the bowls and distribute them across the table.

Walter pushed his way through the door. His expression cooled when he spotted Hyroc. "You're back," he said bitterly. "I was hoping what I heard wasn't true. I was just about to head up to your cabin and see how much I could sell your things for." Helen gave him a sideways glare, and at the same time, Hyroc rolled his eyes. Then the rest of the family entered.

"Hyroc," Svald said in greeting. "Welcome back. You had us worried that something had happened to you."

"I didn't mean to."

Svald gave him a dismissive wave. "Don't think too much about it, all that matters is you're back." Helen shot him a disapproving look. Svald frowned forcefully. "But you had *better not* do it again."

"I won't."

"Good to hear."

"Yeah, I'm glad he finally decided to come back," Donovan said, settling into a seat beside Hyroc. "Hunting hasn't been as much fun since you left." He indicated Curtis with the wave of his hand. "Goober, over there can't hit anything."

"Hey," Curtis said indignantly.

"You have a bow?" Hyroc asked.

Curtis nodded proudly. "Got it a week after you left, and I shot a rabbit yesterday."

"You nicked it," Donovan noted.

Curtis narrowed his eyes at his brother. "It still died!"

Donovan shook his head.

By now, the rest of the family was seated, and they began to eat. Hyroc took a bite, closed his eyes, and sighed happily. How had he made it through the last month without a decent meal?

"You okay?" Donovan asked.

Hyroc gave him a puzzled look. "What do you mean?"

"Nothing, you're just acting like you haven't eaten anything in weeks."

Hyroc smirked. "I wasn't eating your mother's cooking while I was gone." Donovan gave him a comprehending nod.

"So, where did you go when you were gone?" Curtis asked. Elsa's eyes widened into a look of concern. Hyroc sighed to himself and took a bite, acting like he hadn't heard the question.

"I think it's pretty obvious," Donovan intoned. Hyroc and Elsa gave him a startled look. "He was *wrestling bears*, what else would he be doing," Donovan said, with a broad grin. Hyroc swallowed wrong and started coughing.

"You okay?" Helen said, sounding concerned. Donovan gave him a hard pat on the back. Hyroc nodded between coughs as he took a swig of water. "Eat slower."

Hyroc stopped coughing. "You good?" Donovan said.

"Yeah," Hyroc answered. He glanced over at Elsa to see her trying to hide a smile.

"Well, wherever you went, we're glad you're back," Svald said.

A flood of guilt washed over Hyroc. He felt like the most wretched person in the world for what he was doing.

CHAPTER 24

A BETTER IDEA

In the bright morning light, Hyroc stepped outside of his cabin to see Donovan and Curtis making their way over to him.

"Morning," the two brothers said in turn.

"Morning," Hyroc repeated in greeting. Kit stepped beside him and growled. The two brothers regarded the big cat cautiously. Hyroc gave Kit a stiff nudge with his boot. "Hey, stop that, it's Donovan and Curtis." Kit glared at him irritably. Curtis tossed a small piece of dried fish in front of the mountain lion. Kit affixed a startled gaze on the fish. He studied the fish suspiciously, but after an inquisitive sniff, he settled down to eat.

"We figured he might need reminding who we were," Donovan said with a grin.

Hyroc gave him an agreeing nod. "What's up?" he said as he closed the cabin door.

Donovan held up his bow. "Up for some hunting?"

Hyroc shoved down a flare of guilt at the hospitable offer. "I would like that."

"Good."

"But, I need to check my traps first."

"I figured, that'll give us some time to catch up." He indicated toward the back of the valley with his hand. "They're all in about the same places, right?"

"Yes, at least I think I got them back where they belonged." Donovan nodded, and they headed toward the back of the valley. Kit joined them after they passed his favorite tree.

"You okay?" Donovan asked.

Hyroc gave him a nervous glance. "Why . . . why do you say that?"

Donovan shrugged. "Nothing, it just seems like something's been bothering you since you came back from your little trip. How'd that go for you anyway? Find out anything interesting?"

Guilt gnawed at Hyroc's insides. All he wanted to do was tell the two of them why he had actually left. That would make everything so much easier, and he wouldn't have to lie to them anymore. He felt ashamed he couldn't bring himself to do so.

"I'm fine, and no, I didn't find out anything; the whole thing was kind of a waste of time."

Donovan nodded. "Well, that's too bad, but I wouldn't worry, I'm sure you'll find something eventually."

They arrived at the trap at the back of the valley. The snare was tripped, but it hadn't caught anything.

Hyroc spoke as he got to work resetting it. "How's Elsa?" he asked for show, already knowing the answer.

"Still mad at you," Donovan answered. "She's upset you left for so long." Donovan gave him a more serious look. "And to be honest, I didn't like that you didn't tell the rest of us you were leaving. I thought we were supposed to be friends, and that seemed to me like a very un-friend kind of thing to do."

The guilt gnawed even harder at Hyroc. Having finished with the trap, he got to his feet and gave Donovan a somber look.

"You *are* my friends."

Donovan nodded. "Anyway, we're here to hunt, not make this any more awkward." Hyroc gave him an appreciative nod before continuing forward.

217

Not much was said until they arrived at the final trap, and it was the only one to catch anything. Here Hyroc found a squirrel. He dispatched it, gutted it, and hung it on his belt.

"That the last one?" Donovan said.

"Yeah," Hyroc said, as he reset the trap. "Where do you want to go from here?"

Donovan pointed northward. "To the river, that's usually a good spot to start."

Hyroc nodded, getting to his feet.

At the river, they strung their bows. Following along the shore for about an hour, they came across fresh deer tracks. The tracks ran along the shore, ending at a bend in the river. Here, the trail arced sharply away from the water and into the trees. The tracks became increasingly harder to follow among the foliage until they disappeared completely.

"Alright, everyone start looking around to see if you can find the trail again," Donovan said with a sigh. Hyroc combed the ground but found no trace of their quarry. He scowled. Locating a trail wouldn't even be a challenge if he were in his bear form. It stung he was needlessly forcing his friends to work harder than was necessary. He glanced toward Donovan and Curtis. They were his best friends; would it really be so terrible if he told them his secret right now? He planned to do it anyway; what purpose did waiting serve? They might understand. Elsa knew, and it hadn't bothered her. And once he explained the dangers posed to him if they told anyone, he was sure they would keep his secret.

But what if they didn't? What if they weren't as understanding as their sister? He hated those questions constantly interfering with his actions. If he didn't tell them, then they all might end up going home empty-handed, which also meant he wouldn't have anything to eat tomorrow. He shook his head derisively. Getting meat was hardly the issue. He didn't like making his friends waste their time trying to solve an issue he already had the answer to. But was it worth the risk?

Maybe there was a way he could judge their reactions without actually telling them he could turn into a bear. A few carefully phrased questions might do the trick. He gave his surroundings one more hopeful look, and still finding no signs of the deer, walked over to Donovan.

"Find anything?" Donovan said.

"No, not where I came from," Hyroc said.

Donovan shook his head. "I don't know how we lost the trail like that. I was careful too." He sighed. "Well, if we can't find something soon, we'll have to try backtracking."

There was a long pause. "Donovan," Hyroc said, doing his best to keep his anxiety from his voice.

Donovan looked at him. "Yeah?"

"How would you react if you knew your sister was a witch?"

Donovan's expression hardened. "I don't know, but you had better not be suggesting anything."

Hyroc waved his hands apologetically. "No, no, nothing like that," he said quickly. "I was curious about something, that's all."

Donovan gave him a mildly embarrassed look. "Oh, sorry, you caught me wrong with that." He paused thoughtfully. "I'm not sure. I never gave it any thought."

"Well, let's say you saw her turn something like a . . . pebble into a rose, how would you react?"

Donovan cocked an eyebrow. "A rose, seriously?"

Hyroc rolled his eyes. "I was giving *an example*. It doesn't *have to be a rose*; it can be anything you want it to be."

"Well, if I saw that I would be surprised, of course, but I don't think it would bother me terribly."

"Would you tell anyone?"

"Of course not!"

Hyroc breathed a silent sigh of relief at that. Though turning a pebble into a flower was nothing in comparison to transforming into an animal.

"Okay, then what if she made a broom sweep on its own?"

"Now, that would scare me a little, but unless she started flying around on it and cackling or making it whack me in the shin, I wouldn't consider it a bad thing. It would sure save on work around the house." Donovan gave a quizzical look. "Why are you so interested in witches all of a sudden, do you know something I don't?"

Hyroc shoved down a feeling of alarm. "No, I was just curious."

Donovan nodded slowly. An awkward silence passed. "Okay, maybe we should get back to looking for tracks."

"Hold on, one more question, and I'll stop asking."

Donovan sighed. "Okay, one more."

"What if say, she turned a mouse into a chicken."

Donovan gave him a surprised look. "Now that I would like."

Hyroc gave him a look of disbelief. "Really?"

"I might not want to see that as it was happening, but that would still be good. Do you know how many chickens we could have? We'd never run out of eggs."

Hyroc smirked. "Yeah, you could have a lot."

He felt a thrill of relief. He could tell Donovan! All his worrying and delaying had been pointless. Of course Donovan would understand. With the glaring physical differences between them, if his friend were not the understanding type, the two of them wouldn't be friends in the first place. He felt a little daft for not figuring this out beforehand. He couldn't wait to see how many uses they could come up with for his bear form. And the more mischievous part of him looked forward to seeing the shock on Donovan's face when he saw him transform.

"Okay, now let's get back to figuring out where that deer went," Donovan said eagerly.

Hyroc took a breath. "Donovan, there's something I want to tell you."

Donovan gave him a curious look. Right as Hyroc opened his mouth to speak, something caught Donovan's eye. "Is that what I think it is?" Donovan exclaimed as he rushed away. Hyroc stood there with his mouth hanging open awkwardly before closing it and making his way over to whatever Donovan had seen. Donovan crouched over a bed of sweet clover's and pointed down at them. "I think I know where that deer went," he said enthusiastically. "Look." Focusing on the spot where Donovan pointed, Hyroc saw places where the clover flowers had been crushed down into the shape of deer hooves. When he ran his eyes ahead of the tracks, he spotted more. Donovan proudly nodded as he stood. "Curtis, over here, we found some tracks. Sorry about that, what were you going to tell me?"

Hyroc's determination suddenly fizzled out, and he couldn't make what he wanted to say come out of his mouth. A long moment passed. "It was nothing," he admitted in defeat.

"Okay," Donovan answered. "This way." He and Curtis started toward the tracks.

Hyroc sighed irritably. What was wrong with him? He was so close to telling Donovan the truth. He knew he could trust his friend, but he still couldn't do it.

"Hyroc, are you coming?" Donovan called back.

"Yeah," Hyroc answered, starting toward them.

The trail wound its way through the trees, eventually leading them to a rise. Donovan and Curtis stopped abruptly at the bottom.

"Is something wrong?" Hyroc asked.

Donovan pointed to the rise. "We can't go there."

"We can't, why not, that's where the tracks are going."

"There's an old abandoned mine just over that rise. Our father told us not to go there because parts of it cave in sometimes, and we might fall in."

"Oh. So, now what?"

"You want to try fishing back at the lake?"

"Sure, I'll need to get my fishing pole from my cabin."

Donovan nodded, then Curtis and he started away from the rise. As Hyroc turned to follow, he caught sight of Kit's ears pricking up alertly in the direction of the rise. He swept his eyes across it, but there was nothing there. Kit shuffled his feet nervously as he stared intently at the rise.

"What is it?" Hyroc whispered. Kit growled softly. Hyroc had the eerie feeling something was watching them. He looked toward the rise again. He caught movement out of the corner of his eye toward the right side of the incline. When he turned to get a better look, the thing was gone. "Kit, let's get out of here, I don't like this place either." He grasped Kit by the collar, and then, at a brisk pace, eagerly led him toward Donovan and Curtis.

CHAPTER 25

A HUNTER'S MISTAKE

Hyroc glared dishearteningly at the single small piece of bread, a handful of wild strawberries, and fireweed leaves laid across his table beside the fireplace. Having failed to get a deer the day before, this was what he was reduced to eating for breakfast. When he had gone to the lake with Donovan and Curtis yesterday, the only thing he had caught was a trout barely big enough for a single meal, and he was hungry.

With a sigh, he shoved a fistful of leaves in his mouth. Next, he ate his bread, followed by the strawberries. He wasn't hungry when he finished, but it wasn't a satisfying meal. He wiped his mouth, then donned his hunting gear. Outside, he found Kit asleep in the big cat's favorite tree.

"Kit, you coming?" Hyroc called up. Kit twitched his ears but showed no signs of moving anytime in the near future. Hyroc gave him a dismissive wave, then headed toward the back of the valley.

Three of his traps were tripped, but all were empty. From his last trap at the hill on the other side of the creek, he picked his way toward the mountain. Arriving at the mountain slopes, he came across deer tracks intermingled with those of rabbits and some animal he couldn't identify. Carefully sifting through the marks, he distinguished those of the deer and began tracking it. The trail steadily arced away from the mountain before devolving into the familiarly erratic weaving path of an animal searching for food. Then the path curved slowly back toward the mountain, eventually running onto a swath of bare gray rock. Here, he lost the trail.

He scoured the slab of rock for tracks, but the unyielding surface prevented any kind of imprint from the deer's passing. When he made his way past this to softer ground, he still found no prints, and there were so many directions the deer could have gone, it was pointless even to hazard a guess. With a disheartened sigh, he started back toward the rock slab. He really needed to find some meat. The idea of eating fireweed for dinner also was not one he looked forward to. Maybe he could get the Shackletons to give him some food. They wouldn't mind, though after lying to them it felt wrong even to ask.

He stopped abruptly, his eyes lighting with inspiration. There *was* a way he could find where the deer had gone. His sense of smell in his bear form would do it. But was it safe for him to transform only a few miles from Elswood? He swept his eyes through his surroundings. There was nobody here, and besides the Shackletons, he hadn't seen any of the villagers come to this side of the mountain. If he was careful, he was sure he could avoid anyone he might come across.

He removed his gear and stowed it beneath the low hanging skirt of a pine tree. Then remembering what condition the clothes on his upper body had been in when he last transformed from his bear form, he stripped off his jerkin and shirt and put them beside his hunting gear. He started to remove his pants but decided against it. There wasn't much danger posed to them and he didn't relish the idea of being completely naked if, for some reason, he was unable to find his things.

He swept his eyes through his surroundings, reaffirming no one was there. "Anybody here?" he called out. The silence of the forest absorbed his words, and he heard no response. He dropped down on his hands and knees and initiated the transformation process. Moments later, he was a bear. He thought it strange how comfortable he now felt in his altered form. And why should he feel uncomfortable, it was *still* his body? He was still Hyroc.

Sauntering over to the point where he had initially lost the deer's trail on the rock slab, Hyroc sniffed deeply. The dusty smell of birds punctuated the aroma of pine needles, but he easily discerned the deer's scent. Eagerly, he resumed his tracking.

He grinned happily, knowing he didn't have to eat the deer raw this time. He paused. How was he going to cook it—he didn't have hands anymore. He shook his head dismissively. The required wait before he could revert to his normal self would probably have elapsed by the time he tracked, killed, and hauled the deer back to his cabin. Next time, he would try to have a fire already going at his cabin before he transformed again. That way, he could see if it were possible for him to cook in this form. He shook his head humorously as he imagined seeing a bear cooking. Pushing those thoughts aside, he continued onward.

The trail ran along the mountain, then headed gradually toward the river. The deer's scent vanished at the shore as did the tracks. It was obvious that the deer had crossed. He stepped into the water and swam over, shaking once on the other side. Scanning the shore, he spotted deer tracks heading into the trees. Past where the trail entered the trees, he reacquired the deer's scent. The scent trail ran relatively straight, occasionally bending toward a plant the deer must have been interested in. The deer's scent became steadily more defined until he spotted it eating the catkins from an alder.

Making sure he was downwind, Hyroc crept in from behind the deer. He was almost within running distance. It seemed taking down this deer was going to be about as easy as if he were using his bow. The deer's ears suddenly flicked to one side, and it bolted into the trees, jumping over a thick growth of bushes. Hyroc had little hope of passing through those bushes without injuring himself. He blew out an exasperated breath as he stared at the spot where the animal had once been. He was sure he hadn't made any noise, and the wind hadn't changed direction, so why had the deer run off?

He became aware of the sound of dogs barking. He sighed irritably. Those dogs must have been what spooked the deer. And because of some noisy hunting hounds, he might not have any meat for dinner.

The barking was getting closer. He felt a strange sense of alarm at the noises as if he should be afraid of them, but why? The dogs were now very near. His sense of alarm grew in severity. His mind raced as he tried to think of the animals hunting dogs were used to track. They were used to go after foxes, ducks, mountain lions, and even . . . bears. He felt a ferocious thrill of fear. The dogs weren't hunting *something*; they were hunting *him*.

Three barking dogs emerged from the trees to his left, followed by three hunters with bows, flanked by two more hounds. Hyroc's eyes widened with horror as the three hunters leveled arrows at him. He yelped, dashing sideways into the foliage as three arrows whistled past him. Heart hammering away in his chest, he crashed through the trees as fast as he could run.

He could hear the dogs behind him darting through the underbrush. No matter how fast he moved, he didn't seem to be putting any distance between himself and the dogs. How were they so fast? He felt a cold prickle of dread when he realized this was exactly how a bear hunt would occur. The bear attempts to flee from the dogs, running at full speed in a desperate attempt to escape. But the hounds have far more stamina. Once the bear is winded and slows, the hunters catch up, and the bear dies from numerous arrows puncturing its body.

He felt a flood of terror imagining himself being skinned and laid out as a rug. How was he going to avoid that fate? He couldn't hide from them, and he had no hope of outrunning them. That left him with one option—fight. Not just fight, he would have to kill the dogs, *all of them*. Otherwise, the hunters would be able to find him. He hated the thought. Those dogs hadn't done anything wrong; they were just doing what they were trained to do, but it was either kill the dogs or kill the hunters. The dogs were just animals. This wasn't any different from taking down a deer.

Hyroc slowed his pace, turned back, and charged headlong toward the sound of the pack. An instant later he was face-to-face with all five dogs. They skidded to a halt, barking and baying. He barreled toward the nearest hound. The dogs turned to dart away, but Hyroc was on the group before they could even move. He nailed his target in the head with a hard paw swipe, snapping its neck with a sickening crunch. He sank his teeth into the center of the next dog's back and flung it into the trunk of a tree. The dog yelped as it hit with a muffled thud, falling to the ground. The third dog lunged at him. He swatted it out of the air, feeling something break within its body before it tumbled lifelessly across the ground. Using his claws, he slashed open a grievous wound in the fourth dog's shoulder and crushed its neck in his jaws.

When he moved toward the only remaining dog, it bolted. He tore after it. The dog ran with panicked strides, slowing its pace considerably, and Hyroc quickly caught up with it. He slammed headfirst into the dog, bowling the hound off its feet. Before it could regain its footing, he sank his teeth into the dog's skull. The hound cried out in pain as he savagely shook it. He felt its spine beak through his teeth. He unclenched his jaws, releasing the hound's lifeless body. Raising his head, he was startled to see the arrival of all three hunters. Their expressions turned to disbelieving shock when they saw the bodies of their hounds littering the ground. Without any conscious thought, Hyroc drew in a breath and roared. The hunters swore as they lurched back. Hyroc wheeled around and tore off into the trees.

He ran until he was winded. Then he warily made his way toward the river, watching and listening for any signs of pursuit. He arrived at the shore without incident. After sating his thirst, he stepped out into the water and started washing the blood from his face and claws. As he washed, he felt a pang of terrible guilt gnawing at his insides. It bothered him how easily he had slaughtered those dogs. It had almost felt like he was watching his actions through someone else's eyes. What he had done didn't feel at all like killing a deer. It felt like he had destroyed part of somebody's family, as if he had just killed Dilo. He heard the words, "Give in," whispered from the back of his mind. Taking a deep breath, he pushed these thoughts aside. He could feel guilty later; right now, he needed to make sure he left no trail for the hunters to follow.

He submerged his body in the river. After bringing his head above the surface, he swam away from the mountain, continuing until his legs began to tire. Where he made landfall, he thoroughly tore up the ground, rolled in the shed needles of a pine, and trotted down the shore. He randomly zigzagged from shore to shore as he went, repeatedly disturbing the ground. He did this until he was sure there was nothing for anyone to follow. As he started back toward his cabin, he felt the disturbing sensation that something was watching him. When he swept his eyes through his surroundings, something about a shadow on the other side of the river didn't seem right. Focusing on the shadow, he felt a chill ran down his back as it slid out of view. Alarmed, he continued toward his cabin at a faster pace, hoping he had only imagined that shadow.

It was close to dusk when he finally arrived at his cabin. He was dirty and exhausted.

"HYROC," Ursa yelled out.

He felt a surge of anxiety as Ursa sauntered determinedly over to him. He sat, bracing himself for what she was about to unleash.

"Do you enjoy endangering your life?" she glowered.

"Well, how else was I supposed to get out of that?" Hyroc snapped back.

"If you had been paying attention, you wouldn't have even been in that situation in the first place."

"I needed that deer!"

"Obtaining food is pointless if you die in the process!" she growled. "But even that doesn't compare with what you did afterward. How did you get it in your head you needed to slaughter those dogs? Do you not remember what you learned from the shadow, what you learned of what you could become!"

"I didn't have any other choice, unless you're saying I should have killed the hunters. Which, to me, sounds exactly like something my shadow would have done."

Ursa growled in such a threatening manner it startled him. "If you know what's good for you, you *will not* suggest that to me *again*." She paused, shedding some of the irritation from her expression. "You only needed to kill one or two of those hounds, *not the entire pack!*"

"What do you *mean?* I only needed to kill one or two of them? If I hadn't taken care of *them all*, they would have been able to track me back here. And then I wouldn't have a home!"

Ursa shook her head derisively. "If you killed some of those dogs, do you think those hunters would have pursued you and risked losing every single one, and possibly even their lives?"

Hyroc gave her a blank look; he hadn't even considered that. "Well, I was a little preoccupied with *living* to have thought of *that*."

Ursa sighed. "Did you at least make sure to cover your tracks well?"

"I made sure of that."

"At least you remembered *something*." Hyroc scowled. "You won't be recognized in your natural form, that I am sure of. But tomorrow you should go into the town and see what rumors have sprung up regarding an unusually savage bear attack. That way, you'll know what areas of the forest you should avoid in order to prevent any more suspicion being placed upon you. And I would advise you against using your bear form here for several months." She paused. "And for your sake, I would suggest not doing anything else that would put you or your home here at risk. Am I clear?"

Hyroc nodded. "Yes," he said somberly.

"Maybe going to bed hungry tonight will teach you to be more careful in the future."

Movement near the big spruce caught Hyroc's attention. He turned to see Kit dragging a small deer toward them. He beamed at Ursa. "Actually, I don't think I will be going hungry tonight."

She glanced over at Kit and rolled her eyes. "Don't you get smart with me after what you did; I might decide a simple scolding is not punishment enough." She shook her head irritably. "At least one of you did something sensible. I collected the things you left behind when you transformed; you'll find them at the front of your cabin. But *do not* consider that a *favor*, it was merely for your protection."

CHAPTER 26

WHERE TRUST
SHOULD HAVE BEEN

T hat bear came out of nowhere," one man said.

A group of five scruffy men sat around a long table inside the Black Spruce Tavern. Hyroc sat nearby, listening from behind the concealment of a support beam. It seemed reasonable that the three hunters would eventually come here and, as Ursa had instructed, he was finding out what they were saying about the bear they encountered on their hunt.

"And before we knew what was happening," the man continued. "That beast had killed four of our hounds and severely injured another!" He shook his head. "And I doubt that one will see the night out."

"It was as if the beast had no fear of our dogs and knew they posed no danger," another man said. "I've never seen a bear act like that."

"It must have had an arrow lodged somewhere then," another man suggested. "And the pain had driven it mad; I've known of that happening."

"The three of us got a good look at its hide," the second man to speak said in a dismissive tone. "And we didn't see anything that looked like a wound." The man paused. "But now that I'm thinking about it,

230

it had markings I've never seen on a bear. It was dark like a black bear, but it had brownish stripes."

Hyroc felt a spark of fear. He had forgotten that while in his bear form, he retained the coloration of his natural appearance. Those hunters didn't know the bear they encountered was him, but it might seem odd to them he had the same markings as it. Ursa was right, though he hated admitting it to himself. He had done something incredibly stupid.

He felt the familiar cold trickle of dread creeping down his back. What would the Shackletons think when they learned of the bear's features? These hunters wouldn't make the connection even if they stared directly at his face, but the same wouldn't be true for his friends if they heard this tale. The fact that this bear with markings matching his own showed up a few days after he had returned to his cabin made it doubtful they wouldn't figure it out. He should have just told them. How could he have been so stupid? There was no way around it now; he needed to tell them the truth and tell them now. It would be better if they learned it from him instead of someone else in the village. But he couldn't leave just yet. The hunters might say something else useful.

"And I swear I saw it was wearing a necklace," another man said.

Hyroc stiffened in alarm, his hand drifting up to his necklace. If those hunters saw him wearing it, they would surely make the connection. How could he have screwed up so many times in one day? He was an idiot! He hastily removed the necklace and shoved it in his pocket.

"A bear wearing a necklace?" the third man scoffed. "Either your eyes are going bad, or you were played by a trick of the light."

"I was just telling you what I saw," the fourth man admitted sharply.

There was a long pause.

"Well, regardless of what you may or may not have seen, if there is a crazed bear on the loose," another man said, "we best take care of it."

"I agree," the first man said. "It needs to be dealt with before it kills somebody." The other three men spoke their agreement.

"So, where did you run into this bear?" the fifth man asked.

"East side of the mountain, near the river."

Taking note of this, Hyroc crept toward a side entrance of the tavern as the five men began hashing out a plan for killing the striped bear. He felt a strange sense of humored guilt, knowing they weren't going to find that bear and would waste days looking for it.

No sooner had he stepped through the door when a hand yanked him sideways. He fought against the hand's grip, working his way out of it. As soon as he was able to move freely, he spun toward the person holding him, his fist raised, ready to strike. He restrained his fist when he saw Harold.

"Harold?" Hyroc said, confused.

"Not here," Harold hissed. "I need a private word with you." He grabbed the collar of Hyroc's jerkin and roughly pulled him to an empty alley. He released Hyroc, checking both ends of the alley for onlookers.

"Alright, I think we're alone."

"Alone for what?" Hyroc asked irritably, dusting his sleeve off.

Harold fixed an angry look on Hyroc. "I think you know what for," he said crossly. "Did you think I wouldn't figure it out? You're back only a couple of days from some mysterious trip, and I hear about an unusual bear attack by a bear that wasn't acting like a bear."

"Maybe it went crazy from the pain of an arrow stuck in it; I hear that can happen." Hyroc replied evasively.

"Don't toy with me, Hyroc. The bear was black, with dark brown stripes running from its eyes down its back. And I hear some of the hunters say they think it was wearing a necklace. *I know it was you.*"

Hyroc sighed. "Okay, it was me."

Harold shook his head. "So, now you can turn into a bear. How long has this been going on?"

"Since shortly before I left."

"Then, am I right in assuming that your whole trip was a ruse?"

"Yes, I actually went away to learn how to use my new ability."

"Then what I hear is true; you killed those dogs."

"Yes, I panicked, I didn't know how else to get away from them."

"This isn't what I thought I was agreeing to when I decided to keep secret the things I discovered about you and that white bear, Ursa. I will not be an accomplice to such heinous acts. If you are a danger to this village, I will not keep silent, even if that means my death."

"Harold look. I'm not a danger to the village, okay? I made a mistake, a stupid, thoughtless, and irresponsible mistake. I only went after the dogs because I didn't want to hurt any of those hunters, and I definitely didn't want to be killed. It seemed the best choice at the time, but I'm deeply sorry it came to that. It won't happen again."

Harold studied him thoughtfully a long moment before speaking. "Well, now that I know your side of the story, I understand what difficult position you were in and the choice you were forced to make."

Hyroc breathed a sigh of relief. "Thank you."

Harold thrust a finger into Hyroc's face. "But don't think for one second I condone what you did. If I find out you're involved in another incident like that, the deal I made with your mentor is off, and the rest of the village will know the truth, all of it. Got it?" Hyroc nodded. "Good." Harold lowered his finger. "Now that we understand each other, do the Shackletons know?"

"Only Elsa."

Harold cocked an eyebrow in surprise. "Well, that's unexpected. I'll need to have a word with her when this is all under control. You'll need to tell the rest of the family, because if I was able to make the connection between your markings and that bear, they will too. And it will go over a lot more smoothly if they hear it from you first."

Hyroc nodded. "Already figured that out on my own."

"Good, then I'd suggest you get to it. Just remember I'll be keeping a much closer eye on you from now on. Don't disappoint me." With that, Harold walked out of the alley.

Hyroc did likewise before heading in the direction of the Shackletons' cabin at a brisk pace. It may not be the best idea to share the existence of his new ability with the whole family all at once, so as he had already planned, he would start with Curtis and Donovan. Once he showed them his bear form, he could elicit their help in sharing the news with the rest of the family. But even with their help, this was going to be a very strange conversation.

His pace felt agonizingly slow all the way to the trail that led to the Shackletons' cabin. At the trail entrance, he put his thoughts in order, took a deep breath, and started down the trail. As he approached the trail's end, he was overcome with a sense of wrongness. Everything was unusually quiet and something about that stillness made him uneasy. Strangely, when he stepped into the clearing, he didn't hear any barking. Dilo always made noises whenever he arrived, and she was always the first one to meet him. So where was she? As far as he knew, the family hadn't planned any hunting trips and it wasn't the proper duck hunting season. He became aware of a strange smell in the air. He felt a thrill of cold fear engulf him; it was blood!

CHAPTER 27

NIGHTMARES IN THE TREES

Hyroc wasn't sure how he knew the smell was human blood, but there was no doubt in his mind about what he was smelling. Beneath that, he detected a hint of something foul that made the hair on the back of his neck stand on end. He drew his sword and cautiously crept toward the front of the cabin, ready to react to the slightest sign of danger. He started, struck by a wave of fear, when the black mass of an enormous spider came into view on the porch, nailed to the wood with a spear through its head. Another dead spider lay on the ground at the other end of the porch, near the livestock pen, with numerous arrows protruding from its body. He saw red blood smeared across the wood in front of the door. A lone hand spade lay in the garden, and the ground was torn up, indicating a struggle there as well.

He felt a wave of cold flow through him. He stared, transfixed by the scene of violence, unable to think. The implications of what he saw seeped steadily into his mind, sending a flare of pain into his shoulder. The very same monsters that had nearly ended his life a year ago had now attacked his friends. He wished desperately for this all to be some sort of hideous nightmare he could wake up from, wrapped in the warm blanket of his bed. But he knew no such thing would happen. Everything in front of him wasn't the product of his sleeping mind. It was real. Something terrible had happened here. These once familiar surroundings were now alien to him. It seemed impossible for him to have had any good memories involving this place and that so many kind people could have ever lived here.

A faint scraping sound from inside the cabin broke him from the shadows of his thoughts. He clenched the hilt of his sword tighter as he fixed his eyes on the half-open cabin door. Some distant urge in the back of his mind screamed at him to run, but he couldn't force himself to obey. Using his left hand, he slowly pushed the door open. His breath caught when he found a live spider beside the Shackletons' bed. It stood faced away from him, hovering over a white mass as it worked its back legs in a repeating motion. The spider stopped abruptly and turned sideways, so several of its enormous black eyes were looking at him. Repressing the urge to flee under its gaze, he ran forward and rammed his sword through its head before the monster had any time to react. A horrible sounding shriek erupted from the spider's mouth. Hyroc struck in a rapid succession of blows until his adversary went silent.

Breathing heavily in a mixture of exertion and fright, he turned his attention to the white mass. It had the same stringy appearance as the piece of webbing he had found on a rabbit last summer. His eyes frightfully widened when he realized someone was probably in there. He kicked the lifeless spider away, dropped down into a crouch, and eagerly sliced open the webbing with his blade. His elation turned to dismay when he found Dilo inside, with two enormous fang marks on the side of her neck. Judging from the dried blood staining a good portion of her body, he knew the dog had died long before the venom would have had much effect. A thick pink substance oozed out of her nose and the corners of her mouth. Hyroc ran his hands through the fur between his ears, staring in disbelief at the long dead hound. He gently patted Dilo affectionately on the back of the head twice, and got to his feet. He had started to like her.

The spider had been wrapping the body so it could drag it somewhere safe to eat. Just thinking about it sent a shiver down Hyroc's back. That same thing must have happened to the rest of the family, which was why he hadn't found anyone. It hurt him to think about that.

There would be no more hunting or fishing with Donovan, Elsa, and Curtis, and no more dinners with the family—*they were gone*. They were gone, and he was never going to see any of them again. It stung that only one of them had known the truth about why he had left for so long and what he had been doing. He hated himself for not telling the rest of them when he had the chance. They would have understood, he assured himself, but now he would never know. All that would remain of them would be this empty cabin. He felt a surge of guilt. Why hadn't he ever told them about the spiders that had attacked him? Maybe if he had warned them, they would have been more prepared, and none of this would have happened.

He stepped over to the fireplace. Tears welled up in his eyes as he looked at the cooking pot hanging from its hook within the fireplace. He had really enjoyed Helen's cooking. Had she known that? He reached over to touch the cooking pot. The metal felt warm beneath his fingers. He regarded the pot in confusion. He dropped his hand down above the coals. No flames were visible, but he felt a substantial amount of heat radiating from them. The fire had died very recently, which meant the spider attack couldn't have happened that long ago.

A hot surge of excitement shot through him—the Shackletons might still be alive! He remembered his encounter with the spiders. Ursa had told him he wouldn't have immediately died even if she hadn't been there, and it might have taken the rest of the day for the venom to do him in. So, there was at least a chance they were still alive, and that Ursa could cure them. If they were unconscious, then the spiders would have no reason to give them a bigger dose. But that would only hold until the spiders got to a safe place and were ready to eat. The thought sickened him, but he didn't have time to dwell on what-ifs. He wanted to wait for Ursa, but he knew he needed to make every second count. Besides, he knew that as soon as he was in danger, she would come to his aid.

He took a deep breath, sheathing his sword. The first thing he needed to do was figure out the most likely place the spiders were heading. Despite their nightmarish size, bears and wolves might still be threats, so they would need a safe spot to build their nests. He shivered at the mere idea of egg sacks and spiderlings scurrying across the ground. A cave, maybe? He racked his brain, trying to remember any caves he had come across. The only one that came to mind was the cave on the mountain that had served as Huntress's lair, but he hadn't seen anything to suggest the nest was there. Then he remembered Donovan mentioning the mine. Something had disturbed Kit when they were near it. That had to be where the nest was.

He knew it would be dark, and he would need a source of light. Frantically searching through the cabin, he found torches. The flammable material around the tops was blackened from use, indicating they probably wouldn't burn for long. He searched through the kitchen for something flammable to smear on cloth. In one of the cabinets, he found a container filled with a thick greasy substance. When he dripped the substance on the coals in the fireplace, a flame flared up with a delightful whoosh. He ripped off several long strips of cloth from a batch of clothing strewn across the bed and soaked them in the substance. Squeezing off the excess, he reluctantly wrapped the cold, oily strips around his head like a bandanna. He stuffed the freshest looking torch into a knapsack, along with a conk mushroom he had found, placing embers from the fireplace inside of it. Svald had once told him about this hunting trick, claiming that embers carried within would last for most of a day.

He had a source of light. Now he just had to figure out how he was going to get the unconscious Shackletons out of the mine. He could drag everyone out one at a time, but he didn't relish the idea of going back into the mine multiple times, or leaving his rescued friends defenseless in the process. And it seemed unlikely that he would kill all the spiders on his way in and would, therefore, be vulnerable to attack while he did the rescuing. If he died while trying to save them, it wouldn't do anyone any good. In his bear form, he might have enough strength to drag all six of them to safety at once. Of course, he would be much larger in that form and, consequently, a bigger target for a spider bite. One bite may not affect him much in that form, but multiple bites would still disable him quickly.

If he were going to use his bear form to drag them, then he would need rope. He found a length of rope that seemed long enough, and stuck it in the knapsack. He strung his bow, discarding his buckskin tube, sticking as many of the Shackletons' arrows he could into his quiver, and rushed out the door.

As he stepped off the porch to find tracks to follow, movement at the edge of the clearing caught his attention. Snapping his gaze on the movement, he relaxed, seeing Kit plodding toward him. The big cat froze, arching his back and growling as he spotted the spider corpses.

"It's okay, those two are dead," Hyroc called out. Kit moved warily over to him, keeping his eyes glued on the dead spiders. Hyroc crouched down, so he was looking level into Kit's eyes. "Kit, the Shackletons are in trouble, and it's up to me to save them. It's going to be dangerous where I'm going, so I want you to go back to the cabin and wait for me." He stood and started toward the back of the cabin in search of tracks.

He had started walking when he heard the sound of Kit's familiar footfall behind him. Turning, he saw Kit moving toward him. "No, *stay!*" Hyroc said, putting his hand up. Kit stopped and stared at him. "That's a good boy." He turned and continued on his way, but as before, he heard Kit following. He growled irritably as he turned back for the second time. "KIT, I don't have time for this! If I don't get to them soon—," he let his words trail off, what he was going to say was too painful. "There isn't much time, *so please*, go back to the cabin." Kit remained where he was, giving him an obstinate glare. "You stupid cat!" Hyroc bellowed. "Get out of here!" He reached down and grabbed a rock. Kit narrowed his eyes and began to growl. "I don't want to do this, so please, *go back*." The mountain lion remained where he was.

Gritting his teeth in frustration, Hyroc pulled his arm back to chuck the stone. He stopped when he saw a strange look in the big cat's eyes. Kit's expression seemed to say, "My friends were here too." Hyroc glanced through the door of the cabin at Dilo's lifeless body, still wrapped in its webbed cocoon. He felt a twinge of sadness as he remembered Kit playing with the hound. With an annoyed sigh, he tossed the rock aside. "Fine." Kit walked over beside him, with his eyes looking up into his face. "But I want you to promise that if anything happens to me, you'll get as far away from here as you can, and you'll never look back." Kit stared sternly into his eyes. Hyroc nodded in satisfaction.

He studied his companion thoughtfully. "Well, if you're coming with me, then you can carry my rope." He pulled the rope from the knapsack and tied it around Kit's midsection, where it would have the least effect on the big cat's mobility. Kit growled quietly but showed no other signs of protest. "Just tell me if you start getting tired, and I'll carry that."

The two of them made their way behind the cabin. Here, Hyroc found long flat patches of disturbed grass where something had been drug across. He tried not to think about those marks coming from the bodies of his friends being dragged off to a horrible fate. But he would prevent that from happening. This would not be the day he said good-bye to them! He found an accumulation of drag marks at the edge of the clearing near the lake. Breaking into a run, he followed the trails.

He ran until he felt winded, then settled into a more sustainable pace. The forest seemed unusually quiet as if even the trees were hold-ing their breath in anticipation. Time seemed to tick away aggravat-ingly fast as the two of them pressed on. It frustrated Hyroc that he couldn't go any faster. But at the same time, he knew he needed to pace himself; he would be in trouble if they came across the spiders when he was exhausted.

What felt like days passed, days plagued with doubt and gloom before the rise came into view. Hyroc stopped. "Ready for this, buddy?" he said to Kit. The big cat stared anxiously at the top of the rise. Hyroc double-checked his gear, making sure everything was ready, nocked an arrow, then with a deep breath, they started up the incline.

As they arrived at the top, the air gained a sick smell that turned his stomach. Down the other side, enormous patches of ghostly white web-bing appeared plastered to the base of trees, and thick streamers of gos-samer extended down to the ground. The webbing steadily thickened until it reached halfway up the trees, and translucent sheets between them prevented Hyroc from seeing for more than a few yards ahead. He looked empathetically toward a still-living rabbit trapped helplessly in a low hanging web like a fly awaiting its inevitable death. He carefully picked his way through the web sheets, trying not to touch any of them. Soon even the ground gained a thin covering of webbing. He tentatively placed one foot on the covering. It stuck mildly to his boot when he lifted his foot to take another step. Glancing back, he saw Kit shaking his feet in an irritated fashion whenever the big cat took a step.

Hyroc stiffened in alarm when he came around a tree to find a spider webbing up a gap between two birch trees. The spider had scarcely turned to look at him before he shot it with two arrows in rapid succession. The spider shrieked as it died. He saw Kit's ears twitch backward. Snapping his eyes behind the big cat, he spotted a spider emerging from the trees. He nailed it with an arrow as it broke into a charge, then stopped the monster dead with a second. He swept his eyes through their surroundings. Nothing moved. Giving Kit an appreciative nod, they continued down the incline.

Near the bottom, a web-covered structure protruded from the rise. Figuring it was the entrance to the mine, Hyroc moved around it in an arc so he could approach from the front. On his way there, he came across another spider repairing a torn sheet of webbing beside a treeless patch of ground. He lined up his shot then caught sight of a dark shape off to his left near the open patch of ground. He turned to see a spider flying through the air toward him. He dodged out of the way with a quick dive, narrowly avoiding his adversary. Kit hurled himself into the spider as it landed, and the two of them tumbled into the patch of open ground. The first spider Hyroc had aimed at was now charging toward him. Forcing down a wave of panic, he hurriedly leveled an arrow at the approaching spider and let it fly. The spider's legs buckled beneath it as the arrow found its head. When it did not attempt to stand, he pulled his attention to Kit.

The mountain lion lunged on top of the spider and tore into its eye cluster. Kit's teeth sank into two of the spider's eyes, causing them to rupture and splatter the sides of the big cat's face with black blood. Shrieking in pain, the spider scratched at its attacker with two of its legs. Kit jumped backward, snarling as one of the spider's foot claws dug into his shoulder. Rushing over, Hyroc stomped on the spider's blood-soaked head, causing it to stagger, and slammed his sword down through its flesh and into the ground. The spider made a disturbing gurgling noise as it collapsed.

Hyroc quickly gave their surroundings a look, but he couldn't see any more spiders. He turned toward Kit. "You okay?" he asked. Kit glowered back at him. Hyroc looked at the big cat's shoulder to see a small bleeding wound. "You're okay. It's just a scratch." Hyroc continued toward the front of the mine.

A thick layer of webbing covered every surface of the entrance, save for a small circular opening at the center, giving the whole thing the appearance of a gigantic worm's gaping maw. A foul reek flowed from the hole, and Hyroc struggled to keep himself from choking on it. He gave his bow a discouraging look. Arrows wouldn't be of much use in the close quarters of the mine. Reluctantly, he set his bow and quiver against the entrance. He withdrew the torch from the knapsack and used the embers within the conk to light it; then, he unsheathed his sword. He checked the width of the opening, making sure he would fit through in his wider bear form. It might be a little cramped, but it seemed doable. "Ready for this, Kit?" Hyroc asked. Kit gave him an annoyed glare. "Well then, here we go." They stepped into the darkness of the mine.

The entrance webbing eventually thinned and opened up into a tunnel. The light from Hyroc's torch danced orange across the rocky surfaces free of silk as, even this close to the entrance, little light filtered through. The ground sloped mildly toward the blackness beyond the reach of his torch, and dusty wooden beams strutted the ceiling at even intervals. Plastered to the walls were the skeletal remains of animals, their sightless eye sockets staring back at him, pleading with him to turn back. Then cocoons came into view lining the floor and along the walls. A chill ran down Hyroc's back when he saw the shapes of paws pressing outward from within the cocoons as their prisoners tried desperately to free themselves.

The tunnel steadily spiraled to the right, at the end of which it flattened out. It then split in two directions, one to Hyroc's left and one to his right. A jumble of web-encrusted bones lay scattered across the junction floor. Careful of his step, Hyroc crept to the right. The air became fresher smelling. Although pleasant, cleaner air meant this part of the tunnel probably led back out. He heard a scuttling sound emanating from the direction of the other split, followed by a warning growl from Kit. When he turned, his torch revealed the shape of a dangerously close spider. He swung his torch menacingly at the spider, burning a gray line into the air. The spider reared up on its back legs, violently hissing as it swung its front limbs at the torch. Hyroc thrust his torch into his adversary. The flame hissed eagerly as it burned the flesh of the spider. With an alarmed shriek, the spider recoiled. Flashing his sword through the air, Hyroc lopped off two of the spider's legs at the middle joint. Shrieking in pain, the spider lost its balance, collapsing into a growing pool of its blood. Hyroc brought his sword down hard on the spider's head and struck twice more before it stopped moving.

Kit sauntered over, giving him a worried sniffing. "Don't worry, I'm fine," Hyroc assured. "It just caught me by surprise, that's all." He flicked the spider blood from his sword and made his way to the left entrance. After starting down the tunnel, his torch began to dim. Unwrapping a cloth strip from his head, he coiled it around the torch. For a few tense seconds, nothing happened, then the torch glowed brightly again. Crossing through a curving section of the tunnel, it opened up into a wider space.

Hyroc listened attentively for any sign of movement as he passed through the space. He didn't hear anything moving, but he did hear faint and unnerving clicking noises emanating from farther down the tunnel. Kit snarled, and Hyroc turned to see two spiders dropping from the ceiling on filaments of silk. Kit was face-to-face with one while the second circled around to come at him from the side. "KIT, LOOK OUT," Hyroc yelled, as he rushed to intercept the second spider. The spider reared back into a jumping stance and flew forward. Swearing, Hyroc swatted it out of the air with a downward strike. Spurting blood, the spider tumbled across the ground, tripping up the big cat. With an alarmed roar, Kit lost his balance. The first spider immediately lunged forward. Knowing he wasn't going to get there in time, Hyroc flung his sword at the charging spider. The blade sailed through the air, spearing the spider through its head. With a hiss, the spider fell to the ground and slid to a stop.

Hyroc breathed a sigh of relief as he watched Kit scramble free of the dead spider. Then he heard the sound of scraping claws coming from the darkness. Turning, he saw a spider barely two arms' length away. He reached for his knife, but the spider was on him in an instant. It threw him onto the cold floor of the tunnel. His torch flew from his hand, clattering across the tunnel's surface, casting strangely shaped shadows as it came to rest. He wedged his feet underneath the spider, preventing it from impaling him in his throat with its fangs. The spider pressed its body down on top of him. He felt his legs trembling from the strain of holding the spider back. He knew he was seconds from feeling the fangs piercing through his flesh. Kit charged into the spider, knocking it off him. Hyroc watched in horror as Kit and the spider tumbled on top of the torch, and the light went out!

CHAPTER 28

TERRORS IN THE DARK

Impenetrable blackness engulfed Hyroc, an everlasting night the light of the sun could never touch. The only thing he saw was the bluish afterglow of the torch as it faded from his vision. He flung his arms through the darkness, desperate to find anything solid. His hand touched only the nothingness that surrounded him. It took all of his willpower to keep terror from overwhelming him. Even if he found his torch, it would do him no good; he had left the conk on the surface. He imagined spiders rushing through the darkness toward him from every direction. This was where he was going to die, alone in an abandoned mine, far from the warming light of day. His discarded bones would mingle with those of the animals the spiders had already preyed upon. Would anyone know what had happened to him? Would anyone even care? Ursa probably would, and she would likely be the only one to mourn his passing. All of her teachings had been wasted on him. But above all else, he had failed the Shackletons. It hurt him to know he would never be able to apologize for lying to them. Scuffling of feet sounded nearby, followed by a deep growl. And it stung him, knowing he had failed Kit. The big cat's whiskers made him more capable without light, but it was doubtful whether even with that advantage he would make it out of here alive.

Hyroc grit his teeth, a tear rolled down his face. "I'm sorry, Kit," he whispered into the blackness. He remembered the little cub he had found at the stream outside his cabin. At the time, all either of them had was each other. It seemed so unfair that after everything they had been through, this was how they were going to die. He didn't want it to end this way.

As if from some long forgotten place in his mind, he heard a woman's voice. "And for their unwavering devotion to their brethren, Wearla bestowed the Flame of The Sentinels upon them and all their descendants. On this day, the Anamagi were born. And this is our gift to you, Hyroc, my son."

Warmth surged up his arm and into his hand. A sapphire flame blazed into existence above the palm of his hand, bathing the surrounding space in its blue light. He had no time to marvel at the blue flame's sudden appearance, finding himself faced with the open mouth of a spider ready to strike. The spider snarled, recoiling away from his hand. Hyroc instinctively lurched backward. A second spider to his right came into view, and it too snarled. The two spiders hesitated, then angrily hissing, began closing in on him.

Something pounced on the spider to his right. Shrieking, the spider attempted to throw off its shadowed attacker. Hyroc felt a surge of excitement, knowing the obscured creature could only be Kit. He thrust the palm of his hand toward the first spider. The spider reared away from him, swinging four of its legs. Sweeping his eyes through the space, he caught a cold glint of metal in the blue light. He made several jabbing motions at the spider with the hand holding the flame, causing the spider to pull back, then he darted to his sword. The spider charged toward him as he grasped the hilt of his sword with his free hand. He waved the flame in front of the spider, making it come to a reluctant stop and rammed his blade through its jaw. The spider shrieked as oily black blood streamed from its mouth. Hyroc pulled his sword free of its flesh and finished it with a hard, downward strike as the spider fell.

He snapped his attention to the second spider, only to find it lying lifeless on the tunnel floor, with numerous wide gashes slashed across its head. Kit hovered over the dead spider with his eyes fixed on it, ready to resume his assault if it were to so much as twitch.

"Kit," Hyroc yelled out excitedly. The big cat turned toward him, revealing patches of black spider blood splattered across his head and front legs. Kit returned his attention to the spider as Hyroc rushed over. He crouched down beside Kit, breathing a sigh of relief. "I thought we were dead!" Scouring the space, he found his torch at the entrance of the unexplored tunnel. Sheathing his sword, he picked up the unlit torch.

He held the torch up and glanced from it to the flame in his hand, wondering if he could light it. Hoping he could, he moved the flame to the head of the torch. The top of the torch caught fire, burning blue. When he pulled his hand away, the flames turned a natural orange color. Then as the torch burned at its brightest, the sapphire flame shrank until it vanished. Hyroc rolled his hand over inquisitively and ran his thumb over his palm, but he could find no signs that the flame had existed there. Pushing his curiosity aside, he drew his sword and continued into the unexplored tunnel, with Kit following at his side.

The tunnel bent to the right, sloping slightly as it went, then curved sharply to the left. When Hyroc came around the curve, the tunnel opened up into another space, and he was shocked to see large cocoons of webbing mixed with clusters of egg sacks covering the floor and walls, and hanging from the ceiling. Mastering himself, he pressed on into the opening. Within, he found a spider with its back to him and killed it before it had a chance to turn toward him. As he approached the first cocoon, he yelped in disgust when he saw dozens of tiny, white, translucent spiderlings that could have fit in his hand scurry off everything the light of his torch touched. A stream of tiny hissing shrieks rose from the floor. Shutting out the deafening chorus, he walked over to a cocoon plastered to the floor, big enough to hold a person. He carefully set his torch down and used his knife to cut it open. Inside, he found the face of the family's goat covered in a pink substance, and it stared back at him through cloudy eyes. She was dead. He sheathed his knife, picked up the torch and moved on to another human-sized cocoon hanging from the ceiling.

Eagerly, he sliced open the sticky webbing. He was ecstatic to find Walter inside. Hyroc's elation disintegrated when he saw the pink substance oozing out of Walter's nose and the corners of his mouth. Hyroc held his hand over the older man's mouth but found no breath. Placing his hand on Walter's chest, he didn't feel a heartbeat; he was dead. Hyroc felt a stab of sadness as he pulled his hand back. Even though the old man had insulted him at every opportunity, he would have never wished harm upon him. He took a deep breath and moved on to the next cocoon.

He quickly slashed it open, discovering Svald inside. His breath caught when he saw the same pink substance running down the man's face. Frantically he checked for breath and a heartbeat, finding none. He was . . . he was gone. It felt as if all the warmth had drained from Hyroc's body, making him numb. He shook his head in disbelief. It couldn't be true. How could he be dead? The two of them had talked just days before. This wasn't right! After everything the man had done for him, this wasn't how it should end. Now, he was gone, just like Marcus. It didn't make any sense! He hadn't even been able to say goodbye. Tears flowed down his face. He suddenly felt sick. Breathing rapidly through clenched teeth, he stood, pulling himself away from Svald and moved on to the next cocoon.

Within, he found Helen. He tasted bile when he saw the pink substance. Hot tears streamed out of the corners of his eyes. Overwhelmed by nausea, he doubled over and retched, acid burning his throat. He coughed, shuddering with grief. Dropping into a sitting position, he rapidly swept his head from side to side in disbelief, desperately wishing to wake up from this horrible nightmare. Helen was dead! She had been so kind to him. She didn't deserve this! She didn't deserve to die in this stinking hole in the ground; none of them did. He didn't want to believe what he saw. It felt like if he did, then it would become true. But he knew deep down, no matter how hard he tried to deny what he saw, Helen was gone.

Wiping his eyes with his sleeve, he stood, shuddering with misery, and stumbled over to the next cocoon. From the size of it, he knew Elsa was inside. When he brought his knife forward to cut away the webbing, he stopped himself. He couldn't stand the thought of seeing that the lights had gone from her eyes. It would be better if he remembered her as she was and not taint his memory by seeing the look of death on her face. He started to pull his hand away, but something urged him to get it over with.

Taking a deep breath, he sliced open the webbing. He found Elsa inside, and she was . . . she was . . . she was alive. There was no pink substance on her face. Holding his hand over her mouth, he felt the warm rush of breath. She was breathing shallowly, and she was pale, but she was alive. He stared at her baffled, the cold melting away. She was alive! No other thought penetrated his surge of happiness for a long moment. Then it occurred to him; if she was alive, then her brothers might be as well. He sniffed and wiped his eyes before finding the cocoons that held her brothers. They too, were alive, in a similar condition to that of their sister. He hadn't failed them.

Kit growled, breaking him from his jubilation. Turning his gaze toward the entrance, he saw black shapes moving into the opening. He felt a flare of rage engulf him. He gave the spiders a wrathful glare. These monsters had shattered the only kind of family he had. They had taken away the parents of his friends, the only people in the entire village that cared about him, and he would die before he let them take anyone else away. He was going to make sure they never hurt anyone ever again. Clenching the hilt of his sword and the torch in his hands, he charged toward the entrance.

Four spiders entered the space. Seeing Hyroc approach, the spiders arrayed themselves into attack positions. As he drew close, one spider launched itself at him. He sidestepped the spider, nailing it with a downward strike as he moved out of its path. Then the nearest spider lunged forward. He whacked it with the torch, following with a downward stroke when it recoiled. The third spider jumped at him. He made a lateral slice, swatting the spider sideways out of the air. The final spider charged. He dodged sideways and thrust his sword through its head. The spider shrieked and fell to the ground dead. Then he spotted the third spider struggling back to its feet. He rushed over to the injured spider and struck it over and over again, funneling all of his fury into every strike. When the spider was nothing but shredded black remains, and its blood drenched his sword, he stopped to catch his breath.

His torch started to dim, so he coiled another cloth strip around it. When the torch burned brightly again, he made his way over to his friends—keeping his gaze from their parents—and carefully cut them down from the ceiling. He dragged the three of them together, arranging them side by side. He gave the webbing a hard tug to check its rigidity. The webbing stretched, but it still seemed strong enough for use as an anchor for the rope. He cut two holes in the webbing above the heads of his friends and, after relieving Kit of the rope, fed it through each hole. Then he knotted the rope loosely around his stomach and arrayed himself so the rope formed an oval with him at the front and his friends at the back. He removed his sword and knife from his belt and set them on the floor, as they would prevent him from transforming. It saddened him to know he was leaving them here in the depths of the mine. Maybe one day he would have enough courage to come back and retrieve them. Pulling his eyes from his beloved gear, he wrapped the remaining cloth strips around the torch, set it down, then dropped down onto his hands and knees. A moment later, he turned into a bear. The rope cut into him, but the discomfort was manageable. He nearly threw up when the amplified stench of the mine invaded his nostrils. After gagging on the death-reek for an agonizing moment, he was able to shut it out enough to function.

He gazed mournfully at the cocoons of Helen, Svald, and Walter. "I'll get them out," he whispered. "I give you my word." He wiped a lone tear from his eye, then spoke in a firmer tone. "Okay, Kit, let's get out of here." He picked the torch up in his jaws and started toward the surface. Pulling his three friends was easier in this form than he had anticipated, but the ease with which he did so was a painful reminder of what the four of them had lost.

The second space was, thankfully, clear of spiders, but Hyroc had trouble pulling his friends through the preceding tunnels when their cocoons caught on bones or stuck to the smaller cocoons they rubbed against. At the next space, he encountered a spider investigating the corpses of its companions. He charged over, slamming his paw down on its head. The spider's legs buckled, and it collapsed. Kit pounced on the spider, sinking his teeth into the flesh beside its eyes. Hyroc then finished it off with his claws.

A scuttling sound near the exit instantly drew his gaze. He found a spider peeking at him through the entrance of the exit tunnel. Almost without thought, Hyroc roared. The spider hissed acidly before darting back up the tunnel. He waited to see if it would come back with reinforcements and, when no spiders showed up, he continued onward. The air steadily sweetened with the smell of pine needles. Then the entrance of the mine itself came into view. It was a tight fit, but he squeezed through. He squinted beneath the glaring sunlight. It felt like it had been years since he had been out in the sun.

He caught a whiff of something acrid like somebody had lit a foul-smelling mushroom on fire. Turning in the direction of the smell, he was ecstatic to see Ursa. Around her lay five dead spiders and behind her he saw a swath of charred webbing, with a few gossamer strands still burning.

"URSA," Hyroc yelled, his voice cracking as he barely kept himself from crying. Relief swept over the white bear's face when she looked at him. She rushed over.

"Hyroc, *what possessed you to—*." Her words trailed off when she looked at the three Shackleton siblings in their cocoons. She gave him a comprehending look tinged with amazement.

Hyroc felt tears welling up in his eyes as all of his subdued emotions flowed through him. His voice shuddered as he spoke. "I . . . couldn't . . . leave . . . them!"

Her expression softened. "It's okay," she said gently. "You don't need to explain it to me, I understand; you did well. Are you hurt?" Hyroc shook his head somberly. "Let's get the five of you out of here."

Hyroc wiped his eyes as he nodded his agreement. Ursa guided him through the charred webbing back into the green of the forest. They continued until the web-encrusted mine was a distant patch of white through the trees. Hyroc dragged the Shackletons into the shade of a cottonwood. Ursa waved her paw over the rope around his midsection. The rope unknotted itself, falling to the ground. Relieved to have it off, Hyroc scratched with one paw at the band of itchy flesh where the rope had been.

He glanced warily back toward the mine. "Are you sure they'll be safe here?" he asked warily.

"I'm sure," Ursa said, giving him a comforting look. "The few remaining spiders would have fled. And those few won't make it far before predators start picking them off. I assure you we don't have to worry about them anymore." Hyroc nodded, feeling a surge of satisfaction at those words.

Ursa stepped over to Elsa. She held her paw beside the girl, and a blue flame appeared in it. She touched the flame to the webbing. It caught fire, and a blue flame consumed only the webbing, leaving everything else untouched. Hyroc studied the flame thoughtfully. Her flame looked exactly like the one that had saved him in the mine. He refrained from asking her about it as she worked. His questions could wait. The flame died, replaced by a glow across her paw. She moved her paw from Elsa's head down to her feet, repeating the motion several times. Then, in the same manner, she removed the webbing from Donovan and Curtis and waved her paw over them.

"Are they going to be alright?" Hyroc asked tentatively when Ursa had finished working.

"The two oldest ones should, but I'm concerned about the little one. There is only so much my ability to heal can do against the venom. The rest is up to him." Hyroc gave her a concerned look. He opened his mouth to speak, but Ursa silenced him with the wave of her paw. "I know you must have questions, but before I try answering any of them, there's something I must attend to first." She stepped over to the rope. She waved her paw in a circular motion, and the rope wrapped itself around her midsection. "I'll be back in an hour." She turned and headed back toward the mine.

Hyroc watched her leave, then turned his attention to his unconscious friends. As he looked from person to person, trying to figure out if there was some way he could help them, he noticed Curtis shivering. He laid some ferns across the boy, followed by the branches of a pine tree. It wasn't the best kind of cover, but hopefully it would work until he could transform to put his cloak over him. Kit wandered over and lay down against the boy. Hyroc gave his companion an appreciative nod before getting to work covering Donovan and Elsa.

As he put the last branch in place, he heard something rustling loudly through the foliage. Snapping his attention on the sound, he saw rabbits, squirrels, and one or two badgers rushing past. Then he was startled by a loud crack emanating from the direction of the mine, followed by a sound like grinding stone. Then he spotted Ursa making her way toward him. The rope was now in the same sort of oval shape he had used, and there were three cocoons attached to it. He felt a stab of sadness seeing the cocoons. He knew exactly what they contained. Ursa deposited the cocoons behind an alder a short distance from where the Shackleton siblings lay. Hyroc turned his back on the alder, unable to even look in that direction.

"I think you forgot something," Ursa said, coming up beside him. She waved her paw, and Hyroc was surprised and gladdened to see his bow, quiver, sword, and knife, fall from her body.

"Thank you," Hyroc said. He paused. "What did you do at the mine?"

"I freed the animals that were still alive down there, and I figured it was appropriate to get the rest of the family out while I was there."

Hyroc nodded. "What was all that noise I heard?"

"That was me collapsing the entrances so nothing else can move back into that place."

Hyroc nodded then shook his head. He made a confused sweeping motion toward the Shackleton children with his paw. "It doesn't make any sense."

"What doesn't make sense?"

"Why the spiders attacked them. It doesn't make any sense. If the spiders were that close to their cabin, and no one had ever seen them, why did they suddenly decide to attack?"

"I have been thinking about that too, and I may have an explanation. Some residue from the Shade Hunter may have remained in the area. It's hard for me to be positive whether I cleansed all of it. Certain creatures, such as these spiders, are sensitive to Shadow Demon residue and are drawn to it, like moths to a flame. And sometimes, when they come into contact with it, their behavior can change in dangerous and drastic ways. This includes them attacking creatures they would normally avoid for fear of dying, such as people. Your friends likely wandered too close to their nest, the spider saw them, decided they might make a decent meal and they started stalking them."

Hyroc shook his head dismissively. Her explanation seemed too simple. He wanted something more complicated; something that wouldn't make the death of his friends seem like nothing more than an accident. But he couldn't bring himself to attempt coming up with another explanation; it hurt too much.

A long silence settled. Hyroc turned toward Ursa. "How come I was only able to save the three of them?" The words stung as he spoke them, but he needed to know, he needed to know why he had been unsuccessful.

"I believe I also have an explanation for this, but are you sure you wish to know it?"

Hyroc grimaced. "I'm sure, I need to know."

Ursa sighed. "It was because the children were smaller." Hyroc gave her a puzzled look. "As you already know, larger targets require more venom. Since your friend's parents were adults, and therefore bigger targets, the spiders needed to use more venom. Because larger prey poses more of a risk to a spider, the spiders tend to use more venom than is needed. They do this because larger animals are more likely to kill a spider and, as such, the spiders want to take it down as quickly as possible.

"Conversely, when it comes to dealing with smaller prey, the spiders are usually stingier, as smaller prey is much less of a threat. And since the creation of venom costs a spider, they often only use enough to knock their prey unconscious, therefore limiting the amount of venom they need to replace. So, there are two possibilities. The spiders were either stingy because the Shackleton children were smaller, or because they had already used a good portion of their venom on the adults and only had small amounts left to use on the children."

"So, what you're saying is that I wasn't fast enough?" Hyroc demanded.

Ursa shook her head dismissively. "If you had tried going any faster, then you would have made a mistake, and instead of you having to dig three graves for their parents, *I would be digging eight*. It would not have mattered if you had been any faster; their parents were dead long before you could have arrived. There was nothing you could have done for them. You should count yourself fortunate to have gotten *any* of them out alive!"

"Fortunate!" Hyroc glowered. "You're saying I should be *thankful* three people are dead."

"No! It's a miracle your friends are still alive. The spiders may be stingy with their use of venom on smaller prey, but once they get their prey back to their nest, that's where they finish it off. You should be thankful you were even able to get there in time. So, yes, they were fortunate."

Hyroc grit his teeth, reluctantly accepting her words. He swept his paw toward the Shackleton children again, angry tears rolling out of his eyes. "How can I face them, to tell them I couldn't save their parents?"

"I can give you no easy answer to this. Doing the right thing hurts sometimes, but all any of us can do is take solace in the fact that no matter what happens, it was the *right thing to do*. This will be hard on you, but it will be even harder on them. They've lost their parents; their world has been turned upside down. I know this hurts, but you need to be strong for them. You're their friend, and they deserve as much from you."

Hyroc squeezed his eyes shut as hot tears rolled out of them. He felt Ursa's paw press soothingly down on his shoulder.

"No matter what happens, you did an incredibly brave thing by going into that mine. That was a true act of friendship. They will know this. So, I want you to get through your grieving, so you have the strength to tell them what happened. And let them know you're here for them."

Hyroc nodded. "But I've lied to them. Sure, I told Elsa the real reason I left, but her brothers are never going to trust me again after I tell them the truth."

"Yes, you did lie to them, but their reactions may surprise you. And you will now also have to show them your ability. I would recommend doing so before you tell them about their parents."

Hyroc sighed. He was thoughtful a moment. "There are three dead spiders back at the cabin and the body of their dog; I don't think they're going to want to see that so soon after—," he let his words trail off

"I'm aware, and I'll take care of it before they wake up."

Hyroc nodded his appreciation. His expression turned grim when he suddenly felt sick as a thought entered his mind. "And what about the bodies of their parents? When you saved me from my spider bite, I remember you saying the venom also breaks down the bodies of their prey."

"And that is correct."

Hyroc took a breath. "Well, then how are we going to give them a proper burial?" He felt nauseous. "When—," he let his words trail off again—his thought was too traumatic for him even to speak.

"I understand your meaning, and to answer your question, I put an enchantment on their bodies to prevent that. So, they may receive a proper sendoff."

Hyroc nodded thankfully.

There was a long pause before Ursa spoke again. "Now, there's something I need to ask you."

Hyroc wiped his eyes. "What?"

Ursa studied him thoughtfully. "I sensed a strong surge from your Flame Claw from within the mine, which is what drew me to this place."

"Wait, you mean Shimmer didn't tell you I was in danger?"

Ursa shook her head. "He stopped tracking you last night, after that incident with the dogs." She paused. "How did it manifest itself this time?"

Hyroc took a breath. "Well, Kit and I were in the middle of a fight with a spider, and my torch went out. And when I thought I was going to die in that terrible place, I heard a woman's voice inside my head. It said, 'And for their unwavering devotion to their brethren, Wearla bestowed the flame of The Sentinels upon them and all their descendants. On this day, the Anamagi were born. And this is our gift to you,

Hyroc, my son.' And then, a blue flame, just like the one I've seen you use, appeared in my hand. It saved both Kit and my life."

"Ah, you're beginning to control your Flame Claw," Ursa said. "Before the emergence of the Wol'dger, a group of those who possessed the gift of transformation were taught the ways of the beast by a chosen few of their kind, instead of by a Guardian. This was done to give them teachers they were more easily able to relate to. Then, when the curse fell upon the people, these teachers were given the option to remain unafflicted because they had not strayed from Wearla's commandment. They refused the offer as they did not wish to become separate from their people. And so they too were cursed. But because of their loyalty, they were given the gift of the Flame of the Sentinels or Flame Claw, so they may better guide their students. They were known as the Anamagi. And you, Hyroc, are one of their descendants."

Hyroc's eyes lit up as a growing sense of worth surged through him. For the first time in his life, he didn't feel like some monster, he felt special, like everything he had gone through had a purpose.

"Are you going to teach me how to use it better?"

"Yes, there are some things I can teach you about using it, but most of what you will learn about it will simply come from using it." Hyroc nodded. "But I don't want you to think about that right now. I want you to concentrate on what you're going to say to your friends when they wake up."

Hyroc sighed gloomily. "Can I ask you one more thing?" Hyroc asked. Ursa nodded. "That voice I heard—it was my mother's, wasn't it?"

"That seems likely; she probably told you those things when you were a baby, and when your Flame Claw reacted to danger, it also conjured up the buried memory." Hyroc nodded his thanks then turned to leave. "Hyroc, I know it's not what you want to do right now, but you need to think about what you are going to say tomorrow."

Hyroc sighed sadly, wishing his words weren't necessary.

CHAPTER 29

STILL A FAMILY

Hyroc picked his way through the mottled sunlight of the forest in his natural form, searching for something Donovan, Elsa, and Curtis could eat without throwing up when they woke. He vividly remembered how sick he had felt after being bitten by a spider.

It had been a frightening night for him, as Curtis's condition seemed to worsen. He feared they would lose his younger friend, but a few hours before morning, Curtis's body overcame the dangerous effects of the venom. Soon the three of them would wake up. He looked forward to talking to them again, but more than that, he dreaded the things he needed to tell them about their parents.

He spotted a lungwort plant beside an alder, with half its branches broken off. Curious, he tasted a flower and a piece of a leaf. Both tasted to him like they wouldn't upset the stomachs of his recovering friends. He cut off the leaves and flowers and stuck them in his knapsack before continuing on his search. He came across a mint plant and stuck that also in his knapsack. On a tiny rise, he found some cow parsnips. Ursa had told him to find some, and how to prepare them. He cut off a few stalks, peeled them, and stuck them in his knapsack.

The serenity of the forest shattered as someone's screams rent the air. Hyroc felt a surge of fear flow through him, and he ran toward the sound as fast as he could move. When he arrived, he found Elsa doubled over and retching, while Ursa sat nearby with an unconcerned look on her face. Elsa dropped into a sitting position once her fit had passed. Then in a frightened flurry of movement, she started pushing herself across the ground away from Ursa.

"Elsa, Elsa, it's okay," Hyroc said, rushing over to Elsa and trying his best to hold her in place. Her eyes were wild with fear, and she seemed almost oblivious to his presence as she struggled to get away from the bear. Hyroc grabbed her by the shoulders and gave her a shake. Her eyes focused on him. "*It's okay*. She's a friend." Elsa gave him a bewildered stare, her eyes darting confusedly from him to the bear. "She's not going to hurt you, I promise."

"Hyroc?" she said, running her hand over his snout as if trying to make sure he was real. She pointed at Ursa, "That's a bear!"

Hyroc nodded, releasing her from his grip. "Yes, that's a bear. But she's not going to hurt you."

"My name is Ursa," Ursa said. "And I give you my word that I pose you and your brothers no danger."

Elsa's eyes widened with disbelief. "The . . . the bear just spoke. Hyroc, is she a witch?"

Hyroc grit his teeth, and Ursa affixed Elsa with an irritated glare. "I wouldn't call her *that*. She's a little touchy about that, and no, she is *not* a witch."

"Then, she must be the white bear Harold mentioned."

Hyroc nodded. "Yes, she's been helping me."

"Help . . . helping you? Helping you with what, your training?" Elsa swept her eyes through her surroundings. "Hyroc, where am I?" Her eyes settled on Donovan and Curtis. She gasped and rushed toward her brothers with a concerned look on her face. She made it a few steps before falling on her hands and knees, and retching.

Hyroc gave her a reassuring pat on the back. He waited for her fit to pass before speaking. "Try not to move very fast; you're still sick. And you don't need to worry about them; they're going to be fine."

Elsa wiped her mouth.

Hyroc pulled the mint from his knapsack and offered it to her. "Eat some of this; it will help with the nausea."

Elsa studied the plant a long moment before sticking one of the leaves in her mouth. She nodded thankfully then turned her attention back on him. "Hyroc, what happened?" she said, as more of a demand than a question.

Hyroc sighed. "You were attacked by spiders."

Elsa gave him a strange look. "We were *attacked* by spiders?"

"Yes, by spiders." Hyroc indicated Ursa with his hand. Ursa stepped aside, revealing the corpse of a spider.

Elsa started. She jabbed her finger at the spider. "*What is that?*" she exclaimed.

"One of the spiders that attacked you. But don't worry, it's dead."

"I've never seen a spider like that. Where did it come from?"

Hyroc pointed toward the mine. "They were nesting in that abandoned mine north of your place." He paused. "What was the last thing you remember before waking up here?"

Elsa stared at him thoughtfully. "I was out milking Grettle when Dilo started barking at something behind the barn. She barked in a way I had never heard before. I got up from my stool and walked over to the edge of the fence to see if I could spot what she was barking at. Then I heard someone yell behind me. But as I turned to look, something heavy slammed into me. I felt this horrible burning pain on my back, and that's the last thing I remember." Elsa gave him a surprised look. "Hold on, did you go in that mine to save us?"

Hyroc nodded. Elsa opened her mouth, but she couldn't bring herself to speak. Hyroc grinned, understanding what she would have said. Elsa cleared her throat. "Thank—"

Hyroc cut her off by waving his hand. "I know, but I don't want you to thank me."

Elsa nodded as she closed her mouth. She leaned toward him and kissed him on the side of his snout. Hyroc felt a mild warmth seep into his face.

Curtis made a groaning sound. Hyroc helped Elsa to his side. The boy groggily opened his eyes, throwing his arm over his face and rolling over.

Elsa gave him a gentle shake. Curtis groaned again. "Curtis, you need to get up," Elsa said.

Curtis grumbled. "I don't want to get up; give me five more minutes."

"Curtis, get up, or you'll miss the bear."

Curtis was quiet a moment. "Bear?" He rolled on to his back. "What bear?" Repressing a grin, Elsa pointed toward Ursa.

When Curtis looked at Ursa, his eyes widened, and he bolted upright. Hyroc started to warn the boy against that. Curtis paled, doubled over and threw up. Hyroc sighed. They waited patiently for his fit to pass. Curtis rolled into a sitting position and thrust his finger at Ursa.

"BEAR!" he yelled out.

"We know it's a bear," Elsa said. "If she were dangerous, do you honestly think we would have our backs to her?"

Curtis looked thoughtful before he shook his head.

"My name is Ursa," Ursa said.

Curtis gave her a bewildered look. "A talking bear," he said, awestruck.

"Curtis, eat this," Elsa said, holding a mint leaf out to him. Without taking his eyes off Ursa, he put the leaf in his mouth. Just then, Donovan groaned. Curtis stepped over to his older brother.

"Try not to let him make any fast movements for a few minutes," Ursa suggested.

Curtis shook Donovan. "Donovan, wake up," Curtis said. "There's a *talking bear* here."

Donovan pushed Curtis's hand away, rolling on to his stomach. "Go away, I don't have time for your stupidity," Donovan grumbled.

Curtis rolled his eyes, shaking his brother harder. "There's *really* a talking bear here, and her name's Ursa."

Donovan made a sighing noise and rolled on to his back. He lazily opened his eyes and saw Ursa. He bolted up into a sitting position and thrust a finger at her. "Bear, bear!"

"Yes, we see her," Hyroc said.

Donovan gave him a confused look, wondering why all of them were so calm. He spoke with a labored yawn. "Since none of you seem concerned that there's *a very large bear right over there*, may I ask why there is a *very large bear over there looking at us?*"

"She helped me save you from the spiders," Hyroc said. He used his hand to indicate the dead spider beside Ursa.

Donovan started, and yelped quietly when his eyes focused on it. "Woah! *That's a huge spider.*" He paused. "And we were attacked by *that?*"

Elsa nodded toward Hyroc. "And Hyroc saved us from them."

Donovan pointed from Hyroc to the spider. "Really, you . . . umm . . . saved us from that?"

"Yes, and it was the scariest thing I've ever done," Hyroc noted.

"I can imagine," Donovan agreed under his breath.

"But before you get too excited, eat this," Elsa said. She handed him the mint. Donovan gave the plant a puzzled look, then ate some of it.

There was a long pause.

Hyroc took a breath. "Donovan and Curtis," he said. The three of them gave him a quizzical look. He scratched the back of his head nervously. "There's something I need to show you."

"There's more?" Donovan asked. "Giant spider monsters and a talking bear wasn't enough?"

"This might also startle you a little, but you don't have anything to worry about, okay?"

"The fact that you're telling us we don't have to be worried, worries me," Donovan said.

"Just shut up and watch," Elsa said. Donovan shrugged and folded his arms.

Hyroc removed his sword and knife and dropped down on his hands and feet to transform.

Curtis stared at him in awe when he finished.

Donovan frantically shook a finger at him. "You . . . you . . . you just became a bear!" he exclaimed.

"Yep, it's me," Hyroc said. "I'm a bear."

Donovan gave Elsa a strange look. "Elsa, why aren't you freaking out about this too?"

"Because I already knew."

He gave her an even stranger look. "You did?"

Elsa nodded.

"I told her before I left on my trip," Hyroc said. "I was hoping she could help me explain the situation."

Donovan gave him a baffled look. "I guess that makes sense. "

Hyroc stood up on his back legs, surprising himself at how he towered over all of them. "Donovan, come over here, please," Hyroc said.

Donovan stood and walked over to him. "What?"

Hyroc indicated his midsection with his paw. "I want you to punch me right here in the gut."

Donovan cocked an eyebrow. "Okay?"

Donovan punched him in the stomach. Hyroc barely even noticed the impact. "Come on. I didn't even feel that, hit me as hard as you can." Donovan punched as hard as he could.

Donovan shook his hand. "It's like hitting a full sack of grain."

"And the rest of me is just as tough."

Donavan paused, a mischievous grin spreading across his face. "Hyroc, do bears crap in the woods?"

Both Hyroc and Elsa rolled their eyes. "You're such an idiot," Elsa said, repressing a smile as she shook her head.

"Sorry, I couldn't help it."

Hyroc cleared his throat before continuing. "And while I'm in this form, I can also track by scent, and my nose is more sensitive than a bloodhound's. That could make hunting a lot easier for us."

Donovan grinned. "I can imagine it would. How long have you been able to do this whole transformation thing?"

Hyroc grit his teeth, "Over a month."

"A month? Is that why you've been acting so strange lately?"

Hyroc sighed. "I'm sorry I didn't tell you sooner."

Donovan gave him a strange look. "What's there to be sorry about?" Hyroc gave him an astonished look. "I probably wouldn't have told anybody about this either."

"You mean, *you're not mad?*"

"Of course, I'm not mad. Maybe a little annoyed, but with as much trouble as you've been having around the village, I'm sure you thought it was too risky to tell us. That's perfectly understandable to me."

Hyroc breathed a massive sigh of relief, "Thank you," he said. "I hated keeping it from you or your brother."

Donovan gave him a dismissive wave. "Don't worry about it, but I'm happy I know now. Wait until we tell father and mother about this."

Cold dread and sadness engulfed Hyroc as he remembered the terrible thing he needed to tell them. He turned toward Ursa, and she gave him a sympathetic but stern look. He took a deep breath, focusing his thoughts.

"Donovan, Elsa, Curtis," Hyroc said, in a voice tinged with reluctance. "There's something else I need to tell you." The smiles on their faces vanished, replaced with looks of concern. "The three of you weren't the only ones who were attacked."

"Hyroc, you're scaring me," Elsa said.

"Your parents were also taken." Her eyes gleamed with tears. It took all of Hyroc's willpower to continue. His voice shuddered as he spoke. "And I . . . I couldn't save them."

"What are you saying," she said, her voice cracking.

"They . . . they're gone." It felt like a hammer had slammed into his chest. The words hurt more than anything he had ever felt.

Elsa began shaking her head. "No, no, no, it can't be true."

With his eyes misting over, Donovan walked over to Elsa and embraced her. "It's not true!" she said, pushing on her brother. Donovan tightened his hold, and she struggled a moment before relenting and beginning to sob. Tears streaming down his face, Curtis moved closer. Donovan reached down with his free hand and grasped his brother's shoulder. Hot tears began flowing down Hyroc's face, dripping from the corners of his mouth. He turned away, shuddering with sadness, unable to look upon the grief of his friends. Ursa stepped over and hugged him. At her embrace, Hyroc's sorrow broke like a dam, releasing everything he had felt from the time he had discovered his friend had been taken. He needed to be strong now for the sake of his friends.

"Ursa," Donovan said, forcing strength into the word. She stepped away from Hyroc to look at him. "We want to see the bodies."

Ursa shook her head. "No, you do not."

Anger flashed through Donovan's face. "What did you say?"

"You will not wish to see their faces uncovered. You should not taint your memories of them with what you would see; you should remember them as they were." The anger in his face cooled, and he somberly nodded his understanding. There was a long pause. "Whenever you feel strong enough, you may begin the trip back to your cabin."

Donovan looked toward Elsa and Curtis. "Are . . . are you ready?" They nodded slowly.

"Come with me," Ursa said. She led them past the alder to where the bodies of their parents lay.

There was a long silence. "Elsa and I would like to carry our father."

"And if it's okay with you, I would like to carry Helen," Hyroc said. The three of them studied him before nodding.

"And I will carry your grandfather," Ursa said. They nodded.

Using a portion of Hyroc's rope, the three of them helped secure Helen to his back and Walter to Ursa's. Donovan and Elsa hoisted their father onto their shoulders. Then with Curtis carrying Hyroc's things, they began the lonely trip back to the cabin.

It was close to dusk by the time they arrived. Elsa and Donovan indicated for the graves to be dug at the base of a tree behind the barn. Ursa and Hyroc quickly dug three graves, and the bodies were placed inside. Elsa and Donovan delivered loving but deeply sorrowful words of parting. Curtis attempted to speak, but the traumatic event prevented him from doing so. Hyroc thanked Svald and Helen for their kindness and for making him feel like a part of the family. When they had finished, they began the dreaded task of burying their parents and grandfather, never again to hear their voices.

When they completed the mournful task, they made their way back to the cabin. By now, enough time had elapsed for Hyroc to return to his natural form. Elsa pulled out the bowls and utensils and began divvying them out onto the table. Tears welled up in her eyes when she saw she had laid out seven places when only four were required. Hyroc squeezed her hand comfortingly and put away the extras.

Their dinner consisted of cow parsnips and any mild-tasting vegetable they could find, as the sickness of the spider venom prevented them from eating anything else. All four of them picked at their bowls, not really in the mood for eating. A long silence engulfed them. Donovan looked thoughtfully from person to person.

"Curtis," Donovan said. Curtis gave him a somber look. "Remember that time father caught that *huge fish*?" Curtis and Elsa stared at him, then a smile crept across their faces.

"What happened?" Hyroc asked curiously.

"We were out fishing on the lake early one morning," Donovan continued. "We hadn't caught anything for hours and were about to head back home when father got a bite on his line. He must have fought with it for half an hour before we saw it near the shore." Donovan spread his arms apart to show the fish was quite large. "That's how big it was. Father was about to land that thing, but when he positioned himself for the final pull, he slipped and went face-first into the lake." Donovan had to try hard not to laugh. "He lost his grip on the pole and the fish started flopping back toward the water. So, now completely soaked, he charged through the water on his hands and knees and ended up diving onto the fish as it broke the water's surface. But when he grabbed it, he had its tail up by his face and the fish started paddling his face with its tail. And the whole time this was happening, he was yelling our names." Donovan's eyes started watering as he said the next sentence without laughing. "But we were laughing so hard we could barely walk straight!" Donovan said in a loud voice laden with laughter. Hyroc couldn't help smiling a little, and he saw Elsa and Curtis doing the same.

The three of them spent the rest of dinner, and the intervening hours until dark listening to Donovan tell humorous stories about their parents. When Hyroc bid them all a good night and started toward the door, they invited him to stay the night. Feeling a surge of happiness at the offer, he gladly accepted. Elsa made him a place to sleep in front of the fireplace.

Hyroc tossed and turned irritably, unable to find a comfortable position to sleep in, long after his friends had dozed. With a frustrated sigh, he got up, donned his jacket, and quietly made his way outside. He found Ursa sitting near the porch, gazing up into the clear, star speckled sky. Her gaze remained constant as he came over and sat beside her, turning his eyes skyward.

"Hard time sleeping?" Ursa asked without looking at him.

"Yeah," Hyroc agreed.

Ursa nodded. "It's a good night for stargazing."

There was a long silence as the two of them admired the sky.

"So, what happens now?" Hyroc said.

"Well, once they get settled in, I'll begin instructing you on the use of the Flame Claw." Hyroc shook his head humorously. It felt like she had just said that same thing regarding his bear training. One task had ended, and another was about to begin. "But—," Ursa paused. "But once you have mastered that, I'm afraid it will be time for us to part ways." Hyroc gave her a startled look. Ursa looked at him and gave him a placating wave of her paw. "But before you get *too upset*, know that it won't be for a while." Hyroc relaxed slightly. Another silence descended. "Things are going to be hard on your friends, and they don't really have anyone to look to besides you. So, you need to make sure you're there for them when they need you." Hyroc nodded. "That's what a family does for each other."

Hyroc gave her a surprised look. "Family?"

Ursa gave him a humored but proud look. "Yes, the five of you are family. With a bond forged through pain. You all share this in common."

"I'll do my best to protect them," Hyroc said.

"I do not doubt that."

Ursa reached over with her paw, grasping him by the shoulder. She gently drew him closer to her, and he allowed it, thankful for her presence. "You're a good person, and I'm proud of what you've grown into."

"Do you think my mother is proud of me?"

"I know she is."

Hyroc was quiet a long moment before he spoke again. "She was a bird, wasn't she?" Ursa gave him a quizzical look. "Not long before last winter, I had a dream about a talking bird, and the bird's voice was extremely familiar. That's why we seemingly came out of nowhere in Forna. She flew us there."

"I had often wondered if that was what happened," Ursa said. "The frostbite on your ear explains it."

"Because even in summer," Hyroc intoned, "weather cold enough to cause frostbite still exists high up into the air. I know because I felt it during The Choosing when I looked at a bird."

"Yes, well reasoned," Ursa agreed. "She probably flew too high up while she carried you, but when she noticed what it was doing to you, she descended. But not before you sustained frostbite."

"I think I saw her, or a vision of her, the night of The Choosing, right before I came back."

Ursa gave him an intrigued look. "Very likely. Whenever an animal is chosen by those going through The Choosing, that person's memories become a part of the tree. That is why some refer to it as the Tree of Memories. Sometimes, if a person has a strong enough connection to someone and a desire to know more about them, the tree will react to that person's desires and show them glimpses of the person, or persons, they seek."

"So, because I've always wanted to know more about my parents, it showed me something about them?"

"Correct."

"Then, that must mean the second vision was of my father."

"Quite possible."

"But from what I saw, I think he thinks that I'm dead. He talked about getting revenge in front of what looked like three graves. Maybe whoever he talked about getting revenge on was the same person who sent the Shade Hunter after me." Hyroc sighed. "I just wish I knew more about them; I hate blindly guessing."

"Those answers will come; I am sure of it. You've already learned some important things about your mother."

"I guess."

There was a long pause.

"Ursa," Hyroc said.

"Yes, Hyroc?" Ursa answered.

"I need to ask you for a favor."

EPILOGUE

Rays of sunshine penetrated deep into the house's living room as the sun neared the horizon, and a subdued fire glowed in the fireplace. June sat at the desk formally belonging to her brother, feverishly scratching her writing quill across the parchment in front of her. Soon she would be reduced to candlelight and she wanted to get as much written before then as she could.

The new headmaster at the school had laid out a strenuous teaching plan, creating a significant workload for both student and teacher. Even she was having a hard time finding the time to get everything done, but in a way, she was grateful as it kept her occupied and prevented her from worry much about and Light Bringers that constantly harassed her. It had been over a year since "the creature"—as everyone called him, though she never would—had last been sighted in the town. Still, they persisted with questioning her.

She stopped writing and bit her lip in thought as she studied the parchment. Pushing back from the desk, she stood and walked to a bookshelf. Looking through the books stored there, she pulled one from the shelf and opened it to a marked page.

The fluttering of wings drew her attention from the book. On her desk stood a raven flexing its wings. She slammed the book close with a snap and rushed toward the bird to shoo it away before it marked up her parchment by walking through the still wet ink.

"Get out of here!" she yelled, throwing her hand through the air. The bird remained still and regarded her curiously, showing no signs whatsoever of fear. June stepped closer, then tried again. The bird remained motionless. She cocked her head in confusion as she stared at the fearless intruder. As the two of them studied each other, she noticed the bird was standing on only one leg and was clutching something in its claws.

The bird extended its leg toward her as if in offer. She held her hand out, and the raven dropped a green stone into her hand. At the center of the stone was the rune that symbolized courage. She dropped the book she held in her other hand, suddenly recognizing what she was holding. She flipped it over and found the rune symbolizing safety etched into it. Cupping her hand over her mouth, she began to weep tears of joy. All her worry and dread melted away. He was letting her know he was safe. Hyroc had found a safe place to live!

www.ingramcontent.com/pod-product-compliance
Lightning Source LLC
Chambersburg PA
CBHW071828020726
47502CB00004B/1276